THE
NOWHERE
GIRL

BOOKS BY NICOLE TROPE

My Daughter's Secret
The Boy in the Photo

THE
NOWHERE
GIRL

NICOLE TROPE

bookouture

Published by Bookouture in 2020

An imprint of StoryFire Ltd.
Carmelite House
50 Victoria Embankment
London EC4Y 0DZ

www.bookouture.com

ISBN: 978-1-83888-210-5
eBook ISBN: 978-1-83888-209-9

PROLOGUE

'Please,' she whispers, too quietly for anyone to hear. 'Please,' she whispers again. 'Please help.'

But there is no one. Where is everyone? There should be cars filled with people. That's what she's here for – cars filled with people. Help should be racing up the road, screeching to a stop. Help should be here but it's not. Help is as far away as it's ever been.

The road remains empty. A long stretch of darkness leading nowhere. She touches her damp cheek – sweat? Tears?

The heat is heavy, sticky, refusing to let go despite the day ending hours ago, despite it being another day already. She wants to turn around, she wants to run back, back to where it's safe, but it would mean running back through the years. You can't run back to your past.

A truck appears, huge, with more wheels than she can count. Her heart lifts, but the vehicle thunders by, sending bits of gravel flying into the air, leaving behind it the smell of burnt rubber. The driver is only looking forward, staring at the empty road ahead of him. It would be better if it was a woman anyway. A woman, a woman who can think for herself, would help, but a man might hurt.

She is so tired. Tired, scared, heartbroken. She wishes she knew how to not feel anything at all.

Her knees are aching now. She feels old. She is too young to feel this old, to know this much, to be doing what she's doing.

She would like to turn around, to run back home. *Home*, she thinks – such a nice word. For most people it means family and love and comfort, but not for her.

'Not for me,' she whispers. She has no home. She has a house where other people live. Other people who hurt her or ignore her, other people who don't deserve children. That's why she's doing this. That's why it has to happen.

Where are all the people in their cars?

A sleek sports car appears, going so fast it takes her breath away. By the time she realises it's there, it's passed by. It might have been blue or black. It's difficult to tell with only the streetlights on.

'Please help,' she prays, knowing it won't do any good. She swats at a mosquito and wipes her face again.

She feels like she's been here forever.

But finally, finally another car appears. Going slowly enough to see, to register what's there. It stops.

A woman climbs out, young and wobbly on high spiked heels that clip-clop against the tarmac. Bright pink hair shines in the streetlight. She totters over, swaying as she walks.

Is she drunk? the little girl wonders. Drunk isn't good. Drunk means you stop thinking about anyone else, stop feeling for anyone else. She cannot deal with drunk. Not again. She begins to stand up but then the woman speaks.

'Are you, like, lost?' she asks, her voice soft and sweet. 'Are you lost?'

And then she turns and looks back at the car she has just gotten out of. 'We need to call the police,' she yells at the unseen driver. 'Come on,' she says, holding out her hand.

The little girl slips her hand into the stranger's.

She lets out the breath she's been holding. She's done it. She's actually done it.

CHAPTER ONE

Now

Alice

I inch my car forward in the primary school pickup line, glancing at the clock on the dashboard for what feels like the tenth time in five minutes. It's already twenty past three and Isaac will be outside the high school by three thirty. The primary school and the high school are only a few minutes apart but I can't help feeling anxious. I hate being late for him, hate the idea of him peering worriedly up and down the road. I've never actually been late, not once, but I'm always afraid I might be. He'll know I'm coming since I've never let him down, but I don't want him to have to think about it, to have to wonder. It's a terrible thing to be unsure if you will be fetched from school or not. Yet there are worse things. It's a terrible thing to wonder if you will be fed or not, to wonder if you are loved or not. I know that, but still, I cannot help but panic at the idea of being late for my eldest son.

'They will survive... will be fine if you're a few minutes behind, Alice, especially Isaac – he's not really a child anymore,' my husband Jack has said, trying to reassure me. He understands but at the same time he doesn't understand.

I adjust my sunglasses, warding off the glare from the afternoon sun in a cloudless, cold, blue sky.

Finally, I reach the front. I lean forward and straighten the sign lying on the dashboard, making sure my surname is clear to the teachers.

The large group of children waiting to be picked up spills out of the black wrought-iron gates of the school and onto the pavement with two teachers in front of them to prevent anyone from dashing into the road. Despite it being the end of the day, I can see they are still buzzing with energy, shouting and talking, shoving each other and jumping up and down. Uniforms are stained and crumpled and faces are smudged with dirt but there are smiles and laughter, loud conversations and singing all going on at the same time. Pure happiness, pure joy and everything children should be.

As each car pulls into place, there are always two or three kids who recognise the mother or father or grandparent or nanny in the car and alert their classmates to their arrival. As I reach the front of the line, news of my arrival spreads quickly.

'Gus and Gabe, Gus and Gabe,' shouts a little girl whose glasses are secured to her face with a wide strap, 'your mum's here, your mum's here.' The level of excitement that ripples through the group makes me smile. You would think these children were worried about not being picked up despite the guaranteed arrival of a parent or caregiver every single day. This is a privileged primary school in an affluent neighbourhood. These are the children of parents who devote their lives to their kids. School notices contain regular updates about food that's been banned because of sugar content and exhortations to 'buy organic'. These children are shuttled from ballet and football to tennis and violin. They are given everything their hearts desire and can be certain they are loved. Only half the children waiting to be picked up are wearing jumpers despite the cold weather of this first week of winter. I know, without having to think about it, that Gus will not be wearing his jumper, but Gabe will be. Gus's jumper will be in his bag, or in the classroom or somewhere in the playground, forgotten.

I watch as the news of the arrival of Gus and Gabe's mother spreads quickly through the crowd before the teacher in charge of pickup glances at the sign on the front of my dash and lifts her megaphone to her mouth. 'Stetson twins,' her voice booms across the crowd, but Gus and Gabe are already at the car, pushing each other out of the way, trying to be first to get in.

'Augustus and Gabriel Stetson,' she calls, 'you will calm down.' Gus and Gabe immediately stop their pushing and shoving and stand quietly by the car. A hush falls over the group of children, awed by the teacher's loud voice and the reprimand in front of everyone. I want to laugh, I really do, but instead I purse my lips and try to look disappointed in the two of them. I would hate to undermine a teacher. The boys climb, chastened, into the car, bringing with them their little-boy smell of fruit and sweaty hair. Outside, the wind is blowing and there is a chill in the air but, as predicted, Gus is not wearing his jumper.

I nod my head at Marie Winslow, their teacher. She's nearing retirement and I can't help but feel that she's very tired of young children, especially my boisterous twins. My rambunctious little terrors, my beautiful boys.

'Quick sticks,' I say as they shove their bags onto the floor and buckle up their seat belts. I pull away before saying anything else, allowing the next car to slide into place.

'So how was your day, boys?' I ask.

'Me first, me first,' yells Gus. Gus always has to be first; first out of the womb by five minutes means he gets to celebrate his birthday a whole day earlier than his brother. He was first to crawl and walk and talk, and still, at the age of nine, insists on being first at everything. He is running at life at full tilt and I worry that when he's older he will be the kind of child who believes he's invincible, who thinks fast cars are fun and a new drug is worth a try.

'You… you worry too much,' Jack has told me. Of course I do.

'You went first yesterday, Gus,' I say. 'Today Gabe is going first. Gabe, how was your day?'

'Um,' says Gabe and then he is quiet. I can actually feel Gus's frustration. He has so many stories to tell me, he's not even sure where to begin, but I know he won't interrupt his brother. Interrupting means half an hour less on the computer later so Gus keeps quiet, but I can feel his fizzing desperation to speak from the back seat.

'Today in art,' Gabe says finally, 'I drew a picture of our house. It took me a long time because I had to make sure that I got it right, especially the big trees in the front garden where the king parrots like to sit, but Mr Mahmood let me stay and finish at lunch. I was allowed to be in the classroom alone because he says I'm very responsible, and when he came in after, he told me that I'm a real artist. He said my king parrots look friendly. He liked their red bodies and their green wings.'

'Oh, Gabe, how wonderful,' I say, a rush of love for my quiet, serious child filling me. 'I'm so proud of you for taking the time to really work on your drawing.'

'Yes,' agrees Gabe, 'I took my time.'

I risk a quick glance in the rear-view mirror at Gabe's face. He has Jack's deep blue eyes and jet-black hair but my generous mouth, unlike his brother with his striking red hair and emerald-green eyes. 'My Irish great-grandmother making sure we don't forget her,' Jack always says. The boys do not look like twins. They barely look like brothers, and while the idea of identical twins seemed enticing to me when I was pregnant, I'm pleased that they look so different. They are very distinctive children, and their separation in both looks and personality has allowed them to forge their own way forward at school and, I hope, in the future too.

'Okay, Gus, your turn,' I say.

'Yay, I went across the monkey bars three times at lunch and I didn't fall once and I didn't eat my sandwich because I told you I hate cheese and honey or maybe I did hate it at lunch but I ate it now because I was hungry and I don't have homework but Ali says he'll be on the computer at five and I want to be on the computer at five so we can play *Minecraft* together and I was the fastest to finish my maths test today but I got three wrong so Charlie is the best in the class and she said she was the best so I stuck my tongue out at her and then she said she was going to tell so I said sorry and now she's not going to tell but it was only a tongue and what's the big deal and I'm starving, what's for dinner?'

'Goodness,' is all I can manage as his words wash over me. 'What a busy day that was. You can be on the computer at five but only if I can see your diary and make sure you have no homework. And I thought we'd have lasagne for dinner.'

'I like lasagne,' says Gabe.

'Me too!' shouts Gus and the boys laugh as though someone has told a joke. I can't help laughing with them. No one mentions how funny you will find your own children. I don't think there's a day when one or all three of them don't make me laugh.

I pull up into the car park at the front of the high school just as Isaac ambles out, his head down, his thumbs moving furiously as he checks Instagram or texts a friend or does whatever it is he's doing on the phone he is glued to. He looks up and grins when he sees my car. 'Hey, Mum,' he says as he slides into the front seat. 'Hey, you ratbags,' he throws over his shoulder at his brothers.

'How was your day, Isaac?' asks Gabe, and I know I don't have to tell Gus to keep quiet because Isaac is speaking, and as far as the twins are concerned, their fourteen-year-old brother is the closest thing to a real-life superhero they'll ever get to meet.

Isaac is the only one of my children who looks like me. 'Are you sure I was involved with this one?' Jack likes to joke. My eldest has the same shade of dusty-brown hair I do, the same chestnut-coloured eyes and an identical heart-shaped face. He is tall and slim and towers over me already, and I'm sure it won't be long until he's bigger than Jack as well.

'My day was good, Gabe,' says Isaac. 'I've got tons of homework, Mum, and a project for history and another one for science. I don't know how I'm going to get it all done because I have two matches this weekend.'

I throw him a quick smile – Isaac, my gorgeous perfectionist.

'You're going to score the most goals again, Isaac,' says Gus, starry-eyed. 'One day I'm going to be the captain of my football team as well.'

'I bet you are, mate,' agrees Isaac, 'and Gabe will be the best artist in the school.'

'I will,' says Gabe.

'You'll manage to get the work done, love, you always do,' I say to Isaac, remembering him at two years old. He was an absolute terror, refusing to sleep, climbing onto counters, throwing himself at every dangerous thing he could find. But he has matured into a lovely, patient young man who rarely gets angry enough to shout and seems to be managing his teenage years with good-natured humour. He stares down at his phone again, angling it slightly away from me. He is, of course, very protective of his phone.

'Yeah, I guess. What's for dinner? I'm starving.'

'Everyone in this car is always starving,' I laugh.

But as quickly as the laugh bubbles up it disappears. *Don't think about it*, I tell myself as Gus and Gabe chat about moves they will make on *Minecraft* later and Isaac's thumb sweeps across his screen.

I see the kitchen table, round and topped with peeling, grubby laminate, the chipboard showing where whole pieces have broken off. 'Cereal for dinner again,' I can hear myself saying, as though it were yesterday instead of thirty-two years ago. 'No, no!' I remember her shouting. I couldn't blame her really. The sweet, crunchy rings were nauseating without milk, especially when we'd already had them for breakfast and lunch. But it was cereal or nothing. The fridge was empty, the pantry containing only rice and when I looked inside the packet, the grains wriggled furiously, alive and disgusting. 'Please eat,' I remember begging. 'Look, it's delicious.' I filled my mouth, crunching the rings, and then opened wide to show her the multicoloured mess, making her laugh and eventually convincing her to shove a handful into her own mouth.

But that is not my life, not the life my children are living.

I'm not sure I ever meant to be a mother. It wasn't that I didn't want a baby, I did. I wanted one with every fibre of my being but I was terrified to bring a child into the world, terrified of what I would do and who I would become.

In the end Isaac announced himself after a bout of tonsillitis and a course of antibiotics reduced the effectiveness of the pill. I remember being horrified when I looked down at the test. I had taken it just to get the idea out of the way, simply to make sure, not really expecting anything other than one single line letting me know my period was just late. But as I peered down at the little square, in the toilet at work, the second blue line bloomed brightly – so deeply blue that I couldn't deny what I was seeing. I knew the instant nausea I felt had nothing to do with being pregnant. I knew it was fear.

It was impossible for me to imagine the happy future that Jack kept predicting. All I could see ahead were bleak years where all the work I'd done on myself was undone in a haze of sleepless nights that would lead to terrible depression. It was my genetic inheritance and I believed there was nothing I could do to stop it.

'I promise you, you'll make a great mother… a brilliant mother,' Jack told me. But Jack grew up in a different world to me. He grew up with his parents Ida and Lawrence in a house filled with the perpetual smell of baking. He grew up with a family dog and holidays to the coast. He grew up with the expectation that he would achieve something with his life, and the education to do that. He has no idea – no real idea despite having listened to me talk about my childhood – what it's like to grow up deprived of all those things.

It feels far away now, my childhood. It felt far away then, when I found out I was pregnant with Isaac, but it is always there, just there.

There is a feeling I have, when I think about my life, that I exist as two separate people. I compare it to a news bulletin on television where the stories you see on the screen are mostly about local happenings – things like car crashes and fires; but if you read the thread running below, you can see all the monstrous happenings around the world. That thread that moves quickly across the screen is where you read about terrorist attacks and tsunamis and earthquakes in the rest of the world, far removed from where you are. I feel like my life is exactly like that. On the screen you can see me raising my children and eating dinner with my husband, but if you read the words running underneath, you'll see: *Alice is broken. Alice is grieving. Alice was hurt. Alice was abused. Alice is afraid.* The truth of who I am.

'You don't have to go through with it if you're… you're not ready,' Jack said when I told him I was pregnant. I opened my mouth to tell him that I wanted a termination, but when I looked into his hopeful blue eyes, I knew that I couldn't break his heart like that.

The baby hadn't felt real until he'd kicked. I had remained emotionally distant at the first scans, barely looking at the rapid, flickering little heartbeat, and I battled through the nausea without complaint, as though I had a bug that I would soon get over. I got up every morning and dragged myself to work at the suburban newspaper where I had earned my way to editor.

But you can't hide a pregnancy forever, and my colleagues noticed the sickness, saw me resting my head on my desk in the afternoons, watched me as I sometimes ate a hamburger as though I hadn't eaten for weeks. They were delighted for me and naturally everyone wanted to give advice or ask questions. Eventually I took to remaining in my office as much as possible so I could avoid the eager conversations about the gender of the baby and how I was feeling. I believed that if I started discussing it, I would inadvertently let everyone know the truth about how I was feeling. It was easy to picture their horrified faces if I told them about my ambivalence about the idea of a baby, my baby. It was better to keep it to myself instead.

And then, at eighteen weeks, I felt the first kick. I ignored the small flutter the first time, assumed it must be something I'd eaten, but that night I was sitting next to my husband on the couch as we watched television. Jack had his hand resting on my stomach and the flutter came again.

'Did you feel that? Did you feel it?' asked Jack excitedly.

'Yes, and I felt it earlier as well. I think it's just gas.'

'No, Alice, that's a kick. I promise you that's a kick.'

'A kick?' I don't think I believed him, but later that night in bed, I laid my hand across my stomach and felt the small movement inside me. I closed my eyes and took a deep breath. 'Hello,' I whispered, and tiny bubbles of movement answered me back. Just like that, I was completely, totally smitten.

'Pregnancy is not an exam you have to pass, you know,' Jack laughed when he helped me offload the books I had rushed out and bought on my lunch hour the next day.

'I can't get this wrong,' I replied. 'I have to do it right. I can't do what…'

'Oh, sweetheart,' he said, 'I understand, but you're going to be… just wonderful.'

I had no one to look to for an example on mothering, no one to turn to and say, 'I don't know what I'm doing, can you help?' I was so afraid of making a mistake. I was terrified of repeating history.

When my beautiful boy was born, they placed him on my chest and he squealed and wriggled, and I thought, *So this is what people mean when they talk about falling in love at first sight.*

'You're too hard on yourself,' Jack says even now when I question how I'm doing. 'You're doing an amazing job with them. I'm worried for the women they will date and marry in the future because… I can't help but think that no one will stand the comparison to their mother.'

He means to make me laugh when he says such things. I know he does.

He's suggested I return to therapy a few times over the last couple of years but the truth is I don't need to talk about it anymore. Some scars will always be there and some healing can never take place. I'm fine with that.

'Right, here we are,' I announce, pushing aside the morbid thoughts that are always bubbling just under the surface. I admonish myself to pay more attention. I have driven home without thinking about where I'm going. The boys clamber out of the car and race up the steps from the garage into the house. As I push the button to close the garage door, I catch the sweet, spicy smell of a wood-burning fire coming from the neighbour's house. I love the idea of it but I have always been worried about children near an open fireplace. I shiver a little. It's going to be a cold night.

I follow my children into the house, picking up Gus's dropped school hat and two pens that have slipped from Isaac's perpetually open school bag.

I take a deep breath as I enter the living room, embracing the calm created by warm leather and timber furniture. The chocolate-brown sofa glows in the soft light of the living room, and I cannot help but contrast it with another sofa, plastic in feel and touch and peeling from the day it was brought into our house, salvaged from the side of the road. I wrap my arms around myself. It's time to turn on the large gas heater. I'm always surprised by how swiftly winter arrives in Australia. We seem to go from an endless summer to the chill of winter overnight with no pause for autumn in between.

In the kitchen the boys are in the pantry, having shoved their cut-up pieces of apple and orange in their mouths already. Gus has a wedge of orange in his mouth, juice dribbling down his chin.

'Gus,' I say and he shrugs his shoulders at me and spits the wedge into the bin, mostly eaten, I'm pleased to see. I grab a cloth and wipe up a few drops of juice on the floor. I can't stand mess. 'You make things hard for yourself,' Jack says. 'We have three boys.' But he doesn't quite understand the heart-racing panic I feel when things are dirty.

'One snack, boys,' I say as I do every day. The rule doesn't apply to Isaac, who will eat up until dinner and then polish off his food like the hungry teenager he is. I enjoy the comfort repetition brings. I like that I know Gabe will only take one snack but Gus will try and sneak by me with an extra chocolate bar concealed in his pocket.

I grab his shoulder as he walks past me and hold out my hand. 'You always know,' he sighs, and I nod solemnly. 'I always know,' I agree and I bite down to stop myself from giggling as I hear Isaac laughing in the walk-in pantry.

The afternoon flies by in a whirl of homework and mediation. Gus and Gabe inevitably squabble over something, and I like to keep a check on what Isaac is working on. Today it's an English essay, and I go up to his room twice, suggesting ideas, before he actually starts doing anything.

'I'm not telling you two again!' I shout up the stairs for the third time as my phone rings.

'You're going to be late again,' I answer after I see it's Jack calling.

'I am… yes, I'm going to be late again,' he affirms. I hear him tapping on his computer.

'Why do you let the secretary schedule late patients?' Jack has a soft heart for his older patients, who sometimes schedule a visit to the doctor out of loneliness. Lawrence, his father, wanted him to be a surgeon, but Jack was always more suited to the role of a GP and the patience required of that job.

'What can I do, love? I don't want anyone to feel they can't call me when they need me… and they do need me. It's fine, I'll be home by eight. Wait for me to eat, will you?'

'Of course. When don't I wait for you?'

'Never, my love. See you soon.'

'Is Dad going to be late again?' asks Isaac, coming into the kitchen for yet another snack.

'Looks like it.'

'Do you think he'll be able to help me with my science project? I want to do something about genetics.'

'I'm sure, just give him some time to have dinner and then he'll be all ears. Have you finished the essay?'

'It's so unbelievably boring. I hate English.'

'Hate it all you like, Isaac, but you have to do English for the rest of your high school career, so you might as well do the best you can.'

He groans exaggeratedly.

'Muuum!' shouts Gus from upstairs. 'Gabe hit me.'

'No, I didn't!' yells Gabe.

'Oh, hell.' I grab a cloth to wipe my hands after I sprinkle the last of the cheese onto the top of the lasagne.

'Relax, Mum, I'll go. Hey, you ratbags, I'm coming to sort you out.'

I open my mouth to say something but bite down on my lip instead. He's not really threatening the boys, and I know he would never raise a hand to them. Right now, the two of them are probably hiding behind their bedroom door so they can leap out and surprise him. I know that. But certain words… certain phrases will always carry more than one meaning for me.

'A good slap will sort her out,' I hear, his tone filled with anger and contempt, haunting me all these years later.

I pour myself a glass of wine and take a deep breath. Upstairs there is giggling and shouting and then all is quiet. It's 5 p.m., computer time, and all will be silent for an hour.

Opening up my own laptop as I sip the wine, I read messages from the primary school about various events coming up and one from the high school about a cheese and wine evening for parents.

There's a 'Hello, let's catch up' email from Natalia, who's been snowed under with a new job. Both of Natalia's children are in high school, and she's thrown herself back into the advertising world with vigour. I am only mildly jealous of my friend, knowing that every year I stay out of the workforce, it will make it harder for me to get back in.

'You can always hire someone to pick the kids up from school so you can go back to work... a university student... or we could get an au pair,' Jack says time and time again, but I need to be home until the twins are a little older and don't need me as much. Children need a stable environment, and I know myself well enough to know that the stress of a job will not allow me to be the kind of mother I want to be. I overcompensate, I know I do, but it's only because I remember. I remember everything. I'm lucky that Jack is happy to shoulder the financial load, and I will eventually go back to work when the boys are all independent. That time will come soon enough.

The last email has no subject line and it's not from an email address I recognise. As I open it, I realise my mistake because I know this is how viruses are delivered to computers. But it's just a single line. One sentence.

I know what you did.

The glass of wine slips out of my hand and shatters all over the floor.

'You okay, Mum?' Isaac shouts from upstairs.

'Yes, love, fine, just dropped a glass, don't worry.' I can't conceal my shaky voice and I sit very still for a moment, listening for his footsteps, hoping he won't come and investigate.

Alice is mired in guilt. Alice is smothered in guilt. Alice is drowning in guilt.

I take a deep breath and poke my tongue into the hole in the back of my mouth where a tooth used to be. It's right at the back. I lost the tooth when I was ten years old. I lost it after the news on the television revealed the depth of my mistake.

I close my eyes and see it now. I see the mangled red car wreck. I see the police gathered at the side of the road, shaking their heads as the camera moves across the horrific scene. 'Last night,' the reporter said. 'Mount Colah,' the reporter said. Right where we lived. I recognised the road, recognised the car, understood what I'd done.

As the news report ended, I shot up from the couch where I was sitting, turned around, searching for her, knowing she wouldn't be there. I needed to leave, to run, to scream, to cry but I knew to keep quiet. 'I'm sorry,' I whispered, 'sorry, sorry, sorry,' and then I turned around again and tripped, falling sideways and hitting my jaw on the edge of the chipped coffee table.

I woke up after a few minutes and felt something in my mouth – a tooth. I spat it out and rinsed my mouth. I immediately pushed my tongue into the space, worrying the delicate, bruised and broken flesh. *You did this, you did this*, the pain told me. I could have had the tooth replaced when I was an adult but I didn't want to. I don't want to. I need it there. I need it to always be there so I can remind myself that it was all my fault. That I am to blame.

I know what you did.

I watch my own trembling hands delete the email. I'm sure it's just a joke, a spam email.

Unless it's not.

Unless someone knows.

CHAPTER TWO
Molly

Molly chews her lip as she reads, shaking her head, sighing. People are hideous. She feels her eyes well up yet again as she reads about a little boy, 'subject A'. He has detailed his abuse through black crayon drawings. The report, 'The Long-Lasting Effects of Traumatic Childhood Experiences', is on a website filled with research papers on child abuse. The clinical language is juxtaposed with the boy's childish drawings of his experience. He is a stick figure with a permanent rain of tears falling from his circle-shaped eyes. His father is a giant stick figure with shark-like teeth and a long snake-like belt poised to strike. His pictures pull Molly into his turmoil. She can feel his fear, his despair, his sorrow.

How can parents do this to their children? How can people like this be allowed to have children at all? *Poor little boy*, thinks Molly. She would like to wrap her arms around him and comfort him but he is no longer a child; he is an adult suffering from PTSD.

She closes her eyes, imagines herself in a nondescript room, where she sees the boy, to whom she gives blond hair and large, sad, blue eyes. An unmade bed with dirty, crumpled sheets and a box with one or two broken toys complete the picture in her head. She sees a large man coming towards the child, anger scrunching his features. She watches him raise his belt and then she sees herself step forward, grabbing the belt with one hand and landing a forceful punch on the father with the other.

The little boy is safe, but when she opens her eyes, she recognises the futility of the fantasy. No one stopped this man from abusing his child, not until a teacher at school caught sight of his bruised little body when he changed for a swimming lesson. He suffered abuse at the hands of his father for years without anyone helping him at all. Molly thinks about the child's mother, about how she allowed such a thing to happen, and she cannot help a flash of anger despite knowing from all her research that it is most likely she was being abused herself.

The old-fashioned jangle of her ringtone provides a welcome distraction, dragging her away from the disturbing images. She looks out of the sliding glass doors of her apartment that lead to the balcony as she answers the phone. The sky is a perfect cornflower-blue and outside the weather is sharp and cold.

'Moll, what are you doing right now?' Lexie asks.

'Well, hello to you too. I'm doing some research for my next short story.'

'Oh no, not more horrible tales of abused children?'

'Afraid so. You can't even imagine how awful some of them are. I know I have to finish the book but sometimes it's just too much.'

'Why do you have to write another brutal story, Moll? Don't you have enough in the book? What would be wrong with something that has a little happiness and hope?'

'This is the final one, Lex, and it has to bring everything together. The whole book centres on disturbing childhood experiences. That's the concept the publisher bought. This is the final story and I need it to be great, but it's not coming easy I can tell you.'

'You know Mum and Dad are a little concerned…'

'What about?' asks Molly, instantly irritated.

'I don't know. They just don't like your obsession with this stuff.'

Molly is not willing to get into a discussion with her little sister. The truth is she doesn't know where her obsession comes from.

She just knows that she wants to give these children a voice and this is the only way she can do it.

'I'm having enough trouble with this story, Lex, I can't worry about what anyone else thinks.'

'Your muse out to lunch, is she?' Lexie laughs and Molly grins. Her sister has always had the ability to make her smile and laugh. Even when Molly is in the darkest of moods, Lexie never fails to gift her a lighter moment. Lately she can feel Lexie working hard at every conversation, trying to make sure her older sister stays on an even keel.

'I suppose she is at the moment. Anyway, what's up? What do you need?'

'Maybe I just called to say hello to my big sister. I can do that, can't I?'

'Hmm,' says Molly.

'Okay, I was wondering if you would be happy to babysit your niece tonight. You know she goes down at seven so you'll have the rest of the night to lounge on the couch or work or whatever.'

'Where are you going?'

'Owen has a drinks thing for work because they've finished a big project. If I meet him at the bar, we can go out to dinner afterwards and pretend we're a real married couple instead of just two exhausted parents of an eighteen-month-old child.'

'And you want to show off that new dress you bought.'

'Yes,' giggles Lexie, 'and I want to show off the new dress. Please say yes, Moll, it's been ages since I left the house and I'm worried that Owen's going to find another woman to talk to because I'm so boring.'

'Please, that could never happen. Firstly, Owen adores you, and secondly, he's just as tired as you are.'

'Probably, but I don't think Sophie is ever going to sleep through the night so we may as well get on with our lives.'

Molly sighs. Lexie could easily have found a babysitter but she knows how much Molly enjoys time alone with Sophie. A night with her adorable niece feels like it would chase away the terrible images that crowd her mind now. 'Okay, fine, Peter's working late anyway.'

'I counted on that. He always works late during tax time.'

'You sly thing.'

'More like desperate.'

'What time should I be there?'

'Around five, then you can do bath time and story time, and if she wakes up, she'll know to expect you.'

'Okay, see you then. You better leave something nice for me to eat.'

'Chicken pie is in the fridge. Love you, see you soon.'

'Love you too.'

Molly ends the call and goes back to reading. The internet is stuffed full of broken children. On the one hand, she wishes she could write about something different, but she is overwhelmed by the need to tell these stories. She doesn't want these children to simply be statistics, or a short article in the newspaper that people shake their heads at and forget about. She wants to make their pain real, their experiences visceral and the truth of their damaged little lives something that people cannot forget after reading her words.

She clicks on a link to a blog and reads about a little girl who was raped by her father, feeling herself shudder. *Sick bastard*, she thinks.

She has no idea why this last story in her book is causing her so much trouble. It's already written – and according to her editor, 'just fine' – but it doesn't feel good enough. The stories on the internet aren't helping, but sometimes she falls down the rabbit hole. She reads a comment on the website saying, 'We frighten children with stories of monsters like vampires and werewolves but sometimes the real monsters live in your house.' It contains a link to another blog, My Secret, which Molly clicks on. She begins reading at the home page under the heading 'Welcome.'

Welcome

This is a blog for those of us who've been abused and hurt. This is a place to come and share our stories anonymously. I am not a psychiatrist or a psychologist. I am just a woman who survived a brutal, awful childhood. I have had therapy and help and tried to move on with my life, but I still feel the need to tell my story, to have it read by others. I believe that those of us who were hurt as children need to raise our voices as adults. My dream is for no child to ever have to suffer as I did. I hope that by allowing people to share their stories here, we may inspire those who have suffered and even those who are still suffering and feel powerless to reach out.

This blog is an open forum for those of us who have had the very worst experiences that no child should ever have to endure. Please understand that people on here are fragile. Be kind and respectful in the comments. If you would like to read my own history, it's under My Story.

Thanks for being here. I wish you a peaceful day and the strength to deal with your past, your present and your future.

Molly sighs. There are lots of contributors to the blog – all, no doubt, hoping that writing down their trauma will be cathartic. 'All these damaged people,' she mutters.

She looks at the time on her computer. It's already four and she needs to be at Lexie's by five. She really should shower and get dressed, maybe eat some chocolate to help lift her mood, but she clicks on My Story instead.

My name is Meredith.

I grew up in a dark and terrible home. My mother's partner was physically and sexually abusive. The physical abuse began almost as soon as he moved in when I was six years old, the same year my father passed away.

When I was sixteen, I ran away. I spent a year living in shelters and sometimes even on the streets until I managed to get myself some help from a wonderful woman who ran a programme called Finally Home. She got me into counselling and she found me a place in a group home until I was old enough for a place of my own. She helped me navigate all the government resources available to me so I could have money to live on. Most importantly, she helped me go back to school so I could finish and go to university.

I have a good life now. If you saw me at a coffee shop, you would never imagine that I have been through the things I have experienced.

Things come back to me all the time, flashes of memories when I'm in the middle of doing something simple like loading the dishwasher or making dinner. Sometimes it's a smell that brings back a memory; sometimes it's a word someone uses or just a change in the weather.

I don't sleep very well at night. The setting sun still sometimes fills me with fear and despair. My mother's partner used to come into my room at night. I lay in bed every evening, waiting for it to happen, feeling relieved when it was over for that night but terrified of it happening again.

He would walk in and shut the door behind him. 'Put her in the cupboard,' he would say, and I knew that I had to drag my little sister out of her bed and lock her in the cupboard. I would try to make her comfortable in there with her little stuffed green frog and her blanket, and I would pray the whole time that he was there, doing things to me, that she would keep quiet. Once or twice she cried and he opened the cupboard door and slapped her until she went silent. For such a little thing, she learned quickly enough.

I will never be able to forgive him for the things he did, and believe me, I have tried.

I have worked very hard to change my life but the past will always have a hold over me.

I hope that you will leave your own story, and maybe if you have found a way to forgive your abuser, you can help me to forgive mine. X

Molly cannot move. She feels her neck begin to cramp and she wants to take a deep breath but all she can manage are shallow little gasps. She puts her hands down flat on the smooth timber of her desk as her heart races. Next to her computer sits a ratty, worn stuffed frog. He has black beady eyes and a red stitched mouth. His name is Foggy because she couldn't pronounce her Rs when she was little. She has had him all her life. It's just a stuffed toy. It was probably sold in the thousands. But Molly remembers.

She remembers the cupboard. She remembers the sting of the slaps. She remembers the churning fear she felt. She doesn't understand how.

But she remembers.

CHAPTER THREE

5 January 1987

Margaret

Margaret can feel the child watching her even with her eyes closed. Her daughter does that often. She'll tiptoe into the bedroom and just stand there and stare at her, all large, accusing eyes and sharp, angled bones.

Margaret hates her sometimes. But never more than she hates herself. Oh, how she hates herself. It's the only thing she has energy for these days. Even dragging herself to the bathroom exhausts her beyond comprehension.

She keeps her eyes closed, knowing that eventually the little thing will tiptoe out again, taking her accusations with her. Margaret waits until she hears the door close and then slides her body off the bed and gropes around underneath for the vodka bottle. When she grabs it, it is reassuringly heavy. Still full enough for oblivion. She levers her body up, drinks, chokes and coughs quietly.

She can see it's the middle of the day. The burning sun's glare pierces the threadbare curtains. They used to be a deep blue but have faded with the years, disintegrated in some parts, leaving small holes that she has never even tried to repair. She was so proud of them when she first hung them up in a different house, a different home – so entranced by the rich colour and the soft sheen they had. She had never thought she would own something so beautiful.

She spent hours choosing them, poring over the fabric swatches, overwhelmed by the choice, still not believing that she was the one who got to decide. But that was a different life.

Margaret stares at the faded blue as she drinks again. They are beyond repair and too short for the windows they now hang against. Only good for the bin.

'Like me,' she whispers.

The sound of the television drifts through from the living room. The ridiculous music that usually accompanies cartoons irritates her. The child should be at school and the baby should be… Where is the baby? Sweat slides down her body. She would love to be outside. Maybe there would be a cool breeze to stand in, some kind of relief, but outside is impossibly far away.

You need to get up, she tells herself silently. *You can do it if you want to enough. It's mind over matter. All you have to do is swing your legs to the side of the bed and stand up. Shower and get dressed. Leave this room and go and find the two of them and give them breakfast or lunch or something. It's not that hard. People do it every day.* She shoves the bottle back under the bed and stares up at the ceiling. The ceiling fan spins in a slow, dusty circle, moving the heat around the room.

'Lazy cow, lazy cow, lazy cow,' she mutters fiercely, imitating his bitter disdain perfectly. They used to say she could be an actress, but she can't quite remember who 'they' were now. Or she can but doesn't want to.

She closes her eyes and sees herself leaping off the mattress with its sour-smelling sheets, ready to take on the world. But she cannot move. Instead she pulls the bottle out again and drinks. The clear liquid seeps through her veins and soon she can no longer hear the ridiculous cartoon music. One more sip and the voices inside her are silenced as well.

'I'll just take a nap,' she promises herself, making sure to replace the cap tightly so not even a single precious drop is spilled, 'and then I'll get up.'

When she falls asleep, she dreams of a time before. She sees herself, vibrant with youth and possibility, smiling up at him and then gazing adoringly at the newborn in her arms. 'You're going to be the best mother in the world,' he said. How in love they had been, how certain of their future.

It seems impossible to believe now that she was once that woman. Even in her dreams she laughs at herself. 'Stupid, stupid girl.'

She wakes, dry-mouthed and sick with his name on her lips. 'Adam, Adam,' she calls as she struggles out of the dreamscape. The room is dark with only a fraction of light seeping in from the setting sun. A whole day is gone and she didn't even make it out of bed. What did the children do while she slept?

'Stop saying his fucking name, you whore,' he spits. He is on the bed next to her, reeking of cigarettes and sweat and beer; and then as casually as he might scratch an itch, he swings his hand and sends her back into darkness.

CHAPTER FOUR

Now

Alice

I give the boys dinner and clean up after them. I repeat, 'It's shower time,' five times before the twins wash one after the other. Then I empty lunch boxes and pack them for tomorrow. Isaac and I have a long discussion about his idea for a history project based on Roman architecture and I help him find a couple of sites to look at. When he starts rolling his eyes at every suggestion I make, it's time to give up for the day. 'Right, you can sort this out yourself,' I say.

'Yeah, yeah,' he agrees.

I pour myself another glass of wine and slide the lasagne back into the oven as it inches closer to 8 p.m. when Jack will be home. I keep myself busy, cleaning, tidying, organising and talking to the boys, but the words will not stop repeating themselves in my head.

I know what you did.

It must be a joke. That's the logical explanation. Maybe it relates to some old horror movie or perhaps it's simply someone's idea of humour. The trouble is that it doesn't feel like that. I can't dismiss it. I should have kept it to show it to Jack but almost the moment I registered the words I deleted it, unable to stare at the accusatory black letters. I poke my tongue into the space where the tooth used to be. I do it so often the gum is worn smooth.

I'm not sure I would want him to see it anyway. My husband knows a lot. He knows what I suffered. He knows what was done to me. But he doesn't know what I did. The absolute horror of what I did and the terrible result of that choice.

There's no way I could tell him. It took me years to share the truth, or at least part of the truth, with him. I let out small slivers of information, little pieces until he knew most of it. I was always waiting for him to judge me, to look at me and decide that I was too much for him to deal with, but he never did. It's one of the many reasons I love him.

I met Jack at a going-away party for a friend of Natalia's. 'Okay, so he's not really a friend,' Natalia had explained at the time, 'but my dad and his dad are both surgeons and Mark is going overseas to do a fellowship in oncology and he's going to have a whole lot of scrumptious newly qualified doctors at the party and I thought it might be nice to drop by.'

'No way,' I said. 'They'll all think I'm an idiot.'

'You're not an idiot; you're a highly intelligent, beautiful woman who's going to be an important features journalist, and I am also incredibly intelligent and beautiful even though I only want to write about fashion. Those doctors would be lucky to get the chance to talk to us.'

I laughed then because Natalia's confidence always made me smile. She is the only daughter of two surgeons, and in her home, I could see and feel how much she was cherished. I could see it on the walls, adorned with pictures of her at every age, and I could feel it when she spoke to her parents, and in the way they looked at her, listened to her and continually found reasons to offer a hug or a pat on the back. I cannot remember the kind touch of a parent. I cannot remember it at all.

I had never imagined that I would be friends with someone like Natalia. I met her on my first day at university. She rushed into the room, bringing with her a blast of heat from outside, where summer was refusing to let go. There were plenty of empty seats in the lecture hall but she sat down next to me, the flowery spice of her perfume strong enough to make me sneeze.

'Sorry,' she said, 'trying something new, may have to chuck it.'

I looked at her thick black hair and bright red lips and couldn't help smiling.

'Did I miss anything?' she whispered.

I wasn't entirely sure she was talking to me but then I looked at her and she lifted her heavy dark brows, waiting for me to reply.

'Just introductions,' I whispered back.

'Fabulous, I'm Natalia and I owe you a coffee.' I can still remember how hot my cheeks flushed, how my heart skipped at the idea that I would have someone to have coffee with like any other student on campus.

'I'm Alice,' I replied.

I don't think I heard much of that first lecture, as I spent most of the time cautioning myself to not get my hopes up. *It was probably just a throwaway line. She didn't mean it. Why on earth would she want to have coffee with you?*

I was embarrassed at how desperately I wanted to sit in the café amongst all the other students with a friend of my own. Friends had never been a big part of my life. Even when I was at primary school, I knew not to let anyone get too close, not to let anyone see the truth about my life.

When the lecture was over, I took my time gathering my stuff, not wanting to look Natalia in the eye so she could see how much I needed her. I decided that she was regretting the invitation and I hoped she would leave quickly, leaving me to deal with my disappointment privately.

But she stood next to me, studying her long purple fingernails, while I pretended it was of utmost importance that I rearrange my pens in their case.

'Come on, Alice,' she said finally. 'I'm starving.'

I felt my smile spread itself from ear to ear. I think my cheeks ached that night. I've never told her how much that first coffee meant to me. We've been friends forever but I still don't think she could understand that it felt like someone had reached down into the dark space where I was sitting and pulled me out into the light.

'You seem older than me,' Natalia observed over lattes and a shared giant chocolate chip cookie.

'I'm nineteen, nearly twenty.'

'Ah, gap year?'

'Yes,' I lied. I liked the sound of it. A gap year. I could imagine travelling the world, soaking up other cultures as I figured out what I wanted to do with myself.

'What did you do?'

'This and that,' I said. It wasn't a lie, not really. I had struggled to find accommodation cheap enough so that I could save up money to carry me through my university years with only part-time jobs. I had attended group therapy sessions and private therapy sessions in an attempt to heal myself. I had learned to cook cheap nutritious meals and found the best stores for clothing bargains. I had done this and that.

Natalia nodded. 'Cool.'

As we grew closer, I let out small morsels of the truth, hoping that I wouldn't shock my new friend into disappearing. But Natalia never has. Instead, at first, she greeted each shocking revelation with, 'Yeah, I figured.'

The first thing I told her was that I didn't speak to my mother. 'Yeah, I figured,' Natalia replied.

'Why?' I asked, stung that I seemed like the type of person who didn't speak to her mother.

'Well, you never talk about your family. I mean, like, you never complain about them, and I complain all the time because they're such overprotective Greek parents, and even though you've been over to my place heaps, you've never invited me to yours so I figured that there was something going on there.'

I felt some shame at how accurate she was. 'My childhood is not my fault,' I snapped because that's what Ian, my therapist, made me repeat to myself.

'Of course not,' Natalia said. 'How on earth can it be your fault?' We were both curled up on the massive leather couch in the room Natalia's family called 'the media room' because of the giant television with a VHS player and gaming consoles along one wall. Natalia had thrown together a big plate of nachos and we were both sipping on Diet Cokes. A rom-com was playing on the television.

'Not everyone had a childhood like I did, and I understand that,' she said. 'I get that that's not your experience. I don't care either. I think you're fabulous and you listen to all my shit without kicking me to the kerb so you're patient and lovely as well.'

I laughed. 'I like listening to your shit.'

'Lucky me,' said Natalia.

Our friendship only grew stronger from there and Natalia, after over twenty years, is still supportive and unsurprised whenever I reveal another piece of my childhood. But there is one part of my life I have never discussed with her. I've never discussed it with anyone – not Jack and not even Ian. I didn't do the right thing. I didn't make the right choice. And now there's this email, this single line that I've deleted that could blow up my world entirely. Once again, my tongue finds its way into the gap in my mouth.

I take a deep sip of my wine. I don't think I could ever tell my husband the whole truth. I couldn't bear to lose him, to have him look at me with horror and judgement. I simply couldn't bear it. My guilt is an old-fashioned ball and chain I have dragged through my whole life. Some days I don't feel its weight, but on others it feels impossible to move at all.

Back then, I went along with Natalia to the party despite my trepidation. Five minutes after we arrived, I found myself standing in a corner of an overcrowded room. It was nearly Christmas. University was over for the year, and the weather was warm and sultry. I felt light and free in my new white sundress. I was clutching a brightly coloured glass of punch, watching Natalia flirt with three young men at once. I didn't mind. Every now and again she would throw me a look that I knew meant she found all of them amusing but not really worth her time.

'Your friend… your friend is certainly a live wire,' a man said, coming to stand next to me. I noticed his ebony black hair and bright blue eyes and nodded. He moved his hands over his hair and then folded his arms, settling for putting his hands in his pockets.

'She is,' I said, 'and if you wait a few minutes, I'll introduce you.' I was sure Natalia would like this one even if he was a little awkward.

'Nah, I'm… I'm good. I thought I'd introduce myself to you instead. I'm Jack.'

'Oh… I'm Alice.' I couldn't believe he wanted to talk to me. For the first time, I felt seen. I was used to being invisible when I was out with Natalia.

'Med student or already qualified?'

'Um, neither. I'm studying journalism, one semester to go.'

'Interesting. Have you always wanted to be a writer?' he asked. I nodded.

'Maybe we could… discuss this somewhere else?'

'Um… But we can't leave the party? Can we?'

'I think we can leave the party, Alice.' He stopped fidgeting and seemed suddenly much more sure of himself, as though he had access to some book that explained how to be in the world that I had missed out on.

Even after twenty years together I still find myself asking Jack if he thinks a choice I'm making is okay. He always has to think about the answer he gives me, but I always trust that it's the right one.

'You know you don't need his permission, right?' a frustrated Natalia said only last month after I'd called Jack to check if it was okay for me to stay out and have dinner with her after some shoe shopping.

'I know,' I said because it was difficult to explain how much I needed to hear his affirmation that I was doing the right thing. That's what Jack has given me: the gift of someone in my life who is completely certain of his place in the world and of his own opinions, even if he's never quite sure what to do with his big hands and long arms. I can never be as assured as Jack can, and I need him for that. Another reason on a long list of why I love him.

I remember shivering in the warm room at that party as Jack spoke. His voice was low and deep and he spoke slowly and carefully and I felt something stir inside me, something I had never imagined I would feel.

According to Ian, at some point in my past, I distanced myself from my own body and the awful things that were being done to it. I separated my physical and mental self in order to protect myself. 'I want to try and bring those two halves of you back together,' he said, 'because one day that might be something you want.'

When I met Jack, it was the first time that I thought Ian could be right. No one had touched me for nearly six years by then, not even a doctor. I didn't like to think about my physical self. I showered and I made sure that I always looked presentable. I ate food, but I was always aware that I shouldn't enjoy it too much in case there came a time when I didn't have any. I exercised because exercise helped me keep my haunting, troubling thoughts in line, but other than that my body was just a vehicle to get from one place to another. I thought I would be happy with that for the rest of my life. And I could never ignore the small, spiteful voice in my head that sometimes spent entire nights repeating, 'You don't deserve to be happy. You don't deserve anything good at all.'

Jack took me to a late-night pizzeria and we talked over a spicy pepperoni pizza and some cheap red wine. Mostly Jack spoke and I kept him talking with questions about his family and his studies and what kind of doctor he wanted to be and why he had decided to study medicine.

'So,' he said when we were walking back to his car, 'do I get to ask any questions?'

'Um... sure, I mean there's not a lot to know.'

'Oh, I don't think that's true... not true at all. I think there's a great deal to know. I can see what you're doing and that's fine, but I'd just like to know if you're holding back because you don't... like me or if you're holding back because your life is a little more complicated than mine.' He fiddled with his keys while he waited for me to reply.

I was afraid I was going to burst into tears right in front of him. 'I do like you,' I said, 'and my life is a lot more complicated than yours.'

'Okay, then,' he replied. 'Okay... we'll take it really slowly.'

And we did. We dated for a month before Jack tried to kiss me, and then he asked permission first. I didn't expect the softness of his lips or the gentle way he cradled my head. I didn't expect to feel it ripple through my whole body. I didn't expect to want to push my body closer to his. I had never been kissed by a man before and I had always been terrified of it.

'Abuse,' I told him when I trusted him enough. But it didn't really explain anything. It barely scratched the surface.

After a few months he wanted to go further than a kiss, and I wanted to as well. All his awkwardness disappeared when he kissed me, when he touched me. I wanted, I yearned, but as soon as I stopped thinking and started feeling, my brain would reel me back in, a struggling fish on a sharp hook, and I would freeze up. My arms and legs would become rigid and I would have trouble breathing.

'It's okay,' he would soothe, stroking my hair. 'Enough for tonight.'

'I'm so sorry,' was all I could say. 'I really want to be with you but it's just…'

'I know, it's difficult. We'll take it slow… I'm happy with slow.'

'But don't you want a normal girlfriend? Someone who isn't damaged?'

'No, I want you, Alice, with your beautiful brown eyes and those kissable lips and your knowledge on everything under the sun. I know you want to be with me, and I believe… I really believe we'll get there. I can come and see Ian with you if that would help, otherwise I'm happy to take things at your pace.'

Alice is afraid of her body. Alice is afraid of her feelings. Alice doesn't believe she deserves to be loved.

'Have a safe word,' Ian suggested to us, 'something Alice can say and then you know it's time to stop.'

'Would that help you?' asked Jack.

'It would,' I said, relieved that I was allowed to protect myself without consequence. 'It really would.'

We chose 'pineapple', incongruous and so silly it made me laugh when I said it, which helped me relax. And then I let go.

'Even if we break up one day, I will always be grateful to you for giving me the time I needed,' I told him after we first had sex.

'We're not breaking up,' replied Jack. And he was right.

The sound of the garage door drags me away from my memories. The lasagne is perfect, the rich, cheesy smell filling the kitchen, and I pull it out of the oven and cut two pieces.

Jack's arrival throws the whole house into delightful chaos as Gus and Gabe compete for his attention. 'Let Daddy have some dinner, boys, please,' I say, but I don't really mind. I love watching their eagerness to share everything with their father. I love the way they climb all over him and demand his attention. They want to be near him and they eagerly await his arrival every night. They do not cower and hide and hope that tonight he will choose the pub instead of home.

'Agreed,' he says, 'I'm starving. I'll eat with Mum and then I'll be up to continue our adventure with Gulliver.'

'You know they can both read to themselves now, don't you?' I say.

'I do… I do, but soon they won't want me in their rooms at night. Isaac told me he didn't want to be read to when he was about ten so I'm going to enjoy these last few months. How was your day? Anything interesting?'

'Oh, you know, nothing much.' I feel a twinge at my ankle as though I have just added some more weight to the ball of guilt. I shouldn't lie to him. He deserves better than that. My tongue finds the space in my mouth.

Jack looks up from his food. 'Did you go and see your mother? I know you were thinking about it.' Jack thinks that I should see my mother to make sure that I have said my piece, to tell her exactly how I feel.

'I…' I shake my head quickly, my appetite suddenly gone. It's July already and I've only been to see her five times this year. 'I just couldn't.'

'Fair enough. I know things are nearing the end though. It would be good if you could go.' He cannot imagine not speaking to his parents. He calls his mother on his way home most nights, briefing her on his work and his family.

'But I don't want to say anything,' I reply. 'I told you I've forgiven her.'

'Maybe,' says Jack as he cuts himself another slice of lasagne and fills up his wine glass, avoiding looking at me, which I know means he doesn't believe me. And he's right. I never imagined that forgiveness was a daily ritual. I thought that once I said it aloud,

I would be done, but every time a memory surfaces, I have to do it again, affirm that I have forgiven her. It's exhausting.

But forgiving myself is not exhausting; it's impossible, absolutely impossible. *Stop it*, I tell myself.

The words in the email hit me again. *I know what you did.*

I can't forgive my mother but what worries me is that if she knew the truth, she wouldn't be able to forgive me either. How could she ever forgive me for such a thing?

Alice did a terrible thing. Alice made an awful decision. Alice is responsible for something wicked.

That's the trouble with bringing up the past. You can't leave some of it buried.

CHAPTER FIVE

Molly

In the shower Molly concentrates on the hot water pounding on her neck. 'You've been reading too much,' she tells herself in a stern voice like her mother would.

I need a drink, she thinks but she's babysitting Sophie, and anyway she's not drinking right now and definitely not thinking about why she's not drinking.

Chicken pie, she decides. *I need a lot of chicken pie*. Her brother-in-law, Owen, makes his chicken pie with a seasoning mix he refuses to share with anyone. 'I will only pass it on to my first-born child,' he has told everyone.

Molly pulls on sweatpants and a fleece hoodie against the cold. She makes it to her sister's house by 5.05 p.m. and triumphantly slides into a parking space right outside on the cramped street, overcrowded with semi-detached houses.

'I thought you'd forgotten,' says Lexie when she opens the front door.

'I'm five minutes late, Lex, and you look amazing.' Her sister's long blond hair hangs down her back, silkily catching the light. Molly rarely sees it down these days because Lexie ties it up, out of her face and away from Sophie's sticky fingers. Her new deep blue dress emphasises her small waist, rounded hips and full breasts. Molly wouldn't be comfortable exposing that much cleavage but Lexie has always embraced her curves.

'Ah, thanks, and you look…' Lexie stops and looks at her sister, really looks at her. Molly's light brown hair is pulled back and her sweatpants have a small hole at the knee but are so soft and easy to wear that she refuses to throw them out. She braces herself for a lecture from her stylish sister on not leaving the house looking like she's homeless – a lecture she's used to receiving – but instead Lexie is studying Molly's make-up-free face intently. 'Something's happened,' she says. 'What's happened?'

'Nothing, nothing. I was just running late.'

'You're… oh my God, are you?'

'No!' shouts Molly, louder than she meant to. 'No, Lex, do not say it, do not jinx it. Just go out and enjoy yourself.'

Lexie sighs. 'Okay, okay… I'm sorry, but I'm… oh, Moll… I hope… I wish… I pray…'

Molly feels her eyes fill with tears. She hasn't even admitted the news to herself yet, not after last time. She wants to pretend for a little while longer that she has nothing to hope for. Maybe that's why she's had such a strange reaction to the blog. Hormones. The thought comforts her. It's just hormones.

'Moiee, Moiee,' shouts Sophie, toddling in from the kitchen.

'Yes, it's Aunty Molly come to babysit you, you lucky girl,' says Lexie.

'Up, up,' demands Sophie. Her face is covered in whatever fruit she's been eating and her fingers are gummy with food.

'Poor thing, I wouldn't pick her up,' Lexie says, stroking her daughter's soft blond curls as Molly lifts her niece into her arms, earning a sticky pat from Sophie on her shoulder.

'Come on, little one, let's go finish dinner and then have a lovely bath. Off you go, Lex.'

'We'll talk when I get back, yeah?' her sister calls as she rushes around the house looking for her belongings. Her phone lets out a chirp. 'The Uber's here. Where are my keys and bag, Sophie?'

'Dey,' says Sophie.

The keys are hiding down the side of the sofa and her bag has been upended in her bedroom, courtesy of Sophie.

'Lex, we'll talk when and if there is anything to talk about, okay?' Molly says. She gives her sister a stern look. 'Take a coat, it looks like it's going to rain.'

'Okay, okay,' says Lexie, holding up her hands, admitting defeat. She grabs her raincoat from a hook near the front door, plants a quick kiss on her daughter's and sister's cheeks and waves as she closes the front door.

Molly breathes a sigh of relief when she and Sophie are alone. Her niece is easier to be with than her eagle-eyed sister, who somehow seems to know the moment anything happens in Molly's life.

Lexie has guessed every time Molly has been pregnant over the last four years, and she has grieved every time each pregnancy has ended right along with Molly and Peter. Six times. That's how many times Molly has been pregnant. She has lost six babies for no reason that medical science can determine. She falls pregnant easily enough but each time at around ten weeks her hopes, her dreams and another little life are lost. She has tried everything from special teas to progesterone shots, and still her longed-for babies slip away, leaving her empty and devastated. She cannot hope or pray or wish anymore. All she can do is not think about it. It's easier not to think about it. When she and Peter agreed to give it one more go before taking the adoption route, she almost hoped she wouldn't get pregnant. But she did, just as she had with all the others, in the first month of trying. Now she doesn't know if she can survive the heartbreak of yet another ending, so she's not thinking about it, she's simply not thinking about it.

'I just can't, I can't,' she had wailed to Peter as they both stared down at the test.

'But look, babe, look how bright the line is. It's a good sign. I'm sure it's a good sign. Make the appointment with Dr Bernstein tomorrow. Go and see him. Maybe there's something new they can do.' Peter is an optimist. He goes through life believing that everything will turn out all right. He is certain that they will have a child. Just like he was certain that she would, one day, find a publisher for her work. Peter wakes up expecting sunshine every day, but rather than be upset if it's raining, he merely looks forward to the next sunny day. Sometimes he drives Molly crazy but a lot of the time, especially over the last few years, she's grateful for his positive approach to life. After each miscarriage he has picked her up, helped her dust herself off and handed her some hope so she can go on. It's getting harder and harder for him to do, but he keeps trying.

'We've run all the tests we can,' Dr Bernstein explained after the last miscarriage. 'There is no reason for this to keep happening.'

'So, what do we do now?' Peter asked, leaning forward in his chair. Molly wasn't able to say a thing. She was broken and silent in the doctor's office.

'I know it may sound a little callous, but when Molly is fully recovered you simply need to try again.'

'And that's it?' Peter replied, incredulous. 'That's all we can do? There must be a way to solve this problem.'

'I wish there was something we could fix or change but I'm afraid we simply don't have an answer for you.'

Molly has no desire to hear those heart-wrenching words again, so when Peter told her to go and see the doctor, she nodded her head but did nothing. 'Just don't talk to me about it,' she told Peter. 'If he says something you need to know, I'll tell you.'

She could see that he wanted to protest. He has grieved over the lost little souls as much as she has, but she can't allow it to become real only to have her heart crushed once more. If she doesn't see Dr Bernstein, then it isn't real; if she doesn't discuss it, then it isn't real; if she doesn't think about it, then it isn't real; and when it ends it won't hurt so much.

It's been three weeks now and she can see Peter biting back his questions. She hates that she has lied to her husband but she's pretty sure that by the end of next week it will all be over anyway. Why waste the time or the money on a visit?

She sits next to Sophie, who's in the bath, blowing soap bubbles, making her niece shriek with laughter every time she catches and pops one. She can remember her mother doing the same thing for her and Lexie when they bathed together as kids.

Her mother used to sit next to the bath when they were too little to be left alone and blow bubbles for them, perfect round bubbles, growing larger and larger as her hands acquired more and more soap. Occasionally her father would return home early and pop his head into the bathroom. 'How are my two peas in a pod doing today?' he would ask. 'Peafect,' she and Lexie would respond in unison, giggling. He always called the sisters that because they looked so similar, with their long straight blond hair and wide brown eyes. The resemblance in their face shapes seems to have lessened over time. Molly is thinner now than she's ever been whereas Lexie's shape has softened and rounded, even more so with the birth of Sophie. Molly's hair has darkened to a light brown but Lexie's has remained a golden blonde. Their father still calls them his two peas though. They have such similar opinions on everything and are as close as ever, sometimes speaking two or three times a day.

Molly knows that not everyone gets on with their sister the way they do, and she's grateful for their friendship. Even when they were younger, they never fought much. As a child, Molly had always acquiesced easily to her little sister's demands, finding her feisty character amusing and endearing rather than aggravating.

'You're such a good big sister,' she repeatedly heard from her parents and her parents' friends as she grew up. So much so that if she did get irritated with Lexie, she squashed it as quickly as she could, conscious to remain the 'good big sister'.

She feels like the roles are somewhat reversed now with Lexie checking in on her constantly, always trying to make sure she's okay. Lexie is a good little sister, always careful to gauge Molly's mood before she talks about Sophie, and even though Molly knows her sister and Owen want more children, Lexie never discusses this with her, because sometimes hearing about babies hurts so much that Molly feels like she can't breathe.

Now that Lexie has realised she's pregnant, Molly knows she'll want to talk about it because when it comes to Molly being pregnant Lexie can't help herself.

'Only one more week, hey little Sophie, and then it will all be over,' she says, despair colouring her voice. Sophie giggles and reaches for another bubble as it drifts past her.

Molly feels weighed down by sadness. It's more than just the anticipation of losing another child. It is something dark and heavy and old, something she has never felt before. The more she thinks about the cupboard and the frog, the more concrete the memory becomes. There was a smell – a damp, mouldy scent – and her blanket was frayed and pink.

'I'm just making all this up,' she says to Sophie. 'I must be making it up.'

But she is sure that the inside of the cupboard was painted white, and if she couldn't sleep, she would pick at the chipped paint with little fingers, peeling off bits to reveal the board underneath. If she was awake, she felt that she would be locked in the cupboard forever, that she would never be allowed out again. 'Just making it up,' she comforts herself.

'Up, up,' demands Sophie, and Molly wraps her little body in a towel, revelling in the feel of her niece's weight and trust as she rests her head on Molly's chest. Once Sophie is dressed in her lemon-yellow Babygro festooned with white ducks, they sit in the rocking chair. 'Goodnight Moon,' reads Molly, and Sophie points and touches and occasionally says, 'Moon.' All too soon their time together is over and Molly's niece is in her cot, quietly drinking her milk. Molly checks that the heater is on low and half closes the door to Sophie's room.

She tidies the kitchen as the evening yawns before her. Lexie is a haphazard housekeeper, worse since Sophie has gotten bigger and begun the time-honoured toddler tradition of unpacking every drawer, basket and cupboard she can get to. Molly thinks of her own pristine flat. Her black-and-white kitchen was spotless when she left earlier and it will be spotless when she returns, with only an extra coffee cup in the sink if Peter gets home early enough to have one.

Molly clears Lexie's sink of small cups with lids, brightly coloured bowls and cutlery, and tries not to let the loneliness of her clean kitchen and their empty second bedroom overwhelm her.

Once she's done, she cuts a piece of the chicken pie Lexie has left her and puts it into the oven. While she waits for it to warm, she tries Peter at work.

'Babe?' he answers, already worried and panicking, but she senses that he doesn't want her to know he feels this way. He tries to always be positive for her.

'I'm just calling to say hello. I'm babysitting for Lexie. Just thought I'd let you know in case you get home before me.'

'Oh, okay, sorry I just…'

'I know, but let's not talk about it. I'm fine, I promise. I'm about to eat a giant piece of Owen's famous chicken pie and watch some rubbish on television.'

Peter sighs. 'Wish I was there with you. I've just eaten some awful Chinese and I don't think I'll be home before midnight. The computer system mucked up some of the returns and now everyone is in a flap. But I'm sure we'll sort it out.'

'Sounds like a fun day at the accountancy firm then.'

'It's a riot. Anyway, I'll try and be extra quiet when I get home. How did work go today?'

'Okay… I'm reading too much stuff online. I'm starting to feel like I've experienced some of the things I'm reading about. The whole thing is starting to feel depressing. I just want it over now.'

Peter is quiet for a moment. 'Maybe it's more than that. Maybe you need to talk about the… pregnancy. If you don't want to talk to me, I get it, I really do, but maybe go and see that woman that Dr Bernstein suggested. She could be really helpful.'

Irritation flares in Molly. 'I don't want to do that. I don't need to know how to prepare for a miscarriage, Peter. More than anything I know how to have a miscarriage. Please, I know that this is difficult for you, but I need to just let this lie for now. Please?'

He takes a deep breath. 'I understand, I do. Please don't be angry with me. I know you only call me Peter when you're angry.'

'I'm not angry… I'm just…'

'It's okay. I get it. But I think things will be… Look, I better get back to it. I'll be home as soon as I can be.'

'Okay, love you.'

'Love you too, with all my heart.'

Molly puts down the phone, pushing down on her chest where she imagines she can feel pain. 'Love you with all of my heart' is something Peter's parents said to him and something she'd always imagined she and Peter would say to their children. The possibility of those children never existing takes her breath away. It's so unfair. There are people who get pregnant by mistake and then neglect and abuse their kids. There are drug addicts and alcoholics who somehow find themselves parenting, and there are so many hurt children in the world, and yet she and Peter can't have just one to give a lifetime of love to.

Molly resolves to stop thinking negatively, to stop thinking anything, really. She eats far more chicken pie than she wants to and watches a silly movie on television. *I'm not thinking about it*, she keeps telling herself, but even as she laughs at the antics of a couple of teenagers on a road trip, she is aware of a part of her running through different scenarios over and over again. *If I lose the baby tonight, if it lives until next week, if I go for a scan and there's no heartbeat, if I go for a scan and there is a heartbeat, if I manage to get to three months, if I get to four months, if I feel my baby kick.* When Lexie was pregnant, Molly used to sit next to her with her hands on her stomach, waiting for Sophie to turn and kick while her sister read a book or watched television, seemingly unaware of the absolute miracle going on inside of her.

Molly cannot even imagine what the final, joyful scenario, the place she cannot see herself getting to, would feel like. She has never let herself go there, not since the first miscarriage.

Beneath the scenarios playing out in her head there is a darker picture, the one she keeps dismissing. It's a little girl curled up tight on top of a pink blanket clutching her favourite toy. She somehow knows she can hear sounds she doesn't understand. Soft whimpers that are not coming from her and low grunts that sound like they come from a man. *The big man*, she thinks. That's what she called him: 'the big man'. The phrase surfaces in her mind as though it has always been there.

Molly mutes the television and looks around the living room. She feels like someone has spoken the words aloud. The big man. She gets up and checks on Sophie, who is sprawled across her cot, arms above her head, deeply asleep. Unsettled, Molly makes a tour of the small house, looking in Lexie's bedroom, where clothes litter the floor, and making sure the back door is locked.

When there is nothing left to check, she raids Lexie's chocolate jar, pulling out a handful of mini chocolates. She wishes she could have a drink. Finally, she sits back down on the couch and turns on the sound again. 'The big man?' she says aloud. Where did that come from? Is it something she's remembering from a movie or something she's seen on television? Is it something she's read that she's somehow made her own?

The blog she read didn't mention 'the big man'. She's sure none of them have. Molly gives herself a little shake. 'Enough of this now,' she says aloud.

When Lexie and Owen arrive home, they are both slightly drunk. Lexie's cheeks bloom red and Owen keeps touching her hair, her arm, her back.

'Owen, stop,' says Lexie, giggling.

'Time for me to go, I think.' Molly grins.

'Thanks so much,' says Owen and he stumbles towards the bedroom.

'Someone had a good night.'

'I did,' sings Lexie. 'We did. Thanks so much, Moll – you can't imagine how much it means to us.'

'It's a pleasure. Sophie and I had a great time.'

'We'll talk tomorrow, okay?' says Lexie, and Molly simply nods. She doesn't want to spoil her sister's good mood, but tomorrow she'll tell her she doesn't want to talk. Not now and maybe not ever.

CHAPTER SIX

8 January 1987

Margaret

This morning Margaret opened her eyes with the rising sun and somehow found the energy to get up. She is grateful she is up, grateful she managed only a sip of vodka before she got out of bed.

She finds the girls in front of the perpetually on television, watching an endless parade of cartoons.

'Have you had breakfast?' she asks Alice brightly as any mother would.

Alice turns at the sound of her voice. 'You're up,' she states.

'I'm up.' Margaret smiles, hoping for one in return, but her elder daughter simply turns back to the television. 'There's nothing to eat,' she says to the cartoon mouse.

'Li, Li, Li,' says Lilly, patting her sister on the head. It was her first word – her sister's name. Not Mum, not Dad but Li for Alice.

'Stop that, Lills,' replies Alice mildly.

'Do you want to come and help me make breakfast, Lilly?' asks Margaret, but the child doesn't even reply. Her younger daughter regards her as an infrequent visitor. Alice is her real mother. Alice is where she goes for comfort and food and care.

Margaret stares at her daughters. They aren't even grateful she's out of bed. What was the point of her getting up at all? She thinks about her safe sheets and the relief of the bottle, but she is determined not to give in to oblivion today.

In the kitchen she hunts through the pantry and the fridge.

There is nothing to eat but the ends of a stale loaf of bread and two eggs. Alice could have made breakfast for both of them; she's old enough to know how to use the stove. Margaret sighs. *What kind of a useless mother won't even cook breakfast for her children?* the voice inside her asks. 'I'm not useless,' she mutters, 'I'm just tired.'

'What?' asks Alice. She is standing in the kitchen doorway, Lilly's hand clutched in hers.

'Nothing, nothing,' says Margaret. 'I'll make you both egg in the hole for breakfast. Would you like that?'

Alice shrugs and Margaret gets to work, cutting careful squares out of the bread, avoiding the mouldy parts, concentrating hard when she twists on the stove and adds the last of the butter into the pan. *I can do this*, she encourages herself as her daughters watch on. Their silent judgement burns into her back. She knows if she walked out of the kitchen, leaving breakfast to burn, they wouldn't be surprised. They would simply accept it.

I won't do that, she tells herself, *not today*.

She puts the meals in front of them. Alice looks at her for a minute and then she sighs and gets two forks and a knife from the kitchen drawer. She patiently cuts up her little sister's food before beginning to eat her own. Margaret feels shame wash over her. She didn't think to cut up her own daughter's breakfast.

She makes herself a strong cup of coffee, happy to do without the milk and sugar, needing the bitterness to focus her mind and body.

She needs to go shopping, but already she can feel the slithering exhaustion coming to claim her. Why do even the simplest things feel so impossible?

If she can stay away from the bottle for a little while longer, she can stay awake, but she's so tired and now her hands are shaking. It's all just too much.

'Mum,' says Alice, 'we have to go to the shops today.' Her voice is shrill and demanding. Margaret starts, realising that she must have fallen asleep standing up, holding her hot mug of coffee.

She hates the way Alice sounds, the judgement in her voice. She can't stand the disappointment written all over her daughter's face. *You're a failure, you're a failure, you're a failure*, bounces around inside her head.

'I know what I have to do!' she shouts, more to drown out the bouncing words than because she's angry. She's too tired for real anger. She has long given up on anger.

Alice folds her arms and purses her lips. Her mother shouting doesn't bother her anymore; her mother sleeping doesn't bother her either. Margaret knows that if she just disappeared, her daughter wouldn't be bothered at all. *Not true, not true, not true*, she tries to tell herself.

'I'm sorry, sweetheart. I just need a little time, okay? You get Lilly ready and I'll just shower quickly.'

'Okay,' agrees Alice. 'Do you have some money?'

Margaret blushes because she has no idea. She sees her bag on the counter and grabs it to look through. He has left fifty dollars for her with a note: *Fill up the bloody fridge, idiot.*

She crumples up the note. 'Yes, see here, Vernon left us fifty dollars.'

She stands under the shower until the water grows cold. She pulls on jeans and a T-shirt, already sweating in the heat, conscious that she hasn't done laundry for a very long time. The smell of dirty nappies pervades the house so the rubbish bins in all the rooms must be full. 'You need to get your act together,' she mumbles and then she sits down, sweating and shaking from the effort of simply being out of bed. She leans down, grabs the bottle and takes a quick, deep drink. *Just to tide me over*, she thinks and then she takes another. The burning sensation is a balm for her soul. 'Right, let's do this,' she says aloud.

When she comes out of the bedroom, Alice is standing at the front door with Lilly strapped into her pram. It's a wonder she can lift her little sister, who seems about half her size. *I wonder how old she is now*, thinks Margaret. Lilly's clothes are stained and grubby at the edges. Alice's are as well. She stares at a dark spot in the middle of Alice's chest. It looks like chocolate. When last would Alice have had chocolate? How long hasn't the laundry been done for? Her daughter tugs at the T-shirt self-consciously.

'I need to do the laundry when we get home,' says Margaret.

'He said he would do it today.'

'Please don't call him "he", Alice. Call him Vernon or Dad – you know he wants you to call him Dad.'

Alice folds her arms and stares.

'Fine.' Margaret sighs. It would be so much simpler if Alice were an easy child but she's stubborn and angry and each day just the thought of having to deal with her exhausts Margaret as she opens her eyes.

'A little bitch' is what Vernon calls her, and sometimes she agrees with him and then is hit by a wave of terrible guilt. She should love her daughter more. Why doesn't she love her more? But emotions require energy and she doesn't have any. What she mostly feels is blank – a deep, blank nothingness.

She manoeuvres the pram out of the front door.

'You need your bag,' says Alice, her voice flat with disappointment.

'Oh, of course,' replies Margaret, scuttling back to the kitchen.

Once they are outside in the sunshine, she manages to pretend that this is usual for her, that she is someone who thinks nothing of taking her two daughters down to the local store. She doesn't have a car. It broke down weeks or months ago and he said, 'No point in getting it fixed since you're always fucking wasted.'

'Why aren't you in school?' she asks Alice without thinking about it.

'It's the summer holidays, Mum,' says Alice with a sigh.

'Oops, silly me. It's really hot, isn't it? Maybe we can have an ice cream from the shops.'

'Really? Really?' asks Alice, hopping up and down, her worries disappearing with the promise of a treat. She is a child again for a moment, not the jaded little adult she seems to be most of the time. Margaret thinks occasionally of asking her daughter what's wrong but then she realises that she doesn't want the answer. She has enough trouble getting herself up and out of bed. Being a mother is an impossible task. She can remember when this wasn't the case but that was long ago, so very long ago.

'Ice, ice,' says Lilly, interrupting her thoughts, 'weally, weally.'

'Yes, really.' Margaret laughs and tilts her face towards the hot sun. She resolves to be a better mother from now on. She will get up and make breakfast and she will do the laundry and she will stay away from the bottle. But even as she thinks these comforting thoughts she yearns for the bright metallic taste of the vodka.

At the store they meander slowly up and down the aisles, enjoying the blasting, cold air from the air conditioners. 'We need bread and eggs and milk,' Alice says, continuing to point out things they need. Margaret does as she says. She has no idea what her children require. She has no interest in food herself. 'Just like a stringy piece of meat,' says Vernon when he touches her. 'Ugly as fuck.' She shakes her head to get the words to disappear. She knows he's right.

She can almost feel Alice holding her breath as they pass a freezer containing ice cream. 'Go on then,' she says to her daughter.

Afterwards they sit in the sun in the park across the road from the supermarket, watching other families, and Margaret feels the joy of simply blending in. Alice eats her strawberry-flavoured ice cream neatly, catching drips with her tongue before they fall, savouring every precious drop. The baby is soon covered in chocolate but so happy about it that Margaret doesn't worry about being judged. Her own ice cream melts in her shaking hands. She has chosen an ice lolly in lurid green and red, sure she had something similar when she was a child, but one lick tells her it will be too much for her stomach. 'Finish mine,' she says to Alice. 'I'm full.'

'You're always full,' says Alice, grabbing the ice cream away. But then she sidles a little closer to Margaret, sighing happily as she makes her way through it.

'Tell me about my dad, Mum,' says Alice in between licks of the lolly.

She only asks about her father when she feels safe, when she feels happy, and Margaret tries to calculate how long it's been since she's mentioned him. It could be weeks or it could be months. Time disappears into the black hole of her despair. She can feel the exhaustion creeping up on her now. The sun is too bright. The noise of children in the park is like a screeching siren in her head. Oh, how she longs for the acid taste in her mouth, longs for the moment she can close her eyes and sleep.

'He was my first love,' she says tentatively.

'But he died in an accident,' continues Alice.

'If you know the story, why do you want me to tell it?' she snaps. She cannot help herself. Why is it so hot? It shouldn't be this hot. Sweat creeps down her back and her whole face is damp. She would like to climb out of her own skin. She scratches at her arm where the sun is burning it red.

'Sorry, Mum, sorry I'll be quiet.' Alice's eyes widen, her lip trembles.

Margaret wants to feel sorry for her, to feel anything at all. 'Let's get home,' she says, and it takes everything she has to make it into the house. Her feet wade through tar. Alice pushes the pram, back to being silent and resentful. *Don't I even get any credit for trying?* Margaret wants to ask, but children don't give you credit for anything. They take and they take and they take and then when you have nothing left, they take some more.

She leaves the baby in the pram and the shopping bags hanging off the handles. All she wants is the cool burn from the bottle and some rest.

As she begins to drift, she hears the sound of smashing glass from the kitchen. 'Clumsy child,' she mutters. 'He's going to be so angry.'

She wants to get up, to help prevent the blow-up that will inevitably come later when he walks through the door, but she cannot move and very soon she cannot think either. He doesn't care about broken plates really. He simply needs an excuse. Alice shouldn't keep handing him excuses. The child needs to grow up and figure out how to keep herself safe.

Margaret doesn't let the thought form that keeping her children safe is her job. Instead she takes another drink, rubbing out any thoughts at all.

She floats on the surface of her dreams for a while before sinking into the deep sleep that she craves.

CHAPTER SEVEN

Now

Alice

I check my email constantly over the next few days. I think about telling Jack or even about showing Isaac and asking him if he can trace the email address to its owner. Isaac can click through pages on the computer faster than I can breathe. He throws technical terms at me and rolls his eyes and smiles when I don't understand.

I suppose he is typical of his generation. I'm sure he would be able to trace the email but he would have questions. Anyone I ask to help will have questions.

There are no more messages, and my inbox fills up with reassuringly boring missives about school and sales at various clothing stores. But I still find myself struggling to concentrate on anything. I tidy the boys' rooms and reorganise my pantry and chat with another mother about the school bake sale that I have somehow found myself in charge of this year, but I feel like I'm doing everything at a distance. The words from the email repeat on an endless loop in my head.

The Alice thread, the thoughts and feelings that are always there, runs constantly. *Alice is worried. Alice is afraid. Alice has been found out.*

Just a joke, I keep repeating to myself as I poke my tongue into the gap in my mouth.

'Is something wrong?' Jack asks over dinner.

It takes me a second to register his question. 'No, nothing, why do you ask?'

'You've been staring into space for the last few minutes.'

'Just thinking about visiting my mother,' I say because it's an easy excuse for everything.

'Do you want to go on Sunday so I can come with you? It might help if I'm there as well. It might… make things easier.'

'No, love… thanks but I'll be fine. Now how about some dessert? I bought a tub of chocolate ice cream and there may just be some left if the kids haven't realised it's there yet.'

'Sure, sure.' Jack smiles but he can't hide the worry he's feeling. He moves the salt and pepper shakers back and forth across the table.

I know what he's thinking. He's remembering the few dark months after Isaac was born when I became hypervigilant and constantly distracted at the same time. That time feels so long ago and the person I was feels like someone else. I suppose it was inevitable, given how I was raised and my fears about having my own child. But I thought that if I could just read enough, learn enough, prepare enough for his arrival, then I would be fine. I didn't sleep after he was born, but I assumed it was because I was in the hospital where the noise was constant and the nurses came in at odd hours. Isaac didn't sleep either. We spent a lot of time crying together in the middle of the night, me and my baby boy.

Once we got home, I thought things would improve but I couldn't sit still for even a few minutes, leaping up to constantly go and check on the baby. If I did sit, I couldn't concentrate on even the simplest conversation. I didn't sleep at night. I would lie in bed, clutching the baby monitor to my ear, listening to him breathe, waiting for him to stop. When my body was too exhausted to continue, I didn't so much fall asleep as drop into nothingness. Then I would jerk awake and, my heart racing, I would leap out of bed and run to his room to check on him. I thought that something would happen to him if I slept. I thought he would be taken from me if I rested. If Jack was home, I would beg him to sit next to his cot so I could sleep for an hour, watching every breath Isaac took so I knew he was safe.

'You need help,' Jack said after a few weeks. 'You can't go on like this, Alice. You don't sleep and you barely eat. Please, please let's get you some help.'

'I'm fine, I'm just tired, but all new mothers are tired. When he's a little older I'll rest. Now I need to make sure he's okay.'

Jack asked his mother to come over and stay. Ida, bless her, slept on the very uncomfortable fold-out couch in the living room of our small flat, promising to watch Isaac all night, but still I couldn't sleep.

'Enough of this now,' said Jack eventually. 'Something is wrong and we need to fix it. There's medication that can help. This happens to lots of women, Alice, especially women who've had a difficult time as children… I think—'

'I'm fine,' I yelled. I can remember the terror I felt at the word 'medication', at the idea that my brain chemistry would be altered, at the horrifying thought that I would not be fully in control of myself, of my thoughts. If you lose control of yourself, you lose everything and terrible things happen to your children.

I would not perpetuate my mother's legacy. Regardless of how different a person I was to her, I still feared that more than two glasses of wine, more than a few puffs of a cigarette, more than a couple of headache pills would send me spiralling into an addiction I couldn't recover from. I believed if I started taking medication, I would never stop. I was not going to be that kind of a mother. I was not going to blur reality until I had no idea what was going on in my house. I never wanted Isaac to question my love or the safety of his home, and if that meant never sleeping again, I was fine with that.

Jack grabbed me by the shoulders and propelled me over to a mirror. 'Look, Alice,' he said gently, 'look what you're doing to yourself.'

I studied my gaunt face and my sunken eyes and then I hung my head. 'Please don't give me drugs,' I begged.

Jack pulled me to him, held me tight. 'My love, I only want the best for you. We'll find a way to get you some help, I promise we will. Maybe you just need to talk to someone. We can find someone for you to talk to.'

'I can talk to Ian,' I whispered. 'I would like to talk to Ian.' And as I said those words, I felt a profound sense of relief. Ian had helped me put myself back together once before, surely he could do it again.

I remember Ian arrived at the flat in a thick jacket and I had been unable to understand why he needed it. In my sleep-deprived state, I had not noticed the season change. I had not managed to leave the flat since I had returned home from the hospital.

'Tell me what you're afraid of, Alice,' Ian said while I chewed on a piece of skin on my thumb.

'I'm afraid something will happen to him,' I told Ian.

'But he's perfectly healthy, isn't that true?'

'Of course, but what if something happens when I'm asleep? What if he gets a high temperature or throws up and chokes or smothers himself in one of his blankets?'

'There's a baby monitor in the room and you have a monitor under his mattress that will detect if he stops breathing.'

He leaned forward and gently pulled my thumb away from my mouth. It was only then that I noticed I was chewing on it, that I had drawn blood as I tore at the skin with my teeth.

'If you sleep,' I whispered to him, as though I was sharing a great secret with him, 'you don't take care of your children. I have to take care of my child. I'm afraid to sleep,' I admitted, feeling tears on my cheeks. 'I'm afraid if I let myself sleep, I won't want to wake up. I'm so tired, just so tired.'

'You're not her,' said Ian, leaning forward. 'You're not her, you just need some help.' He nodded his head as he spoke.

I found myself nodding along with him. 'I'm going to get help,' I agreed.

Isaac and I had a week's stay at a mother and baby unit where the staff all spoke in soothing voices and I had time to see a therapist. I got better sooner than I expected to but I realised months later it was because Ian had zeroed in on my one terrible fear. I didn't want to be my mother.

'I'm fine, Jack,' I say, tearing myself away from that dark chapter, handing him a bowl with the scraping of ice cream that had been left in the tub, Isaac having obviously discovered it hidden behind some frozen meat. 'I'm fine, let's watch a movie.'

I cover us both with a blanket, sitting close to him on the sofa. I focus my thoughts on the spy thriller we're watching, immersing myself in the character's dilemma of a stolen briefcase, and when it's time for bed I have almost convinced myself to dismiss the email. Mysterious messages about things you've done in your past only happen in the movies.

I check my phone after I start the dishwasher, making sure there's nothing on at school tomorrow that I may have forgotten.

There is one new email. My hands shake so much I have to try twice before I can open it.

I know what you did.

I bite down on my lip, stung by the salty metal taste of my own blood. Who can this be? The message gives nothing away and the email address is just some random letters and a Gmail domain. It could be spam. It has to be.

Ignore it, I think as I listen to the comforting swish and whir of the dishwasher. I look around my kitchen, at my safe space with its dark stained timber doors and white marble countertop. I hate that those words are in my home, hate that someone is tormenting me.

I need to go and see my mother. I need to ask her what she knows, how much she knows. I have never told anyone the truth because I spend every day trying not to think about it, trying not to see her trusting little face, trying not to feel her little hand in mine. I could never have anticipated what would happen. I was trying to help, not hurt. The twisted metal wreck appears in front of me. I poke my tongue into the gap as the lead-like sadness I carry with me all the time takes over my body, and I sink to the floor of the kitchen. *Alice did a bad thing. Alice did a terrible thing.* I didn't help. I didn't help at all.

It's been decades now. Surely if someone knew something, they would have confronted me or told the police. Why contact me now? Why now?

There are only two people I can think of who might hate me that much – and one of them is my own mother.

I look at the words again.

Alice is being hunted. Alice has been caught.

I know what you did.

The words are innocuous and ugly at the same time, and my finger hovers over the button for only a moment before I press delete, and the sentence is gone.

CHAPTER EIGHT
Molly

Molly opens her eyes, her heart racing. Next to her Peter shuffles and mutters, 'Column A,' before emitting a light snore. The bedside clock reads 2.30 a.m. She hadn't felt Peter slip into bed and she curls herself around him now, trying to force the nightmare from her brain.

She was walking alone on a road, covered in small black stones. The tarred road was divided by one thick white line and was completely empty. There were no houses she could see and no cars either, just a long barren stretch of emptiness. There was nothing but the road in front of her and nothing but the road behind her, and she was consumed by a loneliness so profound that all she wanted to do was close her eyes and disappear.

When she looked down as she walked, she saw small bare feet, slightly chubby and rounded. Soft tiny feet padding over stones, maybe not stones but pieces of tar loosened by long-disappeared cars. They would have hurt the delicate skin, she knows that. Now, she touches her hand to her chest as her heart rate slows. She wants to reach out to her child self in the dream and scoop her up, hold her tight. She closes her eyes again, attempting to worm her way back into the dream so she can rescue her little self, but the threads of the image scatter and she is wide awake.

After a few minutes she gets up and goes to the kitchen for some water. The dream refuses to disappear. She places her hand on her stomach. Was the dream telling her that she will lose this baby as well? She goes to the bathroom and checks for the tell-tale signs of blood, the little spots she is so familiar with, relieved and terrified when she finds none. Blood is how it always begins. She knows from all the reading she's done that light bleeding during pregnancy is a common thing and it may mean nothing at all. In the past she believed that and continued to hope despite the dark, relentless stains on her underwear with the first one and the second one. Now she knows that if she sees even the tiniest spot, her body has failed her yet again.

'Stay right where you are,' she whispers, stroking her stomach and then cursing herself for letting her deepest desires get the better of her yet again.

Back in bed she pushes herself up against Peter, but he rolls away from her and curls into a ball. She finds her cheeks wet and realises that she is crying silent tears. She was so alone on the long stretch of road. A great emptiness opens up inside her and she curls herself around a pillow, willing the tears to stop.

'Go to sleep, little one,' she hears and almost immediately she feels peaceful and safe. Sleep descends. She has never heard the words before, and just before she drops into a heavy slumber she wonders where they have come from.

The next morning, she and Peter share breakfast as they discuss the briskly cold weather, Peter's clients, what to have for dinner. Anything but the pregnancy.

Finally, Peter is ready to go. 'I know you don't want to talk about it. I get it, I really do, but it's killing me. I have to know what's going on. I feel like this may be the one.'

'Oh, babe,' says Molly, grabbing him around his waist and resting her head on his chest. 'I promise you that I'll let you know if there's anything to know. So far nothing's happened.'

'I know but you haven't even told me what Dr Bernstein said.'

Molly thinks about keeping up the lie, but it makes her want to wriggle out of her skin. 'I… I haven't been to see him.'

'What?' demands Peter, his face darkening with a rare show of anger. 'You said you had seen him. You lied to me? How could you lie to me like that? That's not who we are. It's not what we do. I'm invested in this too, it's unfair to shut me out.'

'I know.' Molly twists away from him and steps back. 'I know, but I just couldn't do it, Pete. I don't want him to tell me there's no heartbeat or that the heartbeat is slow or that my hormone levels are too low. I don't want to hear any of it because I know it's coming and that the end is inevitable, but I don't want to think about it. I don't want to think about it at all.'

'Molly… sweetheart. You know that thinking about it isn't going to change what's going to happen. You need to see a doctor. You're what now? Eight weeks?'

'Nine,' says Molly, 'and it's always over by ten. I thought I would wait until then, and what difference does it make if I do? If it's going to happen, it's going to happen, and there's nothing I can do to stop it. I promise you that I'll go next week if there have been no… no signs that it's over.'

'Okay, okay. I don't want you to get upset.' Peter sighs, picks up his briefcase and plants a kiss on her cheek before he leaves for work. Molly can see he is full of questions but knows to keep quiet. It's part of his nature to understand when silence is needed. It's one of the reasons she fell in love with him.

Before Peter she had found herself dating men who always seemed full of opinions on what she should do with her life, how she should dress, what she should think.

'I'm tired of dating men who think I need to be rescued and told what to do,' she told Lexie years ago. 'I think everyone needs to stop trying to set me up.'

'Yeah,' agreed Lexie, 'tell that to Emma.'

Emma and Molly worked together. Emma enjoyed match-making and would frequently point out men she thought would be suitable for Molly as they strolled through the door of the bookshop, seeking something to read but not necessarily a date.

'I've got the perfect man for you,' Emma told her one night near closing time, smiling widely at Molly and pushing her glasses back up her nose.

'There's no one in here, Emma,' said Molly. 'You need to finish cleaning the counter so we can go home and stop worrying about who I'm dating.'

Emma shook her head, making her quirky pineapple earrings dance and Molly smile. Emma was so sure of herself, despite her young age, so certain of her place in the world. She dressed in wildly clashing prints and colours, not caring what the latest fashion magazine had to say. Customers had been known to come into the shop and ask for 'the colourful girl' because she always had such good book recommendations, matching stories to customers with an innate ability that had taken Molly years to acquire. Emma was chatty and loud, asking personal questions without a second thought, but Molly was always hyper-aware of saying the wrong thing or asking an insensitive question.

'The last guy was just…' Emma said.

'I know,' replied Molly, 'you don't have to say it.'

Jaxon with an X was a personal trainer. Jaxon had curly blond hair, a very square jaw and a perfect six-pack. Jaxon had told Molly she was 'sexy as hell' and 'a really beautiful spirit', and he had been certain that if Molly just cut wine and bread and sugar and grains out of her diet, she would be much happier, look much better and certainly get her short stories rejected less by publishers. The relationship had lasted about a month before Molly had defiantly ordered a bottle of wine and a plate of creamy pasta for dinner as Jaxon looked on in horror.

'The man I think would be perfect for you is not in here, Molly, not right now, but I can get him over here whenever you want,' Emma said.

Molly laughed at Emma's secretive smile and shining eyes. 'Em, I'm twenty-eight and you're twenty. Who would you know that I can date?'

'My cousin, Peter,' said Emma triumphantly. 'Last year he broke up with an insufferable woman who my Aunt Jenny and Uncle Simon hated, even though they were too polite to say it. Peter's been single for six months now. I've decided he's ready to date and I've also decided that you two would make the perfect couple.'

'You have, have you?' asked Molly, amused by Emma's almost childish enthusiasm. 'And what does your cousin think about that?'

'I told him you were a gorgeous woman with a beautiful smile and the most glorious brown eyes.'

'Thanks, Em, but I don't feel ready for another man right now. Anyway, imagine if we did date and then broke up. You and I couldn't be friends anymore.'

'Oh, please, we'll always be friends. Anyway, you won't break up,' said Emma knowingly.

A week later Molly was unpacking a box of books when Emma came to find her in the storeroom. 'Molly, there's a man here who wants the latest detective novel by that famous writer… What's her name? I've forgotten it.'

'Oh… let me think.'

'Actually, could you just serve him? I'll finish doing this.'

'Sure,' agreed Molly.

Molly found the customer standing in the crime fiction section staring up at the books as though he was overwhelmed by the selection. 'Hello,' she said, 'I believe you're after a certain novel by a woman writer. There was a lot published this year so it's a bit difficult to work out who you might mean. Do you know what it's about?'

'I think,' said the man, 'that it's about a missing child.'

'That's not really…' Molly bit down on her lip to suppress a laugh. 'That's a common theme.'

'I have faith that you can figure it out,' he said and she could hear the smile in his voice.

She looked up, directly at him.

She felt her pulse speed up. He was tall with broad shoulders and vivid green eyes, magnified a little by the rimless glasses he was wearing. An errant curl stood up from his head of thick mahogany hair, and Molly wanted to pat it back into place. When he smiled, lines furrowed his forehead and his eyes lit up.

She lifted her hand, nearly giving in to the desire to touch his face but managing to grab a novel right in front of her instead. 'This is very good,' she said, handing it to him. 'Really well written and...' She was embarrassed to hear her voice tremble and she hoped he hadn't noticed the effect he was having on her.

'Oh, for heaven's sake, Peter, just ask her out,' Emma snapped, making both Molly and Peter jump. Neither had realised she was standing right next to them.

'You're Peter...' said Molly.

'I am, but please don't be angry at us. Emma's a pushy little cousin but she means well and I would like... I would like to take you for dinner or a drink or coffee or whatever you want really.'

Molly wanted to say no. But 'I would like that' flew out of her lips instead.

'Dinner turned into breakfast,' she said, scandalising Lexie the next day.

'I can't believe you slept with him on the first night,' her sister gasped.

'I can't believe we made it out of the restaurant before we did,' Molly said, laughing.

Even though she was intensely attracted to Peter and she'd never experienced a chemistry like it, she kept waiting for him to turn into the kind of pushy, overbearing man she was used to dating.

One night they were discussing her writing career, or lack thereof. 'Every time I think about giving up on it, I'll get a positive reply from an agent or I'll be shortlisted in a competition and I'll think, well, I do have some talent and so maybe I should keep trying. But it's been nearly a decade of really working at it now, and so far, I haven't managed to find myself a publisher. My last agent was lovely but even she wasn't able to get my collection published.'

'Well, you know what I think?' asked Peter.

Here we go… thought Molly. 'What do you think?' she asked.

'I think that you must know what you're doing, and if this is your passion, you should keep at it until it's no longer your passion. You only get one life, after all.'

Molly didn't know what to say to that.

'But you're an accountant – surely that's not your passion?'

'Actually, numbers kind of are. I've always liked the logic of maths. I think there's beauty in the way it all works, but my real passion… my real passion is you.'

'Me?' Molly almost shouted. 'But don't you think I'm wasting my life? Don't you want to ask me how I plan to make money in the future?'

'Do you need my questions, Molly? Aren't you already asking them of yourself?'

'I am,' she agreed, and that was the night she knew she would marry him.

Molly smiles at the memory of that night. She picks up her phone and texts Emma, who is now a qualified physiotherapist.

Want to do coffee on Saturday?

The reply comes instantly:

Would love that but fully booked with sports injuries.

Molly sends back a sad emoji. Emma works with a lot of schoolkids and Saturday is often a very busy day. She sends another text with three different dates, knowing that Emma is never really sure of her schedule until the day before.

Once she has cleared the breakfast things, she sits down at her computer and finds herself drawn back to the My Secret blog. She reads through the woman's story while she holds Foggy on her lap. She shudders as she thinks about little Meredith with a man on top of her. 'The big man,' she says. *Where have I heard that?* she thinks, frustrated that the phrase keeps popping into her head.

On impulse she calls her mother.

'Hello, darling,' she answers.

'Hey, Mum, what are you doing?'

'I'm baking a cake – well, the oven is baking the cake. I've finished the hard part.'

Molly smiles. Her mother is always baking something. Molly and Lexie are fair cooks but terrible bakers, much to their mother's disappointment. 'I suppose you girls have careers,' her mother always says. 'I guess it's one or the other but I was never raised to be anything but a mother and a wife and this is my—'

'This is your art,' Molly always finishes for her.

'Why yes, darling, I suppose it is. Thank you for saying that.'

Her mother now supplies the local nursing home and preschool with baked goods after a thorough inspection by the health inspector, who determined that Anne Sneddon's kitchen was 'sparkling clean'.

'Who's the cake for?' asks Molly.

'It's just for us. Lexie is dropping Sophie over later when she goes to the gym and I do like to give my granddaughter a little something sweet.'

'And what does Lexie think of that?'

'Lexie doesn't mind as long as it's low sugar, which it is. I'm a good grandmother, you know.'

'I know,' says Molly and her voice catches a little as though she has been chastised for not giving her a grandchild, but she knows it's not the case. She can see her mother standing in her kitchen in a dusty apron, the phone tucked into her shoulder so her hands can stay busy, her ash-blond hair tied back into a neat bun.

'What are you doing, love? Have you finished the last story?'

'Not yet,' sighs Molly.

'Your dad and I are so incredibly proud of you, you know that, don't you? All those rejections and you never gave up.'

'I know, Mum, but it's a very small publisher and I'm unlikely to end up in millionaire author territory.'

'Who cares about that? The work is the thing. I've told everyone I know, and the book club is buying copies as soon as it comes out.'

'Thanks, Mum.'

'I've got about ten minutes until the cake comes out – forgive me if I put on a load of washing.'

'That's okay.' Molly laughs. Her mother is never one to sit still. 'So, I have a strange question for you,' she says.

'Sounds intriguing…'

Molly hears the bang of the lid on the washing machine.

'Do you remember when I got Foggy?'

'Foggy? You still have that? Goodness.'

'Yep, still have it. Do you remember when I got it or where you got it from?'

'Ooh, that's a tough one, it was so long ago.'

Molly hears the rushing water of the washing machine filling and she doesn't say anything, giving her mother time to think.

'I think…' says Anne slowly. 'Yes… yes, now I remember. It was in a shop we went into one afternoon in a shopping centre. I remember because it was just before Lexie was born and I was huge and felt like I was ready to pop but I still needed a few things for her, like dummies and some extra nappies. It was just a cheap shop, really, mostly filled with rubbish, but it was close to Easter and the whole store window was filled with fluffy chickens and coloured eggs. You tugged me to go in and I was going to buy you a chicken but you chose the frog. You went straight for it, almost as though you were looking for it.'

'Oh…' Molly replies. 'I thought I'd had it since I was a baby.'

'No, since you were around three, actually. I wanted to get you a chicken but you wouldn't let it go.'

'Oh.'

'What's wrong, sweetheart? You sound upset. Is the work getting to you?'

'I was reading this blog yesterday and it was so sad,' she says, the words tumbling out without her thinking about them.

'I don't know how you do it, love. I would just sit and cry.'

'I do sometimes,' admits Molly.

'Maybe the next book can be a romance or something like that,' suggests her mother.

'Maybe,' Molly agrees. 'I do think it's getting to me. Yesterday I read a story about a girl being abused by her mother's partner and having to hide her little sister in a cupboard when he came into her room.'

'How absolutely hideous. Some people really don't deserve to have children.'

'But the funny thing is… the funny thing is…'

'Is what, darling?'

'She… um… she talked about a green stuffed frog that belonged to the little sister, and when I read the words I could… I felt like I could remember the cupboard and the pink blanket. Everything. I felt like I remembered being the little sister. And I've had Foggy ever since I could remember… so it was really… I don't know, it made me feel really strange. Almost like I was having an out-of-body experience. Do you know what I mean?'

'Oh… oh,' says her mother, sounding unusually flustered. 'I don't think I've ever… I'm sure you're just reading too much of this stuff. Maybe you need to take a break for a day or two, but look, darling, I really have to go now. The cake is ready to come out.'

'I didn't hear the timer go off.'

'I really have to go now. I love you. We'll speak tomorrow, darling. Goodbye.' She ends the call abruptly, leaving Molly staring at her screen in confusion.

Her mother has never hung up on her in her life. 'What was that about?' she says. She calls her again, but all she gets is her voicemail.

Molly wonders for a moment what she could have said to upset her mother but her work pulls her back to her computer. Suddenly she is writing something entirely different. It's a story about a little boy watching his father abuse his sister through a crack in a cupboard door. The story comes effortlessly, as though it has already been written. It ends as happily as possible for a tragic story like this, with the little boy finding the courage to tell a teacher the truth and both children being rescued.

Molly knows the character is a boy, but in her head, she sees a girl, a very small girl with light blond hair and dark brown eyes. She is watching through a crack in the cupboard door, watching the 'big man' peel off his filthy shirt, seeing the little girl's glassy eyes stare at nothing, seeing her clenched fists, knuckles white.

She knows she wants to cry out because it's dark and scary and lonely in the cupboard, but if she cries, he comes and hurts her. She holds her stuffed frog tight to her chest and sucks her thumb, waiting for it to be over, knowing that her sister will come and get her when it is.

Molly writes as she sees the sister focus on the cupboard. Molly sees the sister's mouth move, even though no sound comes out. She doesn't need to think too hard to know what she is saying to the little boy in the cupboard. 'Go to sleep, little one,' the sister mouths. But the words don't fit with the story because it's not her in the cupboard, and in the story she is writing, the girl being abused doesn't know her brother is in the cupboard. Yet she cannot help hearing the phrase.

When the first draft is done, Molly looks up from her computer in a daze. She checks the time and sees that it's nearly 3 p.m., notices that she's hungry.

She stands in the kitchen, cutting some Cheddar cheese and putting it onto crackers. She has never really felt a hunger like this before, as though she is feeding something other than just her own body. She strokes her stomach softly. 'Are you hanging in there, little one?' she whispers.

After she has eaten, she stretches out on the couch, slipping quickly into a deep sleep, only to be confronted with the barren road again. But this time there is something different. She thinks she can see someone in the distance, someone coming towards her. She strains her eyes in the dream until she sees a woman, a woman without a face but with a blur of brown hair. She begins to run towards her but she cannot seem to get to her. She runs faster and faster, pushes harder and harder, but instead of getting closer the woman gets farther and farther away. She wakes up with damp cheeks again, thirsty and despairing. What is going on? What on earth is going on?

CHAPTER NINE

10 January 1987

Margaret

She wakes with a dry mouth and a pounding head. The room is dark and not even the smallest sliver of light slips through the curtains. A storm is coming. They said so on the news tonight, or was that yesterday or last week? She drags herself out of bed and uses the bathroom.

She wants to just lie down again, to return to the darkness, but she needs some water. The tap in the bathroom trickles too slowly, something he's going to fix when he's 'good and ready'.

She shuffles to the kitchen, desperate for something cold in her throat. The bottle underneath the bed is cruelly empty. She will have to beg him to get her another. She will have to beg and plead and he will stand over her and watch her sweating and shaking and then he'll say, 'And what is the lovely Margaret going to do for me if I get her a couple of nice bottles of vodka? What's she going to do for me, eh?'

She will do anything for him, anything at all, but he doesn't even seem to enjoy it now. 'Like banging a bloke,' he sneers. 'Open your mouth and give that a go.'

She wonders sometimes how he had known she was so vulnerable. Was it written on her face?

Alone, that's what she was without Adam, completely alone. Broken, at the funeral, surrounded by his workmates and a few of their friends, she had looked around and pretended that she was not alone, but she was. Completely and utterly. She understood the friends would drift off quickly, not wanting to be tainted by her tragedy. Most of them were only acquaintances because of Adam and his easy smiles.

People found her difficult, reserved and quiet. She didn't mean to be. It was just that it was so hard to relentlessly examine every single word she said before she uttered it that sometimes it was easier to simply be silent. Adam hadn't needed her to speak. He was able to read her, to effortlessly do all the talking for her, understanding that she found it hard.

'She doesn't participate in class,' was what the teachers told her parents. 'We're concerned that she has no friends.'

'She's chatty enough at home,' her mother said, but her mother worked the night shift as a cleaner at the hospital and slept her way through her days, paying the woman in the flat next door to look in on Margaret through the night. Her mother barely exchanged a word with her, preferring to simply bark a set of instructions as she walked out of the door: 'Make sure you use oven gloves to take that casserole out of the oven, throw a load of towels in the washing machine, tidy your room, keep the door locked, don't watch too much television.'

She would return home as the sun began to rise, and she'd fall, exhausted, into bed. By the time she was seven, Margaret knew how to get herself up and ready for school, walking the few hundred metres down the road to join dozens of other children, with parents chaperoning them and words streaming from their lips as easily as water gushed from a tap.

Her father was away for weeks at a time, driving up and down the highways of Australia transporting everything from fruit to furniture.

When he came home, he liked to sleep or go to the pub. He always brought Margaret a present, something small like a key ring or a bookmark. Margaret kept all his gifts in her treasure box, which was just an old shoebox decorated with glitter paint.

On days when she was desperate for someone to talk to, she would open the box and take the gifts out one by one, reading the name written on each key ring aloud in a whisper to remind herself she still had a voice: 'The Blue Mountains, Mudgee, Dubbo, Nyngan, Cobar, Wilcannia, Broken Hill.'

The older she got the less she needed to speak at all. Chatter simply went on inside her head. When her mother said, 'I may be late back from work,' outside Margaret nodded her head but inside she replied, *Have a good shift.* When her father asked, 'How was school this week?' outside Margaret shrugged but inside she said, *I sat next to a new girl at school today. She's Chinese and she has silky black hair but she doesn't speak any English so she smiled at me and I smiled at her. Sharon called me a weirdo and I wanted to cry but I didn't.* Inside Margaret talked and talked but outside Margaret said less and less.

Margaret knows she must have liked to talk at some point but by the time she was ten she spent so much time on her own that silence felt better. And then when she did say something, her voice sounded strange and alien and she knew that what she was saying was stupid. She felt people laughing at her.

'Does she ever talk to you?' she heard her father ask her mother one night. Margaret was watching television right in front of them but sometimes they didn't see her. Her silence made her invisible.

'Of course she does,' her mother replied, irritable and rushing for work. Margaret thought that her mother, Enid, must have an inside Enid and an outside Enid as well. The inside Enid heard Margaret talk all the time so the outside Enid didn't know that Margaret hardly said anything at all.

Margaret liked to spend her lunchtime in the library. 'My little helper,' Mrs Dorio, the librarian, called her. Mrs Dorio liked to talk

about books she'd read and places she'd travelled to and her little
dog called Pugnacious, who was a pug. Margaret liked to listen.
Sometimes Mrs Dorio would stop speaking and say, 'What do you
think, Margaret?' And outside Margaret would shrug but inside
Margaret would say, *I wish I could go to Italy and eat ice cream with
you. I think Pugnacious is ugly–beautiful and I would like to pat him
on his funny nose. I read the book you gave me last week about the
Famous Five and I wanted a new one but I left it at home so I can't swap.*

She met Adam when she was sixteen. She got a job delivering
newspapers for his father's newsagency. Her mother had taken her
in, spoken for her. She didn't mind the work. Even on the coldest
winter morning she could appreciate the silence. She walked the
blocks of her neighbourhood, admiring old houses that had yet
to be torn down and replaced with square blocks of modern flats.
She liked that she was contributing to the family income. 'You
keep most for yourself, just give me a couple of dollars a week,'
her mother told her. A small kindness that Margaret never forgot.

Adam was there one day when she came to pick up her pay. His
voice carried across the shop as he made the woman he was serving
laugh. Margaret watched his father's eyes shine at his boy. *What
would it be like to have someone look at me like that?* she thought.

'Here you go, love,' said Mr Henkel to Margaret. 'You're one
of my best, you know – never late and you never miss a day.'

'You should give her a raise, Dad,' joked Adam, his eyes
sweeping up and down Margaret's body and focusing on her face.
Margaret felt warm. She became aware of her breasts pressing
against her thin shirt, aware of her physical self for what felt like
the very first time.

'How about you treat her to lunch?' Mr Henkel said to Adam.
A wink and a smile. Mr Henkel wanted everyone to be in love like
he remembered being in love with his late wife.

Margaret remembers the panic that washed over her. What
would she say? How would she eat? How long till he declared her

weird or stupid? But Adam had soft brown eyes and wild curly brown hair. She knew she was supposed to protest but she was too busy staring.

'Good idea, Dad. Come on, Maggie, let's order everything they have at Macca's.' No one had ever called her Maggie. She felt that she might be a different person if her name was Maggie. Maggie was everyone's friend and at ease in a crowd. Maggie was pretty and sweet and could be counted on for a good joke. She wanted to be Maggie, to be Adam's Maggie.

He was seventeen and training to be an electrician and he liked to talk, about everything. He barely drew breath sometimes and Margaret was content just to watch his mouth move. Sometimes a word popped out without her thinking, a thought or opinion making its way into the world by mistake, shocking her into clamping her hand over her mouth as she waited for his scorn. But he would nod his head, thinking through what she'd said. 'You might be right about that, Maggie.'

Pregnant at seventeen should have been a tragedy. It was, at least, for her parents, who had been waiting to marry her off and congratulate themselves for having survived a difficult child, though she was really anything but.

'Slut,' whispered her father as he watched her pack to go and stay with Adam and his father. Margaret was going to leave the box of treasures behind but at the last minute she took it with her. She would give them to the baby.

'What did we do wrong?' her mother moaned at her and then she stood and looked at Margaret. Outside Margaret just shrugged, infuriating her mother, who was concerned about the neighbours and the gossiping. But inside Margaret said, *I love him, Mum, he makes me laugh and he even makes me want to let the inside words out. He cares about me, and I love his father too because even when I don't say anything, Mr Henkel acts like I have and says, 'I know that's what you think, Maggie.' And they both call me Maggie, and they don't spit my name but say it softly and lightly so I feel like a different person and I think, I really think, that one day I will be able to speak again if I go and live with Adam and his father.*

Margaret was overjoyed.

Mr Henkel didn't mind her coming to live with them. 'Since my lovely wife Alessandra is gone, it is just me and Adam. A baby is a joy and a blessing. Together we'll be a happy family.'

Adam spoke of his mother with reverence, and sadness darkened his features. 'She was tired, just tired, but Dad thought she should get it checked out, and by then it was too late. We should have known. My grandmother died of the same cancer but we just didn't think it was possible.' He shook his head and then smiled at her. 'Dad is really looking forward to having you live with us – he's been cleaning like mad since I told him.'

She was happy enough to leave school behind and help out in the shop, happy enough to take care of Adam and Mr Henkel, poring over old recipe books left by Adam's mother, trying to teach herself to cook.

Margaret coughs as the memories become stuck in her throat, in her brain. Her mouth could be filled with sand. She hates letting her mind roam around in the past. It never does her any good. It feels like all that was another life, never meant for someone like Margaret, who was too stupid to speak her thoughts to the world. She was a fool to think that could have been her life.

'Why can't we just run away from him?' asks Alice whenever she sees her mother nursing a new bruise. Margaret wants to laugh when she says that. Run away? She doesn't even have the strength to walk away. Where would they go? How would they live?

He gives her money and does the laundry. On school days she hears him shouting at Alice to 'get her skinny arse out of bed and get ready'.

He's not all bad. He can't be all bad, can he?

She makes her way to the living room. The television is on and Vernon and the girls sit staring at it as the ferocity of the coming summer storm is discussed on the weather report. 'Secure garden furniture and keep pets inside,' says the neat weatherman in his neat suit.

Margaret wants to sit on the couch next to the three of them but she also wants to go back to bed, to forget. Lilly has her head resting on Alice's shoulder, sucking her thumb and clutching the ugly stuffed toy she is so fond of. It was a gift from someone Vernon worked with, just a cheap rubbish toy, but Lilly loves it, is permanently attached to the stupid thing, content as long as she has it near her. Sometimes Margaret wants to snatch it away from her daughter so she will learn early on that contentment is dangerous and should never be counted on.

She feels guilty when she has thoughts like that. She stares at the three of them again. If she wants to, she knows she could slip in beside them, snuggle up to her children, despite the sticky heat in the living room. Alice stares straight ahead at the television, her body upright and her teeth clenched. Margaret wonders why she looks so uncomfortable.

She takes a step forward, suddenly keen to join the trio, to play the role of mother. But then she sees Vernon's hand on Alice's leg, up at the top of her thigh. His large hand, covered in calluses with its dirty nails, surrounding Alice's skinny thigh. As Margaret watches, his hand moves even further up her daughter's pale skin. Alice's body turns to stone.

Margaret shakes her head. She is not seeing what she thinks she's seeing. She can't be. She turns away from the living room. Her bed beckons and she can feel beautiful dreams of Adam calling her. That's where she wants to be. That's what she needs. She crawls back into her bed, closes her eyes and sees Adam's smile. 'Hey, Maggie,' he says, 'what have you been up to today?'

CHAPTER TEN

Now

Alice

I park in the shade. It's a strangely warm winter's day, climate change sending everything haywire. 'The cold will be back and with it, the rain,' they said on the news this morning. Making my way slowly up the winding brick path that leads to the front door of the Green Gate Home, I feel like a child, delaying my reluctant arrival at school.

It's a single-storey building that sprawls over a nearly one-acre plot of land in the middle of a leafy suburb. The home gets an offer from an interested developer at least once a week because of its size and location, just twenty minutes from the city. I'm sure it will be sold soon enough, but I don't know what I'm going to do if they close the home while my mother is still alive. I don't think she would survive a move somewhere else.

The actual building is at least sixty years old and was originally built as boarding for the adjacent Green Gate School. It has long been closed and the land sold off by the children of the original owners, but the boarding facilities were turned into an aged care home, specialising in people with dementia and Alzheimer's disease.

Though once beautiful, the building has fallen into disrepair with cracked ceilings and peeling paint, but I can't move my mother out of here. She is frightened of the outside world, terrified of even a walk in the garden, content to be in her small room with her television, her computer and three meals a day brought to her.

As I push open the glass door I am greeted by the usual smell of mouldy carpet and overcooked vegetables. These are details that bother me each time I visit, but I'm not sure a newer, shinier care home would have the same kind of staff I have found at the Green Gate.

Most of them have been here for years and seem to be the kind of nurturing people born to care for others. My mother's favourite carer is Anika, an Indian woman whose quiet grace seems to bring peace to even the most troubled resident. If I'm visiting my mother and Anika walks into the room, I watch her eyes light up, light up in a way that they never do when she looks at me. 'This is Anika,' she tells me every single time, 'she takes such good care of me.'

'And this is your daughter Alice,' Anika will remind her. 'You remember her, don't you?'

'I have a daughter?' is a frequent reply from her. Her short-term memory disappeared first, but now, only a few years after I noticed the signs of dementia eventually diagnosed as early-onset Alzheimer's, her long-term memory has almost gone as well. Some days she struggles to remember who she is, let alone who I am. It is a terrible thing to watch what happens when someone's brain turns against them, to see the strange confusion in their eyes, to witness their hopelessness in the face of their own misunderstanding of the world. For me, it is made worse by our strained relationship, by the fact that I never got to have a proper mother and now it seems she is a child again. I cannot forget everything she did when I was a child and she cannot remember.

Alice loves her mother. Alice hates her mother.

I smile at the nurse at the front desk, a young man I've seen around the home but haven't actually met. 'Hello, I'm here to visit Margaret Henkel,' I say.

'Oh yes, you're her daughter Alice, aren't you? She's having quite a good day today. Seems fairly lucid,' he says with a generous smile.

'Wonderful,' I reply, trying to force a smile back. I sign in and make my way down the boiled-carrot-smelling corridor to my mother's room.

It's a cosy room with just enough space for a single bed, an armchair, a chest of drawers and a small television. My mother is sitting in the chair, looking out of the window at the overgrown garden that has maintained a rough beauty despite a lack of care.

There are gardeners who come once a week to try and keep the weeds and overgrowth at bay, but the task is too big for them. The home can only afford to employ two gardeners at a time, and although it's clear that they always start with enthusiasm, they usually resign after a few months. 'It's too much work,' Anika has explained, 'and once they realise it, they usually leave.'

I see the current two gardeners outside now. Anika has told me they are volunteers. A young man whose mother died in the home and his uncle. 'It's hard for some relatives to let go of the place even when there's no reason to visit,' Anika explained. The young man has a cherubic round face and blond curls, and his uncle is so thin I find myself wanting to bring him a sandwich.

The older man has a long grey beard that hangs almost down to his belt and his cap is pulled down low over his face. They are both hacking at a bush but stop for a moment and turn towards the windows of the home. The older man lifts his hand and waves, as though he knows that there are residents sitting in their rooms, watching him. I watch my mother wave back and I wonder how many others are doing the same. They have little else to do with their time but stare out of their windows.

Next to the television set is a silver framed photo of my mother and my father on their wedding day. You wouldn't know it to look at her but she's five months pregnant in the picture. It's such a beautiful, sad image. My mother is lovely with soft wavy hair, a brilliant smile and long legs, barely covered by her white mini-skirt wedding dress. My father looks so proud of himself. He stares boldly at the camera, his solid, square jaw the epitome of manliness. They both look impossibly young. Whenever I look at it, I feel a strange mix of joy and despair. Joy for the two of them on that day, and despair for the terrible future that awaited the young couple.

The picture used to sit on the mantelpiece above the unused fireplace in our home until *he* moved in. 'I don't need to see that,' he said to my mother. 'I like to think I'm the only one you've ever loved.'

I remember her giggling when he said that, and then taking the picture and hiding it. I can still remember the rage that made my small body tremble as I watched her do it. 'You can't put Daddy away,' I said.

'Don't be so dramatic, Alice – it's only a picture,' she replied. But even at six years old I understood that it wasn't 'just a picture'. It was her past and the love of her life that she was putting away, and along with it, me.

I caught her looking at it often, secretly, so no one would see, only when he was out. Sometimes she would fall asleep holding it and I would creep into her room and return it to the drawer where it lived. I knew what would happen if he saw what she was doing. I felt like I was betraying my father every single time but I needed to keep her safe, even though she seemed to have no desire to do the same for me.

On some visits she will point out my father to me. 'He was the best-looking man I knew and he loved you so much.' But on other visits she is bemused by the photo, assuming it is a stock photo that has come with the silver frame.

'Hi, Mum,' I say.

'Oh, hello, Alice,' she replies. 'I was just thinking about how cold it's getting at night. I don't love the cold but I love the winter colours. I love it when the trees turn but right now, they must be so confused by the heat during the day. Anika says it feels like spring outside.'

'Me too,' I agree eagerly. I can't quite believe this sentence has been uttered by my mother. Lately I have had to introduce myself over and over again, and usually she spends more time muttering incoherently to herself than anything else.

It's been a long time since she was lucid. I know if I came more often, she would have less trouble recognising me. I'm sure there are lots of patients here whose children visit once a week at least. I should come more often. She is no longer the same person she was when I was a child and yet I cannot let go of that. I am not a good daughter and I know it, but each time I visit, I feel like I have allowed another piece of myself to be chipped away. Each time I try to help her or do something nice for her, I feel like the woman who treated me in the worst possible way has somehow won something from me. It's so complicated because there is still some tiny part of me that needs her to acknowledge that she loves me. Perhaps if I came more often, I would receive that affirmation, but I am sceptical about that. I may only receive what I received my whole childhood: nothing.

Alice wants her mother to love her. Alice wants her mother to need her. Alice wants her mother to know her.

'Do you think you could look at my computer, Alice? It doesn't seem to be working.'

'Sure,' I say and I pick up her ancient laptop from the top of her chest of drawers. I start it up and fiddle around with it a little. It's disconnected itself from the internet and I reconnect it. She can't do much with it but I know that Anika finds playing certain videos calms her when she becomes distressed. She's fond of tropical islands and other natural scenes with classical music playing in the background. I wonder what she thinks when she watches these, if she is remembering something from the past or if she is just drifting peacefully in her mind.

I start a video of an underwater scene that looks like it's been taken at an aquarium. 'Lovely, thanks so much, dear,' she says. 'I do love to look at…' She doesn't finish speaking, instead looking back out to the garden. The gardeners are picking up the pieces of bush and weeds they have been cutting, stuffing them into a green bin.

She's lived at the Green Gate Home for six years now. Before that she was in the same hideous rental home she had lived in since we were forced to leave the house she had bought with my father. When I went back to see her for the first time, a decade after walking out on her at sixteen, I was horrified to see the state she was in. After seeing how poorly she was coping, I knew I had to keep seeing her. She was living in almost complete squalor, existing only on vodka and bread.

I went back with Jack, meaning to find them both there, meaning to confront them both and make them acknowledge what they'd done to me, but she was alone.

She answered the door and looked at me for a minute before she said, 'Alice… goodness me, you're Alice.'

'Hi, Mum,' I said and I remember standing straight, my head high and holding Jack's hand as though I needed to hang on to keep from drowning.

'Well, I'm sure I wasn't expecting company,' she said but she let us in and I saw her glance around the living room and register how it would look to us. The same fake leather couch I had always hated was still there, the top coat completely peeled away in some places. One missing foot meant it was at an odd angle. The carpet was stained and a faint smell of urine hung in the air. On the floor under the window were two blinds that had obviously fallen down and never been rehung, and every surface looked sticky with grime. I looked down at the coffee table, covered in watermarks and rings from glasses, and had been unable to say anything for a moment. My tongue darted into the space in my mouth as I stared down at the corner of the chipped coffee table, remembering how dark the bruise along my jawline had been the next day, remembering that she didn't see it until it was fading and then she didn't even ask me about it.

Her shoulders rounded further as she watched me take in the space, and she ran her hand through her mostly grey hair that I could see was dry and filled with split ends. The skin on her chin was rough and peeling. She was as far removed from the beautiful young woman on her wedding day as she is now. It was difficult to believe she had ever been that person.

I had such plans for that visit and so many things I was going to say, but I was so stunned that I found it impossible to do anything other than look around the house, noting the empty fridge and pantry, the layers of mould in the bathroom, the sting of alcohol on her breath.

We left without me asking her or telling her anything, or saying any of the things that had been playing on my mind for ten years. But I returned the next day and cleaned the house, stocked the fridge. While I was there, she followed me around, pointing out what needed to be sorted and tidied.

'Why don't you do this yourself?' I asked.

'I try,' she said softly, 'but some days it's difficult, you know, Alice. I've had a very hard time of it.'

'I notice you manage to get your vodka.'

'Well, that gets delivered. I call the nice young man at the store and he drops some off for me. He's very kind.'

'Have you heard from Vernon, Mum?' I asked. 'Have you heard from him at all?'

'The police came round asking for him... I don't know how long ago that was... Sometimes the days just fly by, don't they?

He got in a bar fight apparently, hit a man and killed him, just like that – one punch. He's in prison now. I asked them to let me know if they found him or caught him, I suppose. He ran away to, um… Queensland… um, no that wasn't it… somewhere, and they called me to tell me he was going to jail. They said he was in a lot of trouble. They said he will be there for… years… I don't know how many.'

'It's where he belongs,' I spat.

'He wasn't that bad, Alice. Life… He was sentenced to life in prison. The detective on the case told me… he told me he was given life. They wanted to know if I would come and testify… Is that the word? Yes, testify, at his sentence hearing. His lawyer wanted me to say some nice things about him and I would have… but I wasn't… well. I should have tried… He took care of you and… Gosh, I'm tired.'

'You're always tired. He didn't take care of me, he hurt me. You know he hurt me.' I was burning with anger, furious that she had conveniently forgotten everything, that she had simply glossed over it all. I scrubbed hard at the bath I was cleaning, feeling my muscles burn, wishing I could erase my painful memories as easily.

'I… I can't talk about this,' she said quietly.

I tried, I have tried, over the years to get her to acknowledge what was done to me, what I suffered through, but she always seemed mystified by my anger. 'It was so hard for me after your father died. You have no idea how hard it was to be a mother. You wait until you have children, you'll see.' She wasn't a mother in any sense of the word, and because of her I have always been a broken child.

Last year Natalia's mother was diagnosed with breast cancer and I couldn't help but compare us as I watched Natalia drop everything to be by her mother's side. She shopped and cooked for her parents, drove her mother to chemotherapy and worked on her laptop while she sat with her. I visited her more than I visit my own mother. I wanted to see her, to let her know that I was thinking of her. I never want to be with my mother. Even now I speak to Natalia's mother more than I speak to my own.

'Don't beat yourself up about it,' Natalia says when we talk about it. But it's not that easy. It's harder to abandon a parent, even a terrible parent, than people might think.

I gave up expecting anything from her and worked on forgiveness. I'm still working on it.

'Vernon was here,' she says to me now, coaxing me away from the memories I am always trying to forget. 'He said to say hello.'

'She talks about him often,' Anika once said. 'Him and your father, Adam. They both visit.'

'One is in prison and the other is dead,' I said when she told me this, 'so I doubt that.'

'It's real enough for her,' Anika chastised me softly.

Today I debate with myself whether to tell my mother that Vernon is indeed in prison as I do every time she says this. I went to the police after she told me about him. I had to call an enquiries line and speak to a police officer in corrections. He is in prison in Queensland, not New South Wales, where I live. I eventually got hold of the right person, who told me that he had been sentenced to life in prison with a non-parole period of twenty years. He began his prison sentence when I was twenty-six. I'm forty-two now. In four years, he might be free. It's a horrifying thought.

'You should tell the police what he did to you,' Jack said, when we learned what had happened to Vernon. 'Get him charged and make sure he never gets out.' But it felt too hard. I imagined recounting the things he did to me, the countless unspeakable things, and having to testify in court. The idea of it made my skin crawl. I couldn't do it. I couldn't expose my child self to the world. I couldn't relive it all, and I couldn't bear to see him again.

Every time she brings him up, he appears before me: huge and hideous. I feel like she's taunting me. 'Hallucinations are part of the disease,' her doctor has told me. 'Your mother will see things that aren't there, people who have died. It's a very common thing. Try to not let it upset you. It helps if she can see family members as often as possible so she can stay connected to reality.'

I nodded, as though it was something I would try to do even as guilt nearly drowned me.

To this day my mother has no idea of the existence of her grandchildren. The few times she's asked me, I've been evasive, just saying, 'One day.'

'You have nothing, nothing to feel guilty about,' Jack has always maintained.

'But I've never allowed her to meet the boys. Maybe if she knew about her grandchildren, if she spent time with them, it would help.'

'There's a reason you've never wanted them to meet her,' he said, 'and that reason is why I never want them to meet her either.'

I don't understand why I'm still so tied to her despite everything she's done, despite her refusal to understand what she allowed to happen to me.

Perhaps it's because of the occasional flashes of memories from before my father died. Images of her baking with me in the kitchen, watching patiently as I inexpertly cut out star-shaped cookies. Or of her standing behind me, slowly working a brush through my hair, gently removing tangles so it wouldn't hurt. But now I wonder if those things actually happened or if I've just made them up, to convince myself that I had a normal childhood, however brief it was. Regardless, I can't seem to let go and just walk away. Mostly I know it's guilt over what I did, over what I took from her.

'Do you know what I feel like?' she says suddenly now.

'What, Mum?'

'Fish with salt and vinegar chips.'

I feel my stomach turn over. The tangy smell of vinegar fills my nostrils and bile rises in my throat, forcing me into the small en-suite bathroom, to vomit until my stomach is empty.

'There's a woman in my bathroom,' I hear my mother say.

'Are you all right in there?' Anika calls.

'I'm fine, thank you.' I rinse my mouth out and leave the bathroom.

'It's hard when they disappear again, isn't it?' Anika says.

I nod as though this is what has caused my distress because I don't have the energy to explain the truth to Anika, and what good would it do anyway?

I know Anika thinks I could be a better daughter, and I don't want to explain to her that that's not possible because her patient wasn't a better mother.

'Maybe I should go,' I say.

'Who are you and what are you doing in my room?' my mother asks, her eyes wide with fear.

Anika shrugs and touches my clammy hand with her dry, warm one. 'We'll see you next time.'

I nod, relieved at being dismissed despite not having asked her what she may or may not know about what actually happened all those years ago.

As I make my way back to the car park I sniff deeply, taking in the earthy smell of the damp fallen leaves, slowly rotting into the soil in the garden. But the smell of vinegar has lodged itself inside me, and as I climb into my car, it drags the memory back, dragging me into my past, into a place I feel like I will never escape from.

Alice is trapped. Alice is haunted. Alice cannot leave her past behind.

CHAPTER ELEVEN

Molly

The next morning Molly calls her mother again but she doesn't answer. She is persistent and finally, after four unanswered calls, her mother picks up.

'Mum,' she says, 'what happened yesterday? Why did you hang up on me?' She fires the questions quickly, not giving her mother a chance to respond. 'What's going on?'

'Oh, Molly, goodness… Let me catch my breath, I've only just come in from the seniors' centre.'

'Why haven't you been answering your phone?'

'I was busy, you know – I read to some of the attendees who have limited sight.'

'Fine,' says Molly, catching a sulky teenage tone to her voice.

'I'm sorry I didn't answer, darling, and I didn't hang up on you yesterday. I said I had to go because the cake was burning.' Molly knows this is a blatant lie. Her mother bakes like she breathes, getting it right every single time.

'Was it something I said, Mum?'

'Oh… no, I just… I really don't think you should be reading those things anymore. You're imagining things. Who is the woman who writes the blog anyway?'

'I don't know. She says her name is Meredith but that could be an alias. Most of these sites are filled with people who want to remain anonymous. And I have to read that stuff, it helps give my work authenticity. It's not as if I have an abused childhood to look back on, Mum. I don't want people to feel I haven't accurately captured their experiences.'

'You had a wonderful childhood, Molly,' says her mother, sounding as if she's close to tears.

'I'm not saying I didn't. Why are you being so strange?'

'I just… There are things, oh, I don't know, I don't know,' she says, and then for the second time in two days, her mother hangs up on her.

Molly sits staring at the phone in her hand, unsure whether or not to believe what has just happened.

She tries her mother's phone again but it goes straight to voicemail, and so in frustration she tries her father. He answers on the first ring, as though he has been waiting for the call. He is retired now but not often at home, preferring to spend his days at the local bowling club, playing a game or two and getting lunch with friends. He is a quiet, dignified man who started his career as a high-school teacher at twenty-one and ended it as principal of one of the biggest public schools in the state. Both Molly and Lexie had attended and both had developed a love–hate relationship with being identified as the principal's daughters.

Molly was a good student, becoming captain of the school and excelling in all her subjects, but Lexie was a rebel, getting into trouble whenever she could. 'As befits a second child,' her father would say wryly whenever he found her outside his office. He was respected and liked by students and teachers, but Molly and Lexie always felt singled out for one reason or another because of who they were.

Molly enjoys an easy relationship with her father now although they rarely speak on the phone. Calling him was an act of desperation. Her mother is usually so open and honest. All through their childhoods, Molly and Lexie were aware that there was no subject that was off limits to their parents. They discussed everything as a family, valuing each other's opinions on everything. Her mother not wanting to discuss something is downright weird.

In the background Molly can hear her mother crying, meaning her father is home in the middle of the day, which is unusual for him. She is suddenly terrified. Something has happened, something terrible, and she has made it worse by haranguing her mother about hanging up on her.

'Dad,' she says, 'what's going on? Why is Mum crying?'

'Molly, sweetheart, listen to me. I don't want you to worry, everything is… I think you need to come over here tonight, you and Peter. Come for dinner if you can.'

'But what—?'

'Molly,' says her father and she recognises that he has switched modes, back into the principal talking to a recalcitrant student, 'I'm not going to discuss anything with you right now. Your mother is a little upset and I need to see to her. Come tonight and bring Peter, all will be explained then.'

'But, Dad,' Molly almost whines.

'No more discussion now. Do as I say, please.'

'Okay, Dad, okay… I'll let Pete know. He might have to work late though.'

'Tell him it's important.'

'I will…' Molly's eyes fill with tears. She can feel her life changing as the seconds pass but she has no idea how or why and she feels powerless to stop it.

'Oh, and Molly,' says her father, 'don't say anything to Lexie, will you? Not until we've talked.'

'Okay, Dad, I promise,' she mumbles before ending the call. The tears come quickly and soon she is sobbing, clutching her phone in her hand. She is desperate to call her sister but she promised her father she wouldn't, and she waits until she has calmed down to call Peter.

'What's up?' he says, and in the background, she can hear the clicking of his keyboard.

'Pete, I'm sorry about this, but can you come to my parents tonight for dinner?'

'Tonight? No, Molly, that's not going to be possible, sorry. Why don't you just go and have a nice meal with them? I should be home around ten, if I'm lucky.'

'No, please, you don't understand,' shrieks Molly, 'something's very wrong. My mother hung up on me and then I called my father and I could hear her crying in the background. I was just talking to her about a blog I read and she… I don't know. I don't know if I've said something to upset her but Dad won't explain and he just said to tell you that you had to come with me tonight and it's important,' she finishes breathlessly.

'Please stop yelling, Moll, it's not good for you or… It's not good for you. I'll rope one of the juniors into staying late and finishing up some stuff for me.'

'What if something is wrong with one of them? What if one of them is sick? What if Mum is really sick?'

'I don't know, love. I'm sorry. What did Lexie say?'

'Dad said I'm not allowed to call her and that makes me think it's something really awful…' Molly feels a hard edge of resentment inside her at having to be the 'good big sister', protecting Lexie, who is an adult and a mother herself.

'All right, let's just take this slowly then. I'll be home by six. Please try not to worry too much. It may be something easy to treat if she is ill. Modern science can do all sorts of things now. Just get through the rest of the day and I'll see you soon.'

'Okay, love you, and thanks, I know it's a bad time.'

'Don't worry, it's fine. Love you.'

Molly cleans and tidies the apartment, too distracted to write. She wipes the white marble counter in the kitchen over and over again, even though it was already clean to start with. She keeps going over scenarios in her head, searching for clues in her conversations with her mother. She hadn't mentioned any tests and she usually would let her and Lexie know after she'd been for a mammogram or a set of blood tests. Molly feels herself grow cold at this thought. Her mother only let them know afterwards when she was sure everything was fine. She never told them before she went.

On impulse she sits down at her computer, and in an attempt to distract herself she rereads Meredith's story on the My Secret blog. Instantly the smell of the damp, mouldy cupboard comes to her, filling her nostrils as though she is inside the cramped space at that very moment. She closes her eyes and tries to see herself there, to imagine herself small and afraid, but then the smell disappears and she is left wondering if her pregnancy hormones are making her mad.

She thinks about Meredith, wonders what she looks like, where she lives, how she manages to get through her days with the horrific baggage of her childhood weighing her down. And then she thinks about Meredith's little sister. Where is she? Was she also abused? What is she doing with her life now?

She looks back at the page with Meredith's story on it. The words are written over a black-and-white photo of the sky filled with heavy grey clouds, the sun piercing through as though a storm has just passed. There is a set of three craggy rock formations in the picture, which Molly vaguely recognises. She sees Meredith, a faceless woman, deciding on the image as a way of reminding herself that she has left the storm of her childhood behind.

The blog has a button to send Meredith a private message, and Molly starts typing before she can talk herself out of it.

Hi, my name is Molly Khan and I'm writing a book of short stories about children in crisis. I read your blog and I wanted to reach out and let you know that I am so sorry you had to go through something like that. I am glad that you have a good life now and I don't want to intrude, but would you be able to tell me what happened to your little sister? I understand if you don't want to discuss it, but if you can speak to me, I would be really grateful. My email is mollykhan@gmail.com. Thanks so much.

She sends the message and then decides on a long shower. Her neck is stiff and her face sticky with tears. She glances at the calendar on her desk. She is nine weeks pregnant today. Her breasts are tender and large and she has to pee every five minutes but she's had no nausea and she knows that Lexie's obstetrician told her that morning sickness is a good sign of a healthy pregnancy. Lexie was sick for months when she was pregnant with Sophie. Molly has never felt nausea with any of the other pregnancies and she cannot help but think this is a terrible sign that this is nearly over, that her time of hoping, of pretending not to hope, and hoping again is almost over. It is the giving up of hope that is the hardest. Without hope she has nothing.

'Are you even alive in there?' she whispers with her hand gently over her stomach. 'Stop thinking,' she admonishes herself. She stands in the shower until the water runs cold and then, shivering in the cool air, she wraps herself in Peter's robe, revelling in his smell of musky aftershave and the ocean-scented soap he likes, and the comfort of the large size.

On her phone she can see there's a new message in her inbox. She is surprised to find it's from Meredith. She hadn't expected her to get back to her so soon or, if she's honest with herself, at all.

Hi, Molly. Thanks for your message. I do have a good life now and I have tried very hard to rise above my terrible experiences. It must be wonderful to be able to write stories and I do admire you for that, but please understand that this is my life and not some piece of fiction. I don't like discussing my little sister but I can tell you that she died very young in a car accident. Best of luck with your writing. Meredith.

'How strange,' says Molly aloud.

She reads the message again. How old was her sister when she died? Was Meredith also in the accident? Was her sister's death reported in the press? Molly shakes her head. She has no idea who Meredith is or how old she is. She could live anywhere in the world. *You're being silly*, she tells herself. *You're fixating on something else so you don't have to think about the fact that you're pregnant.*

She thinks about giving the woman Dr Bernstein recommended a call. 'Olivia Stevens has helped a lot of my patients through their difficult journeys,' Dr Bernstein told her and Peter. 'She's a psychologist who specialises in counselling women who are dealing with infertility and miscarriage.' But as quickly as she has the thought, Molly dismisses it. If she knew for sure that she was on a journey, it would be different. But sometimes, just like she feels in the road dream, there seems to be no end in sight.

She feels like she will be here forever, waiting, hoping, dreaming of becoming a mother but being forever denied it. What's the point in discussing it with someone? She'll never be able to gracefully accept it and she doesn't want to try.

Her mind turns to the dream again, the one she can't seem to shake. Is she alone on the road because her mother is ill and she's going to lose her? Is that what the dream is telling her? Tears threaten again as she considers the possibility of finding out tonight that her mother is ill and then experiencing the cramps she knows mean the end of another pregnancy, the end of another life she loves so dearly.

She picks up her phone and texts Emma.

I keep having a dream that I'm alone on an empty road. Any ideas on what that means?

There is more to the dream but she can't explain it in a text. Emma has always been a huge fan of dream analysis. She's kept a dream journal since she was a child and reads everything she can find on the subject.

'I keep dreaming about Peter in a field surrounded by butterflies,' she remembers telling Emma after they had been dating for a few weeks.

'That means you've met your soulmate,' Emma said sagely.

Molly's phone pings with Emma's reply.

A road symbolises your life path in reality. Would have to know more about it to really work out the meaning. Will chat when we have coffee xx.

She is alone on the road, completely alone. Is the dream telling her that she will always be alone? Her hand goes to her stomach. Is the dream telling her that she will never have a child?

She wishes she didn't have to think about any of this. The churning inside her tells her everything is about to change, about to change in the worst possible way.

She will be someone else after tonight, someone different – she is certain of it.

CHAPTER TWELVE

12 January 1987

Margaret

She swallows another mouthful. The whole country is in the grip of a heatwave and on the news this morning they recommended keeping children and pets inside. She should be drinking water but another mouthful and she'll be back in the past, back where she is happiest.

Margaret remembers pregnancy as a bubble of happy time. When she was six weeks along, the morning sickness set in and would wake her from sleep, sending her scurrying for the bathroom to retch until she thought her whole stomach would come up. Mr Henkel and Adam told her to stay in bed and rest. The shop was below the two-bedroom flat, and at lunchtime Mr Henkel would come upstairs and make Margaret soup and crackers. He would bring her ginger snaps and crystallised ginger and ginger tea to drink to keep the nausea at bay. Sometimes his voice would drift upstairs to Margaret as she watched television and she would hear him telling customers, 'My daughter-in-law is pregnant, and the sickness, we don't know what to do about it.' He was loaded down with advice when he came home at the end of the day: 'Ginger and soda water, crackers and salt and vinegar chips, sour soup and milk.' He was a father and a mother rolled into one, doting and kind, thoughtful and sweet. He was everything she'd never had.

'Sorry if Dad's bothering you with all the stuff he tells you,' Adam said. 'I'll tell him to leave you alone if you like.'

'No,' Margaret almost shouted, 'I like that he cares. Don't say anything.' She wished that she was really Mr Henkel's daughter-in-law and not just Adam's girlfriend.

'When you're feeling better, we'll make it all legal, I promise,' Adam said.

Overnight the nausea simply disappeared and Margaret buzzed with energy. She would help out in the shop in the morning and then go back upstairs and clean and cook for Adam and his father.

The words danced out of her mouth more and more. She flushed with pleasure if she was able to make Adam and his father laugh when she related a story she'd seen on television or something she'd overheard at the store. Other people's voices were easy for her to imitate. 'You're such a good mimic,' Adam said, 'you should have been an actress.'

'Don't give her ideas,' said his father. 'You don't want her running off to Hollywood, do you?'

Margaret felt a laugh bubble up from deep inside her. No one had ever thought her capable of anything in her whole life.

When Margaret was five months pregnant, they got married. Margaret invited her parents, desperate to show them she was doing the right thing as she created her own family, but the painstakingly written letter was returned unopened. She didn't want to risk a phone call, not wanting to hear her mother's disgust over her unmarried state.

'I'll talk to them,' said Adam, his brown eyes dark with anger.

'No,' she said, 'leave it, leave them. It's easier that way.' Her parents only wanted a quiet life, and Margaret realised that her disappearance from their lives would have affected them little as they stuck to their routines.

Only Margaret, Adam and Mr Henkel were at the small wedding conducted by a justice of the peace in a nearby park where the gardenias were in bloom under the hot summer sun. They had a picnic lunch afterwards, just the three of them.

Mr Henkel gifted them a luxurious overnight stay in the Blue Mountains in a room with a four-poster bed and a view of the bushland that made Margaret and Adam feel like they were the only people in the world until they joined the other guests for a sumptuous buffet breakfast the next morning. 'One day we'll come here all the time,' Adam told her as he placed yet another loaded plate filled with fresh pancakes and flaking pastries on their table. Margaret took small bites of everything, wanting to experience the sweetness of the bright red strawberries alongside the saltiness of the bacon. She took her time, lingering over the breakfast, needing to savour the different tastes and the delight of being a married woman on her short honeymoon. She used her left hand for everything, loving the way the small diamond chip on the band on her finger caught the light.

'You're beautiful, Mrs Henkel,' said Adam.

Margaret smiled, concentrating on eating politely, on holding her cutlery properly as she studied the elegant, confident hotel guests. That afternoon they wandered around the small town hand in hand, picking up some souvenirs to take back to Mr Henkel. Margaret couldn't help scanning the crowded streets in the hope of spotting her father, knowing that one of his routes took him right where she was. Her box of treasures from him contained an empty tin that was once filled with chocolates emblazoned with the Paragon Restaurant Blue Mountains logo. Despite everything, she had been overwhelmed with excitement at being able to have lunch at the restaurant her father often ate at when he stopped for a rest. She had never been happier.

Later, things were difficult for Margaret when the baby arrived. They named her Alice for Adam's mother, and Margaret thought she finally had the family she'd always dreamed of. Yet she didn't quite love her child like she felt she should, and the endless sleepless nights made her cry with desperation. Alice woke every forty minutes, screeching at some terror only she understood, inconsolable no matter what her mother and father tried.

'It means she's a smart cookie,' Margaret heard one of the customers tell Mr Henkel. Margaret began to wonder if Alice knew what she was thinking, if the tiny creature was actually smarter than she was.

Margaret wished for her mother but she wouldn't answer her calls. She did everything she was supposed to do with the baby, but most days it felt like she was watching someone else go through the motions. She lusted after sleep as she had once lusted after Adam. She felt like there was a sheet of glass between her and the rest of the world. Everything felt muted and far away.

She envied the way Adam and his father cherished and cuddled and spoke to the baby as though it was the most natural thing in the world. She started to worry that she would accidentally hurt the child or leave her somewhere.

She didn't tell anyone about her thoughts and fears. She gnawed away at her nails and drank endless cups of tea and shoved the words back down inside her, afraid that she was failing so badly that Adam and his father would kick her out of their little family and she would be all alone again.

Meanwhile Adam and his dad were concerned, checking up on her all the time.

'I think you may have postnatal depression,' said the clinic sister when Margaret took the baby to be weighed and measured. Alice was growing fat on her mother's milk, her little hands developing dimples, but Margaret was swimming in the pair of jeans she had worn at sixteen.

'We can help you,' said the clinic sister. 'There's counselling and medication if need be.' Margaret felt ashamed but the woman was kind and Adam took time off work so she could get some sleep. She didn't want to speak to anyone, finding words too difficult, but rest helped a little bit.

The clinic sister recommended a group. Margaret went every week, taking Alice in her beautiful new pram. The women at the group had the same worries and fears she did. She recognised, in their faces, the same despairing defeat she felt at not being able to manage. She never said anything, not even 'yes' or 'no' to questions asked. Instead, she did what she did best. She listened, she collected stories. She became consumed by inside Margaret once more.

One woman, Lydia, also worried that she would hurt her son, Sam, without meaning to, and another, Sandra, checked the back seat of her car over and over again, convinced that she had forgotten her daughter, Mia, there. No one in the group was sleeping. They were all exhausted and tears were shed at every meeting. Each week Margaret returned home and understood that she was not alone and not a failure of a mother.

One night, Alice slept for four hours and then for five and then, eventually, the whole night through. 'I'll get up at night and check on her,' Adam told Margaret sternly, 'you just sleep.'

'But what about work? You have to be able to work.'

'I'll be fine, you just get yourself right, my love. That's all I want.'

The veil between her and the baby finally lifted when her daughter was six months old. Alice slept all the way through the night and Margaret woke up to the morning sun filtering through the curtains, her body rested and her mind calm. At first, she worried that something had happened to her child, and she leapt out of bed and dashed into the living room, where the cot and a change table were set up in the corner. But Alice was fine, lying on her back, playing with her tiny toes, and when she saw her mother, she smiled, her face lighting up with absolute love and devotion. For the first time, Margaret felt a tsunami of love for her child engulf her. 'Hello, darling,' she said, lifting the baby up, and Alice curled her chubby arms around her neck. 'Ma-ma-ma-ma,' she babbled.

And then life was almost blissful.

Margaret stayed home with the baby, finding the joy in her daughter that she had been missing, crooning at her and finding words she never knew she had in her. Alice didn't judge, didn't look at her like she was strange. She thought everything her mother said was gold. She loved outside Margaret.

'I told you you'd be the best mother,' Adam said, laughing as he watched his wife and daughter playing with bubbles in the bath.

'You did,' she agreed, amazed at how wonderful life could be. A life she never thought she would have the pleasure of experiencing.

'What kind of a day did my girls have?' Adam asked every night at the dinner table, and he and his father would look at Margaret and be content with what few words she could offer.

Mr Henkel helped them buy a small house, even though Margaret didn't want to leave him alone in the flat. 'I shall come for lunch every Sunday, Maggie dear. Children need a garden and, God willing, Alice will soon have a sister or a brother.'

Margaret felt as though she had been gifted the perfect life. She took Alice to the park every day after she'd cleaned their house, finding joy in making sure everything looked perfect. Whenever there was extra money, Adam said, 'Why not choose something nice for the place?' Margaret's first purchase was beautiful blue curtains for the bedroom.

When Alice was three, Margaret and Adam began trying for another baby, but after two traumatic miscarriages Adam told Margaret that he thought they should stop. 'I hate how upset you get, Maggie. It can't be good for you, and little Alice takes it so badly. Maybe we were only meant to have one, eh? I think one is just the right number, just you and me and our girl. I couldn't ask for more, and now we can give her everything and spoil her rotten.'

Despite all her heartache, Margaret had agreed easily enough. Alice would soon be ready for school, and Margaret was secretly terrified of finding herself locked back into the cycle of sleepless nights and anxious days.

Now Margaret remembers that time as short – sweetly perfect but so very short.

Not long after, Mr Henkel died suddenly and the debts had to be paid. 'We'll have to sell off everything. He really shouldn't have given us that money. Maybe I should have worked in the shop, helped him to keep it up a bit better.'

'But he was proud of you for going out on your own, he always said so,' she soothed, grieving as much as he was because he had been her father as well.

'You always know how to make me feel better, Maggie.'

Margaret mourned for months after Mr Henkel died. She thought she would never feel completely happy again. But her grief slowly faded, growing more manageable bit by bit, and she and Adam began to laugh as they told stories at dinner about Mr Henkel and his unique brand of customer service. 'I know what you think you need, but let me tell you what you really need,' he would say to people.

'We'll be all right, won't we, Maggie?' Adam would sometimes ask when sadness over his father clouded his eyes.

'We'll be fine,' she reassured him. 'We'll be fine.'

CHAPTER THIRTEEN

Now

Alice

All through the day the memory of what I did keeps hurling itself at me, the smell of vinegar surrounding me, making it impossible to smell anything else. My tongue moves compulsively in and out of the gap in my mouth. At home I grab some fresh rosemary from a pot on the kitchen windowsill and crush it between my fingers, inhaling the lemony-pine scent, but as soon as I move my fingers away from my nose, the vinegar overwhelms me once more, making me gag.

My phone rings with a call from Natalia.

'I've got five minutes and just wanted to invite you to dinner next month – the seventeenth. Does that work for you?'

'Sure,' I say, 'fine.' My voice is stilted and strange. I shouldn't have answered.

'Everything okay?' she asks.

'No... but...' I cannot make the words come out. I let the silence stretch.

Natalia sighs. 'You'll call when you're ready to talk.' She knows me so well.

'I'll call,' I say.

I go out into the garden, where the air is sharp in my lungs and the next-door neighbour's dog barks and barks, but nothing seems to work.

Back inside, I try to lose myself in cyberspace, hoping for a comment from someone or a story not my own that I can read. I need the distraction. I don't think I meant to put my experiences out there for the world to read. I don't talk about what I went through with anyone except those closest to me. I never wanted to expose myself to the judgement from everyone with a computer or smartphone. I hadn't meant to but the words seemed to write themselves. I thought my blog would be an online diary for me, read only by me when I needed to confirm for myself what I had been through but also how far I've come. It's strange how comforting it is to see your life written down. There it is in black and white and no one can dispute it. After so many years of my mother doing that very thing, it was a relief. I hadn't expected that one day there would be other people reading my story.

My first comment came from a young man.

'I'm only seventeen,' he wrote, 'and I found your blog today. Yesterday I left home forever. I'm never going to let him touch me again. I'm never going to let him hurt me again. I hope that I can make a good life for myself the same way you have.'

I cried for hours over that message. And then I looked up some places where he could go for help and put the links on the blog. It's a small thing, and of no importance to anyone but me and a handful of others who stumble across my words, but I like to think that some people are helped by being allowed to leave their stories. 'It never happened,' my mother has said to me. 'You're making this all up. You're exaggerating, and that's not the way I remember it.' There have been moments over the years when I have reminded her of something and I have seen a light of recognition in her eyes, a spark that tells me she remembers the same thing. But then she'll say, 'You have no idea how hard it was for me, Alice, no idea at all.' I have learned that I am not the only person this happens to. Those who leave their stories say the same thing. 'I just want to be acknowledged. I just want him to admit what he did. I want her to tell me she saw it happen.' Murderers stand in court and plead 'not guilty' despite being found standing over the body with a knife in hand. What chance is there that a parent will admit their failings to an adult child? No one wants to see themselves as a monster.

When my mother had no choice but to give up drinking or die, I thought that she would be able to see the past with new clarity. But instead she sobered up into Alzheimer's. I will never get what I need from her.

I click on the link for the blog as I sip a strong cup of coffee, hoping to get rid of the incessant vinegar smell. The smell that lets me know it was all my fault. Vampires cannot enter your home unless you invite them in. I invited him in.

I see myself as I was then, my small pinched face and my long brown hair that was filled with knots because no one brushed it. I know I found the world a terrible, strange place then. I had lost my dad, my lovely dad who danced in the kitchen with me, who took me to the beach and built a whole village of sandcastles with me, who threw me high into the air, making me shriek with a fearful joy because I always knew he would catch me. He was gone. Everything had been perfect but then I had lost everything. Not just him but my mum as well. She was there, still alive, but she'd disappeared, getting fainter and fainter, just disappeared. She slept and cried and slept and cried and I had no idea what to do except watch her and mourn.

Every morning I would wake up and lie in my bed with my eyes closed, hoping that if I could pretend to still be asleep, I would hear my beloved father's voice saying, 'What's up, buttercup?' so I could reply, 'Breakfast time, Mr Lime.' I believed if I could just keep my eyes shut for long enough, he would come into my room, scoop me up and take me to the kitchen, where he would make me blueberry pancakes that were never really round but still tasted delicious. But it never worked and every morning I finally braved opening my eyes to my empty bedroom and my silent house, grief lying in every corner. I imagined that I would cry forever. I cried in the morning and at night and secretly in the toilets at school.

I knew when I got out of bed, I would have to make myself breakfast and pack my own lunch and walk myself to school. I had an old pillow that sat on my bed with a picture of a unicorn on it. My father had brought it home for me one day after work, handing it to me and saying, 'It's magical, just like you are.' I'd had it for years and the stitching at the side had come undone, and the image of the unicorn had faded, and no one had fixed it so the inside of the pillow was falling out. That was what I felt had happened to my life. The stitches were undone and everything was coming apart, and the happy memories were fading, and I didn't know how to fix it. He'd held our lives together and now he was gone.

Sometimes I went and lay down next to her in the big bed, listening to her breathe or stroking her hair. Sometimes she liked that but sometimes she didn't want to be touched and she would say, 'Leave me alone, Alice, I'm tired.'

She tried, I think. I think she tried to carry on. She told me that we would be fine, that we would be a little family, that we would be okay, but then she went to bed and didn't get up again. My father was the one who had made us a family. He was the one who planned family adventures to the beach and special dinners for birthdays. He was the one who made my mother laugh so she was happy, even when she seemed sad. He was the one who kept the stitches closed so nothing came apart. I was so lost without him. We both were.

I walked to school with an empty lunch box. She was never hungry so she didn't care when the food ran out. 'Aren't you an independent little thing?' one of my teachers said, and I know I felt proud of myself for being able to read the kitchen clock on my own so I would know what time to leave for school.

I should never have spoken to him but I was six years old. I had no idea. How could I?

It was winter, sharply cold and overcast, when he stopped the car to speak to me. My father had been gone for three months by then. I was walking to school, hungry and shivering because I hadn't been able to find my jumper and the fridge and the pantry were, once again, empty.

I hadn't noticed the car beside me until he called out to me, 'Hey, Alice, isn't it?' I stopped walking and nodded because he couldn't have been a stranger; a stranger wouldn't know my name. The car was a deep blue colour with a single white door. Something he was always going to fix but never did. It rattled as the engine idled while he waited for me to say something.

I want to shout at that naive little girl, 'Run, Alice, run!'

I should stop thinking about this. I need to get ready to pick the boys up from school. They can't see me like this, but the memory, insufferable and painful, will not be denied. Outside the kitchen window I can see that the sky has turned the same grey it was that day. I watch the wind rushing through the trees outside and remember his voice, deep and rough, even though he was speaking kindly.

'I'm Vernon, remember me?' he asked as I stared at him. 'I was a mate of your dad's. We worked together sometimes.'

I didn't remember him but I didn't want to be rude.

'Can I give you a lift to school? It's really cold.'

I nodded my head as the wind pushed against me and the grey sky offered no warmth, and I climbed into his car.

'How's your mum doing?'

'She's really sleepy all the time,' I said.

'Poor thing, shall I come round this afternoon? Maybe bring some fish and chips?'

I didn't say anything. I was too hungry to think about food.

'What've you got for lunch?' he asked kindly.

I stared at my feet because I didn't want to admit that I had nothing.

I looked up and saw my school and I was so grateful to be there. Something was prickling at me, something was trying to warn me. Instinct had kicked in, and in his car, even with the heater blasting out hot air, goose bumps ran up and down my arm. 'That's my school,' I said and he slowed down and stopped.

'Tell you what,' he said as I opened the car door, 'I'll come round tonight and bring dinner, and you can tell your mum I helped you this morning. And here,' he said, pulling out his wallet from a pocket in his trousers, 'is five dollars for the canteen. I bet that'll buy you a nice lunch.'

I took the money and smiled at him because I knew that the canteen was serving pizza that day, and with five dollars, I would be able to buy two slices and a bag of crisps and a chocolate milk. It seemed to me an unbelievable bounty of food.

'You're pretty when you smile,' he said, smiling back. His face was a shiny pink with a few strips of red where he had obviously cut himself shaving, and his teeth were yellow. His breath was stale, stinking of tobacco. 'Your mum is real pretty too as I recall,' he said. 'I better get along. Off you go now.'

All I had been thinking about then was the silver shutters of the canteen rolling up, releasing the cheesy smell of pizza. My mouth watered through the first few periods of the day. I found myself almost enjoying my hunger, knowing that today, for once, it would be satisfied.

I forgot about him until that night when the bell rang and I opened the door and saw him there. 'Ready for dinner?' he asked. He had a whole parcel of hot chips and another filled with fish.

'Mum's tired,' I told him.

'Let her know I'm here, love. Maybe she'll feel up to dinner.' And she did get up. That was the important thing – she got up. For the first time in as long as I could remember, she got up and got dressed and we all had dinner together and he poured her what I now know was a glass of vodka and she got a bit giggly and I was warm and full and it felt like the answer to all our problems.

I shake my head at my stupidity.

Alice made a mistake. Alice made a mistake. Alice made a mistake.

'It's not my fault,' I say as Ian taught me to say years ago. 'It's not my fault. I was a child.'

He liked a lot of vinegar on his chips and I used to as well. I used to pour it over liberally, savouring the smell. Now it nauseates me because it is the smell of the end of my childhood, the end of my innocence. It's the smell of the end.

There is a jumper I have hidden at the back of my closet. Sometimes I hold it to my nose, pretending that the smell of my father is still here, but I know that the sweet smell of his aftershave is long gone. I know that his touch was kind and gentle but I cannot remember the feel of it. I feel like I have nothing left of him. All my memories of him are overlaid with my memories of the wrong man, of the worst kind of man. And I hate him for that even more than I hate him for everything else he did to me.

I look at my watch – it's nearly time to leave. I touch a key on my computer, illuminating the screen again. There's a new message for me.

Sister, sister, sister. My tongue darts in and out of the space in my mouth.

I feel like my heart may stop. Who is this woman and why is she asking about my little sister? I grow instantly resentful that she thinks she can turn my experiences into a story, into a few minutes of entertainment.

'Leave me alone,' I say aloud as the broken red car returns to my mind. 'It wasn't my fault. I only meant to help her.' I keep repeating these words as I type furiously and reply to this woman on the internet. I hate this stranger with a visceral force for making me confront exactly what I did.

At school I keep my sunglasses on as I wait in the pickup line to hide my puffy eyes. I will not think about it anymore. I won't think about him and I won't think about my sister. My lost little sister with her beautiful smile. My sister who I couldn't save or protect.

Alice is drowning in guilt. Alice is suffocated by guilt.

A tone on my mobile lets me know I have a new email, and I glance down quickly as the line starts to move.

I know what you did. You took everything from me. You don't deserve what you have.

'Oh God,' I moan. 'Oh God, oh God.' Is this the same person who just sent me the message on my blog? Is someone just playing with me? What on earth is going on?

The car behind me hoots and I look up, noting the space in front of me. I slide into position and the boys climb into the car while I squeeze the steering wheel, holding on for dear life as I summon the right questions to keep the boys from suspecting anything is wrong.

I think about the bottle of vodka that has languished in the freezer for months, since we had all the GPs at the practice over for dinner. I know it will take away the pain, erase the memories of what happened to me and what I did. It will numb the guilt. It soothed my mother for years.

'I won't give in,' I whisper.

'What was that, Mum?' asks Isaac, and I realise I am at the high school already.

'Nothing,' I say. 'Nothing.'

CHAPTER FOURTEEN
Molly

'I'm sure it's nothing,' says Peter for the tenth time as he parks the car outside Molly's parents' house.

'What if one of them is sick, Pete? Oh, I can't bear it. I don't think I would survive it.'

'Whatever it is we can deal with it, I promise. We'll deal with it together.' Peter folds her hand in his and Molly takes comfort from his peaceful presence. He reminds her of her father with his pragmatic approach to life. Everything can be dealt with as long as it's approached in a rational manner.

Her father opens the door and offers Molly his customary hug but he holds on too tightly and for longer than normal. Molly's feeling of dread grows.

In the living room her mother is perched on the edge of the couch. That in itself is unusual. The family always sits in the kitchen unless there are too many people. Her mother prefers the kitchen, where they can all congregate around the old table, worn smooth with thousands of meals and swipes of a cloth, so she can keep getting up to put more food on the table or get someone a drink. 'Please sit down,' Molly and Lexie say over and over again while their mother fusses.

'Mum,' says Molly, running over to her mother and clasping her in a hug. 'What's wrong? Please tell me what's wrong.'

'Sit down, Molly dear,' replies her father. 'Can I get you a drink, Peter? Maybe a beer?'

'I'm fine, thanks, Walter, maybe later. Molly's a bit anxious to know what's wrong so maybe we should get straight to it, but I want to let you and Anne know that we're both here for you for whatever you need.'

'Please tell me what's wrong, you have to tell me,' appeals Molly, eyes brimming with tears.

Her mother turns her pale face to her husband. 'Walt, please can you?'

Molly's father sighs deeply, his shoulders drooping with the effort of it. 'Yesterday you told your mother about a blog you read.'

'Yes, but I didn't mean to upset her…'

'And you felt a familiarity with this story?'

'Yes, but I have no idea why… It's just…'

'Darling,' says her father, sitting down next to her. 'We never wanted to tell you this and it's so very wrong of us but we just… I don't… At first we wanted to wait and then it was… I don't know, it just felt too late and we didn't know if we should say anything because we didn't want to upset you.'

'Upset me?' asks Molly, more confused than ever. 'What could you say that would upset me? Wanted to tell me what?'

'The world has changed a lot over the last few decades. We never considered that the internet would take over all our lives. We don't know if the woman who wrote the blog has any connection to you at all, but since you told your mother about it, she has been worrying terribly that we've made a mistake in keeping things from you. We realise that it's now possible for anyone to find you and we don't want to—'

'Wait a second – keeping things from me? What does that mean, and who on earth would be looking for me?'

Her father sighs deeply once more, his face pale, and she can see his hands shaking.

'You are not our biological child, Molly,' he says in a low voice, etched in pain.

'Not your… what?'

'We adopted you. We fostered you first and then we adopted you. I am so sorry that we didn't tell you before, that you had to find out this way. It's unlikely that this woman is connected to you but we thought it best to tell you in case anything ever… anyone ever—'

'Fostered me?' Molly cuts her father off.

'We fostered you,' says her mother slowly, 'and then we adopted you.' She dabs at her eyes with a tissue. 'We are so sorry, love.'

The words don't make sense, none of it makes sense. What her parents are saying is entirely impossible and Molly looks around the living room, waiting for Lexie to jump out with a camera, waiting for someone to laugh, waiting for the punchline of what is obviously a joke. But minutes pass and her mother's eyes shine with tears as her father's face loses what little colour it had. The silence stretches between them.

'That's impossible,' says Molly. Her mouth feels dry and she swallows quickly. 'I'm your daughter, I've always been your daughter. I don't… What about Lexie? I look like Lexie.'

Her father slumps down into the couch and puts his head in his hands. 'You're right, there are similarities, and we were so grateful for that when Lexie arrived, but you have to understand it's never been anything different for us. You are our daughter and Lexie is our daughter. That's all there is to it. We didn't think you needed to know because we had no real idea of where you came from so we just decided that you were ours from the beginning. We didn't want to confuse you, not knowing your past. We thought we were making the right decision.'

'Why didn't you know about my past? Where did I come from? Who were my parents? How could you not know anything about me?'

'If you just give me a moment, I can explain—'

But Molly cannot seem to stop her questions. 'The pictures,' says Molly, recalling the story of the lost album containing her baby pictures that pervaded her childhood.

Her father flushes. 'Yes, well… when your mother got pregnant with Lexie, you were too little to ask questions, but when you were around four and Lexie was just one, you started to wonder where the pictures of you were. It seemed easiest to tell you that we'd lost the albums in a move between houses.'

'Was there even a move? Have you always lived here? Did you really buy Foggy for me when I was three?' Nothing is true, nothing is real. Molly leans down and touches the plush peach carpet with her foot, making sure it's real, making sure she's real. Is this actually happening? Has she really just heard what she's just heard?

'No, darling, not a move that we lost the album in,' her mother says. 'We did move from the inner city just after we adopted you. We wanted you to have a garden to grow up in, and I was pregnant with Lexie by then. We thought it best. And I did buy the stuffed frog for you. I did and I remember it well. I told you…'

Molly can feel her whole body trembling. *Shock*, she thinks, *this is shock*. She cannot process the words her father has uttered. It is completely unfathomable. She cannot be adopted. She and Lexie are her father's two peas in a pod. How can they not be sisters?

'I'm…' she begins and Peter wraps his arm around her shoulders.

'You're shaking. Walter, I think a strong cup of tea is needed.'

'No!' yells Molly. 'I don't want a cup of tea. I don't… I want you to explain this to me. How is it possible that I'm adopted and that you've never told me? How could you not have told me? What kind of a person hides something like that?'

'It was never done to hurt you,' says her mother, her eyes filling up and spilling over. 'We wanted to tell you, so many times we wanted to tell you, but we just couldn't, we couldn't.'

'Why?' shrieks Molly, standing up. 'Why couldn't you? There's nothing wrong with being adopted. You could have told me from the beginning and it would have been fine.'

'Please stop shouting, Molly,' says her father. 'We're sorry, we—'

'No, Dad!' Molly raises her voice another decibel. 'I will not stop yelling. This is my whole life you're talking about. Everything has been a lie. Do you understand what you've just done? You've lobbed a grenade at me and exploded my entire life. Every single memory I have of my childhood is wrong; everything I thought or felt was a lie.'

'Not everything!' her mother yells back. 'Our absolute love and adoration for you was never a lie. Please, please, darling, I know we've done the wrong thing, I understand, but we were afraid.'

'Afraid of what?'

'We were afraid,' says her father levelly, 'that you would go looking for your real family.'

'But lots of adopted children do that, Walter,' says Peter. 'Sit down, Molly, please sit down and calm down.' Molly wants to shout at her husband as well but allows herself to be tugged back down onto the sofa. Peter takes her hand, holds it almost too tightly so Molly wants to pull away, but at the same time she is grateful for the strength there. 'Surely it wouldn't have bothered you if she found her biological family?' her husband asks, voicing the words she is unable to muster.

'It wasn't that,' replies her father. 'We weren't worried for us or because we thought she would reject us. We were afraid for her because we didn't know what she'd find, who she'd find.'

'What? Who did you think I would find? Do you know something about my family you're not telling me? Who are they? Do you know who they are?'

'Now, you need to stop all this and just let me explain,' says her father.

But Molly has no patience for any explanations. 'I can't believe you did this. I just…'

'It was an error in judgement, a terrible error in judgement, and it has been something we've worried about for your whole life. There have been many, many discussions between me and your mother over whether we should tell you or not, but after a few years we decided that telling you would be the real cruelty. We didn't want you to feel different to your sister.'

'Does Lexie know?' asks Molly, afraid to hear the answer. If her sister, her best friend, knows this awful secret, she doesn't know if she will be able to forgive her or trust her ever again.

'No, absolutely not,' says her father, 'and we won't tell her if you don't want us to.'

'Don't be ridiculous,' sneers Molly. 'Of course, she needs to know. I needed to know.'

Molly looks between her parents, struggling to find the similarities in her own face that she always did. She had believed her whole life that she had her father's nose and her mother's eyes, but as she looks at them now their features seem alien. The power of suggestion led her to believe that she resembled them, and now that the truth has been revealed she realises that she looks nothing like Lexie either. She has no idea who she looks like, where she came from, who she is. The revelation winds her.

'This is cruel,' she whispers. 'What you've done is cruel.' She knows she cannot stay in the house for a moment longer. She gets up and leaves, almost running for the door.

She stands breathless in the garden at the front of the house, looking at the street she grew up on, finding the familiar strange, unsettled by everything. She takes in deep, icy breaths of air, trying to calm herself. Small drops of rain begin to fall, but she doesn't move. *Who am I? Where do I come from? How could they do this?* she thinks. She feels her body shudder and wraps her arms around herself. A cold wind pushes against her, making her shiver. She would like to cry, to scream, to do something, but the whirl of emotions inside her cannot find a way out. She could be anyone. Why was her father so worried about who her family was, and if they were scared of where she came from, how on earth could they really love her? Were they scared of her too? When she was little, did they worry about who she might grow up to be? Was that why she was always such a 'good big sister'? Had she realised, on some level, that she was not the same as Lexie, not connected to her parents the same way her sister was? Was she always trying to make up for that by being good, by always doing the right thing? One after another the questions slam into her and she steps backwards as though trying to avoid the onslaught. She wants to clamp her hands over her face and shout, 'Shut up, just shut up.' Who was her mother? Who was her father? Why didn't they love her? The questions keep coming.

After hours or only minutes pass, Molly feels Peter wrap his arms around her from behind. He warms her body, and she leans back into him. 'Perhaps you should come back inside. The rain is getting heavier and it's freezing. Your parents are completely devastated. They're both in tears. We should talk about this.'

'How could they have done this?' asks Molly. She turns around in her husband's arms and rests her head on his chest, listening to the steady beat of his heart. The cold drops of rain dampen her hair, run down her cheeks, mingling with her tears.

Peter lets go of her and then takes her hand, pulling her to the front steps so they are under cover. He holds her gently by her shoulders. 'Listen, I know they've made a distressing misjudgement, and they know it too, but it wasn't done with any malice. They never meant to hurt you.' Everything Peter says is logical as it always is – but logic won't work here. This is not a column of numbers he can correct and explain. This is an awful, tragic mess.

'I can't think about them now. Can you just take me home? Please? I need to go home.'

'Are you sure? Are you sure you want to leave it like this?'

Molly nods silently. The rain is getting steadily heavier and the wind is picking up, but she finds that she doesn't mind standing outside. It's better to concentrate on being wet and cold, better to feel than to think.

'I'll get my keys and let them know we're going.'

'Tell them,' says Molly as Peter turns towards the front door.

'Tell them?'

'Tell them not to contact me.'

Peter nods sadly. Molly knows the words are calculated to hurt her parents but she feels the need to lash out right now – she is capable of nothing else. She is in turmoil. She is angry and sad and almost giddy with disbelief. She knows she needs some time and space.

At home she shows Peter the blog, lets him read the story.

'Do you think she's your sister?' he asks.

'No,' says Molly flatly, exhaustion and despair robbing her voice of emotion. 'I asked her about her sister. She says she's dead. She died in a car accident.'

'Dead?' repeats Peter.

'Yes,' says Molly, 'dead.'

CHAPTER FIFTEEN

14 January 1987

Margaret

She lies with her eyes open in the dark. The alcohol does this to her sometimes – wakes her up without warning, hands her a galloping heart and a mind that won't stop going over the past. She cannot help but feel betrayed by the beautiful liquid whose job it is to keep her floating in her Adam dreams.

The house is silent, heavy with heat but blissfully silent. Next to her he grunts. 'You are such a waste of space,' she murmurs and she knows she's not talking to him but to herself. The clarity that comes from these moments is hideous. Her heart beats so quickly she finds it difficult to take a deep breath. She thinks she may be having a heart attack and is mildly pleased about this. If she dies, right here and now, that's fine.

But what about the girls? She needs to be here for them. *You're not here for them now*, her inner voice whispers. *You are a completely useless mother, a failure of a human being, and all you're good for is being Vernon's punching bag.*

After Mr Henkel died, she thought they had put the worst behind them. They had lost babies and they had lost a father but she was sure that things could only get better. She could never have predicted what was to come, could never have foreseen the terrible tragedy that would take her wonderful husband.

Adam shouldn't have been working in the storm: electricity and rain don't mix. Everyone said it had been a stupid thing to do, no matter how desperate his client was, as though by placing the blame on his shoulders for his own death, they would keep misfortune at bay for themselves. Lightning striking a house was uncommon, so uncommon that Adam hadn't even thought about it. It was a freak accident – but it happened to Adam.

Suddenly, she was a widow. Margaret couldn't make sense of it. Now it was just her and a six-year-old child. She wanted to die with him, to be with him. He was her everything. He was her husband, her friend, her lover and the father of her child. He was her words and without him she had no idea how to speak, no idea how to exist in the world. But she couldn't just close her eyes and join him because she had Alice. A girl who had grown up used to love and attention, chatting to all who would listen about herself and her feelings. She couldn't leave Alice alone and she knew that. She had looked at her daughter and felt a slight edge to the love and responsibility she felt for the child, a small flower of resentment that Alice was keeping her from being with her beloved Adam. She pushed the thoughts aside. She was a mother and she had to be a mother. She wouldn't let her down; she wouldn't repeat history.

'We'll be fine together,' she whispered to her little girl that first night as they curled up in bed together, but Alice didn't seem to believe the words, and in truth, Margaret didn't believe them either. Adam and his father had anchored her in the port of her own life. With both of them gone, she knew she would not be powerful enough to stop herself drifting away.

The anxiety and depression came rushing back and things that had once been simple became impossible. How do you do the laundry so the clothes don't trade their colours? How do you ask the butcher for the piece of meat you want? How do you pay an electricity bill or speak to the bank about needing time to pay the mortgage? Adam was going to sort out life insurance, he really was. But it was too late. Time skips along and the future seems far away.

She dragged herself through mud every day, trying to make things work, but it was too hard.

Only sleep was easy, only that.

People checked up on them for a week or two, but then everyone had lives to get back to. She thought about calling her parents but seven years of silence separated them. It seemed too great a distance.

And then he started popping round: 'Just because Adam was a mate and I can see you're struggling.'

And she was struggling. Her existence was horrible and barren with only the never-ending demands of a small child for company.

She just didn't realise how truly awful things could get.

She hadn't gone looking for him. She hadn't gone looking for anyone. He was a friend of Adam's, he'd said. He saw her at the funeral, told her he was so sorry for her and her poor daughter. Margaret had thanked him and then he had blended into the crowd at the wake.

She hadn't expected him to turn up on her doorstep bearing gifts, offering help, bringing the horrible truth of what she deserved, what she really deserved from her life now that Adam, the man who had always been too good for her, was gone.

She wipes at stray tears. 'Oh, Adam… I miss you,' she whispers. Then she closes her eyes again.

He turns over and throws a heavy arm across her body, trapping her. He smells but she's sure she smells as well. She thinks about that first night, the night she let him in, accepted his presence in her home. Her heart races, her mind twirls and she tortures herself with her mistakes.

She hadn't expected to see him ever again but then one night he turned up on the doorstep, clutching a giant meal of fish and chips. Little Alice had come into the room to wake her although, in truth, the scent had already alerted her to something different.

She hadn't been eating much. She hadn't been doing much of anything except drifting through the hours, half asleep, waiting for every painful day to be over.

Alice had opened the bedroom door and sidled up to the bed. 'There's a man here, Mum.'

'What man? What are you talking about?' The tangy smell of salt and vinegar in the air was making her salivate, but she knew there was no food in the house. There hadn't been for days.

'Vernon, he gave me a lift to school today and he's brought fish and chips for dinner. He was Dad's friend.'

A good mother, a normal mother, a mother worth anything would have seen that as a problem. The Margaret before Adam's death would have leapt out of bed and chased the man away. But Margaret after Adam's death was roiling in pain as soon as she opened her eyes. Margaret after Adam's death couldn't defend and protect her child, couldn't even protect herself. Inside Margaret had long disappeared by then, failing to warn her of the signs.

It was the smell of the fish that got her up, and then once she was dressed and sitting at the table, he poured her a vodka and soda, and for the first time in months, she felt something other than the agonising pain at losing her beloved husband.

There was no attraction, at least not on her side. His blue eyes were too small and his gut hung over his belt, but she invited him back again after that. She liked that he always brought a bottle of vodka, loved the floating, disembodied feeling she got after a few shots. She invited him back again and again, chasing that feeling.

Alice had watched him, suspicious and aloof, every time he came round. She seemed to know that he was a bad idea.

When the money in her account dried up, Margaret knew she needed a job or welfare. She needed something to keep her and her child fed, to keep the vodka coming in. The mortgage was two months behind and the electricity bills were smothered in red. The phone rang with debt collectors. It had only been four months since Adam died but Vernon was round every day by then, a constant presence in the house so filled with grief.

'I'll sort the mortgage and the bills, don't worry. Adam would have done it for my woman. I know he would. You just rest and recover. You've had a terrible shock,' he would say.

She'd resisted letting him inside her until then, kept him satisfied with groping on the couch and blowjobs when her daughter was asleep, but she understood she was making a deal. She hadn't planned on falling in love ever again anyway – her heart wasn't capable – and he was nice to Alice.

He took care of them. He let her lie in bed all day, just needing her at night, and even though it was too soon for her after Adam's soft kisses and gentle touch, at least she didn't have to do much.

Every night she vowed to do better the next morning, to get up and find a job and start running her own life so she didn't need him anymore, but when she opened her eyes to the spring sunshine, the black slobbering dog of depression that had been chained away for years broke free and attacked her, time and time again. 'Who would hire you?' it growled. 'You're a stupid girl with no education. The only thing you've ever done is deliver newspapers and have a baby and you're a crap mother as well. You've got nothing to offer the world. Close your eyes and let someone else run your life; you're incapable of doing it yourself, loser. What kind of a woman sleeps with someone so soon after her husband has died? What kind of a mother can't get herself out of bed to do the washing? It's been months, why can't you get yourself together? You're useless. You never deserved Adam. You're lucky to even have Vernon or you and Alice would be out on the street. You're a waste of space.'

She never ran out of terrible things to say to herself. She never ran out of those words.

'How about I move in with you two, take care of everything so you don't have to?' he suggested one night as they sat on the couch staring at the television. Margaret hadn't really been watching. She had been thinking about the way he smelled, a little like manure because of the smoking. Adam had used a spicy aftershave with a hint of sweetness, a smell that Margaret could still find in the bottle hidden in her side table. One sniff and he was next to her again, telling her about the new house he was wiring, planting gentle kisses on her lips that she never got enough of.

'Um,' she said because she didn't want him to move in. In truth, she didn't want him anywhere near her.

'Think about it, Margaret. You're still not yourself, and the kid and I get along all right. You can take all the time you need, you know, just to recover. I don't ask for much, do I?'

She shook her head because he didn't even need her to talk to him. Not because he understood her difficulty at finding the right words, not because he was able to finish her sentences for her, but because she suspected that he didn't really care what she thought.

'How about we give it a go and then if it's not working out, we can part?'

'Okay,' she said when the words *no* and *I don't want that* and *please go* reverberated in her head. She was so hideously weak.

Alice didn't like finding him in the kitchen in the morning. She was too young to truly understand but even she knew that her dad could not be replaced by Vernon.

'I'll take you to school from now on,' he told Alice, 'give your mum a chance to rest.'

And Margaret had been truly grateful for that. That and the endless bottles of vodka he brought home, so they could drink together and laugh about nothing.

He was an electrician, like Adam had been, but he wasn't at all like Adam. Not even close.

CHAPTER SIXTEEN

Now

Alice

There is no one at the front desk of the Green Gate Home. But I can hear someone shouting and I assume that staff are trying to calm whoever it is down.

I imagine it is terrifying to look around you and not remember where you are or how you got here. 'The lucid days can be worse than the days where they are lost in the past,' Anika has told me. 'They tend to get angry and upset at finding themselves living here when they have assumed they are home.' I wonder if my mother would be pleasantly surprised to find herself in her neat, clean room, rather than the dirty space she used to live in. I immediately feel guilty for this thought.

I pull off my coat, hot in the overheated space after the fresh air outside. I make my way down the corridor, and as the shouting gets louder, I realise, with a panic, that it's coming from my mother's room. I quicken my pace. The door is open and Anika is standing at the computer, tapping frantically at the keys as another young nurse, Isla, holds onto my mother's arms. She keeps trying to hit Anika, her face red with fury.

'You leave that alone!' she's shouting. 'I know what you did. I know what you did.'

The words hold me frozen at the entrance to the room, my heart racing inhumanly fast. I feel sick. 'Alice,' says Anika, turning and seeing me. 'I don't know… The computer, it must be broken, can you help? Can you find the aquarium video?'

I step forward into the room and Anika moves off to try and help Isla hold my mother. I tap quickly at the keys, realising that the computer has somehow disconnected itself from the internet again. As I reconnect it, a Gmail account pops up and then quickly disappears. I shake my head. My mother doesn't have an email account. 'I know what you did,' she yells, sending a shiver right through me, and then she starts to cry. It's a terrible sound, more a wail than a cry, a howl that rips from her body. I find the video and have to click on it twice before it begins because my hands are shaking so much.

Finally, the soothing music plays and the screen is filled with a turtle swimming lazily through deep blue water as a shoal of clownfish swim past.

'See, Margaret,' says Isla, her voice deep and strong, 'see, there they are, look at the fish.'

My mother turns her head, instantly transfixed by the screen. Her body sags and her face goes blank as Anika and Isla lower her carefully back into her chair.

'What happened?' I ask as she stares at the screen.

'I don't know,' says Anika.

'I brought in her lunch and she told me that Vernon had been to visit with Lilly.'

I swallow quickly. 'Why would she say that?'

'She says he's visiting all the time,' replies Anika. 'Sometimes she introduces him to me. I play along because it makes her happy. Today I nodded and said, "That's nice," and she said, "You don't believe me, do you?" I thought the question meant she was lucid so I said, "Well, you know you haven't had any visitors today,

Margaret." And she started shouting, saying that I had made Vernon leave and that I had taken Lilly. Then she told me Lilly was dead because of what I did. Do you have any idea what she's talking about?'

I shake my head. I feel what I can only describe as little electric shocks through my whole body.

'Who's Lilly, Alice, do you know?'

'I… She's…' The words won't come out. I try so hard not to think her name. I slump onto the bed, my legs jelly, unable to hold me up.

'She was my sister,' I say finally.

'I'm sorry, I didn't know,' replies Anika.

'I'll just be at the front,' Isla whispers and she leaves the room after giving my shoulder a quick squeeze. The kind gesture makes me want to weep.

I have no idea why this is happening. First the emails and then the message from the woman about my blog. It's been so many years since anyone has spoken Lilly's name out loud, so many years that sometimes I can almost forget that I had a little sister, that there was someone I loved more than anything in the world. 'She died when she was very young,' I tell Anika. 'Mum hasn't spoken about her for years and years. I assumed she had forgotten about her. She died in a car accident.'

I realise it's the first time I have said the words aloud to anyone but myself. I wrote them to Molly Khan and now I have said them aloud and it feels like I am right back there, like I am sitting in front of the television, looking at the horrifying result of the choice I made. My past has its claws dug into me and it won't let go.

I have mourned her every day for over thirty years. Little Lilly. My darling little Lilly. My tongue darts in and out of the space, in and out of the space. *Your fault, your fault.*

Alice made a mistake. Alice is to blame. Alice should be punished.

'I don't think it's possible to forget about the children we have,' says Anika, dragging me back into the room and forcing me to look at my transfixed mother.

She is absorbed by the fish and the music, her mouth open slightly, a trail of drool running down her chin.

'You don't know what kind of mother she was,' I say in a quiet voice, and then I get up and leave. I need to be outside, away from the smell and the stale heated air. I feel Anika's silent judgement burn into my back. I can't do this today. I can't think about this anymore. I wish there was a pill you could take to erase your childhood. I wish there was a pill for erasing your guilt.

In the car, I take a quick look at my phone. I feel exhausted, drained and weary beyond belief. My heart hammers in my chest as I see there is another email. I click on it, fingers trembling.

I know what you did. You thought you got away with it but I know what you did.

I throw my phone on the passenger seat, the trembling taking over my whole body. I need to tell Jack, maybe bring in the police. The message on my blog must be connected to these emails.

It's all bringing back the past. I hate having to think about him, about what my mother was like and about Lilly. I hate thinking about what I did. All I can remember is the alcoholic, negligent shell my mother became. The fact that she managed to produce lovely Lilly with her big brown eyes and gorgeous smile amazed me. She never understood what was going on in her home and I never wanted her to be able to. The older she got the more she would have seen and heard and the more damaged she would have become. But she was my sister and I adored her. The tears that are always just below the surface appear as I mourn my little sister. The child who never really had a chance.

Alice's fault. Alice's fault. All Alice's fault.

The memories bring only pain and here I am, sitting in my car, and the past is back to torture me.

Someone knows what I did.

I think about the day I finally left home when I was sixteen. I left on the day of my sixteenth birthday. I thought I could leave it behind me finally, that I could just put everything that had happened somewhere in a metaphorical box in my mind, lock it up and hide the key.

When I was twelve, Vernon helped my mother to get the single mother's pension. He was working less and less by then, preferring to join my mother in her drinking when he wasn't at the pub.

'May as well earn your keep,' he told me as he blew a foul plume of cigarette smoke towards me. He had grown fatter with each passing year, and his enormous gut hung over his belt. He suffered from eczema, which made his skin pink and shiny. Even on the coldest day his grotesque body was covered in sweat. He had trouble moving quickly, but no trouble swinging his fists and using his body to hold me down.

He liked to stand in my way if he saw me, forcing me to try and move around him, giving him a chance to grab my breasts. 'I'm going to tell,' I shouted once or twice.

'Who are you going to tell, Alice? Cause if you tell on me, I can tell on you, can't I?'

The blood in my veins ran on hatred for him. I wished him dead every day but he just kept going.

When I was fifteen, he disappeared. Usually it was just for a few days but this time he didn't come back. Not for months.

The vodka ran out quickly.

'Will you get some money from the bank for me and get me some more?' my mother pleaded with me.

'No,' I said, every day. 'No, no, no.'

She lay in the bathroom, suffering through withdrawal, her skin white with a layer of sheen, her body unable to hold down any food. I wanted to feel sorry for her but instead I just felt distant.

'I'm dying here,' she said. 'Do you want me to die?'

'I have school,' I replied. I was cruel, so cruel, but I had been broken. I had been abused, neglected and hurt, and I needed to shut myself down so I could get through every day without thinking about killing myself.

I did bring her water as she lay on the bathroom floor, and when she stopped throwing up, I brought her some thin tinned soup. She stopped asking for the vodka after a week. 'Thank you, love,' she said when I helped her into the shower. 'You're a good girl.'

She was pale and so horribly thin that the bones of her wrists seemed only moments away from poking right through her skin. 'I think I'll be okay now,' she said to me finally. 'I won't need it anymore,' and regardless of how I had hardened my heart, of how I cautioned myself not to believe her, I still couldn't help the hope that filled me.

'I'll get stronger and then you and I can leave and find somewhere else to live. I'll get a job and I'll make more money and I'll give you everything you want.'

'I just want you, Mum,' I said. And Lilly, I wanted Lilly, but she was long gone by then. Lilly was a memory of big brown eyes and a dimpled smile and she was a memory of a mistake I had made. A mistake that cost her her life. I couldn't have Lilly but maybe I could have my mother. I would take what I could get. A sober, awake mother seemed too much to hope for but I couldn't help myself. Abused children never really grow out of wanting, needing the love and affection of a parent.

At school, I had made a friend. My first real friend. Judy was quiet and shy and sat in the library with me at lunch. Her mother overpacked her lunch, and Judy was happy to share if I had nothing to eat, which was most days.

I told her my mother wasn't well, and when she confessed her father was a recovering alcoholic, I told her, 'My mother's the same, only she's not recovering.'

But then, suddenly, she was. She was recovering. She was better. She was trying.

We didn't talk about Vernon at home. It was as though both of us were happy to pretend he never existed. We didn't talk about Lilly either.

Instead we were polite and careful with each other, as though we were both recovering from an illness.

Only once I said to her, 'Do you think he'll come back?'

'I hope not.'

'But if he does, you won't let him in?'

'I hope not,' she said and my heart sank. Hope was not enough. I prayed every day that he was gone for good.

Slowly, things changed in the house. She cooked and cleaned, and although she wasn't strong enough to get a job, she got up every morning to see me off to school. Even though I tried to stay strong, my guard dropped, little by little, each day.

The night before my sixteenth birthday, she suggested a party. Her hands still shook and she was still battling the desire to drink as each moment passed. Vernon had been gone for nearly three months by then. Each day that I returned home and found him gone, I breathed a sigh of profound relief. We were finally the good little family she had promised me we would be after my dad had died.

'I don't really have that many friends, Mum,' I said. 'Maybe you can make dinner and Judy can come over.'

'Absolutely and I'll bake a… a… You'd like a… a… What's the word again?' She forgot words sometimes. It was the beginning of the disease that will soon eat away at her but I didn't know that then. I just hoped she would get better.

'A cake, Mum, yes, I'd love a cake.' I wanted to cry for her, for her desperation to please.

The next day when I got home from school with Judy in tow, both of us excited at the thought of a special dinner and a freshly baked cake, the house was silent. We walked in, a haze and a terrible stench in the air. My mother was asleep on the couch. Vernon was asleep on the floor beside her, his shirt rucked up over his giant hairy belly. Smoke poured from the oven where a chocolate cake was black, close to igniting.

I turned to Judy. 'You should go,' I said.

'But I can help,' replied Judy.

'You should go.'

Judy left and I pulled the blackened cake from the oven and tossed it away. Smoke filled the air, clogging my lungs. On the kitchen table stood one empty bottle of vodka and one full one, and I understood then that nothing would ever be different. She had let him in. She would always let him in, and I felt hope leak from every pore on my skin. I was not enough of a reason for her to stay away from him or the alcohol. I was not enough.

I knew then I couldn't stay. With a heavy heart I searched through her bag, scraping together some coins, and then I found Vernon's wallet on the floor, stuffed full of twenty-dollar notes. I took most of it, threw some threadbare clothes and one of my father's jumpers in a backpack and walked right out. I never went back until after Jack and I got married.

Now, Vernon is in prison. The only other two people who even know Lilly existed are me and my mother. I wonder for a mad moment if she's sending me the emails. She used the same words and I'm certain I didn't imagine the Gmail account popping up when I was fixing the computer.

'Ridiculous,' I say now. My mother rarely knows what day it is. She would not be capable of sending me an email, and why now?

Why now, when for years we've always had a silent agreement to never mention Lilly again? Why now?

I take a deep breath and start my car, pulling out of the car park of the Green Gate Home.

At home I open up the email again, deciding that the best defence is a good offence. I will frighten this person back just as they are trying to frighten me. I find one that I've deleted and return it to my inbox.

I know who you are and I'm going to the police if you don't stop.

I send the email and wait. Eventually I get up and put on a load of washing. When I return to my computer there's already a reply.

What a good idea, Alice. Go to the police and then you can tell them what you did. What happened to her, Alice? What did you do?

My body starts to shake. Blood pounds in my ears. I want to scream and scream. Instead I delete the email, and then as terror and fury swim through my body, I pick up the laptop and raise it above my head. I smash it onto the floor. The sound of the computer hitting the tiled kitchen floor rings through the house, the screen cracks and the hinges split.

I stare at the machine, shocked by the violence of my own behaviour.

Going to the freezer, I grab the vodka. My skin sticks to the freezing glass, stinging. I open it and take a long drink, feeling it burn its way into my stomach.

What is happening to me?

'This is not you, Alice,' I say aloud. 'It's not you and you don't want to do this.'

Filled with shame, I shove the vodka back into the freezer and go to the pantry, where I find a half-eaten block of chocolate, sickly sweet and filled with caramel.

I shove the pieces into my mouth so fast I almost choke. Chocolate doesn't wipe out your thoughts, doesn't let you ignore the world, doesn't force you into bed. Chocolate is just a rush of sugar. It isn't enough.

I stare down at the mangled computer, wondering what I will tell Jack as another email notification beeps on my phone.

Didn't like that idea, did you, Alice? I left you a little present – in your post box. I hope it brings back memories.

I cover my mouth where the chocolate is coming back up. I rush to the kitchen sink and vomit, my whole body trembling, until there's nothing left.

Whoever this is, it feels like they can see me, like they're watching me. I think about what I did, about the terrible consequences of that choice, and I feel my body heave again. I retch, spit into the sink and then run hot water, erasing my shame. I rinse my mouth, ridding myself of the taste.

I rush to my front door, open it cautiously and peer into the garden and the street beyond the wall. It is quiet. Nothing stirs and there is no one around. I walk slowly to my post box, hoping there is nothing there, praying I am merely the victim of a sick joke.

There is something soft inside, roughly wrapped in newspaper, clumsily taped as though it was done in a rush. I sniff the paper in case it's something disgusting, hold it gingerly between my finger and thumb. But I can only smell the chemical scent of newsprint.

I take whatever it is back inside with me, snapping on a pair of gloves. Then I slowly open it.

It is a stuffed green frog. Her stuffed green frog. She used to have it with her all the time. She carried it everywhere. I hated it because it came from a friend of his. In my rush to leave all those years ago, I forgot to take it. It had been hidden between my mattress and headboard for six years by then, and I simply forgot to take it with me. I never forgave myself for that, but I could never go back for it and I could never find it when I went back to see her when I was twenty-six. Now, I stare at it for a long time, and then even though I know I shouldn't, I hold it to my face as I cry.

CHAPTER SEVENTEEN
Molly

Molly wakes from the road dream. The aching loneliness she felt when she was standing in the middle of the barren road overwhelms her. She turns over once, twice and then looks at the clock next to the bed. It's 3 a.m. She wants to be asleep. She wants to forget. She has no desire to think about her parents' revelation but her mind races along. She thinks about the street where she grew up, about the double-storey cream-coloured house with a bright blue door she has always called home. She thinks about Carol and Frieda from next door, who have lived on the road as long as her parents have, smiling and waving as she and Lexie used to run past on their way down to the park at the end of the road. 'There go the Sneddon girls,' Frieda would always say. But she wasn't a Sneddon girl, not really.

She turns over again and feels a sudden ache in her pelvis. She lays her hand gently on her stomach. 'Oh no,' she whispers. She remembers this feeling, she knows what it means. She thinks about waking Peter but realises his side of the bed is empty. 'Oh no, oh no, oh no,' she whispers.

The empty road is her life path in reality. That's what Emma said the dream means. A quick jolt of pain forces her to take a deep breath. She moves her feet and can almost feel the small black stones on the road. She will be alone again very soon. She knows it.

She slides out of bed and walks slowly to the bathroom, bent over because the ache is stronger when she stands up. 'Please, please,' she whispers but she knows it's no use.

She uses the toilet and then wipes, closing her eyes, trying to find the strength she needs to deal with what's coming. When she looks down at the toilet paper in her hand, she sees it. A light pink stripe. It's over. Numbness cloaks her. It's too much, just too much. She closes her eyes again, trying to imagine a white light surrounding the small being inside her as she has done all the times before, but she can only conjure the colour black. It's over again. Once again, it's over.

She finds Peter in the kitchen, standing at the kettle, staring into their darkened living room.

'What are you doing up?' she asks him, and he starts, her voice breaking his reverie.

'I just, I don't know… Thinking about it all… What are you doing up? You need to rest, darling.'

'I'm bleeding.' She feels strangely detached as she says the words. She's done this before. She knows how it goes.

'Oh, babe,' says Peter. He moves towards her but she steps back. She doesn't want comfort. She doesn't want platitudes about it not being their time, about how they'll find a way to be parents, about how everything will be okay. Everything will not be okay. Everything is not okay.

'I think I'll just take a sleeping pill and go back to bed,' she says. 'No reason to stay away from them now.'

'No,' says Peter firmly. 'We're going to the hospital.'

'What for?' she asks and the numbness disappears, cracking her open. She leans against the kitchen counter, the ache in her pelvis steady, and covers her mouth with her hand. She bites down on her fingers to stop herself from screaming, tears dripping off her chin.

'Oh, Molly, Molly, my love,' says Peter and he holds her tight, waiting for her to run out of despair.

'Come now,' he says as she shudders and breathes, 'get dressed and we'll go and see what's happening.'

Molly does as she's told, pulling a tracksuit on and tying her hair back, grateful to be told what to do. She doesn't want to have to think. She wants to be a child again, safe in her illusions, blissfully unaware of just how awful life can be.

On the way out of the apartment she passes her desk and grabs Foggy, holding him against her as she hasn't done since she was a child. She imagines she will seem strange to the people in emergency, a grown woman clutching a toy, but she cannot care about that now.

They drive to the hospital in silence. There is nothing to say.

In the warm emergency room, the bright lights immediately give Molly a headache. She sits on a moulded plastic chair, incapable of doing anything but staring at the television up on the wall, playing a rerun of an old sitcom. A woman comes in carrying a child who is sniffing and coughing, whining with tiredness. 'Never a moment's rest,' she says to Molly as she settles herself into a chair opposite her. The little girl stares at Molly through sleepy eyes. 'Tell them her temperature is over forty,' the woman says, calling across to a man talking to a nurse at the counter.

What I wouldn't give, thinks Molly longingly, trying not to stare at the woman and her daughter.

Peter talks to the triage nurse and then comes over to get Molly. He helps her out of the chair as though she's unable to stand alone, which is exactly how she feels. Her legs would like to collapse under her. She would like to curl up on the floor of the brightly lit waiting room and close her eyes until her life changes. She has a sudden clarity of the mind of a drug addict or alcoholic, understanding the fierce desire to wipe away every single thought in her head, to sink into oblivion.

Molly answers the questions from the young nurse, who looks worn down by the long night, before she even finishes them.

'Nearly ten weeks along, ache in my pelvis, light pink blood, I haven't seen a doctor, six miscarriages,' she reels off robotically. Her hand strokes Foggy's head compulsively, seeking comfort in the toy.

The nurse nods her head at the word 'six'. Her professional mask slips for a moment and she looks at Molly, sadness warming her dark eyes. 'You poor love,' she says, covering Molly's cold hand with her warm one, stopping it from moving. 'You poor love.' Molly can only nod. The nurse's kindness nearly destroys her. She bites down on her lip as tears cascade off her face, soaking her jumper.

'We'll get you seen as soon as possible,' she says as she takes Molly's blood pressure and temperature.

'I understand you've been seeing Dr Bernstein,' she says gently. 'He's in the hospital now. He's just delivered. Would you like me to see if he can take a look at you?'

'What for?' Molly shrugs.

'Actually, yes, that would be great,' replies Peter. Molly wants to argue with him but finds she doesn't have the energy.

'Can you do us a urine sample while you wait?' the nurse asks, handing Molly the specimen jar.

In the bathroom Molly fills the jar. She tucks Foggy into her top first, keeping him safe the way she hasn't been able to keep this baby safe. There is less of the pink blood but she knows that soon it will be a heavy dark brown and then a violent red. Her babies' lives end in an array of colours.

The nurse directs them to a room with three beds in it. She shows Molly to the bed at the end and pulls a curtain around it, separating her and Peter from the room, cocooning them in their sadness. 'Dr Bernstein says he'll be here soon. Just rest for now.'

Peter paces the small space around the bed. Molly stares at the ceiling, catching stray tears with her hands every now and then. The strong hospital smell of antiseptic turns Molly's stomach. She hates this smell and everything connected to it. On the wall of the white room is a clock that ticks loudly. With the curtain closed they can only hear the sound, and Molly concentrates on the tick, tick, tick as the last seconds of her pregnancy are counted down.

The door to the room is flung open, startling them both. Dr Bernstein's head appears around the curtain, which he then pulls open, filling up the space with his large, shaggy frame. His white hair stands on end and he looks tired, but he smiles kindly at Molly. 'Hello there, I didn't know you were pregnant again. Why haven't you come in to see me?'

Molly shrugs, crushes Foggy against her breast.

'She wanted to wait,' says Peter. 'Well, you know.'

Dr Bernstein nods. 'I do…'

Peter carries on, 'We hoped…' and then he simply stops speaking. From somewhere inside her own anguish, Molly is aware of her husband and his feelings. He puts a hand on her shoulder and she leans her cheek against it. She has not just lost her baby but his baby as well.

'Well,' says Dr Bernstein, 'let's take a look. I brought the portable ultrasound so we can get a clear picture and then we'll know if you need a curette or not.' He sounds matter-of-fact but Molly knows that he understands how difficult this is for them. When he told her that her sixth baby's heart had stopped beating, she was alone in his office. She had just gone in for a check-up, believing, as she had for every pregnancy, that this was the one, and after he gave her the news, he stroked her head and then held her as a father would a child while she sobbed and howled.

'I hope not,' says Molly because at this point, she feels that being allowed to just go home and curl up in bed is the best she can hope for. She doesn't want to don the hospital gown and shiver as they insert the needle to put her to sleep. She doesn't want to wake up in recovery and be consumed by emptiness. She's done that too many times before. If the pregnancy comes away by itself it's easier.

Peter helps her off with her trousers and underwear as Dr Bernstein fiddles with switches on the machine, allowing her a small measure of dignity. When the sheet is draped over her legs, her husband grabs her hand and she curls her fingers into his, holding Foggy between them.

She flinches when the wand is pushed inside her and then she wills herself to relax. It's less painful if she relaxes. The ache in her pelvis has subsided a little because she is lying down.

She closes her eyes. Under his breath, Dr Bernstein hums a tune. He always does when he's concentrating and Molly wonders if he's even aware of it.

'Well, that's interesting,' he finally says.

'What is?' asks Peter.

'Take a look,' replies Dr Bernstein, and he turns the screen he has been watching so Molly and Peter can see. 'See there,' he says, pointing.

Molly and Peter both squint at the screen, where a small, alien-looking form moves back and forth – a little heartbeat drumming fast and strong.

'It's alive?' asks Molly in disbelief.

'Very much so,' says Dr Bernstein, 'very strong heartbeat, looks very good and I would say that you're closer to eleven weeks now than nearly ten. You're only a week away from being out of the danger zone but I'm very optimistic about this, very optimistic indeed.'

Molly gazes at the moving image on the screen. She can make out arms and legs and hands as her baby squirms inside her. But what she mostly stares at is the heartbeat, the flickering, rapid heartbeat of a living baby.

Dr Bernstein begins to pull the wand out.

'No, wait,' says Molly, 'please can we look just a little longer?'

Dr Bernstein chuckles.

'Look, Moll, I can see little hands, can you see?' Peter's voice is filled with wondrous joy. Molly glances at him quickly and sees the face of the little boy she remembers from pictures his mother shared with her. She smiles at his open, unguarded amazement at what he's watching. 'Hands, I can see little hands,' he repeats.

Molly nods, her tears of joy falling onto Foggy. 'I can, I can see them.'

They both watch for another minute, stunned at the beautiful sight.

'So,' says Dr Bernstein, removing the wand, 'I'm sure you're on your vitamins and doing everything else you need to do. You need to book in for the twelve-week ultrasound and the nuchal test. They do it here at the hospital. The nurses will give you the information on the way out.'

'But the bleeding…?' says Peter.

'It may just be a small blood vessel. I'm not concerned but stay off your feet for the next few days and then call me.' He stands up and goes over to a basin in the corner of the room to wash his hands. 'I think we may have a winner here so let's just take it one week at a time. Call the surgery in the morning and hopefully I'll see you in the next couple of weeks after your test and then it's full steam ahead. Six and a bit months from now, you'll be two very tired parents.'

'I can't imagine anything better,' says Peter. Molly can see the shine of tears in his eyes and he takes off his glasses and wipes his face quickly.

'Yes, I imagine so,' replies the doctor, and he sweeps out of the room, dragging his machine behind him, leaving Molly and Peter to stare at each other, delight written on both of their faces.

'Do you think something will—'

'No, let's not do that. Let's just believe it will all work out this time, okay?'

'Okay,' she agrees, 'okay.'

They leave the hospital with Peter supporting her elbow, holding her gently.

'You must be exhausted,' he says when they're back in the car.

'I should be but I'm not, I feel… exhilarated. He said it looks good, can you believe it?'

'I heard him myself. It looks good.' He laughs. 'It looks good.'

Molly laughs as well, holding her husband's hand. 'If I wasn't pregnant, I would say we should find a pub and get a drink.'

'Straight to bed for you, but I do know of a twenty-four-hour drive-through where we can pick up some milkshakes. What about that?'

'That,' says Molly, 'sounds perfect.'

CHAPTER EIGHTEEN

15 January 1987

Margaret

She wipes the kitchen counter lightly with a filthy rag. It really needs a good scrub but a quick wipe will have to do. She is up and cleaning in a desultory fashion. The girls are playing in the garden, running through the sprinkler in their underwear. The grass in the garden has been browned by the sun and she can hear the roar and click of the cicadas in the few trees that line the street. Adam used to take her to the beach on Sundays in summer. He loved swimming in the waves and she remembers him holding Alice tightly as she dangled her tiny feet in the water when she was a baby. 'She'll be a surfer when she grows up,' he liked to say. Margaret used to love summer.

She looks out of the window at her daughters, watching how Alice gently encourages her little sister into the water, drying Lilly's eyes with a threadbare towel when she squeals.

She's sure she never meant to get pregnant with Lilly.

It was an act of desperation, she knows.

She knows she made the suggestion but she's also sure it wasn't her choice. She'd handed her choices to him by then. In the back of her mind she knows that she had imagined she would lose the baby. If she hadn't been able to keep the babies made with Adam, the babies made with so much love, then she was sure her body wouldn't want to hold onto something created as she gritted her teeth and tried not to smell or feel or touch the body on top of her. Yet fear led her to make the suggestion. Fear that she would be left alone again with Alice and would somehow have to work out how to survive.

The first time he disappeared for a few days she was frantic, filled with panic that he'd never come back again and that she'd be left trying to raise Alice alone. Some small part of her felt relief, as though the air in the house had cleared of his smell and his cloying presence, making the rooms seem larger, freer. But mostly she was afraid.

She had twelve dollars in her purse and an empty fridge. She was running out of vodka. That was the worst thing, the level on the bottle going down, steadily emptying. Alice was happy he was gone. 'I hope he never comes back,' she said over their modest dinner of noodles and tomato sauce. 'Then how are we going to eat, Alice?' she snapped at her child. Her daughter's small shoulders sagged. 'I can get a job,' she whispered.

'Stupid child,' hissed Margaret. Words her mother might have used, words designed to hurt and humiliate. Words she had never imagined she would use on her own child but words that came out of her mouth all the time since Adam's death. She was turning into someone she barely recognised.

'Can't we get money from the prime minister?' seven-year-old Alice asked, used to the sharp words of her mother stinging her by then.

'It's called welfare,' said Margaret.

'Welfare,' repeated Alice. She was chasing her noodles around the bowl, reluctant to eat another serving of the same bland meal despite her obvious hunger.

Margaret thought about applying for welfare but was weary at just the idea. There were forms to fill in, questions to answer, people to see. She didn't have the energy to go and wait in a queue for her number to be called so she could explain what a useless mother she was.

She lay awake at night, listening for the sound of his footsteps, feeling herself flinch at every slam of a car door, her heart racing with anxiety.

Finally, he came back. When she questioned him, he was contrite. He brought bags of groceries into the house and bottles of vodka as though he'd only been to the store around the corner rather than away for days on end. Margaret understood on some level that she was being given a message. It was a warning and a test of some sort. He wanted to see her reaction when he showed her what he could do, how powerless she was, and her tears at his arrival had pleased him. It was absolutely clear to both of them then. He had control.

Vernon had only been living with them for six months. Violence had not become an entrenched part of their partnership yet. He had shoved her once or twice and given her a quick slap, not something Margaret had ever experienced before, not something she believed would become an everyday part of life.

She'd assumed the first slap had been a mistake and then she had caught the smile on his face as he waited for her to react. She had hunched her shoulders and walked away, letting him know that there would be no consequences for his actions, and later, when he came into the bedroom, where she was drifting along with her memories and the vodka, he ordered her to get him a beer. She had not said, 'I'm tired,' or, 'Get it yourself,' or, 'Why have you come in here to tell me to get you something when you're already up?' Instead she had dragged herself off the bed, dizzy and weak, stumbling to the kitchen, where Alice sat at the table, colouring in a picture of a princess in front of her castle, and grabbed a beer for him. And then she had taken more vodka out of the freezer and poured herself another generous serve. She had been trying, until then, to only drink when her despair grew so wide and so deep that she felt she couldn't breathe.

'Can I have a snack, Mum?' Alice had asked.

'Get it yourself,' Margaret had mumbled and she had dragged herself back to the bedroom and handed him the beer and then she had sat down on the bed and finished her drink in one burning gulp.

He had laughed at her then. Margaret had still been able to feel the sting on her cheek from his hand, but she had laughed along with him. The vodka helped her see the funny side of it.

The violence grew after that. One slap led to another and then a slap wasn't enough so he needed to land a punch to her stomach. And each time he did, Margaret watched him step over a line; each time she let him get away with it, he needed to get away with more. The vodka migrated from the freezer to live under her bed, and sometimes when he hit her, she didn't even feel it.

Disappearing was a new trick for him, a new line to cross, a new test for Margaret to pass.

'I just need to get away sometimes,' Vernon explained that first time when he was still treating her as though she mattered. 'You have no idea how hard it is to be raising another man's child, especially a friend's child. I'm sorry, Maggie, love. It won't happen again.'

'Don't call me that,' she wanted to tell him. 'I was Adam's Maggie and Mr Henkel's Maggie. I am not yours and I will never be your Maggie.' But she swallowed the words, trying to work out how to keep him tied to her, to keep him paying for everything and bringing her the sweet relief of the alcohol.

'We could have a baby together,' she offered in a quiet voice one day, even though the thought of another screaming, needy creature was horrifying to her. But babies tied a man to you and she needed him tied to her. Sometimes her skin crawled when he touched her but it was easy enough to close her eyes and pretend it was Adam.

'Yeah, yeah,' he agreed, 'a baby that's mine, a kid that belongs to me,' leaping on the suggestion as though he'd just been waiting for her to make it.

Margaret watched his face light up, tried not to see seven-year-old Alice frown with understanding at the words. *We really shouldn't talk like this in front of her*, she thought. Vernon wanted to start trying right away.

'Let's give it a go, eh?' He smiled crookedly.

'It's the middle of the day and Alice needs her lunch. Let's wait so we can really be together.' She said it gently, trying to make him understand that she would fulfil the promise of the conversation later that night.

'Don't be a cock-tease, Maggie. She can watch if you want but I suggest you get that arse into the bedroom now.'

Margaret met his eyes, saw the challenge there and understood another line was being crossed right then and there. She turned the television on for Alice, turning the volume up, grateful some cartoon was on.

She studied the ceiling as he grunted and pushed. *How has this happened?* she thought. *What have I let happen?*

She prayed for the blood to arrive, for his invasion of her body not to take hold. But the little life was determined. When she showed him the test, smiling shyly, she hoped it would make him happy. She hoped things would change. She was stupid to think anything could change.

He threw away all the bottles of vodka. 'No, no, no,' she begged, watching the precious liquid trickle down the sink.

'You don't want to give birth to a monster, do you?' he said. 'I've read what happens to babies whose mothers drink. It's fucking horrible.'

She hated that he had taken it away from her, was certain that the vomiting and the chills of the first few months were withdrawal as well as her raging hormones. She loathed him for taking away her life support but was paralysed by the vomiting and the ache in her bones so there was little she could do.

'Don't let them give you any rubbish to take,' Vernon told her when she explained that the doctor thought she needed treatment for depression. 'It'll hurt the baby.' And she had listened. She missed so many appointments anyway, needing to rest, unable to move. Pregnancy was hard. Her body was out of control. She ate to keep the nausea at bay, then threw up everything she consumed. This time no one brought her little treats to help, no one asked her how she was feeling. This time no one seemed to care as long as she stayed quiet.

'Leave your mother alone, she's resting,' Vernon yelled at Alice in the morning and in the afternoon and at night. She dreamed about the clear burn of the vodka, slipping down her throat, numbing all the pain, missing its anaesthetising charm. It didn't stop him landing a blow when he got angry, but now, she could feel the bruise flower and the sting of a split lip. He kept clear of her stomach, protecting his seed.

When her symptoms subsided, she felt a streak of determination. She wouldn't stand for it anymore. She would get up and get away with Alice and she would try to make some sort of life for her and her children. She would save them all.

But the tiredness was part of her bones, locked into her body by her faulty brain. And on days when she felt like she had the energy to get up, she realised what she'd done. Babies tied you to a man forever. She almost laughed at the hideous irony.

She could try and walk away with Alice, could apply for welfare, could attempt to make a life for her and her children, but she would never get rid of him. He had rights. She thought about giving up the baby, about handing the child over to him and just leaving. She could leave Alice as well. She could walk her useless self right out of the door and be free.

Yet she slept instead. She grew fat with the baby, like an incubator that needed food. She wondered sometimes at the love she used to feel for Alice, at where it had gone, or whether she'd imagined it in the first place, but she never wondered for very long.

'I can have one drink, can't I? I'm six months along, everyone says it's okay.'

'Don't you fucking touch a mouthful, you idiot. Everyone says it's wrong. All you have to do is lie there and get fat, stop fucking complaining.'

She lay in her bed, growing bigger and bigger, and when the nausea disappeared she stopped complaining, learned to shut up. She drifted along in her dreams, living her life with Adam.

She hadn't minded the birth because at least she felt something other than the despair. She hoped she would die as her new daughter slithered out of her.

'We're moving,' he announced when she came home from the hospital. He hadn't liked the way the social worker lectured and the doctors worried, all the questions thrown their way. He was way behind on the mortgage anyway. The bank had been sending threatening letters for months. So they moved in the middle of the night. Margaret took the beautiful blue curtains that had been hung up with such hope when she and Adam had bought the house. A tiny piece of an old life filled with hope to remind her that such a thing was possible. Their faded glory mocked her now.

After the move, she was far from even her most tenuous of acquaintances in a filthy, run-down rental house. But at least it was close to the shops and to the new school Alice went to.

'I miss Mrs Walton,' Alice told her.

'Who's that?' Margaret asked, not caring about the answer. She was exhausted.

'The librarian at school.'

Margaret smiled at her daughter, remembering her own safe place. 'Tough,' she said.

Eight-year-old Alice doted on her new baby sister, taking over for her mother whenever the tiredness struck. Vernon was delighted at first, less so after he realised the work a baby brought with it. He disappeared a lot more after that.

When he came home, he wasn't evasive anymore, rather defiant and angry at the existence of the woman and two children he needed to support. 'I've been out so don't fucking ask where. Not everyone is a whinger like you. Some women appreciate a real man.'

He began to cross more and more lines, stepping over them like they weren't even there.

The first punch to the face, the first kick, the first rape.

She went back to her vodka and began crossing lines too. The first time she had a drink in the afternoon, before lunch, at breakfast.

It's all a bit of a blur when Margaret thinks back on it now.

'Useless drunk cow,' Vernon observed from time to time, but he kept buying bottle after bottle of vodka, making sure she was well supplied. He kept hitting her, but sometimes she felt it was simply to let her know who was in charge rather than out of any rage he felt towards her. And then eventually the rapes stopped as well.

Margaret before Adam died would have worried about that. Margaret after Adam died, after Vernon moved in, after Lilly was born didn't wonder at all why he suddenly had no interest in her sexually. All she did was enjoy the relief of not having him near her.

She sighs. It does her no good to go over all of it again and again. She looks around the kitchen, seeing the sticky dirt everywhere. The bin is overflowing and in the living room she knows the dust lies thick on top of the television. She hardly notices the dirty nappy smell in the air anymore, unless she goes outside, and she rarely does that. She stares at the sink, piled with dirty dishes. It's no use. She would need to clean all day. She drops the cloth onto the filthy counter and goes back to her bedroom, back to her bed, back to her bottle of vodka, leaving the sound of her children behind. Leaving everything behind.

CHAPTER NINETEEN

Now

Alice

I curl my arm, bringing the hand weight to my shoulder, feeling the burn and watching the muscles in my shoulder separate. Next to me a man strains as he lifts a heavy weight and I breathe in the smell of sweat, not minding it because at least it's not the stench of vinegar. A country music song is blasting in my ears and I try to concentrate on the singer's words about loving and missing his wife, but it's not working.

Instead, even as I stare in the mirror and can see that no one is touching me, I feel his hands everywhere.

Alice is afraid. Alice is disgusted. Alice is thinking about dying.

I have hidden the stuffed green frog in the back of my closet but can't stop myself from going back to it every few hours.

This morning I googled Vernon, just to check, just to be sure. I thought I would find nothing but there are two newspaper articles. One, dated 2002, talks about what he did, and the other, from 2003, is about his sentence.

The Courier Mail
15 March 2002

Sickening Attack

Police and paramedics were, last night, called to the Blackwater Tavern in Sunnybank, Queensland, where a brawl had erupted between two men. Paramedics found Micah Jones (19) on the footpath. He had suffered catastrophic injuries after allegedly receiving a single punch from Vernon Howell (44). Despite Mr Jones being on the footpath and not in a position to defend himself, witnesses say that Mr Howell continued to kick and punch the man until police arrived. A young woman, Leslie Saunders (19), was also injured in the incident. Mr Jones was taken to hospital but died en route.

Mr Howell is now helping police with their enquiries.

The Courier Mail
20 June 2003

Life Sentence for Unprovoked Attack

Vernon Howell (45) was today sentenced to life in prison for the unprovoked attack on Micah Jones in 2002. Mr Jones was only 19 at the time of the attack and died as a result of his injuries. His girlfriend, Leslie Saunders, who was also 19 at the time, is still suffering from the damage inflicted upon her. 'I cannot sit for long periods of time because of the harm done to my spine as I was trying to pull him off Micah. It was a vicious and violent attack and my life will never be the same. Micah's family are devastated and may never recover from the loss of their beautiful son.'

'This was an unprovoked attack for no rhyme or reason and the defendant has shown no signs of remorse during his time in custody; therefore, the full force of the law must come to bear,' Justice Ben Smith said upon sentencing Mr Howell to life in prison with a non-parole period of 20 years.

The article went on to talk about how Vernon had devastated yet another family but I couldn't read anymore. He's in prison.

That's all I needed to know. He could not have sent me the frog – so who did?

It would be impossible for my mother to hand-deliver a parcel to me.

I like to think that I have locked my painful memories away in a box. In my mind it's a large wooden box, decorated with the images I have of myself as a child. For years, whenever a moment from my past came back to haunt me, I would imagine myself forcefully grabbing it and shoving it into the box. It isn't that I pretended it didn't happen or that I didn't work through the trauma of it with Ian, I just allowed myself to lock it away so I didn't have to dwell on it until it drove me crazy. But I have been kidding myself. The thread is always running beneath my daily life, proving that those memories have not been locked up tightly enough. The endless, relentless, truthful thread.

The emails and the message from the woman on my blog have unlocked the box without my permission. All of the hurtful memories have escaped and are now roaming around my mind, forcing me to experience them again. They are worse than the thread because they are dominated by the smell of vinegar, cigarettes and sweat; by the feel of rough hands, bruised skin and dirty sheets; by the taste of hunger; by the sounds of a broken heart.

The first time he hit me it was because I stepped in front of the television during a football game. I was getting my book from the chair where I'd left it. I didn't even think about it. He had only been living with us for two weeks then. He'd already stopped pretending to be kind to me – that had only taken a matter of days – but he hadn't done anything more than call me stupid for dropping a glass. But I believe I knew something was coming, something worse. I found it difficult to eat dinner when he was at the table. The shiny pink of his skin, the way he looked at me as he drank one beer after another, the way he smelled – it all made my stomach churn.

And then I stepped in front of the television for a moment and he stood up from the couch. He roared, 'Out of the way, you silly cunt,' and his big, meaty hand swiped across my face, knocking me over.

I stayed on the floor, shocked, my hand over my burning cheek, as an advert for a beer came on displaying the camaraderie of a group of friends at a pub. I have never been able to drink beer or tolerate the smell of it. After he smacked me, he stumbled off to the kitchen for another can, just as the advert needed him to do. I couldn't believe what had happened. As soon as he was out of the room, I jumped up and ran to my mother's bedroom, where the curtains were closed, despite it being a Saturday afternoon. The whole room smelled of sweat.

'Mum,' I cried, 'he hit me, he hit me. Vernon hit me.' I knew she would be outraged and shocked. I assumed that this would be the last straw for her, that this would galvanise her into getting up and getting on with her life without this nasty man.

I saw her jumping up off the bed and confronting him, throwing him out of the house and then hugging me to her chest. I thought she would be horrified at what he'd done but instead she sat up a little on the bed, her eyes glazed, and said, 'I was sleeping, Alice.'

'But, Mum, look he hurt me,' I shouted, pointing to my fire-red cheek so she would understand.

'Just stay out of his way, you're always in the way,' she muttered. Then she turned away from me and closed her eyes again. She turned away from me.

'I wish Dad was here,' I whispered, feeling my unstoppable tears return.

'Just get out,' she murmured, rolling over.

It's a terrible thing to understand at six years old that you no longer matter to your mother; a terrible, incomprehensible thing.

He hit me a lot after that. He kept away from my face but I usually had a bruise somewhere on my body. I tried to stay away from him. I spent my nights in my bedroom, even eating dinner there. I didn't ask my mother for help again.

But as I grew older, he sought me out. He made me return to the table for dinner and he asked me questions about school and what I was reading. He hit me less and I thought that he was trying to be a better person. But he was always watching me. He would walk in on me when I was in the bathroom so I started locking the door, but then he beat his fists on the wood, making holes and splinters, screaming, 'No locked doors in my house, it's dangerous.' I started showering only when he was out and tried to go to the bathroom only when he was asleep.

I put down my weights, longing to escape the clutches of these memories. I am drenched in sweat because I spent forty minutes on the treadmill, running away from my thoughts, but here they are again.

The first time the ugly thing happened – that's what I called it in my head as a child, the ugly thing – I was ten years old. My guard was down on that particular day because he came home from work with a whole bag filled with new clothes for me.

'Here you go, love,' he said, and a wide grin spread across his face, exposing yellowing teeth.

I took the bag from him and peeked inside. It was filled with clothes. 'Oh,' I said and I know I smiled back at him.

'I noticed you were growing out of everything, so I thought… well, a young lady needs to look nice, doesn't she?' But I wasn't a young lady. I was a child.

His voice was soft and smooth and I should have dropped the clothes and run but everything I owned was too small for me; even my underwear left red rings around my waist and legs where it dug into my skin. I had asked my mother and she'd promised, time and time again, to take me shopping when she wasn't so tired. I was old enough by then to know that she was always going to be tired.

'Go on,' he said, 'try it all on.'

'Thank you,' I said, turning to leave the room.

'No,' he said, his voice growing an edge, 'here. Here or I'll take it all away.'

'I don't want—'

'Take off your clothes or I'll crack you hard.'

As I was changing, my hands trembling so ferociously I couldn't do up zips or buttons, his octopus hands went everywhere.

'Stop!' I shouted and then he hit me across my head, knocking me over, making my ears ring and my lungs contract.

I was wearing a pair of shorts with sparkly purple butterflies embroidered on the front, and he ripped them down. I heard the fabric tear, and in that moment, I wanted to cry because the shorts were so pretty and I had loved them the moment I saw them.

I tried to fight him but he hit me twice more and then… and then…

'You'll get used to it,' he said afterwards, leaving me on the floor with blood on my legs. 'And if you say one fucking thing to your mother, I'll snap Lilly's neck while you watch and then I'll snap your mother's neck and then I'll snap yours, just like that.' He clicked his fingers.

Lilly was sleeping and I was grateful for that, grateful she didn't have to see what had happened to me. My mother was also having a nap or she hadn't woken up yet. All I know is that she didn't hear me shout, she didn't hear me cry. She slept through the whole thing. The whole thing.

I head home from the gym and jump into the shower, where I scrub at my skin. I can't get clean enough, can't wash away his smell and his germs, and I hate whoever is sending me the emails for bringing it all up again.

Are the emails and the message on my blog connected? I haven't said anything to Jack yet, and I know I should, but I have no idea how to explain it all, no idea what to say.

I think about my mother uttering those words, shouting at Anika, 'I know what you did!' What was she talking about?

I need to speak to her again.

I may get lucky if I go over now and find her in a more lucid state.

As I drive, I remember what it was like when he started coming into my room at night. The first time he touched me gently, so gently that, as I woke from sleep, I thought it was my father. I opened my eyes, a smile already on my face, relieved that the last four years had simply been a bad dream. But then I realised who I was looking at. 'Don't say a word,' he said and his hands crawled over me.

'Lilly will see,' I whispered, trying to keep my voice calm, even though I wanted to scream and scream.

'Put her in the cupboard then,' he said. I was so grateful I could hide her somewhere. I didn't want her to see. I dragged her out of bed, taking her pink blanket and her frog, and I made a little nest for her. She barely opened her eyes and she slept until he was done. Throughout it I stared at the dark ceiling, removed myself from the body that was being hurt, drifted away to the beach where the sun was shining and my father and I were playing in the sand. The salt smell of the sea surrounded me, and the hands that were clutching the sheet beneath me felt the soft heat of beach sand.

Parking outside the Green Gate, I take a deep breath. I need to be calm before I speak to her. It's colder today than it has been for a while and I pull my coat tightly around me as I walk up the path to the front door. The young gardener is watering some pot plants at the front, and he smiles at me.

'Cold today,' he says.

'It is,' I agree, almost pleased that I can carry on such an innocuous conversation while my thoughts are in such turmoil.

'It's so nice to see you again,' says Anika once I'm inside, 'but I'm afraid she's not having a very good day.'

My heart sinks. 'That's okay,' I mumble, 'I'll just sit with her.'

'You smell nice,' my mother says when I lean down to kiss her.

'Hi, Mum, how are you feeling today?'

'I'm fine, love. Vernon popped over to say hello. He said to give you his best.'

I nod, because what else is there to do?

'Oh, there he is now,' she says, waving frantically at the window. I look outside to see the young gardener dragging a lawnmower across the grass.

'That's not…' I begin but then I give up.

'Vernon knows what you did, you know,' she says mildly.

I open and close my mouth once or twice, gaping like a fish out of water, struggling to get enough air into my lungs. 'What…?' is all I can manage.

'To Lilly,' she says, turning to look at me. 'He knows what you did to Lilly.' And then she returns her gaze to the window.

I almost fall down onto her bed. I drop my head into my hands. I can't think straight. How is this possible? Is my mother really the person sending me emails? Is she also the woman on my blog? Is she even suffering from Alzheimer's?

'Who are you?' she asks.

I look up at my mother, who is staring at me, staring at a stranger.

'I'm your daughter Alice, remember?' I reply quietly.

'I have a daughter? Who would have thought. My mother said I would be a dreadful mother. She said I wasn't cut out to take care of a child.'

I nod my head. The grandmother I never met was right. My mother should never have had one child, let alone two. I thought that when she got pregnant with Lilly everything would change. A second child, a second chance of being a mum. He took her vodka away and I thought that would help her get up and out of bed but I thought wrong. She just slept her way through her pregnancy and then left it to me to take care of Lilly after she was born, sleeping through motherhood. I didn't mind. When they brought my sister home from the hospital, I thought she was the most beautiful thing I'd ever seen. Her perfect tiny hands curled around one of my fingers and I was in love. I didn't even mind that we moved houses and I had to move schools. I had Lilly and she was everything.

'Take her for me, I'm just exhausted,' she would say the moment I got home from school.

Sometimes I would find my little sister screaming in her cot, red-faced and smelly. But taking care of her was the best thing that had happened to me since my father died. I loved her with a fierceness I had never thought possible, with a fierceness I never thought I would experience again until I had my own boys. Whatever I did and why I did it, I know that I loved Lilly. I loved her more than her mother did and more than her father did and that's why I can't forgive myself. You shouldn't hurt someone you love that much. It is simply unforgivable.

If my mother is sending these emails, I don't blame her for her anger. I wonder how long she has known, how long she has wanted to let me know that she's aware of what I did and what happened because of it. I wonder how deeply furious she is at me. I imagine her thinking of going to the police and then dismissing the idea. How would she have explained everything? How would she have explained my battered body and the filth we lived in? How would she have explained how she had simply checked out of motherhood?

Anika comes into the room. 'Isn't it nice to see Alice again so soon, Margaret?' she says.

'Who's Alice?' my mother asks, and before Anika can answer her, I stand up and shake my head.

Alice's mother is not here. Alice's mother was never here.

'It doesn't matter,' I say, even as tears are running down my cheeks. 'It doesn't matter.'

CHAPTER TWENTY
Molly

After three days of lying in bed Molly feels she might be going mad. 'I think I need to get up today,' she tells Peter as she watches him dress for work. She likes watching her husband get dressed, going from rumpled and casual to professional. She enjoys the way his muscles work as he pulls on a deep blue shirt.

'Molly, if Dr Bernstein told you to lie in bed for the next six months, you would, wouldn't you?' he asks as his hands expertly knot a paisley tie. He smooths his hair down and Molly resists the urge to leap off the bed and grab him. She sits up instead, pushing her pillow behind her. She can remember Lexie saying that in her second trimester she couldn't keep her hands off Owen. 'It's all the hormones,' said her sister at the time, 'Owen has no idea what's going on.'

'But he's enjoying it, I bet,' Molly had teased.

She smiles – she is so close to her second trimester – and then she feels her stomach twist. It would be unimaginably terrible to lose everything now. She shakes her head at her thoughts. She is alternately delirious with happiness and awash with terror.

'Of course, you know I would. I would do anything it took,' she replies.

'Right,' he says triumphantly, 'then a couple more days won't make a difference. Maybe call Dr Bernstein and let him tell you if you can get up or not. Otherwise the scan is on Thursday and we'll know more then.'

'Easy for you,' mutters Molly.

Peter comes over to sit down on the bed next to her. 'I know this isn't easy but you can do this. In a few days, we'll be able to celebrate together. I'll book La Trattoria for dinner and we can start arguing about names.'

'Arguing about names,' Molly says with a laugh, 'how incredible would that be?'

'In the meantime,' says Peter, standing up, 'I really think you should return your mother's calls or at least return Lexie's.'

'How many are we up to now?' asks Molly.

'Your mother has called eleven times: five times before I told her to give you some space and six times after that. Your father has called at least three times and Lexie has called at least double that. They're going crazy, Molly, and I know, despite everything, that you miss them. You need to call them and talk about what's happening with you and the pregnancy, and you need to be able to ask all the questions you want to ask.'

'I don't know if I'm ready for that yet,' says Molly. She cups her hand protectively over her stomach. 'I don't know if we're ready for that.'

Peter leans down to kiss her on the forehead. 'I'm sure he's ready. He needs his grandmother in his life.'

'He?' Molly smiles.

'Yes,' says Peter, 'he until we find out he's a she. Either of which will be the most spoilt baby on the planet.'

'Amen to that.'

She lies down in the bed again, turning on her side and staring out of the bedroom window at the blue sky. She is warm but she knows that outside the air has a tinge of ice in it. Her baby will be born in the summer when the days are long and the heat wraps itself around everything. 'Breakfast, baby?' she asks as she hears

Peter call goodbye and shut the front door behind him. *My baby*, she thinks and joy suffuses her heart. *My baby.*

She has been telling herself that the reason she talks to the baby is because right now she's not talking to anyone else. She has asked Peter to wait until the twelve-week scan before he tells his family. She doesn't want to have to go through what they went through all the other times she was pregnant. Emma was so excited the first time that she turned up the day after they'd told her with a bagful of baby clothes and toys. 'I couldn't help myself,' she said, her eyes sparkling. 'I'm going to be the best second cousin and I'm going to tell her that I'm the reason she was born.' Telling Emma about the miscarriage was excruciating. Her eyes filled and tears spilled down her cheeks. 'I'm so sorry, I shouldn't have bought anything, I'm so sorry,' she sobbed. Molly found herself comforting Emma; in fact, she found herself comforting everyone around her, spouting the platitudes she had read and heard over and over again, all the while trying to conceal her own devastating heartbreak.

They have told fewer and fewer people with each subsequent pregnancy, not wanting to raise anyone's hopes but also not wanting to open themselves up to discussions that seem to inevitably take place. Molly knows that if Peter hadn't told her to take a test this time because he had learned to recognise the signs, it's possible she wouldn't have even told him.

She would love to tell everyone now, would love to be able to discuss their happy news with her mother and her sister. At the thought of her family Molly feels a moment of dark despair. Who is her family? Who is she? Why were her parents so scared about her past? She pushes the thoughts away and heads to the kitchen where she fills the kettle and switches it on. She hasn't had the road dream for a few days and she's trying not to think of her parents' revelations because every time she does, she can feel her pulse race and anger rise inside her. It can't be good for the baby.

It's better if she doesn't talk to her mother. It's better for her to keep the pregnancy a secret for now. She doesn't want to admit the flower of hope pushing stubbornly through the concrete inside her. She doesn't want to admit to herself that she is starting to plan a nursery, that she's painted the walls a neutral beige and decorated the room with a frieze of Disney characters. That she's imagining her eyes and Peter's mouth, that she dreams of little fingers grasping her thumb. She wishes she could tell her parents, wishes she could talk to Lexie. Lexie will be over the moon to know that they've seen a heartbeat and that this pregnancy has a real chance at success.

In the kitchen her phone is on the counter, missed calls from her mother and sister listed. She picks it up and considers taking the first step. She wants to know the truth about who she is, needs to know. She is bringing a child into the world and knows nothing of its genetic legacy.

Her father telling her they were afraid of what she would find if she went looking for her parents comes back to her. How terrible a family must they have been?

More than anything she wants nothing her parents told her to be true. She wants to be Lexie's sister and her parents' daughter in every sense of the word, but she knows wishing won't change anything.

Her own future motherhood colours everything now. She is filled with love for everyone one moment and furious with everyone the next. She has never cried as much as she has cried over the last few days, tears of joy mingling with tears of devastation, and she can never be entirely sure which particular tears are dripping off her chin. She would like to concentrate on just this baby growing inside her.

Even her work holds little interest at the moment. She has sent off the last story to the editor and hopes that the publishers accept it. Now she will wait months before she begins editing. She can feel there is a new story brewing, a story about dreams fulfilled and a family created, but she is afraid to write down the words. She is afraid to create a character who succeeds at something she has been trying to do for so long, lest she, herself, fails at holding onto this baby, this child.

'We're planning publication in July next year,' her editor, Sandra, has informed her. Molly has calculated that the baby will be six months old by then. She would like to tell them that they need to allow her to finish editing the book before the baby is born but she cannot mention it to anyone yet.

She scrambles herself an egg and covers a piece of toast in peanut butter. She would like a cup of coffee in principle but right now coffee smells wrong to her, as though it's been burnt. A common side effect of pregnancy, she has read. She makes a cup of green tea instead. She has never allowed herself to read past the first trimester of pregnancy websites, not after the first miscarriage. Now she finds herself skimming through advice for the second trimester and then feeling guilty, as though she is doing something she shouldn't.

After breakfast she clears up, puts a load of washing on and distracts herself with a crime series on television. She falls asleep in the middle, something that happens often, which she attributes not just to the pregnancy but also to the stress of waiting for the twelve-week ultrasound and trying hard not to think about all the questions she has about her past.

The doorbell wakes her and she sits up, dazed, not sure if she's heard it, but it chimes again. She stands up and wipes her mouth. She has no idea what the time is. She peers through the peephole to see her mother and Lexie. Their worried faces loom through the tiny circle of glass.

Molly thinks about pretending she isn't home.

'We know you're in there, Moll,' calls Lexie. 'Peter called us.'

'What?' she says, yanking the door open. 'When?'

'Oh, Molly,' says her mother. Her arms are filled with a cake tin, and Lexie is holding Sophie and a bag of groceries.

'Moiee,' shouts Sophie, flinging her arms up at her aunt.

'No, Soph, Aunty Molly can't hold you now. She has to rest.'

Before Molly can mount an argument, her sister and her mother have bustled inside. Lexie puts Sophie on the floor and surrounds her with toys Molly keeps in a basket by the couch for when she visits. Her mother puts the kettle on and opens up her cake tin to reveal a sumptuous carrot cake with cream cheese frosting – the same cake Molly has requested for every single birthday from the time she was five years old.

'You just sit down, darling,' says her mother. 'I'll bring you a slice of cake and some tea.'

Molly cannot summon a reply so she sits on the couch, trying to stop the turmoil going on inside her. She has specifically told her mother not to contact her, and yet here she is. She also told Peter not to tell anyone about the pregnancy, and yet from the way her mother and sister are treating her, they obviously know about everything that happened at the hospital. She is furious with everyone but desperate for a piece of cake and overjoyed at the sight of her sister. Her mother and sister chat brightly in the kitchen as Lexie finds cups for tea and boils water in the kettle. Molly can hear the forced joviality.

Once they are all sitting down, silence descends. Lexie and Molly and their mother exchange glances like strangers at a party, waiting for someone to make the first move. Finally, Anne says, 'I have something for you, love. I've kept it for a long time because it was always my intention to tell you the truth.'

She gets up, goes to her capacious handbag and pulls out a folder. Inside is a series of news articles.

'You can read them now or after we've left, and I will try to tell you everything I know and remember. There aren't enough sorrys in the world, I know. I cannot apologise enough for keeping this from you, but I also can't lose you, Molly, not over this. Your father and I won't survive it. So, whatever we have to do to make this right, we'll do. I won't let this get between us. You're my daughter, regardless of your biological composition you're mine, and nothing is going to take you away from me.'

Molly recognises a streak of hidden fierceness that occasionally surfaces in her mother. Her mother is always calm, always serene, always busy helping others and keeping her house and her family running smoothly. But there have been times when she has shown a side that made everyone in the family aware of just how formidable a force she could be.

'I just can't think about you right now, Mum. I need to get this straight in my head,' she says slowly. She clutches the folder lightly, not wanting to hold too tightly onto something that will cause her pain.

'I understand how angry you are,' says Lexie. 'When Mum told me, I was just as angry as you are. They've done the wrong thing. They should never have kept the truth from you, it was very unfair. I yelled a lot.'

'She certainly did,' replies their mother lightly, although Molly can see the pain of that exchange on her face. Her parents have let Lexie down as well.

'You and Dad lied to me my whole life,' says Molly, mashing a bite of her cake with a fork, concentrating on mixing the rust-coloured cake with the snow-white icing.

'We did,' agrees her mother. 'We did and it was a terrible thing to do to you and to Lexie, especially when we have always been honest in our family, but I'm hoping you will eventually see that the decision came from a place of love.'

'Molly might find that a little difficult to do right now, Mum,' says Lexie. She lays her hand softly on her sister's arm. Molly stills herself, understanding the gesture means she has her sister's unequivocal support.

'I know that,' Anne whispers.

Molly looks at her mother. Her shoulders are hunched and her face is pale, her lips almost white. Her mother has not eaten any of her cake and her mug of tea remains untouched. Molly glances at her sister, who has also been studying Anne, and without having to say anything, they can both see how burdened their mother is. Through the whirl of emotions inside her, Molly feels sorry for her mother. She shakes her head at Lexie, indicating they should just leave this now.

'So, Peter told us about the hospital,' says Lexie with a small smile, and Molly can see she is switching gears.

'He shouldn't have done that,' says Molly woodenly. She takes a bite of the carrot cake, comforted by the familiar, sweet taste and grainy texture. It feels like another betrayal. She doesn't want to discuss the pregnancy yet, but she also desperately does. She wants to talk about it with her loved ones and so part of her is grateful that Peter has taken this out of her hands. Now that there is finally a chance of things working out, Molly hated that she was hiding things from her family.

But your mother hid things from you, she thinks and then she grows irritated with herself. *Stop it, enough now.* She takes another bite of cake.

'No, he shouldn't,' agrees Lexie, 'but he's so excited, Moll, and terrified.'

'We're both terrified,' says Molly, tears making an appearance without her thinking much.

'Oh, darling,' replies her mother, and she comes over to where Molly sits and wraps her in her arms. 'This is going to be the one. I feel it. It won't be long until Sophie has a little cousin to boss around.'

'I hope so,' says Molly and then she lets herself be hugged and she lays her head on her mother's shoulder, allowing the tension of the last few days to float away.

'It's going to be fine,' Anne says over and over as she pats Molly's back, and Molly is reminded of when she had her tonsils out. She was six years old and frightened of the needle and terrified of the idea of the doctor cutting something out of her throat. Then her mother had held her as well, had told her that it was going to be fine. And it was fine. Molly had absolute faith in her mother's power and her mother's love then, and now as she holds onto her, she understands that power and that love have not gone away. She needs answers about her past but she can absolutely count on her mother right here and now. The realisation is a relief.

'I'll read these later,' she says, dropping the folder onto the coffee table. It holds her past, the secrets of her life, but she needs to be alone to focus on that.

'So how are you feeling?' asks Lexie.

'Coffee smells weird.' Molly smiles and the conversation turns to pregnancy cravings and everything else Molly has to look forward to. Sophie is the centre of attention as usual until she becomes irritable. 'Sleep time, I think,' says Lexie eventually.

When she and Sophie are at the front door ready to leave, Lexie grabs Molly in a hard hug. 'You're my sister,' she says. 'I don't care about anything else. If I could have chosen a sister, I would have chosen you, and nothing has changed as far as I'm concerned. If you need to talk, just call me, okay?'

Molly nods and Sophie protests at being slightly squashed between her aunt and her mother.

'I think I'll go too, darling,' says her mother, gathering up the empty cake tin. 'You and Peter finish the cake.'

Molly cannot help feeling awkward now that her sister has gone.

'I hate that we've done this to you,' says her mother. 'I can't apologise enough, Molly. All I can do is let you know how much we love you and tell you that if you want to find your biological family, we will do everything we can to help you. The government has a registry for adopted children but…'

'But?' asks Molly.

'But they never found your family. The police… the social worker would have told us if they did. We asked to be told because we were so worried. Read the articles because they explain a lot. Read them and then call me and we'll talk.'

Once her mother has gone, Molly slumps onto the couch, resting the folder on her lap. What horrors can it hold? She opens it up, reads the first headline and feels her lungs expand with shock as she confronts her past.

CHAPTER TWENTY-ONE

18 January 1987

Margaret

She wakes from an afternoon nap, or early evening nap, something. The streetlight shines through the gap at the side of the curtains and she kicks her legs to remove the light blanket that is making her sweat in the heat. She can't remember if she went to the shops that morning or two days ago or two weeks ago. She slides out of bed, shuffling out of the bedroom, noting that she's wearing jeans and a T-shirt so she must have gotten dressed today, or some other day. Her head pounds with each step she takes. Her mind flits briefly to her daughters. She has a ten-year-old and a two-year-old. She really should know what day it is. She really should know a lot of things.

In the kitchen she drinks two glasses of water quickly. The pounding intensifies. She rifles through the cupboards, chancing on pain pills, swallowing five without thinking. She holds her head and starts her slow shuffle back to bed when she hears a sound. A muffled cry, a whimper. The sound of hurt, the sound of pain.

She doesn't want to know, doesn't want to see. She just wants to return to bed but her feet carry her to the girls' room, where the door is open just a crack. She pushes it, hearing the hinges protest.

She is immediately assaulted by the dirty nappy smell that pervades the whole house. It is strongest in here where Lilly and

Alice sleep. Margaret knows that this room is very different to the lovingly decorated room Alice had at the old house. There, she and Adam had painted the walls a light rose pink and thrown a bright pink rug on the floor. There, toys lined the walls and the room carried the sweet smell of baby powder and shampoo even when Alice got older. Adam used to love bathing her when she was a baby. He would hold her in his hands, tightly enough to make her feel secure but gently enough so that she knew she was loved, moving her tiny body through the water. He would sing a lullaby his mother had sung to him. The words were in Polish and he couldn't remember what they meant anymore, but Alice loved the song, would smile her gummy smile up at her father, and Margaret would understand that this was what true love looked like.

This room has smoke-stained, peeling painted walls because the last tenants were heavy smokers and Vernon told the landlord he would paint the house in return for a reduction in rent. He never has, of course. He will 'get to it when it fucking suits me'. The smell of cigarettes lingers but is overpowered by all the other smells that Margaret would never have tolerated once upon a time when her life was a fairy tale.

The soft whimper comes again. She thinks perhaps one of the girls is having a nightmare.

There is a nightlight in the room, miraculously working after all this time. Margaret's eyes adjust to the dimness and she is able to see everything.

She can see Lilly's bed, empty with the covers thrown back. The pounding in her head makes her teeth ache. She hopes Lilly hasn't fallen out. *I should check*, she thinks but then she looks over at the other bed and her daughter's wide eyes capture her. In the nearly completely dark room, Alice's eyes are large circles of black in her small face. Her daughter is staring straight at her but not moving.

He is there. He is above her, moving, grunting, sighing. Margaret feels the vomit rise in her throat.

'What?' her voice cracks. She slams her hand over her mouth, cursing the word that has escaped.

He stops moving and she sees Alice give her head a little shake, telling her mother she shouldn't be here.

'Run,' Alice mouths. 'Run,' says her ten-year-old child as she's being brutalised. 'Run.' But Margaret cannot move.

He stands up and she can see what he's been doing. Oh, it's sick, sick, sick. Her little girl, her little girl is being... The word disappears, too awful to think.

She keeps her hand over her mouth, holding in the vomit. He stands tall, defiantly staring, willing her to say something else. Willing her to confront him, to tell him to stop. Willing her to show that she is something other than the empty husk of a human being she is.

The three of them are frozen in the dim light from the night-light, a tableau of horror. Alice on the bed, her skinny legs slightly open, bony knees angled, Margaret in the doorway, her body hunched in horror, and Vernon with his trousers around his ankles.

A howl escapes from behind Margaret's hands, a scream of anguish, and he is jolted into action. He yanks up his trousers and lurches towards her.

'Stupid cunt,' he spits and he is on top of her in two steps. His fist smashes into the side of her head, making her stagger and cover the floor in bile. She lifts her arms to try and fend off the next blow but she is dizzy with alcohol and painkillers. The fist comes again and again and again, each time with more ferocity, each time with more fury. He swings and hits and swings and hits, and every moment of pain he has ever had in his life, every flash of fear he has ever felt, is pounded into Margaret.

And then she can't feel anything anymore. She can't feel and she can't hear and she can't see. There is nothing, just nothing. And her last thought is that it's better this way. It's better.

*

When she opens her eyes, it is daylight and she is lying on her side with a pillow under her head. At first, she thinks Alice may have given her the pillow but then she has a vague recollection of crawling to the couch and grabbing it for herself before black sleep claimed her again. She sniffs. She is surrounded by her own vomit and blood. She moves her neck and sees her daughter. Alice is staring down at her, holding a dripping wet cloth in her hands. Her lips are set in a thin line and her brown eyes are dark with hatred. Margaret can see her daughter's disgust for her, can feel it coming off the child in waves.

'He said you need to clean yourself the fuck up,' says Alice, and Margaret feels a flash of terror at the perfect imitation of Vernon's voice. The incongruous harsh tone slipping so easily out of her daughter's mouth is frightening. The wet cloth is dropped on her head.

Margaret knows that the child Alice was is gone just like the Maggie she was is gone. The open, bubbly girl Alice was has been gone for a long time and she can understand why. How could a child survive this life?

A memory surfaces of a time when Alice was four and Margaret had the flu. 'Stay in bed,' Adam said. 'I'll be home from work early. You'll look after Mum, won't you, Alice?' The child nodded eagerly, always so happy to please, and Margaret remembers that at the end of the day she had five cups of water by her bedside and packets of biscuits from the pantry because Alice had been taking care of her. She had sat next to her mother on the bed, reading from memory her favourite book, *Madeline*, reciting the words she knew so well and stroking her mother's head, and Margaret had remained silent, revelling in the feeling of so much love directed at her.

But today, 'Clean yourself the fuck up,' Alice repeats before stomping off to the kitchen, where Margaret hears her singing to Lilly.

Margaret wants to yell, to scream her pain and frustration at her daughter, but she cannot even open her mouth. The girl is right to hate her. She has let her down and now… now he is using her. *What kind of a mother are you?* repeats in her head. She doesn't deserve these children. She doesn't deserve to be loved. She deserves only pain and derision. She is no kind of a mother at all. She is no kind of human being at all.

I have to get out of here, she thinks. *I have to take them away and save them.* But as she struggles to pull her damaged body off the floor, she understands that escape is impossible. She hobbles to the bathroom and confronts her puffed, broken and bruised face. The pain in her side tells her a rib is broken, maybe two or three, but broken ribs heal by themselves. There is a ringing in her head and the sounds on one side seem muffled. His fists have probably burst an eardrum. She cannot see Margaret reflected in the mirror, only a shattered monster. She would prefer to be asleep, unconscious, unaware of it all.

She knows this is not how a mother should feel, not how a mother should behave, but she cannot feel anything for them. She cannot feel anything for herself. 'Piece of shit,' she mutters through blown lips at the mirror.

She runs the shower, bathes in the tepid water, every muscle aching, every piece of flesh screaming, and cleans up as best she can. She pulls on some clothes, dirty, unwashed clothes, but at least they are not covered in blood. She sinks onto her bed, her safe space, her oasis. There are two bottles under the bed, unopened, brimming with the promise of a blackout. An apology of sorts, she supposes. A bribe to silence her. *How much is that?* she wonders. *Sixty dollars?* She is worth so very little now, and by extension her children are worth even less. It was up to her to show them and the world their worth, and that is perhaps her greatest failure of all.

'Mum,' says Alice, and Margaret sees her standing by the bedroom door, her little sister's hand clenched in hers. 'Mum, we're hungry.'

'I'm not well, Alice,' she murmurs, twisting off the bottle cap. She takes the first delicious sip and then another and another. The alcohol pours into the cuts on her lips, burns and stings, but it's the burn she craves. She curls up around the bottle, feeling safe, feeling protected from the ugliness she has seen.

'He hurts me, Mum,' whispers Alice. 'He does stuff to me that's for grown-ups.'

'Leave me alone, Alice,' she says, the alcohol numbing everything. 'I'm not well and I'm tired.'

CHAPTER TWENTY-TWO

Now

Alice

I lie in my bed, staring up at the ceiling. It's Tuesday morning and after ten, and I'm still in bed, cocooned by my heavy duvet.

My head is pounding. When the alarm went off at seven this morning, all I could do was groan.

'I think I've caught a bug,' I said to Jack, who was getting ready to go downstairs for breakfast. 'Do you think you could get the boys to school for me?'

I rarely ask him to do this. It makes him late for work and his patients and throws his whole day off schedule.

'Sure,' he said, 'and then when I get home tonight, we're going to… we're going to talk and you're going to explain exactly what's going on.'

I groaned again. Jack rarely gets angry, rarely raises his voice. I could hear him controlling his fury at me, and when I looked up at him, I could see that anger came from fear. He is terrified for me.

I haven't caught a bug. I'm dealing with what I assume is my very first proper hangover, and for the first time, I understand why people cannot function with one. The sour taste in my mouth brings back the smell of my mother's breath in the mornings. She felt like this every day for years and years.

When Jack got home last night, he found me in the kitchen with an empty bottle of vodka on the counter. The boys were already upstairs getting ready for bed and I was drunk, not tipsy, but drunk.

'Alice… Alice what…?' Jack said, his shock obvious in his high tone. 'Are you okay? What's going on?'

'I'm fine, just fine.' I giggled because right at that moment I was fine. One shot had been followed by another and then another. The first one had burnt, making me cough, but I noticed that it slowed my racing heart and warmed my anxious stomach. I started thinking about the emails and the stuffed frog.

I know what you did.

I thought about the things my mother had said, trying to work out if her words had just been coincidental and the product of her fading mind or if she was actually capable of sending messages to taunt me. That made me start to panic again so I took a second shot and then another two and the alcohol hit me like a sledge-hammer and suddenly everything was funny instead of terrifying.

'Where are the boys?' he whispered fiercely.

'Oh, they're fine, Jack. My mother was drunk more than she was sober, and I turned out just fine.'

'Alice, what's wrong? What's happened? I've never seen… Why don't you go and have a shower and I'll get the boys to bed, and then we can talk… We obviously need to talk.'

'Don't you stand there judging me,' I hissed at him, furious. I picked up the bottle to pour myself another slurp of vodka but my hands were unsteady and the lip of the bottle hit the rim of my glass, sending a long crack snaking down to the base. The bottle was already empty anyway.

'Oops.' I laughed and then I felt the vodka rise in my stomach. I covered my mouth with my hand.

Jack took the bottle away from me gently, but even in my haze I could see that he was deeply sad. Shame washed over me, shame and fear that the boys would be downstairs any minute to greet their father and that, horrifyingly, they would find not their mother, but my mother. My drunk, neglectful, self-absorbed mother.

'Go and have a shower, Alice. I'll tell the boys you don't feel well.'

I was only able to nod, and all the way up the stairs I held myself rigid in case one of my sons saw me. In the bathroom, I stuck my finger down my throat, forcing the alcohol from my body. I had only taken the vodka out of the freezer to look at it, to try and once again determine what it was about this particular spirit that had meant so much to my mother, so much that she sacrificed one child and lost another.

I'm sure I hadn't meant to take that first shot.

'You're just like her,' I whisper in my bed, punishing myself for my behaviour. I break out in a sweat and sit bolt upright, my head thumping in pain, bile rising in my throat. 'No, I'm not!' I shout, grateful for the empty house.

I get out of bed and into the shower, where I stand until my fingers prune.

Downstairs I eat breakfast, toast and peanut butter to soak up the alcohol. I drink two cups of strong, bitter coffee, and when I can put it off no longer, I open my new laptop. 'I was carrying it and I tripped over something and it just fell out of my hands,' I told Jack. The lie slipped out of me so easily.

'What did you trip over?'

'Um… a ball, you know those small bouncy balls the boys are always playing with. One of them was on the floor.'

'I told Gus and Gabe last time that if they left them on the floor again, I was going to take them all away and throw them in the bin.'

'No, don't do that. It was an old computer and I needed a new one anyway. I'll talk to them tomorrow, remind them about putting the balls away.' I felt eaten alive by guilt. What kind of a mother blamed her children for something she'd done?

The new shiny machine looks incapable of harbouring a distressing message.

But there is another one, just as I knew there would be. It occurs to me that since the emails have begun, I have seen my mother more than I ever have. Is that what she's trying to achieve? And if she's capable of thinking like this, then why is she where she is?

I know what you did.

My whole body shakes. I cannot let this go on. I need to talk to Jack and the police. I pick up my phone but then I immediately end the call. It's my fault she was there.

Alice did a terrible thing. Alice did a horrible thing. It's all Alice's fault.

I drop my head in my hands. 'But I didn't mean to,' I say. 'I didn't mean to. I was trying to help. I was trying to help. Please, I didn't mean to.' I don't know who I'm pleading with.

I stare at the email and then I type:

What do you want?

Maybe this will mean a request for money or something tangible. While I wait, I check my blog but there are no new messages.

Finally, my inbox pings.

I want everything you have, Alice. Everything.

My whole body trembles, my hands immediately clammy. Jack and my boys are everything. Is that what this person wants? My breakfast rises in my throat and I make it to the bathroom just in time.

Panting and sweating, I sit back down and stare at the email for a long time. Then I pick up the phone and call Jack, leaving a message for him to call me back. 'We have to talk,' is all I say.

CHAPTER TWENTY-THREE

Molly

Sydney Morning Herald
20 January 1987

Toddler Found Wandering on Pacific Highway

Asquith

A toddler was found wandering along the busy Pacific Highway at roughly 2 am this morning.

Two members of the public found the child near the intersection of Rupert Street and the Pacific Highway. Police were immediately notified and have issued an appeal for the parents of the toddler to come forward. The little girl is aged between eighteen months and two years old. She was wearing a red T-shirt in a size 10 and a nappy. Police think the T-shirt may have once belonged to an older child.

Constable Berriman of the Hornsby Police Department says a young couple heading home from a party saw the child and stopped to help her. They then transported her to the Hornsby police station.

Police took a photo of the child door to door in the surrounding neighbourhood but nobody recognised her.

The child, unable to communicate with police, cannot tell them her name or give any identifying information.

Constable Berriman says nobody has filed a missing child report prior to or since the child was found. 'We just want to see this child reunited with her family,' he said. Anyone with any information is urged to contact the Hornsby Police or to call Crime Stoppers on 1800 333 000.

The child is now in the care of the Department of Community Services.

Molly reads the article twice. The print has faded but she can still clearly see that the picture is of her. Her parents have a lot of photos of her from two years old on or what they have always assumed was two years old, and this little girl is the same child. This is her. She was left on the side of the road like a dog, like a piece of rubbish. She shivers, thinking of her niece wandering alone in the dark wearing nothing more than an old T-shirt and a nappy. The road dream washes over her, forcing her to slump back down onto the couch. She has been remembering more than dreaming. She has been remembering. She must have been so scared. *What goes through the mind of a child in that situation?* she thinks. When Lexie was pregnant with Sophie, she shared everything she was learning about motherhood with Molly. 'Do you know that when you leave a small baby alone to cry, it feels like it's dying because it has no concept of time or place yet? Imagine how hideous that must be.'

At eighteen months, Sophie understood so much. She knew if someone was angry or happy or sad.

'I was all alone,' she says, staring at the article unearthing her past. She looks over at Foggy, her stuffed frog. If she had been found with him, she would have been certain that she and Meredith, the woman from the blog, were connected. She has only had Foggy since she was three years old. There was a whole other life before that, a whole other family – a family who didn't want her.

The second article is from a week later.

Sydney Morning Herald
27 January 1987

Parents of Toddler Still Not Located

Asquith

Police are desperately trying to find the parents or carers of a little girl found wandering on the Pacific Highway last week. She was dressed in a large red T-shirt and a nappy. Despite repeated appeals on television and radio and in the press, no trace of her parents or carers has been found. 'It's not possible that no one knows who this child is,' Constable Berriman of the Hornsby Police said. 'We understand that there may be difficulties in the lives of this little girl's guardians, and we are fully prepared to help.'

The child has been temporarily placed with a foster family until her relatives can be located.

Crime Stoppers 1800 333 000

Molly wonders if she was immediately placed with her parents or if she was with another family. She would like to call her mother and ask but she can feel her eyelids getting heavier. The stress of the last few days feels like it has caught up with her. There are more articles to read but she assumes they will be more of the same, more heartache spelled out in black letters. Obviously, they never located her parents; obviously, no one came forward. Obviously, no one wanted her. This thought makes her want to weep. All along she has been drawn to stories of the unwanted and unloved children of the world, never realising that she is one of them. The irony is not lost on her, and she would laugh if it weren't so tragic. She slides down on the couch and closes her eyes, giving in to the sleep trying to claim her.

She dreams of the road again, can feel the stones poking into her soft little feet, can smell the tar that still holds the heat of the day. She sees Foggy in her arms, her small arms, and then suddenly her arms are empty and she knows in the dream that she has nothing and no one to comfort her.

When she wakes up, feeling lethargic, still in the claws of the dream, she can see the sun is setting. Hunger twists her stomach and she goes to the kitchen and grazes from the fridge, indiscriminately eating fruit and cheese and cold leftover pizza until she feels satiated.

When she is done, she thinks about calling Peter, who is once again working late, but decides against it. She wants to be able to study the articles alone for just a little while longer. She's not ready to discuss this yet, not until she knows how she feels, because right now her reigning emotion is confusion.

There are four more articles in the folder, each one shorter and shorter and further and further back in the newspaper as interest in the abandoned child waned.

Sydney Morning Herald
31 January 1987

Toddler Unclaimed

Asquith

A toddler found wandering on the Pacific Highway in Asquith 11 days ago is still living with a foster family. Relatives have yet to come forward to claim the child. 'She's doing very well with her foster family but we would like to see her reunited with her parents,' Constable Berriman of the Hornsby Police Department told reporters. Another appeal will air on television and radio in the coming days.

Sydney Morning Herald

5 February 1987
>   Police Appeal for Relatives of Abandoned
>   Toddler to Come Forward

Asquith

Constable Berriman of the Hornsby Police Department has issued another appeal for the parents or caregivers of a toddler found abandoned on the Pacific Highway to come forward and claim the child.

'We have had many calls but none of them have led to the location of any of the child's relatives,' he told the press. 'As a father myself I cannot imagine that this little girl's parents are not concerned about her welfare. We would really like the family to come forward and we are prepared to offer all the help they need.'

Sydney Morning Herald
20 February 1987

>   Toddler to Be Given Permanent Foster Family

Asquith

A toddler found wandering on the Pacific Highway in Asquith in January will now be moved to a more permanent care situation. She will reside with a foster family, who will be able to keep her long-term. Police have once again appealed for the family of the child to come forward.

The final article is from a year later. Molly cannot help her tears as she realises that this last article means that all hope of finding her family, her real family, has been lost.

Sydney Morning Herald
21 February 1988
                    Abandoned Toddler Adopted

A toddler who was found wandering along the busy Pacific Highway in Asquith last year has been adopted by her foster family. The family declined to be identified but did say, 'We are thrilled to be able to provide a permanent home for her. She is our child in every sense of the word and we look forward to watching her grow up.'

No one has ever come forward to claim the child.

Molly goes to her computer and tries to find more articles about her, but there is nothing else. 'Where do I come from?' she asks Foggy, who answers with his lopsided stare. 'Nowhere,' she says sadly, 'I'm from nowhere.'

She looks up sites that help adopted children find their parents and parents find their children, but before she even begins to read about the process, she realises that her family wouldn't be on the site. They didn't want her then and they certainly wouldn't want her now.

She shuts down the laptop and opts for a long shower. She has no idea what to do with the information she now has. Meredith from the blog told her that her sister died. It is possible that her feeling of familiarity with the story is simply because she went through a similar situation, not because that was her situation.

She wishes she could just leave the information alone now. What good would it do to try and find a mother and father who abandoned her? And if she is remembering her past when she thinks about the cupboard, how terrible were the people she lived with? Does she want to find them, to know them?

She steps out of the shower and studies herself in the mirror. Her breasts seem to be getting bigger every day, and her normally flat stomach now strains at the waistband of all her trousers. She rests her hand where she thinks her baby lies. She needs to know where she came from and who she is, if only for the child she is carrying. 'I will find the truth,' she promises the child inside her. 'I will find it for you.'

CHAPTER TWENTY-FOUR

22 January 1987

Margaret

The vodka only lasts three days and when she wakes up, already in withdrawal, Margaret realises that he has probably not come back to the house in that time. She knows he would have placed the two bottles under her bed before he left, making sure that she drowned the memory of whatever he'd done. It was easy enough to do; Margaret has been drowning memories for years. *Stay gone*, she thinks. *Come back*, she thinks. *I'm thirsty.*

Now she knows why Alice is the way she is. She didn't know why, had seen what was going on, had not seen. 'Turning a blind eye,' is what they call it. Margaret isn't that kind of person. Is she that kind of person? She is sure that once upon a time she wasn't that kind of person. She closes her eyes, trying to erase the terrible images of what was being done to her daughter, to her child, her baby. He will keep doing it, she knows he will. He has all the power and she has none. He is aware that she cannot protect herself from him and so is unlikely to be able to protect her child.

She needs to do something, really needs to do something, but what can she do? Who can she tell? Who would help her? She is utterly alone. She tries to imagine going to the police but she can only conjure up judgement from those she would confess her failures to.

She drags herself out of bed to the kitchen, her empty stomach grumbling for something.

Alice is alone in front of the television with the blinds closed. The room is a suffocating oven. She is sprawled on the couch in a singlet and shorts, eating cereal out of a box with her hands. Margaret studies her chest where tiny breasts are beginning to bud. She is a child with the body of a child. *Her* child. Who goes to a child for such a thing? Was that his plan all along? Did he worm his way into her home in order to get at her daughter, and how could she not have known what he was doing? She is a failure. The worst kind of mother.

She believes grief and despair blinded her. She tells herself that this is the truth even though somewhere inside herself she admits that she has sacrificed her child to save herself from the reality of having to handle her life. She has betrayed her little girl.

She immediately longs for a drink, for something to wipe that truth away, to purge it from her brain.

The clock on the wall tells her it's after five. 'Where's Vernon?' croaks Margaret.

'He's been gone for three days,' says Alice, her voice stilted and dry. Margaret can feel Alice building a wall between herself and the rest of the world. She doesn't blame her. She wishes she could throw up some bricks to protect herself, wishes she wasn't so weak.

'You were sleeping. You've been sleeping and sleeping,' her daughter says.

'Where's Lilly?'

'She's gone too,' replies Alice. Her eyes are fixed on the television with its lurid colours and flashing lights.

'What? What do you mean?'

'Just that,' Alice shrugs turning around to look at her mother, 'she's gone. Why don't you go back to sleep?'

Margaret and her daughter lock eyes and Margaret shudders at the coldness there. She can't blame her really. There's only so much betrayal a person can take.

She stumbles back to her room and takes a comforting sip of the last mouthful left at the bottom of the bottle. There's something she should be thinking about but she can't quite remember. She'll rest and then she'll know what it is. She's sure of it. She was hungry but now she's not. She was going to get up but here she is in bed again. What is it? What is it? She really needs another drink. She closes her eyes and wishes for a drink and then she keeps them closed.

She wakes with Vernon shaking her violently. Her first thought is to smile because he will have a bottle for her but he doesn't smile back.

'Where the fuck is Lilly, you silly cow?' he spits.

'Lilly?' she murmurs. 'I don't know, she's asleep or outside. She must be with Alice.'

'That silly little bitch won't tell me anything. She's my kid and I want to know where she is.' He drags her out of bed and shoves her into the shower. 'Get yourself together for fuck's sake.' He turns on the cold water, soaking her, stinging the places that are bruised and cut, only just starting to heal. When she tries to climb out, he shoves her back in. He stands and watches her.

'Just pathetic,' he says, his arms folded. Margaret doesn't tell him that he should be the one to wash. He stinks as though he's been living outside for the last three days. There is beer on his breath. It mingles with the smell of cigarettes and the stench of his body odour, and Margaret thinks she catches a whiff of something else as he manhandles her out of the shower and stands, feet apart, arms folded over his fat belly, watching her as she gets dressed into dry yet dirty clothes.

Perfume, she thinks, trying to place the cheap chemical smell. He's been with another woman. Margaret feels her heart skip a beat. Maybe he'll leave now, go and live with some other woman, but then she looks at him and she knows, she knows he's not going anywhere. No one else would tolerate being treated this way, and anyway he's not really interested in women. She knows that now. Her stomach twists. It's sickening, sickening.

She is shaking. 'I need a drink.'

'Not until you find Lilly. Get Alice to tell you, she won't tell me.'

She looks up at him, meets his gaze for only a moment as the thought of defiance rises inside her. He takes a deep breath, his chest puffing out, slowly clenching his fists. She doesn't think she will survive another beating, and that would be fine were it not for the daughter she would leave behind at his mercy. She is sober now, sober enough to feel everything. She drops her gaze to her feet and, shoulders rounded, she shuffles off to find Alice.

Alice is in the kitchen, one side of her face puffing up, the eye swelling closed.

'Alice,' begs Margaret, 'you have to tell us where Lilly is. What happened to her?'

Her daughter is holding an ancient bag of frozen peas to her eye and Margaret wonders where she learned to do that. Then she remembers her daughter at five, getting hit in the face with a ball at school. Adam left work to pick her up because Margaret was feeling tired and needed to rest. When she woke up, she found the two of them in the kitchen, Adam gently patting a bag of peas on his daughter's eye. 'See,' he said, 'this will take the pain away and help stop the swelling.'

Margaret is cut by an anguish so deep she cannot stay standing. She slumps into a chair at the thought of not just everything she has lost but everything Alice has lost too.

'Please, tell us where she is,' she pleads.

'Dead,' whispers Alice harshly. 'Dead, dead, dead,' she repeats, the words getting softer and softer, and even though she is holding the bag of peas to her eye, Margaret watches tears trace their way down her cheek.

Vernon lifts his hand and swipes it across her face, grunting as he moves with the effort of the smack. Her little body flies off the chair she was sitting in, across the room, crumpling in a corner. 'You'll kill her!' screams Margaret.

'She doesn't deserve to live, neither of you two do. What kind of a stupid cow of a woman can't keep an eye on a two-year-old?'

'Have you looked everywhere?'

'I've been home for nearly a day, of course I've looked everywhere. Lilly isn't here. Where is she, you little bitch? What have you done with my kid?' He runs at Alice, slumped in the corner, and slams into her with a strong kick. Alice's body moves a fraction but not much, as if she has given up. Margaret feels the pain of the kick ripple through her own body, feels the physical pull of her child. She tries to stand up from the chair, meaning to grab him away, meaning to tend to her daughter.

'Sit the fuck down,' he roars and Margaret's bruised body obeys. It cannot stand another beating.

'We should call the police,' says Margaret, desperation making her throw the suggestion at him. 'They need to help us find her.'

'The police? Are you fucking kidding me?' he asks. 'What are the police going to say about all this then?' He sweeps his arm around the squalid kitchen and Margaret follows where he points. The rubbish bin is overflowing onto the floor. Crusted pots and pans fill the sink and a putrid smell tells her a rat is dead somewhere. 'We could clean up,' she says lamely, 'tell them we woke up this morning and she was gone. Maybe someone took her or she wandered off – I heard about that on the news… about a toddler wandering off… I think.' Her whole body is shaking, fear and withdrawal combining to produce a sickening, suffocating nausea.

'And what do we do about that, eh?' he says, inclining his head towards the little ball of Alice.

'You shouldn't have hit her. It's not her fault. She's only ten,' she whispers, wanting him to hear the words but terrified of what will happen if he does. Margaret bites down on her lip, opening the cut that has only just healed. She is only ten. What kind of a life is this for a ten-year-old? She believed that she had suffered because her parents were absent, but how much better off would Alice be if she and Vernon were gone? *How have I let this happen?* she thinks for the tenth, twentieth, hundredth time. She has never found the answer to that question and today it doesn't materialise either.

'You shouldn't be allowed to have children, Maggie, you're a useless piece of shit,' he sneers. The same thing her mother said to her, more or less. They are both right. She should never have had children. 'I'm leaving now. Sort this shit out yourself and find my fucking kid or I'll come back here and kill you both.' He stomps out of the house, unconcerned with Alice, and Margaret is pretty sure he doesn't really care where Lilly is either. She feels a sharp pang when she thinks of the baby even though she hasn't had much to do with her in a long time. Alice has been her mum, really. Margaret crouches down next to her daughter. 'Alice, love, are you all right?'

Alice moans and Margaret summons all her strength to lift her up and take her back to her bed. She lies down next to her, sucks desperately at the bottle for the last drops and then they sleep together. Margaret finds she cannot recall Lilly's face. It's only been a few days but she has no idea what the baby looks like.

A day passes, heat soaks the house, it is night and then the sun burns through the curtains again.

Margaret worries that Alice won't wake up. Alice sleeps and sleeps and sleeps and Margaret tries to stay awake to watch over her. She cleans her face, wiping away the blood. Her body glows with bruises. The bottle underneath the bed calls but is empty, no matter how many times she checks it. She shakes and sweats but she keeps wiping down her little girl.

Finally, the child wakes. Her eye is glued closed and she rolls off the bed like a frail old woman, clutching at her insides.

'I should take you to a doctor,' says Margaret.

'No, Mum,' replies Alice, her voice low and creaky.

Maybe Alice is worried that questions will be asked about Lilly. What has Alice done? Has she hurt Lilly? Margaret wouldn't have thought it was possible for Alice to hurt her little sister. She loves her so much but then she remembers Alice's dead eyes and the spitting anger when she talks. She thinks about what he does to her, wipes the thought quickly away, wishing he would return with something for her to drink. She hates herself for wanting him back, for needing the alcohol so much.

'Where is Lilly, Alice?' she asks.

But her daughter says nothing. She shakes her head and takes herself off to the bathroom.

She's fine, Margaret reasons with herself. 'I'll make us some dinner,' she calls, 'and we can talk.'

'I'm not hungry,' replies Alice, which Margaret knows is a lie. She can't have had a proper meal in days. She hears the shower start. In the kitchen, with trembling hands, she throws together what's left in the fridge with a tomato sauce and makes a passable pasta dish. She nearly drops it when she takes it out of the oven because her hands are shaking so much.

'Alice, dinner!' she shouts, as though it's something she does every night. As if she is a homemaker. She is surprised when Alice appears at the table, still clutching at her ribs with bruises yellowing on her face.

The house is quiet without the chatter of the baby. Margaret remembers screaming at Alice, 'Shut that child up for God's sake.'

I shouldn't have said that, she thinks. Is that what Alice did? Did she shut Lilly up for good? Did Alice get rid of Lilly? She closes her eyes at the thought. Her ten-year-old daughter couldn't have harmed her little sister, could she? That wouldn't be possible, would it? But of course, anything is possible, Margaret knows that now. The very worst things in the world are possible whether you believe them to be or not.

'Where's Lilly?' she whispers as she watches her daughter painfully spoon small amounts of pasta into her mouth.

'I don't know, Mum,' says Alice, 'where's Lilly?'

Margaret shakes her head. She cannot eat, cannot even hold the fork she is shaking so much. She wishes for Vernon to return, bearing another apology bottle of vodka.

'I may just go lie down,' she mutters to Alice.

'Yes,' agrees Alice, wincing as she chews, 'that's exactly what you should do.'

CHAPTER TWENTY-FIVE

Now

Alice

I rearrange my pantry while I wait for Jack to call back. Even after all these years I still take comfort in the neat rows of tinned goods and different kinds of pasta. The bottom shelf contains cleaning products and I line everything up, noting things I'm running low on. My pantry is overstocked and overfilled so my boys never have to wonder if there is anything to eat. Finally, half an hour before I am due to pick up the boys, he calls back.

'I've only got about five minutes until the next patient so I can't speak for long but I'm glad you called. Is everything okay? Are you... okay?' I can hear him rearranging things on his desk, can hear the click-clack of the balls of the Newton's cradle as he shifts it from one side of the desk to the other.

'I've been getting some strange emails and I'm starting to worry about them.'

'Strange emails? From who?'

'I don't know and that's exactly why I'm starting to worry about them.' I should tell him about the frog, but the words stick in my throat.

'What do they say?'

'They have all mostly said the same thing: "I know what you did."'

'I know what you did? What could that mean? Perhaps it's a scam email... you know, one of those where they ask for money or gift cards or something. Have they asked for money?'

'No, and the thing is, Jack... I think they might be from my mother.'

'Your mother? But she's not capable of using a computer, is she?'

'The other day I was there and she told me that Vernon knows what I did.'

Jack is quiet for a moment. 'Alice, love... isn't Vernon in prison? And your mother... well, you know how far her Alzheimer's has progressed. She doesn't recognise you most of the time. I'm sure she's said something random to you and you've connected it with some spam emails. Things are difficult... I know that.'

'I really don't think it's just spam, Jack.'

'Those kinds of emails get sent all the time. Our practice was sent one last year that accused us of all sorts of things. It accused us of malpractice and threatened to sue unless we paid them. I'm sure it's rubbish, Alice... it has to be. Please don't worry. We can try and trace where they're coming from. Don't let it distress you. We'll get to the bottom of it, okay?'

'Okay... okay,' I mumble, wanting to believe him.

'I'm so sorry, I have to go, a patient is coming in. I really have to go. Love you.'

He hangs up and the words I want to say die on my lips. 'There are things you don't know,' I should have told him, 'things I've done.'

But I couldn't say the words, couldn't admit the truth. Lilly died. Jack knows she died in a car accident. Everyone close to me except for my boys knows about the little sister I once had. What they don't know, what I never want anyone to know, is my part in that. I poke my tongue into the space where my tooth used to be. *Look what you did*, I think. *Look what you've done.*

Jack wanted to know more about Lilly when I told him about her. But I never wanted to discuss her. 'I just can't,' I told him.

Lilly was a child who slipped through the cracks of the social system, just like I did.

Someone should have helped us before I made such a drastic choice. The system should have saved us but no one ever asked, no one ever questioned my bruises or the way I shrank back from everyone who came near me, no one noticed. No one ever asked the questions that should have been asked. It was a different time but I still resent the fact that no one reached out to me. We moved soon after Lilly was born, and I'm not even sure my mother registered her birth. Few people knew when Lilly was born and even fewer realised she was gone.

I think about the possibility that Jack is right, that the emails are simply a scam of some sort and that my mother couldn't possibly be sending them. He's probably right. The message on my blog is just from some voyeur. I mentioned the stuffed frog when I wrote about my life on the blog and maybe whoever is sending the emails had a similar toy? I feel like I'm clutching at straws but who knows how far someone would go to simply torment me.

The woman has no connection to the emails.

As I get ready to go and pick the boys up from school, I resolve to seek some help. I shouldn't be obsessing over this and I certainly shouldn't be drinking like I did last night. Whatever happened, whatever I did in the past, is long gone and I have to believe that no one is coming back to make me pay.

And yet… and yet I cannot help but feel that this is exactly what I deserve. I was a child but I was old enough to know what I was doing even though I could never have predicted the terrible consequences. I close my eyes and see my sister's little face. 'I'm so sorry, Lilly,' I whisper. Words I have said almost every day for more than thirty years. 'I am so sorry.'

CHAPTER TWENTY-SIX
Molly

Molly hears the alarm and rolls over onto her side, reaching out for Peter, who pushes back against her. 'I read those articles,' he says. Molly groans. She wanted, needed, just to stay in that blissful moment between sleep and waking for a little while longer. Last night she had not even felt her husband get into bed. Her sleep had been heavy, almost suffocating and silent of dreams.

'What are you going to do?' asks Peter, turning over to face her.

'I'm… I'm going to go over to my parents' today and ask every question I have, and then I'm going to try and find my birth family. Yesterday I realised that I need to know who they were and why they abandoned me. What if there's a genetic history of something awful that we need to know about? What if there's a specific reason for all my miscarriages that could affect this baby?'

'I understand you needing to know, Moll. I do, of course I do. But what if there are no records for you to follow? There'll be some old police reports, that's all.'

Molly slides out of bed and pulls on her dressing gown. 'I have to try, Pete. I don't know who I am. I can't look at my sister and my parents and see where my chin or my eyes came from, and that kills me. I watch you and your father together, and whenever I ask him a question, he tilts his head a fraction, exactly like you do, and then he takes a breath before he answers and I know that's because he's thinking through what he's going to say because it's exactly the same thing you do. All the traits I have I've attributed to my mother or my father but the whole time I was wrong. I am nothing like them. I don't come from them and that hurts. I feel so stupid for thinking that my sense of humour is just like my dad's or that Lexie and I look so alike. I feel like every thought I've ever had about my family is tainted.'

'I can't even imagine how that feels, I really can't. But I don't want you to get hurt. I'm afraid of you suffering even more. And I don't want you to stress yourself out over something that may have no conclusive answers, especially not now.' Peter gets out of bed and walks over to her. He cups her face and lays a gentle kiss on her forehead. 'We're so close to everything we've always wanted. I want you to enjoy this, to be happy… not to be consumed by the past.'

Molly studies her husband. He's not wearing his glasses and so looks younger, more vulnerable than he usually does. Logically she understands that he wants the best for her and the baby but he also needs to understand that logic has nothing to do with anything right now.

'I will only get stressed if I have to pretend that I don't have this information now. My parents have just dropped a bomb into the middle of my life and you can't expect that there'll be no fallout from that.'

Once Peter has gone to work, finally acquiescing, she showers and dresses, tying her hair back without even brushing it and ignoring how pale she looks in the mirror.

On impulse she sits down at the computer again and types in the headline from the first news article, as if it's possible that today there will be something more. But, of course, there's nothing.

She types 'toddler' and '1987' into her search bar and scans the articles about a toddler rescued from a well in Texas and about a toddler kidnapped in Canada. She clicks through to the second page, and right at the bottom she finds an article about a toddler killed in a car accident.

Sydney Morning Herald
21 January 1987

Questions Asked After Toddler's Death

Questions about child safety are being asked after a toddler was killed in a car accident on the Pacific Highway near Mount Colah last night. It is understood that the toddler was unrestrained in the back seat of the car when it veered off the road and into a pole. All three occupants, Deidre Olsen (18), Jason Burke (19) and an unidentified child, were killed.

'We are concerned that parents are still not complying with rules for child restraint,' Constable Symons from traffic control said. 'Parents who do not restrain their children correctly risk their lives. It is possible that this child would have survived the accident if she had been in a properly fitted seat.'

The mother of the young woman, Deidre Olsen, said, 'She was a wonderful girl, loved by everyone who knew her. She had only just started dating Jason. I didn't know he had a child but it doesn't surprise me. I knew that boy was trouble. I knew the way he drove was dangerous.'

Jason Burke's parents refused to comment but are cooperating with police. The mother of the toddler has not come forward.

Molly notes the date on the article. She experiences a moment of profound gratitude that her life did not end the same way.

She grabs her coat from the rack near the door and leaves the apartment. She will ask her mother all her questions and see if there is anything more to know.

She shouldn't really be out of bed at all but she needs to speak to her mother. Dr Bernstein's nurse assured her, when she called early this morning, that if there had been no more bleeding it was fine for her to move around a little. 'But don't overdo it,' she said sternly.

Her mother opens her front door as though she has been standing behind it, just waiting for Molly to push the bell.

'Why didn't you use your key?' she asks.

Molly shrugs.

'I'm baking, so come into the kitchen,' her mother says with a sigh. Molly can see that her mother looks tired. Her normally immaculate make-up is haphazardly applied and there are dark circles under her eyes.

Molly sits on a barstool across from the kitchen counter where her mother is baking chocolate chip cookies.

'Do you want some tea or something to eat? Are you feeling okay? Any nausea?' asks her mother all at once.

'I'm fine, Mum, I just need you to answer some questions I have.'

Anne nods, swiping at her face where tears have appeared.

'Why are you crying?' asks Molly, more stridently than she intends.

'You called me Mum. I was worried, I thought… I don't know.'

Molly looks at her and for a moment she glimpses a much younger, less sure woman. She gets up and goes around the counter, places her arms around her mother, who turns and sobs in her arms. 'I'm so sorry,' she says as she cries. 'I was so afraid we'd lose you.'

'Oh, Mum, how could you lose me? I'm yours.'

'I'm all right,' her mother finally says, breathing a sigh of relief. 'Sorry, love, it's been a long night. I didn't know if you'd forgive us or if you'd ever want to see us again. I just didn't know.'

'You're my parents, whatever happens, but you understand that I need to know more, right? I want to let it go, but I can't. I feel like I have to know everything, for me and for whoever this is.' She touches her hand to her stomach.

'I understand,' replies her mother, picking up her rolling pin and working the cookie dough again. Molly knows she needs to keep her hands busy. Some conversations are easier to have when you're not looking directly at the person you're talking to.

'Can you explain to me how it happened? How I came to be with you and why you decided to become a foster parent?'

'It feels so long ago now. Sometimes the memory is a bit fuzzy but not the feeling, not the overwhelming joy of holding you and having you with us.' Her mother stops rolling out the dough and looks at her. Molly sees the shine of love in her eyes, and for a moment she is angry at herself for pushing this. Surely it should be enough to know how loved she is, to be able to look back at her childhood and know that she never felt anything except loved and protected and taken care of?

'Whatever you can remember, Mum, please,' begs Molly because in her heart it's not enough.

Anne is silent for a few minutes, pressing out star shapes and placing them carefully on a baking tray. Molly chews her bottom lip, knowing that her mother is organising her thoughts.

'The second school your father taught at was in a very disadvantaged suburb. There were a lot of housing commission flats and unemployment as well as people with drug and alcohol issues. Your father loved the school. He instituted a breakfast programme because he knew that a lot of kids came to school hungry. Once news spread, more and more children began attending, knowing that at least they would get one good meal a day.'

'I bet you got involved with that,' says Molly.

'I did.' Her mother smiles. 'Your father and I had only been married for two years when he was posted to the school. I had been a secretary before that but couldn't travel for an hour each way to get to my job so he encouraged me to look for something closer. When he started the programme, he asked me to help. Of course, I couldn't resist getting involved. I used to work with some of the older girls in the school kitchen, baking muffins for the next day. I really enjoyed spending time with them. They had so little and came from such difficult situations at home but a tiny bit of praise about their baking made them beam like sunshine.'

Molly can see her mother as a young woman. The picture of her and her father on their wedding day stands on the mantelpiece in the living room. Her mother's blond hair is a halo of artful curls with a comb attached to her veil and she wears a simple lace wedding dress. She is a beautiful woman who looks a little incongruous standing next to her husband, who is five years older but looks even older than that. Her father has always looked older than his age and his beard gave him the serious demeanour of a politician.

'The more I worked with the girls,' continues her mother, 'the more I heard about their lives, and I began feeling that I wanted to do something to help; so many of them were responsible for their own lives at such young ages. A lot of them were in the foster system and they told some terrible stories of homes where they were abused or neglected – as they had been in their own homes – and of having to move over and over again because of the poor quality of care. It's better now, I think, with more stringent guidelines for foster parents, but back then standards weren't that great. I floated the idea of becoming a foster parent with your father. We were trying for a baby of… for a baby.' Her mother stops abruptly and blushes.

'For a baby of your own, Mum, I get it,' says Molly. 'You don't have to start watching your words around me.'

Her mother nods. 'We were trying for a baby but month after month, nothing was happening. I wasn't concerned because I knew my own mother had taken a year to fall pregnant with me, but I did know that either way I wanted to foster a child who needed our help.'

'I bet Dad agreed.'

'He did. I thought it would be a long process but it wasn't that strict in those days, which is probably why a lot of children landed up in unsuitable homes. Your dad and I got approved almost immediately. We were the ideal couple, I suppose – we were young and he was a teacher and I would be able to be a stay-at-home mother. You were the first child they brought to us, and the way things worked out the last one as well. They weren't even sure exactly how old you were but estimated you were close to two years old. We had no idea what you'd been through before you came to us and I knew I needed to be prepared for some difficult patches.'

Molly thinks about a picture her parents have of her at what she has always been told is two years old. It must have been one of the very first photographs they took of her. In it she is sitting on a swing in a park, and she knows that every time she has looked at the image, she has wondered what the child in the swing has to look so concerned about. It all makes sense now. She swallows as she tries to imagine what it would have been like for her to find herself first alone on a road and then with a strange new family. It is no wonder that the child on the swing looks watchful, wary, and that she has no smile for the camera.

'And were there difficult patches?' she asks, wondering about the possibility of broken nights and tantrums. She would have been so confused about her life.

Her mother stops making star shapes and turns, sliding the first baking tray into the oven. 'Funnily enough there weren't,' she says as she begins to fill another tray. 'I always felt as though you understood on some deeper level that we were trying to help you.'

'Do you know why I was given to you?'

'No idea, really. Luck of the draw, I suppose, and I have always considered the day you arrived to be the luckiest day of my life.' Her mother looks up at her, a small smile playing on her lips at the memory. 'I told them I would be happy with a child of any age but you were the one they brought. I had seen the appeals on television and read the newspaper reports and felt so sorry for the little girl who'd just been abandoned, but I never dreamed they would bring you to us.'

'And… what was I like?' asks Molly nervously.

'You were the quietest child I had ever met. So quiet that we worried about you.' Her mother slides the next tray into the oven. 'It's such a long time ago. They gave us so little information. They knew nothing themselves, of course. It seems impossible that your parents just left you on a road and disappeared but it's what happened.'

'They didn't want me,' says Molly, and the enormity of that statement washes over her, lodges in her heart. They didn't want her. Who were these people? Why did they even decide to have a child at all? Had they wanted a boy and been unhappy with a girl? Had she been a difficult baby? What kind of a mother does what her biological mother did? She wants to try and understand it. Perhaps it was postnatal depression or a violent partner or perhaps she was very young and had no money, but no matter how much she tries to explain it to herself she cannot. No reason would be good enough. And she worries that this obvious lack of a mothering instinct present in her mother may be present in her. What if she has this baby and it doesn't sleep? Will she also want to simply get rid of her own child?

Her mother looks at her, her eyes brimming with sympathy. 'Maybe they couldn't look after you. Maybe they were addicts or very young. We don't know but I do know that from the moment our social worker handed you over to me, I loved and adored you.'

'Maybe I could contact the social worker, maybe she would know more about where I came from?' she says, hope flaring inside her.

'Oh, darling, Sarah was in her late fifties when we fostered you. She died about five years ago. We kept in touch, sent her pictures and that sort of thing.'

'And yet you never told me any of this?' says Molly. 'How could you have just kept it from me?' Suddenly she is angry again.

Her mother's hands cease their continuous movement and she looks up at Molly. Molly can see her getting ready to apologise again, to tell her she made a mistake, and she shakes her head. She doesn't want to hear the same things over and over.

Her mother goes back to cutting out the cookies, biting down on her lip to prevent any more apologies floating out.

'Could I speak? Did I have any words at all?'

'You could say single words. You said words like "cat" and "dog" and "up". Things that I would expect to hear out of the mouth of a one-year-old rather than a two-year-old.'

'Anything else? Anything that could help me find out where I came from?'

Her mother sighs, picks up the last full tray and slides it into the oven. The smell of baking cookies fills the air, reminding Molly that she's in a safe space. The scent always makes her think of home, of the sweet warmth that has always permeated her mother's kitchen.

'Mum,' she says now, aware that her mother hasn't answered the question. 'Anything else?'

Her mother takes a deep breath. 'You cried very quietly.'

'Well, that must have been good.'

'No,' says her mother, shaking her head, 'it wasn't good. The first week you were here you bumped your head on the edge of a bookcase and I saw you do it but you just kept on walking so I thought you were fine, but then you sat down to play with some toys and I came over to where you were and there were silent tears running down your cheeks. You had hurt yourself, you were in pain, but you didn't make any noise. It was… it was awful.'

Molly stares at her mother and is overcome with a deep sadness. For a moment she forgets where she is sitting and she feels far away. She feels another space around her, a cluttered, dirty space filled with harsh smells. She hears her own voice but it doesn't feel like her voice. 'I wasn't allowed to make a noise. If I made a noise, then he hit me again,' she says quietly, the words escaping her lips.

Her mother stares at her, takes a deep breath. 'How… how do you know that?' she asks, shock making her pale.

'I…' Molly shakes herself a little, bringing herself back to the bright, clean kitchen and the smooth countertop beneath her hands. She rubs the surface compulsively, seeking comfort. 'I don't know, I just felt it… I mean, I read about it on the blog, but right now, right now I felt it. I wasn't allowed to make a noise.'

'Have you spoken to the woman who wrote the blog? Have you asked her about your situation?'

'I have but it has nothing to do with me. Her sister is dead so it can't have anything to do with me.'

'Are you sure she's telling the truth?'

'Why would she lie? Meredith could live anywhere in the world. I imagine I just connected with the blog because I've had a similar experience.'

'I don't know, Moll, I looked it up after you told me about it and I don't know how it's possible that you would remember the things she writes about if you weren't involved in some way. I think she's Australian.'

'Why do you think that?'

'Maybe it's the way she writes but also the picture she uses on her blog – the one with the clouds and the sun peeking through has the Three Sisters in it; you know, the formations in the Blue Mountains.'

'Yes!' exclaims Molly. 'That's why it was so familiar.'

'It may just be a stock image off the internet but it may mean she's Australian, and if she is… you just never know, do you? I don't want to send you off in the wrong direction but I cannot believe that you would have had such an emotional reaction to her words if you weren't connected in some way.'

Molly knows that this must be true. 'Why did you call me "Molly" she asks suddenly, hoping that she had somehow managed to tell the police her real name.

'Oh,' says her mother, 'we had always planned to name our first daughter Molly, after the books I used to love as a child, you know, the *Milly-Molly-Mandy* stories? I think I read every story at least a hundred times when I was growing up. I planned to have three daughters, one name Milly, one named Molly and one named Mandy. Your father thought that wasn't a great idea but he did agree to your name. We read the books to you, remember?'

Molly does remember. 'I loved that she shared my name.'

'You did.' Her mother smiles.

Molly rubs her eyes with her hands, feeling a headache coming on. It's too much. The emotional toll of the discussion is simply too much.

'I should go. I think I need to lie down.'

'You can lie down here, love, you do look a bit worn out. You need to rest as much as possible.'

'I know, but I think I want to go home. I'll be fine, Mum. Thanks though.'

Anne comes over to the other side of the counter where Molly is sitting and wraps her in a long hug.

At the front door, Molly kisses her mother on the cheek. 'I'll call you later,' she says.

'Molly, one last thing…'

'Yes?'

'In the beginning you were terrified of Dad, of your father. You wouldn't let him near you for months. You didn't scream or cry but if he came near you, you would run away and climb into your bedroom cupboard.'

'Right into the cupboard?' Molly asks woodenly, smelling again the mould smell, seeing the paint she would peel with little fingers.

'Right into the cupboard. You would only come out if I came and got you.'

CHAPTER TWENTY-SEVEN

2 February 1987

Margaret

Vernon doesn't return for over a week. Margaret sleeps as much as she can and Alice's bruises fade and mottle. 'Stay inside,' Margaret tells her, and Alice rolls her eyes at her mother's stupidity. She should be back at school but there's no way she can go.

When Vernon returns, he brings fish and chips for dinner and the promise of oblivion in the form of two large bottles of vodka. 'Thought you two might be hungry,' he says, his words slurring a little. He studies Alice. 'You should be more careful,' he tells her.

Alice doesn't greet him but gobbles the fish and chips. The fridge and the pantry are empty. Margaret feeds her body the only thing it needs. She noticed this morning that she was feeling a little better, that the shaking had diminished and her nausea was not as bad, and she thought, *Maybe I can stop, just stop.* But then he walked through the door and the spirit called to her like a lover would, its gentle warmth more precious than anything in her world.

Margaret sips at the vodka she has poured into a glass. If it's in a glass, then she's just having a drink with dinner, like so many others do; slurping it from the bottle is different. Margaret wants to be the kind of woman who just has a drink with dinner. She tries to not see the way Vernon looks at Alice, letting his eyes roam up and down her skinny body. 'Alice is going to sleep with me tonight,' she whispers, the burning alcohol giving her a moment of courage.

'Like fuck she is,' sneers Vernon.

Alice doesn't even look at her, just drops her shoulders, surrenders to it, surrenders to it all. Margaret wants to save her daughter, to grab the child by the hand and run as far as they can run, but the creeping tiredness is upon her again, bringing her hopeless reality into focus. She cannot even take care of herself.

'Clean up this fucking mess,' Vernon says after dinner. The promise of punishment for not doing what he says is blatantly clear.

Alice slides off her chair. 'I'm going to watch TV.' Margaret knows she will sit hunched on the couch as long as possible, hoping that Vernon will pass out before he can touch her. She can remember doing the same thing when he first moved in.

Why can't you do something, you stupid woman? she asks herself but doesn't have the energy to reply, even in her own head. She wishes she was dead and gone. She eyes the kitchen knives, wondering if one of them would do the job. The idea of being asleep forever is liquid and beautiful inside her.

She shuffles around the kitchen, shoving things in cupboards slowly as though her bones are wearing away with each movement.

The fish and chips came wrapped in white paper with a newspaper cover. 'Just like the old days,' Vernon said when he first started buying them from the shop at the end of their road.

Margaret picks up some paper that has dropped on the floor and peers at it. It's old, from more than a week ago.

Sydney Morning Herald

21 January 1987

Questions Asked After Toddler's Death

Questions about child safety are being asked after a toddler was killed in a car accident on the Pacific Highway near Mount Colah last night. It is understood that the toddler was unrestrained in the back seat of the car when it veered off the road and into a pole.

Margaret stops reading before she gets to the end. The accident happened so close to where she lives. She imagines it had been her, that her car had been drivable and she had been on the road, alcohol controlling her body, her mind. She also didn't have a car seat for Lilly. She closes her eyes and sees her car smashing into a pole on the side of the highway, hears the crunch of metal and the shattering of glass. Would that be an easy way to die? Would she have taken her children with her? Would they all have been better off?

She thinks about Alice, sitting rigid on the couch, and about Lilly. Where is Lilly? She stares at the kitchen wall where the wallpaper is peeling and curled. It's strange to think she had almost forgotten about Lilly, waking last night to question if the child had ever even existed. Time trips over itself and even the most significant things can be forgotten. Could Lilly have wandered away and been picked up by strangers? It's possible and it would explain why Alice won't tell them what has happened to her. Alice was supposed to be watching her, after all. She closes her eyes and sees her baby daughter on a road, lost and confused. She sees her get picked up by a stranger and then she sees the car she's travelling in veer off the road and into a pole. It's possible. Lilly could be dead. Lilly probably is dead. Vernon hasn't asked about her again. Maybe he knows what happened to her. Could Vernon have done something to Lilly? Had he started to do the same things to her that he was doing to Alice? Did the baby fight his touch and get hurt for it, too hurt to recover? Margaret's stomach bubbles with nausea. She cannot think about this. She grabs the bottle and takes a swig, letting the liquor burn away her thoughts.

She scrunches the newspaper into a ball and then she gets up and pushes it into the bin, on top of the greasy remains of the fish. Wherever Lilly is, whatever has happened to her, Margaret is sure that she is better off than she would be here.

CHAPTER TWENTY-EIGHT

Now

Alice

On Monday morning, I call the number Jack has given me for an appointment with a new therapist. I wish, not for the first time over the last few years, that Ian was still alive, that he had not been taken by his damaged heart. He would only be seventy now and I would love to be able to talk to him again. I'm grateful he was still here after Isaac was born, grateful that I got to speak to him again. He went into hospital to have a stent fitted and never came home, but luckily I visited him the day before the operation.

'Too much booze and too many cigarettes,' he said wryly when I wished him well.

'You wouldn't be the first, Ian, and they can do wonders these days. I'll see you when you've had a chance to recover a bit.'

'You were one of my greatest success stories, Alice, you know that, don't you?' he said, a smile on his lips.

'I bet you have thousands of success stories,' I said, so grateful for the man who helped me turn my life around. And then a nurse came in to do some blood tests and I had to say goodbye. I didn't know it would be goodbye forever.

I shake my head, thinking of Ian. 'Why didn't you go back to therapy sooner, Alice?' he would have said. That could have prevented me from letting myself slip into the bottle the way my mother did.

'Going to therapy means you're *not* your mother,' I hear him say and I try to rid myself of the gloomy feeling I have. I'll go and see her again today. My first therapy session is in two weeks and I want to be able to tell the therapist, a woman named Amelia, that I have said what I needed to say to my mother.

I am hit by a sharp wind as I get out of my car at the Green Gate. It will soon be the worst month of winter. The wind and the rain and the cold will make everyone miserable and it will feel like summer will never return.

Anika is at the desk when I sign in. 'Your mother is not in her room,' she tells me and she sounds quite excited by this fact.

'Where is she?'

'Out in the garden.'

'In the garden? But she never leaves her room.'

'I know but today she insisted she go outside.'

'Isn't it cold?'

'We made sure she was all wrapped up. She said she wanted to see Vernon and Adam.'

'Vernon?' I almost shriek.

'Well, that's what she says, but of course only Ed's outside at the moment. She seems to really like him though. They speak every now and again.'

'Who's Ed?'

'The young man who does the garden, the volunteer.'

'Oh, yes… Is she this way?' I ask, pointing at a door that leads out to the back, and Anika nods.

I find my way to the vast, overgrown back garden and look around, finally spotting my mother sitting on a bench. In front of her is the young gardener that Anika has identified as Ed. As I walk towards her, I can hear her talking to him. I am quite cheered to hear her so animated.

'Hello,' I say when I get to the bench.

'Hello,' she replies, looking up at me, and then her eyes light up. 'Hello, Alice, are you home from school?'

'Yes, Mum,' I say, disappointment settling over me.

The young man, who is currently pulling at some weeds around the bench, looks up and nods at me.

'Vernon and I were just talking about you,' says my mother.

I swivel my head around desperately but obviously there is no one but the young gardener, me and my mother.

'I'm Ed, Margaret, remember,' he says softly.

'Oh… oh, yes, Ed of course. You're not Vernon. You're too young.'

'That's right,' he says.

'Vernon went to prison. He killed a man and he went to prison. Did you know Vernon went to prison, Alice?'

'Yes, I know, Mum. I don't think we've formally met before, I'm Alice,' I say, holding out my hand to shake Ed's.

He stands up, wipes his hands on his trousers and then clasps my hand in his. His hand is freezing and rough, splattered with leftover soil. 'Yes, I've heard all about you,' he says.

'Ed helps me with my computer,' says my mother.

'That's… nice,' I respond.

'I'm only a volunteer here,' he replies. 'I'm doing a degree in computer science.'

'That's great,' I say. 'Where has the other man gone – the older man?' I ask.

'My uncle,' says Ed, 'he's not been well.' He resumes his digging.

I watch him for a moment, wondering at the futility of trying to keep such a large, wild expanse of garden in shape. He stands upright, shaking his head, and then he looks around him. 'I never seem to achieve anything,' he says to my mother.

'I think you do a beautiful job, Vernon,' she replies.

'Who's Vernon?' he asks me.

'He's a man we used to live with, a terrible man,' I say without looking at him.

'He's not terrible, Alice, and you know he wants you to call him Dad.'

He's not my dad, he's not my father, he's not my anything. I remember shouting those words at my mother when I was twelve years old, horrified that she kept exhorting me to call the man who was abusing me 'Dad'.

I look down at my feet. I don't know why I keep doing this to myself. She doesn't understand what she's saying and I'm sure there's no malice behind it, but it feels malicious. Malicious and hurtful.

'I'm cold, Alice,' says my mother. 'And very tired. I think I need a nap.'

'I'll take you in then.'

Ed walks away from us, carrying a handful of weeds.

'Are you sending me emails, Mum? Did you send me Lilly's stuffed frog?' I whisper just loud enough for her to hear. I don't expect a reply but I need to ask the question, to voice my fears aloud.

She catches my gaze, her eyes bright, and I feel almost burnt by the intensity of her gaze.

'Maybe I am… I know how to use the computer, you know. Vernon taught me.'

Shock renders me silent.

'Why would I send you emails?' she asks and she smiles. 'What did you do? What did you do, Alice?'

I shiver but not from the cold. I hear a ringing in my ears. It's her, she's doing it.

'Do you know where my daughter is?' she asks.

'I…' I begin but before I can form a coherent sentence she sighs.

'I wish she would get home from school. She's been there a long time. Do you know where Alice is?'

'No, I'm sorry,' I say. 'I have no idea where she is at all.' I push my tongue into the gap in my mouth. I am sitting with a stranger.

I have no idea what's going on in her head and I feel too weary to try and figure this out.

'Let's go in,' I say, helping her stand up from the bench.

'Goodbye, Vernon,' she calls as we walk away but Ed doesn't reply, just raises a hand in goodbye.

Once we're back inside, I help her to her bed, and in a few minutes she's asleep. I have once again lost the chance to talk to her, losing her to sleep like I used to all those years ago. Instead I take a look at her computer. It's still connected to the internet and the search history tells me that they've been using the soothing videos a lot but nothing else. I search up Gmail and, using my phone, I type in the username of the account I got the emails from. As my fingers hit the keys, I'm aware of feeling slightly crazy. My mother has not been sending me emails, it's impossible. The account name pops up and asks for a password. 'Well, of course it does,' I say to myself.

'Stupid,' I say, shutting down the computer. I have no idea what I thought I'd find. I leave my mother sleeping, leaving the things I wanted to say unsaid.

CHAPTER TWENTY-NINE
Molly

Molly sits in front of her computer trying to summon up the courage to do what she's going to do. She looks through Meredith's blog again. The woman says her sister died but what if that's not the truth? She has read hundreds of blogs as she researches her short stories and she has never felt a connection like this with any of them. She has read Meredith's story at least twenty times, and each time she feels her skin grow cold and the smell of the mouldy cupboard assaults her. There is something here. She is sure of it. What if she is Meredith's sister? What if Meredith has no idea her sister is alive? What if? What if?

She has decided to give this another try – to see if she can get Meredith to talk to her, really talk to her. She has laboured over her message for hours and now she knows she needs to just send it, just send it and hope. She reads through it one more time.

Dear Meredith,

I know you don't want to speak to me about your experiences or discuss your little sister but I wanted to ask you to reconsider. You see, I recently found out I was adopted, and when I read your blog, I felt like I remembered some of the things you were discussing. I feel like I remember, and I think that maybe, maybe I'm your sister. I know how crazy that sounds, especially in light of what you've told me about her.

Please forgive me for contacting you again if this isn't the case. I just really want to find my biological family. I'm pregnant with my first child and I feel like I need to know what kind of genetic history I come from. I hope you will consider replying to me, and I would also love to be able to meet you someday. You can get me at mollykhan@gmail.com.

Many thanks,
Molly Khan

Molly's finger hovers over her keyboard. She is harassing a woman who specifically asked her not to contact her, but she has literally nothing else to go on. She hits the button and the message is sent.

Needing to get out of the house, she decides to go for a slow walk. She cannot sit in the apartment for a moment longer. She has had no more bleeding and Dr Bernstein has assured her that it's fine for her to walk around now even though they haven't had the scan yet.

'If the bleeding has stopped there is no reason to stay in bed but don't overdo it,' he instructed, just like his nurse instructed, just like everyone keeps saying.

Outside, the winter sun is weak and offers no warmth at all. Molly is grateful for her beanie and gloves. She finds herself increasing her pace in time to her music and then having to force herself to slow down.

She tries to imagine what it will be like to be walking through the streets of her neighbourhood a year from now with a baby in a pram, stopping to point out the cute boat-shaped post box or picking a daisy for little hands to feel and a little nose to smell. She feels a rush of joy that is quickly tempered by the onslaught of fear. It must be so easy for women who fall pregnant when they want to and then go on to have a healthy baby without any drama. It must be so easy for them to imagine their future, to plan a nursery, to pick out names and to wander into children's clothing stores, deciding what kind of onesies to dress their babies in. She will never have this ease, this peaceful journey to parenthood, but if it's the price she has to pay for a child, she is willing. She will accept the months of terror because for the first time in years it seems as though there may be a reward at the end.

'Don't go getting ahead of yourself, Molly,' she mutters aloud.

She stops in front of a small house with a for sale sign attached to the surrounding sandstone wall. It has a bright green patch of lawn and a decorative brick pathway leading to a wood panel front door. An old-fashioned bell on the wall next to the door begs to be tapped.

The sign advertises three bedrooms and two bathrooms with a big overgrown back garden. It appears that money was spent to smarten up the front of the house but not the back. Molly imagines herself pulling out the rampant weeds and cutting back abundant shrubbery to clear a space for a table and chairs.

Peter has been saying for a while that they should try and upgrade but Molly has feared the emptiness of a house without children. Now, she thinks, now it may be a possibility. A house with a back garden for a little girl or boy. But she shakes her head and continues walking, resting her hand on her stomach, imagining the little being inside her surrounded by a white light of protection. The scan is in two days. In two days, they will know more, and for the first time ever they will be past the three-month mark. She will be just over twelve weeks when she has the scan. Yet the minutes and hours tick by so slowly that Molly sometimes feels time is moving backwards.

She wonders about the mother who simply abandoned her on a road in the middle of nowhere. Did she touch her stomach like this when Molly was inside her? Did she long for a child, or was her pregnancy a mistake? Did she ever love the child inside her at all?

Sometimes this feels like too much. She's nothing but a jumble of questions and fears.

Once she's home she opens her computer to check if Meredith has replied but there is nothing.

Her heart sinks. Meredith probably won't reply. Molly can imagine the woman's horror at getting another message from her, at having someone on the internet declare that she believes herself to be her sister. Meredith must think she's insane. She rubs her eyes, trying to hold back tears. This feels impossible.

There is nothing else she can do, nowhere else she can go from here.

CHAPTER THIRTY

Now

Margaret

Margaret watches the bird methodically strip the branches of the tree where he sits, occasionally pausing to work at something in his beak. She wonders what the bird is called, is sure it's something she used to know. She looks down at her hands but they can't be her hands. They're the hands of an old woman and Margaret is still young. She's waiting for Adam to come home. He said they could go out for Italian tonight. Margaret is looking forward to an evening out with her husband, and her mouth waters at the thought of freshly baked, buttery garlic bread. She turns around and looks at the door her husband will soon walk through. Her house is smaller than she remembers… or is it?

Adam will be here soon. Mr Henkel will need dinner as well so maybe he should come with them. 'Call me Max,' Mr Henkel says but Margaret can only call him Mr Henkel.

There is something she is forgetting, something she needs to remember, but she's not sure what. She'll have to ask Alice. Who is Alice? Margaret watches the white bird. The yellow thing on top of its head makes her want to laugh. What is the yellow thing called? Where is Adam and what must she remember?

The door to her house opens and Anika comes in. Margaret smiles. She remembers Anika with her soft skin and jasmine scent. Anika is gentle and kind.

'Morning, Margaret, are you ready for breakfast? Would you like to eat in your room or in the dining room?'

'Oh, I'm just waiting for Adam. He says we're going out to dinner.'

'How lovely, but maybe have some breakfast first, just in case he's late. Would you like me to help you to the dining room?'

Margaret looks at the door and feels her hands begin to shake. She can't go out there. She has no idea what's out there or who's out there. 'No, no,' she says. 'I can't leave.'

'That's fine, don't upset yourself, I'll just nip out and get a tray for you. You stay here and rest.'

Margaret nods her head although she doesn't really feel tired. She used to feel tired all the time, she used to want to sleep and sleep, day after day. She can't remember when that was.

But Adam is coming home and they will go for Italian. Margaret goes back to watching the bird. She wonders if Lilly would like to see the bird. She would ask her but she has no idea who Lilly is.

CHAPTER THIRTY-ONE

Alice

I pack the last of the shopping bags away, ready for next time, and open the fridge to get some cheese out to have on toast for lunch.

As I place the bread in the sandwich press, the door knocker sounds. I feel a jolt of fear. Everything feels like a threat now. The person sending me the emails knows where I live. He or she could be at my door right now.

I wait for the knocker to sound again but there is only silence. After a moment I summon up the courage to go to the door and nearly cry with relief when I see it's just a parcel on the front step left by a delivery man.

It's a rectangular box, addressed to me. I ordered some signs for the bake sale at school – they were designed by the children and I know that before this all began, I was excited to see how they turned out. I turn the package over in my hands but the name of the company I used isn't on it.

It takes only a moment to open but there are no signs inside.

Instead there is a filthy pink blanket. I yelp and drop it onto the kitchen floor, and then I stand looking at it, my heart racing. I lean down and pick it up, recognising this blanket. I know this blanket. I know that it used to be edged in satin but that when that started coming off, no one fixed it. I know that it used to be in my cot and then on my bed. I know that it used to be mine and that I loved its soft texture and so I gave it to her because I loved her more than anything.

The only other thing in the box is a printed note.

I wonder if you think about her every day, Alice.
I wonder if you regret what you did then.
I wonder if you're afraid of what's going to happen now.
I'm locked up in here and you're out there and really it should be the other way around.

My scream of anguish fills the house. Is this Vernon? He's locked up in prison but my mother must feel she's locked up as well. If it's Vernon, he can't get to me, can't hurt me, but how did he find my address? Who told him where I live?

When is this going to end? How is it going to end?

Frantically I open my computer to see if there is another email. There isn't but then when I check my blog there is another message from Molly Khan.

She is hunting me, haunting me, harassing me. Who is she? Is Molly Khan my mother? Is my mother masquerading as someone on the internet to torment me?

It's too much. She won't let go. She won't let me be.

I scroll back through all my posts, my hands vibrating with fear. I look at all the messages that have come to me over the years. I should never have written anything down, never have released my story into the world.

Slowly and deliberately, with great care, I delete my blog and everything to do with it.

Only when there is no evidence that it ever existed do my hands stop shaking.

CHAPTER THIRTY-TWO

Molly

She checks her email every few hours, hoping that Meredith may have decided to respond, but eventually, after the continued silence, she understands that she has to give up. She goes back to take another look at the blog, hoping that there will be a new post that may give her a clue as to what Meredith is thinking, but when she clicks on the link, the blog is gone. She retypes its name, searches different words, goes back to the first place she found it but she finds nothing. Meredith has completely disappeared. She is gone.

Molly feels the warmth of fury spread through her. Meredith is hiding from her. Why is she doing that unless she knows something more? Did she lie about her little sister being dead?

Is Meredith related to her? Is this all her imagination? The questions come thick and fast, her hands trembling.

She searches for another few minutes but it's as though the blog never existed, and for a bizarre moment she thinks she may have imagined the whole thing. But she dismisses the thought quickly. Peter has read the blog and so has her mother. She is not going crazy.

Molly would like to close her computer and leave Meredith and her past life where it belongs, but something gnaws at her. Some truth is trying to crawl its way out of her brain and she knows, even as she goes to the kitchen to prepare her hungry body something to eat, that this will not be the end of her search.

CHAPTER THIRTY-THREE

Now

Margaret

'How are you feeling this afternoon, Margaret?' asks Anika cheerfully.

Margaret knows this is Anika because she sees her every day. Anika is… Anika is kind. She helps her get washed and dressed and brings her food but Margaret has no idea why she does this. Anika is kind. She smiles at Anika. 'I'm… I'm…' but then the words disappear and she cannot say it. The words are stuck inside. Inside Margaret says, *I don't think I slept very well. I've been watching the garden but there's no one working in it today. I keep thinking about Lilly and Alice but I don't know who Lilly and Alice are.* But outside Margaret cannot make the words release themselves.

'I'll bring in your tray for lunch, unless you want a nap before you eat?'

Margaret realises she is very tired. 'Yes,' she says, 'a nap.' The word feels strange in her mouth. Anika helps her onto the bed and tucks a blanket around her legs before leaving. Margaret has just begun to drift off to sleep when a man comes in.

She's sure he shouldn't be here. She would like to ask her mother why this is but she can't seem to find her. She must have just been here because Margaret just heard her say, 'Keep that door locked while I'm at work.' It was just moments ago.

But then she recognises him and smiles. 'Hello,' she says. She likes to see him.

'Missed me, have you, Maggie?' he asks.

Margaret nods because she has missed this man. She loved this man… she thinks.

She tries to sit up but suddenly there is something heavy on her chest, pushing down, holding her to the bed. She looks at the man. He is smiling and she opens her mouth to tell him about how heavy it is on her chest. But the words won't come out and he keeps smiling and smiling as she opens and closes her mouth, struggling to get the words out.

She tries to take a deep breath but her lungs won't inflate. She cannot get any air into her body. 'Oh,' she pants and then she feels her bladder go, the bed suddenly wet, her legs sticky. The pain in her chest is enormous. There is a rock on top of her, a mountain sitting on her chest, and she cannot move or breathe for the pain. Her heart begins to speed up. It goes faster and then faster and then faster again and then it just… stops.

Margaret looks around her as the world is blanketed in silence. She sees Adam standing next to her.

'Hey, Maggie, I've been waiting for you,' he says.

'Oh, Adam.' The words come rushing out of her mouth. 'I've missed you so much. Where've you been all this time?'

'I've been here, Maggie. Right here, my love, right here waiting for you.'

CHAPTER THIRTY-FOUR

Alice

I don't tell Jack about the blanket or the frog. I don't mention the emails again. I decide that I will confront my mother first. I don't want him to question me about this. I don't want to hear that my mother isn't capable of harassing me. Because I think she is. I think she's more lucid than she lets on. It must be her sending the emails and probably the messages on the blog as well. No one else would have had the blanket and the frog. She must have hidden them from me and now that she is nearing the end of her life, she is tormenting me this one last time. Perhaps she blames me for everything. I know she blames me for Lilly but perhaps she is angry about my very existence.

I am putting on a load of washing before I leave when Anika phones me. I'm immediately anxious when I see that the call is coming from the Green Gate Home. I have never received a call from them. They usually email me with any changes to my mother's medication and my bill for each month.

'Hello?' I answer.

'Alice, it's Anika from the Green Gate.'

I can't manage more than, 'Yes.' My mouth feels dry and sticky.

'Alice, I'm so very sorry to tell you that your mother has passed away.' I hear her voice catch as though she is trying to prevent herself from crying. She liked and maybe even loved my mother.

Over the last few years, she has been by my mother's side far more than her own daughter.

My mouth opens and closes as my brain tries to catch up with what I've just heard until eventually I'm able to ask, 'When?'

'I think it was sometime in the last hour. She told me that she wanted to nap before lunch and so I left her to sleep, but when I brought her a tray, I couldn't wake her. I'm so terribly sorry.'

'But… but what happened?'

'I think she passed away in her sleep. Her health was, as you know, very poor. I wanted to tell you myself. A doctor will be here shortly to sign the death certificate and try to determine what happened, but I'm fairly certain it would have been her heart.'

'But she was fine. I saw her yesterday, she was fine, she even went outside.'

'Alice, I'm so sorry. I understand how difficult this must be for you, and I'm so terribly sorry there wasn't any warning. It's not unusual for our residents to rally a little in the days before they pass on. I did attempt CPR while we called an ambulance but I'm afraid it was too late.'

'Too late,' I echo her words. It was too late, too late for everything. I never got to say the things I wanted to say to her, never got to hear the apology I have been chasing all my life. It was too late.

'If you'd like to come over and have some time with her, that would be fine,' she says.

'Yes,' I answer, 'yes, I'm coming.' I hang up the phone. My hands are trembling as I end the call. I take a deep breath, feel acid rise in my throat. I feel cheated. I was going to confront her about the emails and now I can't. I feel cheated and angry and filled with despair – a whirl of emotions, because I am not sure how a daughter should feel when her mother dies, but I am sure it's not like this.

I know I should text Jack and let him know but I don't think I have it in me to have a conversation with anyone right now. I need to be alone with this news, alone with her.

In the car, as I pull out of my garage, I have a vision of her before my father died. I am lying next to her on their bed and she is stroking my arm as she sings. It's an unexpected memory, something I haven't thought of for years, and I try to conjure up the words of the song as the sensations of that moment wash over me. It must have been summer because the bedroom was warm although not too hot, and I remember the sweet, flowery smell of her perfume, of her. It was the scent she had before she started drinking, and it was the scent of safety, security and love. I take a deep breath, trying to hold onto the memory of it, and sitting in traffic, I am suddenly howling for my lost mother. My mother is gone. I sob as I drive, wiping at my face, as an overwhelming sadness lodges itself inside me. My mother is dead.

I am an orphan. A real orphan, although in reality I have probably been an orphan since I was six years old and my father died, taking the best parts of my mother with him.

Anika offers me a silent hug when I arrive, tear-stained, at the home.

I follow her slowly down the passage to my mother's room. I stop just before I get there and lean on the wall, feeling dizzy. I'm not sure I can do this. I'm not sure how to do this.

Anika doesn't say anything. She touches my elbow lightly to encourage me to continue.

After a moment I stand up straight, push my shoulders back. I have to do this.

My mother is lying on the bed, her hands crossed over her chest. Her skin has retained its slightly olive tinge, a result of her failing liver. I had assumed that she would look relaxed, finally released from her pain and the confusion she was living with, but even in death she looks slightly perplexed as though she has no idea what's happened to her. I question again how severe her Alzheimer's was and then realise that there is no point in that. She is gone.

'I'll leave you alone,' Anika says.

I sit on a chair next to my mother's bed and place my hand over hers, feeling her paper-thin skin. It's dry. I should have bought her some special hand cream to help with that. I should have sat at her bedside and massaged it into her skin, giving her the small pleasure of some physical contact, which she has been denied for so many years. She looks so small and thin, so vulnerable, so powerless. She always seemed powerless and yet she managed to ruin my life, and she was on her way to ruining Lilly's. I brush my hand across her sparse grey hair. As a child I thought her beautiful. It's been a long time since anyone thought her beautiful, I imagine. I feel tears begin to fall again at the thought of how she wasted her life, at how she drank away or slept away all the years she had until she couldn't remember what she was running away from.

After half an hour I sigh and stand up. I will need to pack up her things, I'm sure. I open her bedside table drawer and stare down at the few things she owned. A pair of glasses and her engagement and wedding rings sit next to a packet of sweets I brought her months ago. A brush and mirror with carved timber backs are wedged next to a plastic packet filled with key rings and bookmarks. The grandfather I never met gave them to her, she told me all those years ago when I was little, telling me that we would visit all the places her father visited one day. Decades later, when I moved her out of her house and into this room, I found them all in a rotting shoebox, tattered and covered with bits of glitter.

There are no photos, no cards or drawings from grandchildren, like there should be. She never even knew she had grandchildren.

I pick up the rings from the drawer and slide them onto her finger. They kept slipping off because she's lost so much weight in the last few months. I look at the thin gold bands, put on with such hope, on her birdlike hand, wondering if I should take them for myself, but I decide against that.

I don't know if I want anything from her, and that makes me sadder than anything else.

It's then that I notice the music that is playing softly in the room. I glance at her computer, where it's coming from. A kind gesture from Anika.

I go up to it and tap a button, illuminating the screen. The aquarium video is playing, the same turtle swimming lazily through a deep blue sea across the screen, but another tab is also open and I click on it. It's a composed email, not yet sent.

I know what you did.

I flush, sweat beading my body, my stomach churning. I can't believe this, it's not possible. Dead women don't write emails. I hit send on the email, and a moment later my phone pings to let me know it's there.

A knock on the door startles me and I hurriedly close the screen, making sure the tabs stay open.

It's Anika with Dr Townsend behind her. 'I'm so sorry for your loss,' he says, his young face solemn with responsibility.

'Thank you,' I reply. I stay where I am so he can conduct an examination of my mother, but the room is small and I keep having to step aside for him.

'If you'd like to leave for a few minutes,' Anika says, 'I can make you some tea.'

Wordlessly I follow her out of the room. It's cold in the corridor and Anika hurries to close a door that leads outside.

She sits me down in the visitors' lounge and brings me a cup of tea from an urn they have on the boil all day long.

'Are you okay?' she asks.

I nod. 'Can you tell me…?' I begin and then I bite down on my lip.

Anika nods.

'Did my mother ever use the computer?'

'Not that I ever saw, no.'

'Because it looks like someone has an email account open on it. I saw it just now.'

'Perhaps that's from before? It's a very old machine. How long has she had it?'

'Years, but…' I trail off. The explanation would take too long; where would I even begin? I will take the computer with me and show it to Jack.

I have no idea what to think anymore as thoughts tumble and whirl through my mind. Why would she have sent them to me? How was she even capable of doing it?

'Maybe ask Ed to take a look,' says Anika.

'Ed?'

'The young man who works in the garden. He fixes all our residents' computers. He's studying computer science at university.'

'Ed,' I repeat. Ed, who my mother thought was Vernon. Why on earth would he be using her computer to send me emails?

The doctor comes to find us in the visitors' lounge. 'A huge heart attack from what I can see,' he says. 'We can do an autopsy if you'd like but her health was very poor. There's bruising on her chest, most likely from Anika's attempt at CPR.'

I think about her heart finally breaking under the strain of a terrible lifestyle and endless poor choices, breaking under the strain of too much tragedy and despair. Her poor broken heart.

Anika nods, her cheeks flaming. 'I didn't want to hurt her, but I had to try.'

'I've signed the certificate and you can organise with your funeral home of choice to come and pick her up now, unless there's anything else?' the doctor asks.

'No,' I reply, my voice thick with emotion. 'Thank you. I'll make some calls after I fetch the boys from school and get everything organised.'

'We can do most of it for you, if you're happy to use Sutton's funeral home,' Anika says.

'Thanks, I am.' I smile gratefully at Anika.

I make my way back to my mother's room and head straight for the computer. When I open it up, the aquarium video has changed to one of puppies playing around in a garden. The Gmail tab has disappeared, even though I left it right here.

I look around the room, at my mother who hasn't moved, and I wonder if I'm going mad. I feel like I'm going mad. Has someone been in here? Was whoever it is going to send me the email? Were they interrupted by me coming into the room? I think about Anika, who had the most contact with and the absolute trust of my mother. Has my mother told Anika about Lilly? Is Anika involved in some way?

I look at my phone, see the email there, confirming what I know. I go to the window and look out but there is no one in the garden.

Grabbing my mother's laptop, I make my way back to my car, looking behind me as I walk, turning back at every step.

Someone is watching me, I'm sure. I can feel someone's eyes on me.

In the car I lock the doors, rest my head on the steering wheel.

I wish, just for a second, that I didn't have a husband and children, that I could simply pack my bags and leave, just pack my bags and run. But the moment I have this thought, I dismiss it. I am not her. I will not run from my life. I will not drown out my life.

I am not her.

CHAPTER THIRTY-FIVE

Molly

'I don't understand,' says Peter, 'why would she have deleted the blog? She told you her sister died.'

They are sitting in their favourite Chinese restaurant, sharing an entrée of spring rolls.

Molly takes the last one, finishing it in two bites, and Peter laughs. 'I only got one of those, you know.'

'Oh, sorry, I didn't even think. I'm just so hungry these days.'

Peter smiles. 'I like watching you eat; I love it in fact. You're getting that glow.'

Molly looks down at her lap, folding and twisting her hands in her white napkin. 'Don't say that, please, not yet.'

His face falls. 'Okay… but when will it be safe to say it? When do we get to enjoy this?'

Molly looks up at him, feels her eyes filling with unwanted tears. 'I don't know. I wish I did know but I'm just so scared to hope even a little bit.'

Peter leans across the table and wipes a tear off her cheek. 'Don't be scared. Don't be scared because no matter what happens, we're in this together. Now,' he sits back and picks up the menu again, 'I know we've already ordered but since you ate my spring rolls, I think I deserve some prawn toast.' Molly laughs but her laugh feels empty, fake.

'So, why do you think she deleted the blog?' he asks.

'The only possible explanation is that she was lying. She couldn't deny it when I told her that I remembered some things. She had to disappear.'

'Or she thinks you're a crazy woman who's stalking her,' says Peter gently.

'Maybe, but then why not just reiterate that her sister died and ask me not to contact her again? Why vanish altogether?'

'She asked you once not to contact her and you did anyway. It could be that she thinks you're an internet troll or something.'

'So you think this is my fault?' Molly hears the high pitch of her voice, recognises the roiling anger that seems to assault her these days.

'I really didn't say that, not at all.'

The waiter drifts past their table and Peter stops him and asks for the prawn toast before he wafts away again. There is only one other table of diners in the restaurant, and the waiter, who is usually run off his feet, looks bored. Outside, the rain pelts down. They almost decided against going out but Molly is finding her long, lonely hours in the apartment stifling. A dinner out seemed a good way to get away from her circular thoughts.

Molly feels slightly sick, unsure if it's pregnancy nausea or because she's eaten too many spring rolls or because she is devastated at having lost Meredith's blog, her one link to what she believes is her family.

She sits back in her chair, rests her head and closes her eyes.

'Moll, it's only one night until the scan. Perhaps we should leave this for a bit until we know what's what, and then if everything is good, we can talk about what to do. You've got enough on your plate.'

'But what is there to do, Pete? I don't know her name, I don't know anything about her. She's just some random person on the internet. I will never find her again.'

'Except nothing on the internet is ever lost. If you can wait a few days, I can talk to Will at the office. I think he might be able to find the IP address and that could lead you to the person who set up the blog. Everyone needs to use email and nothing can really be hidden; even the smallest detail can help you find out who a person is.'

Their waiter arrives just then with the prawn toast and their main courses. Molly is hungry once more with the kind of insatiable hunger that only pregnancy brings, but she's almost too excited to eat.

'Oh my gosh,' she says, eyes widening. 'So, you think Will could really do that?'

'I do, yeah. He's a whizz at that kind of stuff.'

'So, let's say I find her email address after tracing her IP address. Then what?'

'I guess you have to see what the address is. Maybe he can find a phone number associated with the email and maybe even a physical address.'

Molly feels little flutters of excitement in her stomach. 'Can we really do it? You'll ask Will?'

'I'll ask him. He may not be comfortable because it's not exactly legal and it's basically stalking, but yes, after the scan, I'll ask him. I know how much this means to you.'

Molly stands up and walks over to Peter's chair. She leans down and gives him a quick kiss on the lips. 'You are the best husband a woman could have,' she says.

Peter laughs and touches her cheek. 'I'll do anything I can to help you put this behind you. I want you to be able to enjoy what's coming. I want us to move on and finally settle into the kind of life we've been longing for.'

Molly sits back down and takes a mouthful of noodles but doesn't reply. She doesn't want to tell Peter that she doesn't know if she can ever move on from this. She was abandoned by her mother and now she has been abandoned by the woman who is possibly her sister. There's no way of letting this go.

*

The next morning Molly wakes up with the rising sun. She lies in bed, listening to her husband's even breathing. In her sleep she placed her hand on her stomach, surrounding, protecting the little life inside. *Who will I be after today?* she wonders. The scan is at 10 a.m. and afterwards she could be a joyful expectant mother or a woman devastated by yet another failed pregnancy. One of those possibilities is almost inconceivable and the other feels like the alarming truth.

She has never experienced anything beyond the very beginning signs of a pregnancy. She would like to see it as a sign that this time she will be allowed the happy ending she sees around her every day. This time it will be her turn. But she's sceptical. Why would it have worked this time?

She turns over in bed. She would like to go for a run. She would like to run until her body is exhausted and her mind is empty of anything except the pain in her lungs and muscles. She sees her mother – her biological mother – a faceless woman who never wanted her, who probably never wanted children at all. Did she count down the days of her pregnancy? Or did she simply ignore the whole process and hope it would just go away?

'What are you thinking?' asks Peter, interrupting her thoughts.

'Nothing,' says Molly, because she cannot lay her fears bare over and over again, she cannot suck him into the whirlwind of her emotions when she needs him to be her strength. There is little, truly, he could say to comfort her.

They eat breakfast in silence, Molly forcing herself to chew a piece of toast. She sips at a bottle of water continuously, knowing that her bladder needs to be full for the scan. It is eight o'clock and then it's eight fifteen and then it's eight twenty-five and Molly feels like she may be going crazy. She can't read or watch television or concentrate long enough to even unload the dishwasher.

'Why don't you give Lexie a call?'

'I don't think I can speak to anyone until it's over. Maybe we should just go to the hospital and wait there? Being there will help, I think.'

In the car they crawl along with the other commuters. Molly knows they could have left later and avoided the morning rush, but somehow just being on the road feels better, as though they are at least moving forward. That's what she wants most out of today: permission to move forward with her life.

By the time they are seated in the waiting room for an ultrasound, Molly's bladder is uncomfortably full. She and Peter page through old magazines, filled with pictures of mothers and babies, smiling out from every page.

Molly looks around the room at the other couples. One woman has a prominent belly and looks to be only weeks away from giving birth. She is scrolling through her phone, ignoring the toddler by her feet, who is singing to himself. Another couple holds hands, occasionally turning to smile at each other with secret joy. Molly remembers looking at Peter like that in the first few weeks of her first pregnancy. They thought they had found the key to pure happiness, and Molly couldn't believe that anyone in the world could be as ecstatic as she was right at that time. And then the first miscarriage happened. This is the first time she has had a scan that wasn't simply to confirm a miscarriage.

'Molly Khan?' says a young woman dressed in pink scrubs. Molly and Peter stand.

'This way,' she says, gesturing. Molly follows her, finding her heavy scent of perfume nauseating. 'I'm Michelle and I'll be doing your ultrasound today,' she says as Molly lies down on the bed. Michelle beams at them both, probably used to excited couples waiting for their first glimpse of their baby. When she receives nothing back, her face falls a little and her blue eyes cloud.

'We're a bit worried,' explains Peter.

'Oh, don't be worried, it's a very standard test and I'm sure it will all be fine.'

'I've had six miscarriages,' replies Molly bluntly, unable to hide her nerves.

Michelle nods. 'Well then, let's see what's going on.' She is subdued now as she spreads the clear gel on Molly's stomach. She moves the wand back and forth and Molly waits for her to tell them about the heartbeat, to say anything at all, but Michelle is silent.

Molly feels the cold air against her skin, feels the warning tightness of a headache, her throat swelling with anguish. It's happening again. It can't be happening again.

'Molly, can you do me a favour?' asks Michelle, and Molly can do nothing but nod. 'Can you go to the bathroom and empty your bladder a little? It's making it difficult to see because it's slightly too full. Just try to get rid of about a cupful for me.'

Molly gets up off the bed, wondering how on earth you measure a cupful. She risks a glance at Peter and then quickly looks away when she notices a shine in his eyes.

In the bathroom, she takes a deep, laboured breath and tries to calculate the right amount. 'Okay,' she says quietly to herself. 'You know how this goes. It's over. Get it done and then you can leave, and later you can have a drink or scream or cry or run until you want to pass out. Just get through the next few minutes.'

Back on the bed, Molly grips Peter's hand. Michelle slathers the gel once more and the wand begins to move across Molly's stomach. She is silent for a minute and then two minutes. Molly feels the truth of a broken dream lodge itself in her heart.

'There you go,' says Michelle.

'There you go what?' asks Peter.

'There's your baby, see here?' She turns the screen to face them. 'Sorry, sometimes the little things hide, but there it is, see that heartbeat? It's really strong. He or she is waving at you, hi, Mum, hi, Dad.'

Molly and Peter watch the image on the screen, the tiny hands, the moving feet, the fluttering beat of a heart, and Molly can no longer hold in her anguished relief. 'Oh God,' she sobs, squeezing Peter's hands, 'oh God, oh God, oh God.'

'Shush, shush, it's okay, love. It's all okay,' he comforts, stroking her head.

Molly doesn't hear Michelle explaining about the measurements she's taking; she doesn't do anything except stare at the moving image of her child, of their child, wonder in her heart.

'Okay, all done,' says Michelle finally. 'Do you want to wait for the results or shall we send them to your doctor?'

'We'll wait,' says Peter, 'we'll definitely wait.'

An hour later, Molly practically skips back to the car, clutching the ultrasound pictures and the report that details a healthy growing baby.

'Now can you call your mum?' says Peter as he reverses out of a parking space, but Molly is already dialling Lexie, who cheers with excitement when she hears the news.

She calls her mother next, who bursts into tears. 'I knew this was the one, Molly, I just knew it.'

'We need a big celebratory lunch,' declares Peter. 'I feel like Italian. What about you? I know you can't resist a good garlic bread.'

'I feel like I'm going to be a mum.' Molly laughs, and it is only after lunch, after too much bread and pasta and the tiniest sip of Peter's white wine, when she lies down to rest, that a stray thought makes its way into her conscious mind. *Will my mother love this baby, this child who is not related to her at all, as much as she loves Sophie?*

She drapes her hand over her stomach. 'I will love you enough; your dad and I will love you more than enough,' she murmurs, and then she falls asleep.

CHAPTER THIRTY-SIX

Alice

I drop my flower into the open grave. I pull my coat tighter around me as the wind whistles through the cemetery. Grey clouds gather and merge as a storm threatens. The weather is terrible but perfect for a funeral, perfect for the deep well of sadness that has opened up inside me. I hadn't expected to feel sad. I had expected relief, I think. I imagined that I would be relieved that she was no longer in the world because if she was no longer in the world, then I would not be able to try and tell her, once again, what she had done to me. I would not feel that I needed or wanted anything from her. I would not have to constantly work at forgiving her. If she was no longer in the world, then it was over and I needed to finally lay my past to rest and walk away from it. But I don't feel relieved at all. Instead all I feel is an overwhelming sadness about who she was at the end, about her confusion and her bewilderment at the world. I feel sad that she never got to know her grandchildren, that she never got to sit around our dinner table at Christmas and enjoy the company of my boys. And I am sad for the life she lived, for all that she suffered. The sadness is deep and dark and I would like to sink to my knees and weep, while Jack and the boys stand solemnly behind me.

Alice doesn't have a mother. Alice never had a mother.

It was a small funeral, quickly organised. Only Anika and Mary from the Green Gate had been able to leave the home to attend.

Natalia was here as well. I watched Anika through the ceremony, watched how she wiped her eyes and shed tears and I tried not to wonder about her. I tried to only be grateful that she had taken such good care of my mother, but I cannot forget that Anika was always in my mother's room and Anika is computer literate.

She and Mary left soon after the priest finished speaking, as the other residents needed to be taken care of. Natalia had to attend a meeting at school for her daughter and left soon after. I cannot remember my mother ever having any friends, even when my father was still alive, so very soon it was just me and my family at a cold gravesite under a grey sky.

Gus and Gabe had been given a lecture by their father all the way to the church about 'appropriate funeral behaviour'.

Now I can see that Isaac has a firm hand on each boy's shoulder, making sure that the boredom of a funeral for someone they never met doesn't lead to poor behaviour.

The priest described her as a loving mother and a loyal wife. I didn't know what else to tell him, what else to say. I didn't say loving and I didn't say loyal. He added those words. I didn't know her, not the person she really was behind the alcohol and the depression. And the good memories I have of her are not concrete so I'm never certain if I made them up or if they actually happened. How awful it is that I have only vague memories of her not drunk, not sleeping, not mired in depression.

As we turn to go, I let my eyes sweep across the cemetery. There are people dotted here and there, visiting graves, replacing flowers and cleaning headstones. I wonder if I will ever come back, but in all honesty, I don't think so. I start therapy next week and I need to find a way to live in my present, to finally put the past behind me.

I told Jack about the latest email and the messages from the woman on my blog and he agreed that I was right to delete everything.

'You should have told me about the messages. I would have linked them to the emails,' he said. 'Whoever was doing it might be some sort of lunatic. Perhaps the blog wasn't a good idea. I mean, you never know how damaged the people are that you're connecting with.'

'I think it was my mother... I think it was her sending the messages, and on the blog,' I told him.

'I'm not sure that's possible... I don't think it could be possible,' he said, as I knew he would.

'Maybe she had help.'

'From who?'

I shrugged my shoulders then.

'Isaac is looking at the emails, and with a bit of luck he'll be able to figure out who was sending them. If he finds something concrete, then we can take it to the police.'

'And what about the young gardener? The one she kept calling Vernon.'

'But what would he have against you? You've only spoken to him once, maybe twice. Perhaps you should talk to Anika about him, get the full story.'

I agreed I will talk to Anika in a few days. Then I can ask her about the frog and the blanket.

I am going to tell Jack about the blanket and the frog. I will need to tell him everything, to explain what really happened to Lilly and my part in it. He's here today but he is caring for two dying patients at the moment, and more often than not, he doesn't come home until very late. I will tell him, just not yet.

It is quite possible that my mother has had the frog and the blanket all along, and that she encouraged Anika to send them to me or that Anika took it upon herself to do so. Who knows what they talked about in all the hours they spent together? I cannot imagine what Anika would have against me although she may have been angered by what she regards as my poor treatment of my mother. She doesn't know the whole story, so how could she ever understand?

I hope this is all over now. Just over.

Thankfully, there have been no more emails since my mother died.

I look down at her grave again. Despite everything, despite believing that she is behind all of this, I can't quite believe she's gone. I wipe away my silent tears, making sure not to turn around, not wanting to distress the boys. *My mother is dead*, I test out in my head but the words don't seem real.

'I'm sorry, Mum,' I whisper. 'I'm sorry you had such a hard life. I think you would have loved me if you could have.' As I utter the words, I realise that I believe them. She wasn't capable. That's the stark truth. She just wasn't capable. 'I… I forgive you,' I say quietly. 'I forgive you,' I repeat with a little more force.

'What did Mum say?' I hear Gabe ask.

'I'm cold,' says Gus.

He's right. It's freezing. The clouds above merge and there is only grey as rain begins to fall. 'I'm ready to go now,' I reply. Something inside me feels lighter.

Turning away from the grave, I follow my family back to the car. Taking one last look around the cemetery, I spot a man standing behind a tree, a red cap on his head. But when I look back a second later, there's no one there.

I shake my head. 'Enough of this,' I whisper to myself. 'Enough.'

CHAPTER THIRTY-SEVEN

Molly

Molly gets home and throws her shopping on the bed, easing off her shoes, which have grown tight over the hours she and her mother and sister have walked. Her phone rings and she smiles when she sees it's Peter.

'I just bought some leggings and tops so I don't have to worry about tight jeans anymore. I hope you're prepared for a fat wife,' she says, laughing into the phone.

'I am… You'll be beautiful.'

'Are you okay? You sound weird.'

'Yeah… it's just, Will found the woman from the blog using your computer history. He found her and her real name and her address, everything. It only took him half an hour.'

Molly sits up straight on the bed. Goosebumps tsunami over her arms. 'Where is she? Who is she?' The questions burst out of her.

He takes a deep breath. 'Her name is Alice Stetson and she lives in Greenwich.'

'Greenwich… Where, in England?'

'As in Greenwich, the suburb next to ours.'

'I don't understand,' says Molly because she cannot comprehend what he has just told her.

'She lives in the suburb next to ours, Molly, Will confirmed it. He says she's definitely the woman who wrote the blog.'

Molly squeezes her fingernails into her palm. 'So close,' she whispers. Her mother was right. Meredith or Alice is Australian and she has been here all along. The irony of it is cruel.

'Yeah. She may not be your sister, you understand that, right? It may just be a huge coincidence. She may not want to talk to you even if she is, and we'll have to respect that. I know how hard that will be but we'll have no choice.'

'I know,' says Molly. She releases her fingers, marvelling at the perfect crescents on her palm. She runs a finger over them, enjoying the sting.

'Can you text me the address? I just want to look it up on Google.'

'Okay…' He hesitates. 'I'm sending it through now but please don't do anything until I'm home later. You should wait for me. We'll figure out what to do together.'

'Of course,' says Molly lightly, knowing that she is lying. 'I'll see you at dinner – do you feel like a curry?'

'Yes, yes good, I'll see you at dinner.'

She holds her phone as she waits for the text to come through. The woman she thinks might be her sister lives in the suburb next door. They have probably stood behind each other in line at one of the local coffee shops. Molly could have smiled at her in the supermarket as they both reached for the same kind of juice. She could have hooted at her if she swung out of a parking spot too quickly. They could have been in the same doctor's office, Molly with a cold and her sister – yes, the words feel right: her sister – Alice with a sick child. Does she have children? Did she also suffer from miscarriages? They could have both gone out to dinner with their husbands and sat at tables next to each other and neither had any idea. Her sister has been right here all along and she's never had any idea. But if she is her sister, if she really is her sister and they have seen each other… why didn't they recognise each other? Surely, she should have known her if she saw her?

And why would Alice lie about her sister being dead? What kind of a person does such a thing?

Her phone pings, and she opens the message. She gets up off the bed and goes to her iPad, where she looks up the street. So close, so very close. She slides her shoes back onto her feet.

She needs to know for sure; one way or the other she needs to know for sure.

There's no way Peter actually believed she would wait for him. No way at all.

CHAPTER THIRTY-EIGHT
Alice

I sit in my kitchen, staring into space. In front of me is a cup of coffee in a bright blue mug, decorated with sunflowers. The mug was a gift from the twins last Mother's Day. They had demanded Jack take them to the shops and they had wandered around with serious expressions on their faces, clutching five dollars each as they searched for the perfect gift. The large blue mug was an obvious choice to both of them. 'Because you like a lot of coffee and this is really big,' said Gus.

'And because you like flowers and this is pretty like you,' explained Gabe. I found it difficult to conceal my tears. I'm still amazed after all these years to be the recipient of such an enormous amount of love and devotion. I don't think I thought it possible when I was a broken ten-year-old just trying to survive each brutal day of my life.

I hear a ping on my phone indicating an email has arrived. My heart races as I look down and then I remind myself that I have had no new emails since my mother died. It will be from school about the bake sale – emails have been coming in over the last few days from the other mothers letting me know what they'll make. I glance down at my phone and open the email without looking at who it's from.

It's not from a mother at school. It is not from someone wanting to bring in something sweet to sell. It's another email from him. From her? Another one.

I know where you live. I know where you live with your sons and your husband.

I feel my hands get clammy and my top lip beads with sweat. How can there be another email?

My mother's computer is here in my home and my mother is gone and yet another email has arrived. A clear, threatening message from someone who knows more about my life than they should.

Whoever this is, is serious. It would have been easy enough to find me on Facebook. Alice Stetson née Henkel is listed as my name, and my profile picture is one of the three boys. My account is set to private but any half-decent hacker could get in and find all the information they needed. I think I may have even been stupid enough to add my address or telephone number as the site kept asking me to do. I log onto my Facebook and delete my account. I wish I was more tech savvy so I could wipe the internet of any information about me. I shake my head, once more regretting the blog and my desire to tell my story. I should have just kept quiet.

It's time to get the police involved.

But police ask questions. They investigate things and they will look into my history. They may even ask me about Lilly and I will have to tell them the truth. *But it's time to tell the truth now*, a voice in my head whispers. I've been running away from what I did for too long.

I need to protect my children now, that's all that matters. Whatever happens to me, happens.

The sound of the door knocker makes me jump. I sit for a moment, trying to still my pounding heart, and the sound echoes through the house again. I cannot take another delivery from my past. I cannot take another reminder. I will not answer it. I will not. But the door knocker reverberates through the house again and again.

I stand up, testing my shaking legs. I will have to answer.

I look through the peephole but the man standing there has his head down. *It's probably a delivery*, I reason, squaring my shoulders and pulling open the door.

The young gardener from the Green Gate is standing on my front step.

I just stare at him for a moment and then he smiles at me. 'Hello, Alice,' he says.

'Hello,' I reply. I wait for him to say something else. I have no idea what he's doing here. I start to say something but then realise I don't know what to say. He must be here to pay his respects. I wonder why he didn't come to the funeral.

'I'm sorry about your mother,' he says slowly.

'Thank you.' I nod.

'Can I come in?' he asks. It's a simple enough request but when he smiles again, my instinct prickles. There is something about the way he is looking at me. I find myself angry at Anika or whoever has provided him with my address. Surely that's not allowed?

'I'm actually quite busy at the moment,' I reply. 'But thanks for coming. I know my mother liked you.'

'Yeah,' he says. He looks behind him. 'She's here,' he calls. Then he looks back at me.

'Thank you again, but…' I begin but he turns and walks away, almost running down the front path to get to the gate and the street, and then, from the side of the door, someone else fills my vision.

It's the older man, the other gardener. He is wearing his cap but as I look at him, he pulls it off his head and I see his drawn, wrinkled face. Large brown liver spots cover his hands and cheeks. His grey beard is bedraggled and his hair is sparse on top. His eyes are sunken into his skull. I have no idea why Ed ran off but as I look into the man's eyes something inside me shudders and my skin prickles all over. I am suddenly afraid, very afraid. I need to slam the door. I start to push against it with everything I have but he sticks his foot in the gap. I hear him shout, 'Ouch, you bitch!' Then he pushes the door open, forcing me backwards.

He smiles at me and it is only then that I recognise the vastly changed man before me. The monster who physically and sexually and emotionally abused me for years. His yellow teeth, his stench, are imprinted on my brain. As he steps closer, I inhale the thick smell of a committed cigarette smoker as well as the dark, sweaty scent of beer.

Vernon.

'Look a bit different, don't I? Liver cancer. I didn't deserve it after all I've been through but there you go. We don't always get what we deserve, but today, today you're going to be one of the lucky ones because you... you, Alice, are getting exactly what you deserve.'

CHAPTER THIRTY-NINE
Molly

Molly programs the address into her GPS with shaking hands.

'She may not be your sister,' she says to herself. 'This may all just be a coincidence of timing and your own imagination.'

The afternoon sun glares through her windscreen, making her squint as she drives. She slips her sunglasses onto her face but they do little to help. Her GPS tells her she will be at the house in ten minutes. The school traffic has yet to begin and the afternoon rush hour hasn't started yet, giving Molly a clear run.

She glances at the houses she passes. Greenwich is a more established and expensive suburb than where she lives. Liquidambar trees standing naked in the winter wind line the wide streets.

Molly parks outside the house on the nearly empty road. All of the homes have double or even triple garages so Molly assumes that everyone is either at work or parked snugly inside.

She has never been envious of those with more money, of people with large mansions and fancy cars, because she has never thought those things would make her happy. She knows that when Peter becomes a partner at his firm, they will be well off, more well off than she's ever experienced, but she has never really cared whether that does or doesn't happen.

Now, looking at the gabled two- and three-storey houses in the well-kept street, she feels a touch of longing for a home that's so beautiful, so large and inviting. She imagines that the back gardens hold sparkling pools and tennis courts, wonders what life is like for the people who live in these homes.

'So, what now, baby?' she says, stroking her stomach. She feels a fluttering inside her and smiles. It's too early for her to feel any kicking, she knows, and what she feels are nerves and anxiety, but the fluttering makes her feel as though the baby understands where they are and what she's about to do.

She climbs out of the car, her heart rate accelerating. Meredith, or Alice, she corrects herself, could be out or she could have recently moved. If she's home, she could have a sophisticated security system and refuse to answer the door, or she could answer and when Molly explains, she could slam the door in her face and call the police.

Or she could not be her sister at all. She could feel sorry for Molly and her ridiculous quest to find the family who never wanted her, and she could prove to Molly that her little sister is dead and send her away with no more answers. Molly would have to admit then that she will never find the truth about her past. The road comes back to her, the road she travelled alone. Even though she is surrounded by people who love her, she knows that there will always be that well of loneliness inside her if she cannot find out who she is and where she came from.

'Go to sleep, little one,' Molly hears as she stands on the pavement, taking deep breaths. The words her sister said. Are these the words of a memory or the words of her imagination?

Molly stands at the arched front gate for a moment before giving it a push. It's not locked, sliding open. The house has a steeply angled roof and small windows at the top. Molly imagines an attic room where she could sit and drink tea and stare out into the street, watching the seasons change.

A neatly tended garden path made from large stepping stones leads to the front door and Molly smiles, despite her nerves. Large evergreen trees block most of the house from the street, protecting those inside from being seen.

It's a lovely home, old but charming, and she feels a moment of happiness for Meredith or Alice, that after the terrible childhood she endured she has found herself in a happy marriage, perhaps with children, and a home straight out of a fairy tale. She hopes that Alice is happy now, that she has managed to leave behind the horrors of her past, and then she feels momentarily guilty at what she is about to do. Perhaps this will be too much. If she is her sister, what terrible memories will she be bringing with her? What will she force this woman to relive, and how can she do that to someone when she has been asked not to?

But it is too late to turn back. She takes slow steps up the stone path, admiring the rich red of begonias clashing with bright purple sage.

At the door she stares at the large round iron ring for a moment. It could be a door knocker or it could simply be for decoration. She searches the walls either side of the door but finds nothing.

Taking a deep breath, she lifts the iron ring, liking its solid weight. She lets it fall once before repeating the action. Then she stands and waits.

CHAPTER FORTY

Alice

I step back, further away from him. He is unrecognisable as the man who hurt me. A third of his size, his body eaten away by the cancer that looks only days away from killing him. He looks ancient but I know he can only be in his late sixties.

'You're… you're…' I stutter, 'you're in prison.'

'Was.' He smiles. 'But they let you out when you're dying. Ed was good enough to say I could come and stay with him. His mother, my bitch sister, hated me, told all sorts of lies about me, but Ed and I get along all right and she's dead now – went nuts just like Maggie. Ed was the only one who wrote to me in prison. He told me he'd found Maggie at the same home his mother was at – imagine that? I never thought I'd get to do anything about that but then… along came cancer. I've waited for this a long time, Alice. A really long time.'

I step back further, terror clawing at my skin. My phone is in the kitchen. I need to get to the kitchen. How quickly could I get there? I take another small step backwards and he takes one towards me.

'There's only one thing I need to get right with before I die; well, there was more than one but Maggie's gone now, isn't she. Didn't take much.'

I hear what he is saying but cannot quite comprehend it. What did he do to my mother?

'They were so excited that Ed – lovely Ed – brought his uncle in to help with the garden. They don't ask volunteers about their history. Free is free, right?'

My stomach turns and my knees sag a little. I feel so stupid for not recognising him. How could I have missed him? He has stalked my nightmares for years. But back then he was a big man, a giant scary man with a belly that hung grotesquely over his belt, with a pink shiny face from all the alcohol abuse. I could never have imagined he would turn into this.

'You look more like your mother now, skinny and dry, but that's fine. I don't want to touch you. You're not my type. I prefer a fresher face, a smoother body. You liked it when I touched you, didn't you, Alice? Oh, you pretended you didn't, but I know you did. You wanted it. Had a bit of fight in you too. I like a woman with fight.' His dull blue eyes are bright for a moment and he licks his dry lips.

'I wasn't a woman,' I croak.

'You were woman enough.' He smiles and I feel sick to my stomach.

'You need to leave,' I say, my trembling voice suddenly high and squeaky. I move slowly backwards again, heading for my kitchen. He doesn't look very strong, this Vernon, but I am still beyond terrified of him. I know what he is capable of. Images of him above me, of his hands all over me, of his fists battering at me, his feet kicking out at me assault me, flashing rapidly through my brain. I'm going to be sick. I gasp desperately, unable to get enough air into my lungs.

'I have this here, see,' says Vernon, and he pulls a large knife out of the back of his trousers.

'You… you… you have to go,' I try desperately as I shiver at the sight of the knife. He wants to hurt me, to really hurt me, to even kill me.

'Nice place,' he says, looking around the living room as I continue taking small steps backwards, and he follows, stepping forward.

'What do you want? Why are you here?'

'I want you to say sorry for what you did, to be sorry for what you did. You took my Lilly away from me. She was beautiful, my Lilly. Her skin was so soft, and her face was so pretty, and she's gone because of you.'

I am nearly in the kitchen and I risk a quick look behind me, spotting my phone in its dark red case on the kitchen table. Would I even have time to get the words out to the police before he catches me? How fast can I move?

I think the door from the kitchen that leads to the terrace is unlocked after I went out there to refill the bird feeder. Did I lock it? I don't think I locked it. If I can grab my phone and get out the door, I can run across the garden and jump over the back fence. Mrs Chan is always home. How fast can I run? How fast can he run?

'What happened to Lilly wasn't my fault,' I say, knowing that I need to keep him talking as I mentally plan the moves I need to make.

'Course it was your fault. You were supposed to be taking care of her. You knew your useless mother wasn't doing it. I just want to know how you did it. Where did she go? Where did you take her? You said she was dead. How did you know she was dead? What did you do to my Lilly?'

'I never meant… I never meant,' I stutter.

'Yes, you did!' he roars, waving the knife, and spit lands on my cheek. I cannot help the shudder of revulsion that runs through my body.

'You were jealous of her because she was so soft and so sweet. You were jealous. Tell me! Tell me now how she died.'

'It was an accident… a car… a car accident.'

For a moment he looks like he's going to cry. 'A car accident? But why was she in a car? Why was she near a road? You were supposed to be watching her.'

'I…' but I can't say anything. What am I going to tell him? That I was the reason she was in the car? That she wasn't just on the road but in a stranger's car? I shake my head.

'It's your fault. You didn't keep her safe. You basically killed her. And now I'm going to kill you. I'll slice you up nice and neat, Alice, and then…' He looks at the photos on the wall in the living room, photos of my boys from the time they were babies that cover one whole wall. 'And then,' he says slowly, 'then I'm going to wait for your little boys and I'm going to kill each one of them, just like that.' He snaps his fingers. He starts laughing. Seconds later his laughter turns into a hacking cough and he doubles over, gasping and wheezing. I see my chance.

I dart into the kitchen and grab my phone. My hand is on the door handle when I feel him behind me. He grabs my hair, yanking me back hard, forcing me to lose my balance. I land on the floor with a thud and he holds the knife up to my neck.

'Don't try that again.' He spits right into my face and I feel bile rise up in my throat. 'Don't fucking try that again.'

'Please,' I whimper. I hate myself for how weak I sound. I'm not ten years old anymore. Logically I know that. He is old and he is debilitated by illness, I know that. But my body, my heart, the small child inside me who was sent flying across the room by his giant, nicotine-stained hand, cannot understand that.

'I was a good dad. I was good but your mother was a rotten mother and you were a shit sister. You should have kept her safe. But you didn't and now I have nothing and no one to leave behind. She could have grown up and gotten married, had kids… anything could have happened. I would have been a good grandfather. I know I would have. But I have nothing because of you. No one's going to care when I'm gone, Alice, and that's your fault. All I had left of her was that stupid stuffed frog and her blanket – can you imagine how that made me feel? You did that. I bet that was what you wanted all along.'

He wipes at his face with the hand not holding the knife and I realise he is shedding a few tears of self-pity. He is clearly absolutely mad, moving from laughter to tears in a moment, and I am certain that he does mean to kill me and then attack my family. He is dying and he is sorry for himself and cannot take any responsibility for what he did and the life he created. He is actually sorry for himself.

I think about my boys, about the minutes that are ticking away until pickup time. I won't be there for them. For the first time in their lives I won't be there. And then they will come home and find me. I cannot stop the tears from falling.

'Tell me you're sorry, Alice,' he says menacingly, tears disappearing into his disgusting beard. 'Tell me you made a mistake and you're sorry.' He waves the knife in front of me. 'Go on, just say the words and maybe I'll go. Maybe I'll forgive you and I'll just walk out of here and not see you again.' He moves back a little and he laughs, yellow teeth on display. I know that he is not going to walk away from me. He's dying. He has nothing left to lose. He's not going to leave me alive.

'Killing me won't bring her back,' I say softly, hoping a change in tone will help, hoping to appeal to the tiny shred of humanity he must possess.

He steps right up to me and touches the knife to the tip of my nose. 'Tell me you're sorry, Alice.'

Alice is afraid. Alice is terrified. Alice is going to die.

I know that when I utter the words, it will be over. I know that if I don't utter the words, it will be over. I could refuse to speak but something inside me, some part of me that has carried the guilt of her death for all these years, needs to apologise out loud to him, to my mother, to the world, to my long-gone sister. I'm going to die but, unlike my mother, I need to apologise for what I did before I do.

Alice is sorry. Alice is so, so sorry.

I close my eyes and take a deep, shuddering breath. There is nothing I can do now. Time has slowed down. I watch him move the knife back and forth in front of me, watch it catch the light and glint in the weak sun. And in that moment, I regret that I never told the boys I loved them this morning. I do it at night, before they go to bed, but I wish I had said it this morning as well.

'I'm—' I begin.

The sound of the door knocker fills the house, shocking both of us.

The words I was about to say disappear and my mind is suddenly racing.

This does not have to be over. This does not have to be it. If I can scream loud enough, whoever is at the door will hear me. If I can make a run for it and just scream and scream, I may have a chance. But I need him to step back, away from me. I need him to back off, just a little.

Adrenalin courses through my body, focusing me right on this moment. 'It's my friend Natalia,' I say quickly. 'If I don't answer, she'll know something's wrong. We're supposed to have coffee.'

'Fucking liar,' mutters Vernon.

My body is screaming at me to run, to simply bolt for the front door, yelling my lungs out as I do, but he's too close to me, the knife is too close to my throat.

I lock eyes with him. Mercifully the person on the doorstep does not simply leave. Instead the knocker sounds again.

'She'll know something's wrong,' I say again. Even though my whole body is shaking, my voice is firm and strong. I am trying to save my life, to save my boys from heartbreak.

'Fine,' snarls Vernon. He grabs my arm, pulls me up from the floor and shoves me roughly in front of him. I feel the point of the knife against the back of my neck. A sharp pain tells me he has pushed it into the skin. I feel a dribble of warm blood and I bite down on my lip. I need to get closer to the door before I scream. If I startle him, I may be able to wrench it open. I take a deep breath and prepare myself to scream my lungs out.

'Tell her to fuck off or you both get hurt.' He shoves me towards the door.

'Coming,' I call.

I grasp the handle and pull it open. He stands behind me with the knife hidden by my hair.

I ready myself to move but I am not ready for who is standing on my doorstep.

She is a young woman with dusty-brown hair and deep brown eyes just like I have. She has a heart-shaped face and she is slim and tall just like I am.

I feel my whole body sag because it cannot be possible, and yet, it is. I know it to be the truth with absolute certainty. I feel that truth ricochet around my body.

Everything I have known, everything I have thought for the last thirty-two years is wrong because here she is.

Here she stands.

My sister.

CHAPTER FORTY-ONE
Molly

She shivers as she feels the temperature drop in preparation for a cold night, but she also feels sweat under her arms. Her mouth is dry and she swallows, hoping to get rid of the feeling.

'Coming,' she hears from somewhere inside the house. The voice has a slight echo. The house must be larger than it looks.

'Come on, come on,' whispers Molly. She can feel her feet turning ever so slightly and she knows if she has to stand here for much longer, her courage will fail her and she will simply walk away.

But finally, the door swings open.

Molly studies the woman's dusty-brown hair and dark brown eyes. She notes her heart-shaped face and her slim build and the dimple on her chin. Her mouth is too dry for her to speak. *You're imagining this*, she inwardly tells herself but she knows she's not. Her own face looks back at her, older, more lined and paler, but she feels that if she reached forward and touched the woman's cheek, she would feel it on her own skin. It has not been her imagination. She has only been remembering. She has been remembering a life before, a different life, a different child. She lifts her hand to reach out and touch the woman for fear that she's not real, but then she drops it again. Her stomach churns and her heart races. She has no idea what to do or say. She can smell smoke from a wood-burning fire, hear the call of cockatoos in the trees, feel the sharpness of the wind whipping up dry fallen leaves. Every sense captures this moment.

There she is.

There she stands.

Her sister.

The woman looks directly at her, stares at her for a moment, and then she covers her mouth with her hand. Molly cannot find any words as she watches the woman's eyes.

'Oh… oh,' she says, 'you shouldn't have come. You shouldn't have come, Lilly.'

Her voice is warm, deep with a tremor that Molly is sure is not usually there. Molly has heard this voice when she, herself, speaks. They look like each other and sound like each other.

Here they stand: sisters.

CHAPTER FORTY-TWO

Alice

'I'm not Lilly,' says the young woman, and I feel like I am hearing myself speak. Her voice is deep like mine, like our mother's was before age and alcohol deformed it. 'My name is Molly Khan.'

'I know,' I whisper, 'I know who you are.' I shouldn't have used her name. I shouldn't have said it out loud. I feel like I might be going mad. How can this be? I thought she was gone. I thought she was dead and it was all my fault and yet here she is.

On any other day, at any other time, I would not be able to prevent myself from flinging my arms around her, but not today. I have put her in danger. I have put her in danger again.

'You're Alice, aren't you? You're Meredith from the blog but your real name is Alice.'

'My real name is Alice.' I can do nothing but repeat her words. I had a plan. I was going to scream and I was going to run but I hadn't thought about who might be at the door. I hadn't considered that. How could I have ever considered this?

'Hello, Molly,' I say loudly, hoping that he has not heard me call her Lilly. 'This is not a good time for me, I'm afraid. You can't be here.'

I wonder if she can see that something's wrong. If we had grown up together, we might be able to communicate without speaking. But we didn't. Will she still know what I'm trying to tell her? I twist my body a little even as the knife digs in deeper. If I scream, will she turn and run with me? Will we both be able to get away?

'I should go,' she says, and I watch her face fall, her eyes shine with tears. This is not what she expected. I can see that. She doesn't understand what I'm doing, why I look so strange. She doesn't understand.

'You should go,' I say quickly. 'You should go,' I repeat, even as I realise that she is my last hope for saving myself. If I scream, she will know, but if I scream, he will hurt her. I tried to save her once and thought I'd failed. I won't make that mistake again.

I bite down on my lip as a single tear traces its way down her cheek, and I feel her heartbreak as my own. She thinks I'm rejecting her, that I'm abandoning her just as I did all those years ago. I cannot explain that I'm saving her. I couldn't explain it then and I cannot explain it now.

She turns to go and then she turns back to me. 'You don't even want to—'

I shake my head. 'Just go,' I say.

She starts to move off and then she stops, as though she has realised something, as though she has understood.

'Are you okay?' she asks. 'Because you don't look okay.'

I blink rapidly. 'I'm fine.' *Please understand me. It's not safe. It's not safe. Run, Lilly, run.*

She nods as though she has heard what I've said and then she turns to go, but once more she turns back around, making me want to scream with frustration.

'Look,' she says, 'are you okay? You don't seem well at all. Shall I call someone? Shall I call an ambulance?'

I feel him move, the knife releasing its sting from my neck, and then he is out in the open, looking at her.

'Oh, I didn't...' she begins and then she sees the knife he is holding and I watch as her lips pale to white.

'Maybe you could just fucking come in, eh?' says Vernon and he lifts the knife, this time to the front of my throat.

'Run,' I rasp.

Vernon peers at her. His face blanches as he recognises the woman standing there. 'You're her. You're her! You were, I thought… Well, you could knock me over with a feather. I thought you were gone. I thought you were dead but there you are, there you are, my little girl.' I can hear joy in his voice and for a moment I think it might be okay. He can see it's Lilly. He is as shocked as I was but now that he can see her, it might be okay. He might be so happy he will forget what he's here for. I want to believe that but I can't take that chance. Vernon cannot be capable of a happy family reunion.

'Run,' I say to her again.

'If you do, your big sister won't last another five minutes. Now step inside before I fucking slice her up.' And just like that there is no more joy or happiness in his voice. He is not overwhelmed to see his long-lost daughter. He is hell-bent on revenge.

I watch her hands fly to her stomach, a protective gesture that I recognise, and I remember that she's pregnant. She told me in her message. I close my eyes, vowing that I will not let him hurt her and her child. Whatever he does, whatever happens now, this time I will keep her safe.

CHAPTER FORTY-THREE

Molly

Molly cannot quite believe this is happening. The skinny man with the bedraggled beard is smiling at her with yellow teeth that disgust her but somehow look familiar. She bites down hard on her lip because the urge to vomit is suddenly overwhelming. She should never have come here. She has no idea who these people are and what they're capable of. This woman is her biological sister, that much is clear, but why is this man calling her his little girl? She cannot help touching her stomach. She needs to keep the baby safe. She cannot let anything happen to the baby. But the man is holding a knife. She could turn and run right now but he says he will hurt Alice. She could run. She owes Alice nothing but she can't seem to abandon the woman. She has no choice but to step inside.

It is warmer inside the house than outside with only a fraction of light coming in through the leadlight windows at the side of the door. The pattern of coloured triangles throws shapes on the tile floor. Molly cannot help looking around, noting the wood panelling on the walls and the ornate carved timber sideboard with a large multicoloured glass vase in the centre.

Alice told her to run. She should have run. She shouldn't have run. She could have run.

The man shuffles around, closing the door behind her. He pushes the knife against the back of Alice's neck, and even through her hair, Molly can see a small trickle of blood snake its way down her back, staining the white shirt she is wearing.

Alice is terrified, frozen, ghost-white.

Molly struggles to find words, to do anything. The man with the knife feels surreal. Alice's face and the blood trailing down the back of her neck are a scene in a movie. This cannot be happening and yet it is. Molly can think only of the baby, of protecting the baby, and she feels a sense of what motherhood must be like. Thoughts tumble through her mind and she cannot form a coherent plan because all she can feel is a terrible fear for her child. She will not let this child get hurt. She will not. She will not.

'I think you should just leave,' she says, in what she hopes is a firm voice. 'Put the knife down and leave and no one has to know you were here. I have some money in my purse. Take it and leave and we'll keep quiet about this. We won't tell anyone.'

The man laughs and shoves Alice forward. 'Let's all have a cup of tea, shall we? There are things you need to know, Lilly.'

'Why are you calling me Lilly?'

The man laughs again and then he hacks and coughs for a minute. He stinks of cigarettes. Molly swallows the bile that rises in her throat.

'As plain as day it is,' he says as he marches Alice to the kitchen at the back of the house. He shoves her hard down into a chair and she sags weakly.

'Please,' says Alice, 'please don't hurt her.'

'Please don't hurt her,' the man mimics. 'She's my kid. I'll do what I want.'

My kid, Molly thinks. He seems to be referring to her. Her hand flies up to her mouth. 'I'm going to be sick,' she says.

'Take deep breaths,' says Alice, 'just deep breaths.' Molly does as she's told. She takes in a huge gulp of air and locks eyes with her sister, who shakes her head and mouths, 'I'm sorry.' The nausea abates.

'You,' says the man, gesturing at Molly with the knife, 'put the kettle on.'

Molly looks slowly around the kitchen until she locates the kettle on the counter. She goes over to it and pushes the button to start it. Scenarios run through her head. *If I grab the knife and she pushes him, if I scream and distract him, if I can find a knife on the counter, if my phone rings and I scream help into it, if I can text Peter somehow, if I can call the police.* Her heartbeat feels as rapid as the little flutter she had seen on the ultrasound. *I'm sorry, baby,* she thinks. She should never have done this. She should never have put her child in danger.

'She looks just like Maggie, doesn't she?' says the man to Alice.

Molly watches as her sister nods weakly, as though her head is too heavy for her neck.

'I bet you're wondering what this is all about, aren't you, love?' says the man to Molly, his tone liquid and sweet.

Molly nods but doesn't say anything.

'You're my little girl. I would have known you anywhere. I mean, you're not little anymore but you're my girl all right. You look just like your useless mother and like your big sister here.'

'I don't understand,' says Molly, buying time to think. She is sure that keeping him talking is a good idea. If he is talking, then he is not hurting them. Is he her father? It's a hideous thought and she feels a desperate rush of desire to turn back time so she can remain ignorant of who she really is.

'Tell her,' says the man to Alice, pressing the knife against her cheek.

'Don't,' says Molly, her heartbeat a runaway horse.

'Alice and I used to have some fine times together, didn't we? You liked what we did, didn't you? You missed out on the fun, Lilly. We were going to have so much fun, me and you, but you didn't get to be a good daughter to me because Alice here made sure you disappeared.'

'Please,' whimpers Alice, 'just let her go.'

The man laughs. He plays with the knife, occasionally running his fingers up and down the smooth blade. 'You coming here today, Lilly, is such a wonderful coincidence.'

'My name is not Lilly. It's Molly. I'm Molly Khan. You need to let me leave now. My husband will be looking for me. He'll be worrying about me. He knows where I am. I told him I was coming here and I told him to come looking for me if I didn't come back in an hour.' Molly tries to convince herself that what she's saying is the truth.

'You may be whoever now, but you were my kid once, my little girl until this bitch took you away from me,' he says. 'I thought you were dead, gone. I would have looked for you if I'd known. I promise.' He smiles and Molly feels the horror of that idea churn inside her. Imagine being found by this man.

She looks at him, at his sunken eyes and grey skin, and she wants to cry. How can this awful human being be her father?

'Tell her it's the truth. Tell her what you did,' says the man to Alice, and he grabs her ear, pushes the knife down on top of it, 'or I'll slice your fucking ear off.' Molly watches Alice wince as the knife makes contact with her skin. 'Tell her,' he growls.

'You're my little sister, Lilly,' Alice whispers. 'That was your name – Lilly.'

'But you said your sister was dead,' says Molly. 'I asked you and you said she was dead.'

'I thought…' says Alice. 'I thought you were killed in the accident… the car accident. I saw the car on television… the red car. It said the accident happened in Mount Colah, where we lived. A toddler was killed. It was on the same day I… on the same day…'

'But I wasn't found in Mount Colah,' says Molly. 'I was found in Asquith, that's one… Yes, one suburb over.'

'I thought…' says Alice, 'I didn't realise I'd walked to the next suburb. I thought you died in the car accident… but I was wrong.'

CHAPTER FORTY-FOUR

Alice

I watch her face as she leans against the kitchen counter for support. It is silent in my kitchen except for the whooshing sound of the kettle boiling. I see confusion, fear, disgust and horror march across her features as she tries to comprehend what I'm saying. She came here looking for her sister but she never had any idea of the terrible truth she would find. I curse my blog and myself. I have done this. I have made this happen.

'I don't understand,' she says.

I don't know how to explain it to her. The story would take too long so all I can say is, 'I wanted to keep you safe.'

I flick my eyes towards Vernon. 'This is the man I wrote about,' I say, and I watch as she remembers, as she makes the connection.

'Oh,' she gasps.

'What the fuck are you talking about?' says Vernon, and the knife slices further into my skin. The pain is agonising. My body begins to shake. I have to do something.

I lock eyes with my sister before focusing quickly on the boiled kettle and then back at Lilly, looking between the two.

'What are you doing, bitch?' says Vernon. 'What's going on here? Why were you writing about me?'

I hunch my shoulders as the knife pierces my skin further. I can feel blood running down the side of my face.

I flick my eyes at the kettle again.

'We should have tea,' says Lilly. I can't think of her as Molly. She is Lilly, so clearly Lilly. Her voice is weirdly cheerful. 'Wouldn't you like some tea… Dad?' she asks.

Vernon looks up at her and grins; the knife releases its pressure. Lilly steps towards the kettle.

'Where are you going?' shouts Vernon.

'Tea,' she says brightly, 'you said you wanted tea, Dad. We can all have a cup and talk. You can catch me up on your life.' The use of the word 'dad' disarms Vernon again and he nods.

She lifts the heavy kettle and holds it. Her wrist bends a little with the weight but she doesn't put it down.

'So, make tea,' he replies.

'I don't know where anything is,' she says, and she makes a big show of looking around the kitchen in a confused manner.

'Tell her,' says Vernon to me.

'Behind you, in the cupboard,' I respond.

Lilly holds the kettle in one hand and opens the cupboard behind her. She rifles through the boxes I have there. 'You don't have any hot chocolate, do you?' she asks.

I nod. 'I do, it's—'

'Can't you just show me?' she says.

Vernon steps away from me to point out the tin of hot chocolate that is obviously on the counter. 'You can see it—'

My body springs into action. I leap out of the chair and shove him hard, forcing him to take a few steps back, his arms outstretched to prevent him from falling. I dart over to where Lilly is standing and grab the cordless kettle out of her hands, holding it tight around its boiling steel body. I gasp as the heat instantly burns my hands but I don't let go. I won't let go. Vernon recovers his balance and starts towards us, a low growl vibrating in his throat, his yellow teeth bared. The boiling water is the only weapon I have, but before I can use it, Vernon is almost upon

us and I don't have time to do more than lift the kettle up, my
muscles straining at the weight of it, my hands on fire, and I throw
it towards him, hoping it hits its mark.

It hits him in the chest and he screams and rears back. The
kettle bounces onto the kitchen floor, spraying water everywhere.
Vernon holds his knife in front of him and steps forward but he
slips on the water, going down with a thump.

'Run!' I scream at Lilly. 'Run.'

She stares at me for a moment, her lips quivering, her face pale,
and she seems unsure of what to do.

'Run!' I shout again.

Lilly moves quickly over the wet floor, careful movements in
case she slips. She is out of the kitchen and heading towards the
front door when Vernon stands up and roars in frustration, 'I'll
fucking kill you!'

He moves quickly, following her. I am close behind. Lilly pulls
frantically at the handle, but before she can open the door he is
right there and I watch him raise his hand, see the shine of the
steel blade, hear him yell with anger as he plunges it into her back.

'Oh,' she says, 'oh,' as her legs start to go out from under her.
She sags a little.

I come up behind Vernon and watch as he raises the knife to
hurt her again.

A blinding fury rises up inside me. I let her go to keep her
safe and now he's hurt her. All I ever wanted to do was keep
her safe and he's hurt her. I grab the huge glass vase on the sideboard. I lift it high above my body and I hit it against Vernon's
skull, the force from the blow reverberating right through my
body. 'Leave her alone!' I scream.

He lifts his hand, panting, as though trying to locate the source
of his pain, and then he falls over and lies still on the floor, his head
hitting the stone tiles of the entrance hall with a clunk.

I place the unbroken vase gently back on the sideboard. And then I drop onto the floor and crawl over to my sister. My sister, who I loved more than anything and who I thought was gone. My sister, who I only wanted to keep safe.

CHAPTER FORTY-FIVE
Molly

Molly holds her hand to her back where the knife has gone in. She can feel the dark, wet blood that she knows is coming from inside her.

'Oh,' she hears herself moan. She is lying on the floor on the cold tiles of the entrance hall. She would like to close her eyes. She cannot feel any pain, and she has no idea why this is. She turns her head to see the man, the man who called himself her father, lying silent and still. She watches as Alice crawls over towards her.

'My baby,' she says to Alice because she knows that she is going to lose him or her.

'It'll be okay,' replies Alice, stroking her head. 'I need to get help. I need to call for help. Don't close your eyes, Lilly, don't go to sleep.'

'You... you used to tell me to go to sleep,' says Molly.

Alice nods and Molly can see the tears dripping off her face.

'Go to sleep, little one,' says Alice. 'That's what I used to say, but don't close your eyes, Lilly, please don't go to sleep.'

'Just for a bit,' murmurs Molly, 'just a few minutes.' And then there is nothing.

CHAPTER FORTY-SIX
Alice

I pace up and down the waiting room of the hospital. I've already had three cups of tea and I can't possibly drink anymore. Every time I sit down, I'm overwhelmed by all that has happened and have to jump out of my chair again and start pacing once more. My hands are loosely wrapped in gauze and they've given me something for the pain, but I can still feel the hot sting of my burns, taking me back to that terrifying moment.

I've been here for four hours already. I called an ambulance, screaming my address at them, and they arrived, sirens blaring, with the police not far behind. I refused to answer any questions until I'd called Jack.

'You have to pick the boys up from school,' I yelled before he'd even had time to say hello.

'What… why? Are you okay?'

'I'm going to the hospital, but you have to pick them up from school but don't take them home. You can't take them home.'

'The hospital, Alice, what's happened… what's happened? What's wrong? Why can't I take them home?'

'I'm okay, Jack, I'm… Just promise me you'll fetch them and take them to your mother. Fetch them and then come to the hospital.'

I am waiting to see Lilly or Molly as her name is. I am waiting to see my sister. My breath catches in my throat. I am waiting to see my sister.

When we got here, I had no idea how to explain things to the nurse. I told her I was a friend of Molly's, and they used her wallet and phone to call her husband and her parents.

'She's pregnant,' I told the nurse.

Once she'd been admitted and my hands had been seen to, Constable Ferris had taken me to a small, sterile room and asked me to explain. Then he asked me to explain again and again.

'You'll need to speak to one of our detectives,' he said, scratching at his blond hair, still confused about my story.

'I understand, but I need to be here for now.'

'I should really take you in to the station straight away.'

'I feel sick,' I said. 'You can stay with me, but I'm not going anywhere.' I wasn't going to leave her. Not again. Never again.

He's sitting a few chairs away from me now. 'A detective will be here soon,' he said.

Constable Ferris is the one who keeps bringing me cup after cup of tea.

'He forced his way into my house,' I told him. 'He was my mother's partner for many years and he came back to hurt me.'

'But why?' he asked, and I shrugged my shoulders. I can't explain it now, relive it all. I'll save my energy for the detective, and I may also need a lawyer before I say anything else. I slump down into a grey plastic chair. I cannot believe what has happened, but a small part of me is relieved that I was actually getting emails from someone who wanted to hurt me, and not my mother, or Anika. I'm not going mad. He was using my mother's computer or getting Ed to use it to torment me. I think about how confused she must have been to see him and about how terrified she must have been at the end. No one believed her when she said he was visiting, but how could we have known? I'm certain he caused her death. She was so weak, so sick, it wouldn't have taken much to force her body to shut down. Her chest was bruised from Anika attempting CPR, but what if it was bruised from a blow delivered by a monster? The relief I feel mingles with a terrible sadness at how she died, alone and afraid.

Another part of me is almost leaping with joy. Lilly did not die in a car accident. Lilly was adopted. Lilly was saved. Lilly is back. It doesn't feel real and I stifle an overwhelming urge to walk around the waiting area saying to people, 'My sister isn't dead, she isn't gone,' until this wonderful truth sinks in.

Alice has a sister. Alice has a sister. Alice has a sister.

I watch as a tall man walks quickly to the front desk. He runs his hands through his curly dark brown hair, breathing so fast he almost can't get the words out. 'Molly Khan,' he says, 'my wife, she's pregnant.'

I stand up, wanting to go to him, but then I sink down again. What on earth would I say?

A few minutes later two women and a man fly in, also asking after Molly. The women are both blond and beautiful, obviously mother and daughter. I can see terror and desperate love on both their faces. Lilly has been loved, loved and cared for. Relief fills me right up. Lilly is alive and she is here and she is loved.

My phone rings. 'What happened, Alice?' says Jack the second I answer.

'The boys?' I ask. 'Are they okay?'

'They're with my mother, she'll give them dinner. I told them you had to go and meet some mothers about… about the bake sale.'

'And they believed that?'

'Isaac said… he said it was unlike you to schedule a meeting at pickup time.'

'Smart boy,' I say. I can't help smiling but then I feel a stone of sadness crush my heart. What if I lose all of them when the truth comes out, when they know everything? What if they can never look at me the same way? Will Jack resent the lie I've held onto my whole life? Will he resent it too much to stay married to me?

'It's a long story, Jack,' I eventually reply. 'I don't even know where to start.'

'Well, it's going to take me twenty minutes to get to the hospital… so I have time and I'm listening, Alice… I'm really listening.'

I look at Constable Ferris, but he is on the phone as well. I turn my body away from him and I begin. The hidden story of my little sister flows into the world, feeling too fantastical to be real. The fear that has consumed me these past weeks makes me shiver as I speak. I don't leave anything out. I tell Jack everything and then I am silent, waiting, expecting judgement and derision, waiting for him to tell me that my life as a wife and a mother is over.

'Oh,' he says, 'my poor darling. I can't believe you've been dealing with this alone. Why didn't you tell me this before? Why didn't you tell me all this before?'

'I was afraid, afraid you would hate me for what I did, afraid that you would make me go to the police, afraid that the whole world I built for myself would just collapse. And I thought she was dead. I thought I was the reason she was dead. I thought it was all my fault.'

'You were ten years old. You were being horribly abused and there was no one to turn to for help. I have no idea how you coped… but you did, and what happened… it wasn't your fault. You had no idea what you were doing. You thought you were helping her, and all these years you thought… you thought she was dead. I cannot imagine what that has been like for you. You were a child, Alice… just a child, only a year older than Gus and Gabe are now… I just… I understand why you're so protective of them… I get it… you were so little and you had to make such a terrible, terrible choice.' He stops speaking and I can hear him sniffing and I know he is shedding tears for me, for the child I was. It's a different reaction to what I expected, and I realise that even though I have always trusted him, I have not trusted him enough, have not trusted his love enough.

My eyes feel heavy, my body is exhausted and I need to sleep. My revelations have depleted me.

He takes a deep breath. 'Look, I'll be there soon. I love you, Alice – I love you so much,' my husband says.

'Love you too,' I reply in a whisper.

I end the call and look up as the tall man, Molly's husband, walks towards me. I stand up and straighten my shoulders, preparing myself for whatever is coming.

'I'm Peter, Molly's husband,' he says, holding out his hand, but then he looks down at my bandages and smiles gently, dropping it.

'She's awake and talking and she'd like to see you,' he says.

'How… how…?' I stammer.

'She's fine. It was just a flesh wound. She'll be a bit sore but she's had ten stitches and she'll be fine.'

'The baby?' I ask.

'She told you?'

'She… wrote… Yes, she told me.'

'The baby is just great. It's our first, you know.'

I nod, tears filling my eyes.

'Come on now, you've both had a rough afternoon, but she'll be fine and she wants to see you.'

I look at Constable Ferris and he nods his head.

Lilly's husband places his arm around my shoulders and I know it's because I look like I might fall over. The doors at the front open and Jack walks in. He sees me, sees Peter's arm, and I watch him tense as if afraid that I am being hurt.

'Oh, my husband,' I say, and Jack walks up to us. Peter immediately holds out his hand. 'Peter, Molly's husband.'

'Molly?' says Jack.

'Lilly,' I say, 'he's Lilly's husband.'

They shake hands. They are the same height, but so very different in looks, Jack with his ink-black straight hair and Peter with his brown curls.

In Lilly's room, I look at the two women sitting by her bed. My sister is sitting up, her cheeks rosy, a smile on her face.

She is talking fast and I immediately worry about how she will feel when the adrenalin wears off.

'Here she is,' she says, 'she saved my life.'

'Oh, Lilly, I'm so… so…' I start but then I can't go on.

I feel Jack's arms around me as he pats me on the back. 'It's okay,' he murmurs, 'it's okay.'

After a few moments, someone produces a chair and I sink gratefully into it.

I drop my head into my hands, wincing as the gauze presses against the skin. Everyone in the room remains silent until finally I take a deep breath and look up at the assembled group.

'What happened, Alice?' asks Lilly.

'You know, you were there,' I say.

'No, I mean what happened when I was little? How come I was out on that road alone? Why did you think I'd been killed in a car accident?'

'It was my fault,' I say.

'Your fault?'

'Yes,' I reply and then I tell them. I tell them everything.

CHAPTER FORTY-SEVEN

Then

19 January 1987

Alice

It wasn't something I planned.

That morning after my mother saw what he was doing to me, she lay crumpled on the floor, beaten so badly that I thought she might be dead. We crept past her, my little sister and me.

'Mama sleep,' said Lilly because that was all she knew about her. Mama sleep.

I leaned down and touched her hair, already stringy and threaded with grey like she was an old lady. Then I put my hand on her chest, felt the rise and fall.

'I made bacon and eggs,' he said jovially, standing in the kitchen like it was an ordinary morning. I felt sick, too sick to eat, too sick to believe how he was behaving, as though she wasn't lying still on the floor covered in blood. He stared at me until I dropped my gaze and I picked Lilly up, putting her in her high chair. He put a plate down in front of her with the toast cut into little squares as though he was the perfect parent. As though he hadn't just battered my mother into oblivion.

'You're a good sister,' he said. He came and sat down at the table with us, bringing his coffee with its strong smell of the whisky he always added.

'When she finally wakes her lazy self up, you tell her to clean herself the fuck up,' he said, looking at me over the rim of his coffee cup as he drank.

'Tell her to clean herself the fuck up,' he said again. I practised the words in my head, the ugly brutal words. *Clean yourself the fuck up.* I hated her, hated him, hated myself for letting him do what he did, for being powerless to stop anything.

He smelled like Lilly's nappies and he was only wearing his underwear. Everything flopped and bulged on his body. The eggs I was forcing down my throat started to come back up. I grabbed a piece of toast, chewed and swallowed quickly, hoping it would keep everything down.

'She's a pretty little thing, isn't she?' he said, looking at Lilly, who smiled at him, her big brown eyes lighting up her face.

'You and I are going to be great friends, aren't we, Lilly?' he said with one of his nasty smiles. He reached out and touched my little sister's hair, so gently, so softly that it could have been a touch coming from some other man.

'Yah,' said Lilly.

I grew cold in the hot kitchen.

'You won't give me trouble like your mother and your sister, will you, love?' His hand moved onto Lilly's face, down her neck and chest.

I put some eggs on a spoon and fed them to Lilly. My head was filled with white noise.

How long does she have? I wondered. He had started with me when I was ten but would he wait that long with my sister?

She held up her stuffed frog for him to see. He smiled. 'You like that, don't you?' He made to grab it away from her and she held it close to her again, making him laugh. 'You'll learn,' he said.

He got up from the table, stretching so she and I could see everything. I looked away, down at my plate.

'I'll be home for dinner, I think, or maybe I won't be. I need a break from all this shit.'

I watched my mother after he left, willing her to wake up and tell me we were leaving. Willing her to stand up and say, 'It's enough, I won't let him hurt you anymore.' But she slept on.

'Clean yourself the fuck up,' I spat at her when she finally opened her eyes.

'What's wrong with you?' she whined. 'Can't you see I'm hurt? Can't you see I'm tired?'

I understood that nothing was going to change. Nothing was ever going to change, and one day, one day very soon, he was going to start hurting Lilly. Little Lilly, who still thought the world was good because she had me, but I knew I wasn't enough. I wasn't strong enough, and I wasn't powerful enough to protect her.

I looked at my little sister, speaking nonsense to her stupid stuffed green frog, and I knew I couldn't let him hurt her.

The hours trickled along. I played with Lilly, made her afternoon tea and dinner. At least the fridge was full. When it was so late that I could no longer keep my eyes open, I knew he wasn't coming home. He didn't want to have to clean up his mess.

I fell asleep next to Lilly, waking hours later from a nightmare of him dragging my sister by her leg, a broken doll, her little face too bruised to see properly.

I climbed out of bed, stripping off my sticky, sweaty pyjamas, throwing on shorts and a T-shirt.

He was going to do it to Lilly. I knew he was going to do it to her too. But I couldn't let him. She was so tiny. She was so small she wouldn't even have the words to describe her pain.

I wouldn't let him hurt her.

My eyes were burning and I was tired again, so tired, but I knew I had to save Lilly. I tried to wake her but she was deeply asleep so I dragged her out of the bed into my arms, grabbing only her frog, thinking that at least she would have him. She was dressed in an old red T-shirt of mine that hung down on her like a nightie.

It took me ten minutes to creep out of the house because I kept expecting my mother to wake up and stop me, but finally, I was outside in the heavy, humid air. I lifted my head and felt the slightest of breezes. I could smell the jasmine in the air.

I started walking. I needed to get to a road, a big road, a road where there would be a lot of people and cars no matter how late it was. I knew it couldn't be both of us who got saved. I was old enough to speak. I would be forced to tell people my name and address and then back we would go. It couldn't be both of us.

I kept walking with Lilly getting heavier and heavier, our bodies stuck together in the warm, dark night. It felt like I had been walking forever. I expected someone to stop me, someone older and stronger than I was to rush out of their home and stop me, ask me what was wrong. I wished for someone to stop me but no one did, and I walked on, more determined. No one was ever coming to help us. I had to save Lilly myself.

I stumbled once, twice, and Lilly woke up just as I heard the swish of traffic on the road ahead of us.

'Down,' she demanded and I let her walk, watched her flinch as her soft feet encountered stones and scraps of rubbish at the side of the road. I wished I had thought to bring her one and only pair of shoes, small for her already but better than nothing. She held my hand, walking silently, patiently next to me, not complaining. Her frog was in her other hand, grinning madly, his beady eyes shining wildly whenever we were near a streetlight.

We stepped out from a small side street onto the big road, the road that would have cars soon but was, just for a moment, empty. I pulled Lilly over to a bush at the edge of the road. 'Ow sore,' she said, sitting down. I looked at her little foot and brushed away some small stones, placing a gentle kiss on her dusty skin.

Two cars raced past us, their lights illuminating the bush we were crouched in, the curious look on Lilly's face as she wondered what we were doing out, the little foot I was holding.

Lilly held her frog tight and sucked her thumb, happy and safe because she was with me. A truck rumbled by and I felt the noise of it rattle inside me. I knew that I shouldn't be out with Lilly, so close to a main road. I should have been home and safe in my bed, but home wasn't a safe place, not for me… and soon not for Lilly either.

I watched the truck disappear into the distance and then all was silent. 'Come, Lilly,' I said and I dragged her out onto the side, visible to all who would come down the big road.

'Home,' she replied. She didn't want to be out anymore. But she could never go back. I knew that.

The road was empty and I knew I wasn't going to get another chance. I grabbed the frog from her and threw him as far as I could.

Lilly screamed, 'No, no!'

'Go get him, Lills,' I said, holding back my tears. 'Go get Foggy.'

She took off at a run and I hid in some bushes at the side, crouched down, folded myself up.

My little sister picked up Foggy, dusty from the road, and looked around her, her little face crumpled. 'Li, Li,' she called. I put my hand against my mouth, biting down hard on the clammy flesh to stop myself from answering her, my heart aching at not being able to.

She sat down on the side of the road and cried and called for her big sister. I bit harder into my hand, taking comfort from the pain I was causing myself, stifling my sobs. 'Please,' I prayed, 'please someone help.'

Lilly cried for a long time and then she grew tired of crying and sat staring at the road.

I waited and waited. I wouldn't move until I knew my sister was safe.

Finally, she started walking, back to where she thought I was. My body cramped, my heart broke at my own cruelty. She walked right by me, sniffing and occasionally saying, 'Li, Li.'

She was sad and lonely, lost and afraid, and she needed her big sister, but I knew she needed to be away from her terrible family even more. I didn't believe in God, not anymore, but crouching in the bushes I prayed desperately. 'Please let someone come and find her, please I beg you, I'll let him do anything he wants to me just please let someone come.'

And finally, someone came. A car had gone past Lilly. She was far away from me when it happened and I could only just make her out under the streetlights, holding tightly onto Foggy. The car screeched on brakes and reversed, and then a woman got out and swayed over to Lilly. She looked very young and like she'd been drinking, and I almost stood up to snatch her away. She needed a good home, not another drunk mother, but the girl said, 'We need to call the police,' and I felt my body relax. She held out her hand and Lilly, having no choice and no one to turn to, took it. I watched her walk towards the car. Lilly said, 'Ow sore,' again and the girl reached down and picked her up. 'Thank you,' I whispered and I closed my eyes. I opened them again to see Lilly arching back in the girl's arms. 'Foggy!' she shouted. 'Foggy, Foggy!'

'Shush, kid, I'm trying to help you.'

I watched her little hand open and close desperately and saw where she was looking. On the ground lay her stuffed toy. She had dropped Foggy.

The girl didn't turn around. She didn't look back. She climbed into the car, which I could see was a shiny red under the street-light, a silver H on the bonnet. '"H" is for Honda,' I whispered. I remembered my father teaching me the alphabet, pointing out cars we drove past. 'A' is for Audi, 'B' is for BMW. 'H' is for Honda, I knew. 'A red Honda,' I repeated, holding onto the last time I would ever see my sister. In a moment the car was gone, roaring away into the night, my little sister safe inside.

I crept out of the bush, picked up the frog and held it to me. I comforted myself that at least she was safe – or so I thought until the news report. I watched that night – to be sure, to be certain – and that's when I found out. She wasn't safe. I had made a mistake. All I saw was the car – the shiny red car. The shiny red car, crumpled and broken, the H glinting in the sun. 'A young man and a young woman,' the reporter said. 'An unrestrained toddler in the back,' the reporter said. 'I didn't know her boyfriend had a child,' the mother of the young woman said. I knew whose child it was. At least, I thought I knew.

I trudged home after I left her, my heart broken, my soul heavy. She was the only thing I truly loved, the only thing that mattered, and now she was gone.

At home I climbed into bed and slept and slept because I finally understood why my mother needed to sleep so much.

There was no reason to wake up, no reason at all.

CHAPTER FORTY-EIGHT

Now

Molly

Molly shivers despite her warm coat. It's the last week of winter, and the intensity of the cold snap has taken everyone by surprise, making spring seem very far away. This morning, as she waited for Alice to pick her up, her phone told her it was only three degrees outside. The wind seems determined to push her off her feet and force its way into even the tiniest gaps in her clothing.

'We should have done this another day,' says Alice.

'Who knew the weather was going to turn like it has?' replies Molly.

'Are you sure you're warm enough?'

'I'm fine,' Molly says, smiling, 'stop fussing.'

Alice laughs. 'I'm making up for lost time. Come on, it's just down this path.'

The two women lower their heads down against the wind and trudge forward.

'Here,' says Alice, 'just here.'

The wind quite suddenly dies down and a weak sun emerges from behind clouds. The cemetery is silent and empty except for the two sisters. Large evergreen trees block out the small slices of sun as it struggles through the clouds. Molly looks up and down the rows of gravestones in black and grey granite. Some of them are empty but some are covered in flowers, wilting and blowing in the wind. 'Beloved mother and grandmother,' Molly reads. 'Much-loved wife and sister,' she sees on another.

Molly sweeps her eyes across the manicured green lawns. Everyone else has stayed home, safely cocooned from the cold weather. Margaret's grave is at the end of a long row, the second last grave. Next to her a fresh mound of earth tells of another family and another loss.

Alice stares down at the simple white headstone. The inscription 'Margaret Henkel' is followed by her date of birth and the date of her death. Unlike many of the other stones the two women have passed, there is no mention of her being a wife or a mother or a grandmother. There are no loving words or lines of poetry, just the bare bones of when she was born and when she died.

'I was going to write beloved wife and mother,' says Alice, 'but when the time came it felt like the wrong thing to do. I didn't know if I would ever come back to visit her, but I knew that if I did, I would probably be infuriated by those words every time I saw them.'

Molly looks at her sister, at her wide brown eyes that shine with tears. 'Oh, love,' she says, and she puts her arm around her shoulders, bringing them closer.

Alice shakes her head. 'It's weird. I didn't think I would miss her. I mean, she wasn't even really herself for a good few years before she died, and before that, well… she was hardly a mother at all.'

Molly and Alice have talked it all through, have discussed where Molly came from and who Margaret was over and over. Alice has explained about the news report and the accident. 'If I hadn't left you, you wouldn't have been in that car. That's all I knew – that I had left you and the girl had put you into a car and then there was an accident.'

'You were a child,' Molly keeps saying when they discuss it, 'just a child.'

Despite Molly still feeling that she should have been told she was adopted, what she mostly feels is an overwhelming gratitude that she was given the chance at a life like hers, that she was saved from the trauma that Alice went through.

When she recovered from her stab wound, she was afraid for Alice, for what would happen to her, but the sisters sat together and told the police the truth. Jack had hired a lawyer to represent Alice in the interview, but in the end he was unnecessary.

'You were a child,' all of the constables and detectives they spoke to said. 'You were a child and you felt you had no choice. Someone should have seen what was happening to you. Someone should have helped you. We're sorry no one helped you. We're sorry the system failed you.'

Detectives had, of course, wanted to question Margaret and Vernon, but Margaret was dead and Vernon in a coma, and there was no one to tell the story but Alice.

In the end, the case was closed and everyone was allowed to move on with their lives.

Alice told Molly that she thought her tears of relief, of closure after a lifetime of being broken, would never end.

Vernon never woke up from the blow to his head. He had been in a coma for weeks until hospital staff had called Molly, as his only living relative, to make the decision on whether or not to withdraw care. Ed had disappeared. He was Vernon's nephew but he had left the country the day after Vernon had come to Alice's house. Molly would like to speak to him, to find out more about her father and her family, but so far, he hasn't responded to messages on Facebook. She will keep trying. She wants to know more, wants to know why he helped Vernon do such terrible things, wants to understand it. She hopes that if she understands it, she won't be so angry about it.

'There's been no brain activity for weeks,' the doctor told Molly when he called to explain what was happening with Vernon.

'I can't tell you what to do,' said Molly. 'He is my biological father only. Please do whatever you feel is right.'

They withdrew care, and a few days later, Vernon died. Molly was notified of his death but chose not to go to his funeral. Peter paid for him to be cremated. 'You don't have to do that,' Molly said, 'he was an awful man.'

'I know but I don't want you to ever regret not doing it, not sending him off to wherever he's going.'

'Hell, I imagine.'

Alice and Molly began to take tentative steps towards each other, towards a relationship that they both longed for, as Molly's stomach grew with her child. Everyone was cautious and polite at first. Jack and Peter talked about work and sports, and Molly and Alice talked babies, but little by little the truth of Alice's story emerged. Molly spent many hours holding her sister's hand, weeping with her over all the pain and suffering she had endured.

Sometimes when Alice talked about the things he did, Molly felt a raging, burning anger on behalf of her sister. She hates to think it but she is glad that he's dead. It is all he deserved. She can't remember much about the time that she was with Margaret and Vernon, but what she mostly remembers is the feeling of fear associated with him. He hurt her, she knows he hurt her, but he hurt her beloved sister more.

'When was I born?' was one of the first questions Molly asked Alice.

'On the 10th of January. You were a summer baby. You'd just turned two when I took you to the road – not that we had celebrated or anything. When is your birthday now?'

'The 20th of February. It was the day I was given to my parents.'

Molly's parents were overwhelmed by it all.

In the beginning they couldn't help being afraid that Molly would embrace her new family over them, would want to be closer to her own sister than she was to Lexie. But Molly understood quickly what every mother does: there is no limit to the number of people you can embrace, no limit to how much love you can experience.

When they'd all met for the first time outside the hospital, Molly had stood back, letting Alice and her family and her parents and Lexie decide how things should go. After a few quiet minutes in Molly and Peter's living room, Lexie had stood up and gone over to Alice. 'Thank you for saving our sister,' she had said, putting her arms around Alice. And just like that, the ice was broken.

Molly studies the gravestone before them. 'I wish I remembered something about her, anything at all really, but I don't. I mean, I don't remember much, but sometimes I get a flash, an image that I know is from before, and it's always of you.'

'I was the one who took care of you.'

'I'm sorry you had to do that. You were so young, and I'm sorry you had to take on that responsibility.'

Alice turns to look at her sister. 'Don't be sorry, don't ever be sorry. I loved you more than anything in the world. You were the best reason for me to get up in the morning and the best reason to come home to that house.'

'I don't know how you survived it,' Molly whispers, 'and I feel so… so guilty that you were there alone.'

'Don't,' says Alice, 'it's over, really over now.'

The wind picks up again and the women stand in silence, staring down at the gravestone. Molly folds her hands over her growing bump.

'I felt a kick last night,' she tells Alice with a smile.

'Oh, how wonderful,' says Alice. 'Did Peter feel it too?'

'He did.' Molly laughs. 'We were reading in bed and I felt like… bubbles inside me, I guess. At first, I thought it was my stomach gurgling but they came again and I realised what it was. I just burst into tears and Peter didn't know what was wrong. I was crying so hard that I couldn't explain so I just grabbed his hand and put it on my belly and then it happened again.'

'I am so happy for you,' says Alice, grinning back at her sister. 'I remember the first time I felt Isaac kick. It was the first time he became real to me, really real.'

'I wish I could just enjoy it. I wish I wasn't so afraid all the time.'

'It's going to be fine, Molly. I promise it's going to be fine.'

Molly feels her sister beside her, a little taller than she is but with the same shaped face and the same colour hair, and she marvels at the changes the last few months have brought to her life.

She could never have imagined finding out she was adopted and then being lucky enough to find her sister. The awful truth about her father and who he was is not something she dwells on too much. Who her parents were and how they treated her and her sister wakes her from sleep some nights as long-ago images of two lost little girls insert themselves into her dreams, but she tries to not think about Vernon during the day.

'Do you think…' she begins once they are both back in Alice's car and out on the road. Then she falls silent, unsure of how to ask her sister the question that has begun to take up space in her mind.

'Do I think…?' prompts Alice.

'Do you think it's possible that I'll be a mother like her? I mean, I'm part of her and part of him, and they were both so… I wonder sometimes what I've inherited from them.'

Molly has asked this question of her mother and Lexie in the weeks since she got out of the hospital, unable to shake off the awful thought.

'That's not possible,' Lexie has told her. 'It's just not who you are.'

'It won't happen,' her mother has assured her, but Molly continues to worry.

Alice doesn't speak for a moment as she manoeuvres into a parking space outside a café that has become a favourite place for her and Molly to meet for lunch or tea.

Once she has turned off the engine, she turns to Molly, covering her sister's hand with hers. 'I know it worries you, love. I know because it worried me. It worried me so much I went overboard with Isaac. I wish I could tell you that everything will be fine, but motherhood can be really, really hard. There are days when it can feel like everything has been taken from you and you still have to give more. What I can tell you is that you are surrounded by people who love you, just like I was. Peter will be there and so will your parents and me. If it feels like you're drowning, don't just sink. We will help you stay afloat. Promise me that you'll say something.'

Molly grabs onto Alice's hand, thankful that she hasn't just dismissed her fears, thankful to be truly listened to. 'I won't sink,' she says.

'Okay, then. I think we should start with dessert today.' Alice gets out of the car and waits for Molly. When her sister is standing beside her, she grabs her quickly in a hug. 'I'm so grateful you found me, so grateful you're here,' she says, her voice muffled against Molly's coat.

'Oh, Li,' says Molly, unable to stop a few tears, 'I'm grateful too.'

'I won't let you go again.'

'As if I would let you,' says Molly through her tears. 'Now come on, I'm buying lunch today and you can get next time. I'm starving.'

'I have something for you first,' says Alice, and she extracts a picture from her pocket, well-worn and with fold lines running through it. It is of two girls. Molly can see the younger one is about a year old, which means, she knows, that the older one is nine. They are sitting in the garden on a summer's day, smiling at the person taking the picture. Molly traces each face, noting the similarities there. It is her and her sister. Just an ordinary picture of two sisters, but pictures can lie.

'And I know you have your own one, but I have this too,' says Alice, and she reaches inside her handbag and pulls out Foggy wrapped in a frayed pink blanket. He is grubby and worn but Molly takes him and holds him to her face, and he still smells familiar, just like the blanket.

'That's why I went straight for it in the store. I thought I'd found him. I lost him and I thought I'd found him.'

Alice nods. 'I'm happy you thought that. You loved him very much.'

'Hello, Foggy number one,' whispers Molly.

Alice looks at the picture Molly is holding. 'She took the picture on one of her very rare good days, and it was the only one I could grab when I left home. I have looked at it secretly every day since then.'

'Every day?' repeats Molly, staring at her own little face, forming a possible picture of the baby to come. 'Can I…?' begins Molly.

'It's for you,' says Alice.

'I feel like I'm going to cry again but I don't want to cry anymore. I'm tired of crying.'

'Me too.' Alice wipes her eyes and smiles. 'Time for lunch.'

As they walk into the café, Molly shakes away the cemetery and thoughts of Margaret and Vernon.

It is just her now, just her and her sister, and they have, against all odds, both been saved.

CHAPTER FORTY-NINE

Alice

I straighten the sign on my window and move my car forward a little.

My phone pings with an email and I glance down quickly. It's from Molly. 'Chapters for the new book' is written in the subject line. It's a novel about sisters. She writes brilliantly and I wait eagerly for new chapters every week. I will read these tonight and send her my thoughts.

I look up again. There are three cars ahead of me but Isaac is going for a burger with some friends so I don't have to pick him up until much later.

I can see Gus and Gabe watching for my car.

I smile and wave, and both of them jump up and down and wave back.

Without thinking, I run my tongue along the new implant in my mouth. A tooth has been added, a gap has been filled and a memory released.

I inch my car forward again, smile widely at my boys and wait for them to open the car door.

Alice has been healed. Alice is whole. Alice is happy.

EPILOGUE

Molly shifts in her hospital bed, groaning as she feels her stitches pull. 'I never thought it would be this hard,' she says to Lexie, who laughs.

'You'll be surprised how quickly it gets better. You'll be back to your old self in no time.'

'I can't wait to get home. I miss my bed.'

'Don't rush it, Moll. Once you're home, you're on your own.'

'Peter's taking a few weeks off.'

'Ah, paternity leave, those blissful few weeks when you have a helper right there with you. When Owen went back to work, I think I cried for half the day.'

'What did you do then?'

'Called Mum of course.'

Molly laughs. 'Of course.'

There is a knock at the door. 'Is that Alice and the family?' asks Lexie.

'Yes, they've been dying to come but wanted to wait a couple of days.'

Lexie gets up from her chair and opens the door. Alice smiles brightly at her. 'Hello, Lexie, is this a good time?'

'Perfect, Peter just went to get a late lunch and I need to get Sophie from my mother so she can come and visit.'

'Wonderful.' The Stetson family crowds into the room. Molly sits up straighter, holding her arms out for Alice to give her a hug.

'I'm so proud of you, darling. Peter told me you did so well,' says Alice.

'I certainly have a new respect for you doing it with twins – that pain was…' Molly laughs.

Isaac is standing behind his mother and he screws up his face. 'Sorry, Isaac,' says Molly. 'TMI. Come and meet your new cousin.'

'Hands in your pockets, boys,' Alice says to Gus and Gabe, who have been standing shyly by the door. Both boys eagerly shove their hands into their pockets and crowd around the bassinet. Isaac stands a safe distance away and glances inside.

'She's sooo tiny,' says Gus. 'Can I hold her?'

'No, because you have too many germs,' says Gabe. 'Mum says we can when she's a bit older.'

'Look at her fingers, just look at her tiny fingers,' says Gus. All three boys stare down at Lila, who is fast asleep despite the noise.

'Does she do anything else except sleep?' asks Gabe.

'She cries,' says Molly.

'Oh.' The boys look at their mother, clearly bored with their new cousin who hasn't yet deigned to open her eyes.

'Isaac, can you take the boys for a milkshake in the cafeteria, please?' says Alice. She hands her eldest son some money.

'Sure, let's go, ratbags. See you soon, Aunt Molly.'

'See you soon, Isaac,' says Molly, still smiling at the novelty of tall Isaac calling her 'aunt'.

'I might tag along with them,' says Jack. He folds his arms and then unfolds them and puts his hands behind his back. 'Well done, Molly. I've had a word with Dr Bernstein and he says she's textbook perfect… just perfect.'

'Thank you, Jack. I hope you won't mind a few panicked phone calls from a new mother.'

'I'm always ready to help.' Jack smiles before following the boys out.

'So,' says Alice, sitting down, 'do you want to take me through the gory details?'

'No,' Molly laughs, 'I think I'm good.' She is not ready to tell the story just yet, not ready to share it with anyone as she keeps it close to her so she can marvel at her luck, at the miracle of her daughter.

She had been two days past her due date, uncomfortable but not enough to stop her from being out and about. 'It's because you're a runner, just like me, and you haven't stopped exercising,' Alice told her in one of their twice daily phone calls. 'You're fit and strong.'

Molly had smiled at the words 'just like me', because the sisters are so similar. Molly can see an older version of herself every time she looks at Alice.

The night Lila arrived, Molly and Peter had been for a long walk and finished the evening with some spicy Thai food in an attempt to kick-start labour. Molly had fallen asleep easily but woken an hour later, fear gripping her heart, absolutely certain that something was wrong.

The baby wasn't moving. She had tapped her stomach gently, something that usually led to a response from the child inside her, a kick or a small movement, but this time nothing happened. She had stared at the ceiling in the dark, creeping fear overtaking her for a few minutes before she knew she had to wake Peter.

'Pete, Pete,' she had said, prodding him with her elbow.

'What?' Peter mumbled, going from fast asleep to sitting bolt upright in the bed. 'Is it time?'

'She's stopped moving.' Ever since the eighteen-week ultrasound when both Molly and Peter had agreed they wanted to know the gender of the baby, they had alternately been referring to the baby as 'she' or by her full name, Lila Grace. Lila because they both loved the name and because Molly always wanted to remember that she was Lilly first, and Grace because she only existed by the grace of God.

'Are you sure?' Peter asked, switching on the bedside lamp and putting on his glasses. Molly nodded wordlessly, her hands around her stomach.

'Dr Bernstein said she would move less now, she hasn't got a lot of room.'

'I know but she usually moves all night and now…'

'Okay,' said Peter, 'let's go to the hospital.'

Molly nodded and climbed out of bed, grateful that her husband had not tried to calm her down or reason away her fears. It would be the sixth time they had made a dash to the hospital in the middle of the night when Molly was worried, and she had stopped counting the number of times she had dropped by Dr Bernstein's office during the day if she felt the baby was too quiet.

'In for a quick check?' his receptionist always said, a wide smile on her face. 'Have a seat and he'll be with you in a minute.' And a minute was all it usually took for Dr Bernstein to locate the heartbeat and send Molly happily on her way. No one in her family, not Lexie or her parents or Alice or Peter, had tried to dissuade her from checking on the baby so much. Everyone understood. Of course they understood.

Molly dressed quickly in the dark but just as they were about to walk out the door, she was gripped by a contraction so strong it took her breath away.

'Ooh,' she moaned as she grabbed Peter's hand and squeezed hard.

'Right,' he said when she felt the contraction release its hold, 'I'll get your bag. We're coming home with a baby, Moll.' He was unable to keep the excitement out of his voice.

Molly had only allowed herself to embrace the excitement of it when the monitor was strapped to her belly and they could hear Lila's heartbeat safely echoing through the room.

Lila had been in a hurry to arrive, and two hours after they got to the hospital, Molly had asked for an epidural only to be told by the midwife that it was too late.

'You're ready to push, my love,' the woman said. Molly liked her sensible grey hair and large strong arms. 'I'll page Dr Bernstein. He's run off his feet tonight. Three babies, must be the full moon.'

And despite the pain of the seemingly never-ending waves of contractions, Molly laughed.

It took an hour but finally, when Molly felt that she could no longer push, Dr Bernstein helped Lila into the world. There was a moment of silence after she was out, when Molly again felt terrible fear grip her heart, but then baby Lila let out a wail and Molly shouted triumphantly, 'You cry, baby girl, you cry.'

They placed the little baby on her chest and Peter leaned down to kiss her head. 'Welcome,' he whispered as his tears mingled with his child's damp curls. 'Welcome. Love you. Love you with all of my heart.'

Now Molly says, 'I can't believe it, really. I can't believe how lucky I am. Even when she's sleeping, I'm finding it hard to sleep because I keep checking to make sure she's still there.'

'She truly is a miracle, Molly,' Alice agrees. 'Try to rest when you can. Rest makes everything seem manageable.'

'I know,' Molly nods, 'don't worry, Peter and the nurses are watching me, and my mum too.' She feels tears spill down her cheeks.

'Oh, sweetie,' says Alice, sitting on the bed and taking her hand.

'Sorry, it's just… I feel so strange calling her Mum in front of you.'

'But she is your mum, more of a mum than Margaret ever was.'

'I know.'

'And you have me too. Wild horses won't keep me away from my new niece. I never got to experience having a little girl. I can't wait to shop for her. I'll be over as many times a week as you'll let me.'

'You're a good big sister,' says Molly, and Alice laughs at the wonder of it all. At how much her life has changed, at everything she now has, at how far she has come from the terrified little girl she was, at the marvellous ways the universe works.

She laughs, even as more tears fall. She laughs.

A LETTER FROM NICOLE

Hello,

I would like to thank you for taking the time to read *The Nowhere Girl*. If you did enjoy it, and want to keep up to date with all my latest releases, just sign up at the following link. Your email address will never be shared and you can unsubscribe at any time.

www.bookouture.com/nicole-trope

For a long time, I was told to 'write what you know', but that never really worked for me. Instead I write what I fear.

I write about families in crisis, about lives changing in the blink of an eye and about people who somehow manage to survive very difficult situations.

I think it must be difficult for readers to sometimes find that the same themes are repeated in many books, especially when they are about the lives of women. The idea of domestic violence and child abuse seem to come up again and again. Because I am a reader, I understand that feeling. But as a writer I would have to say that these themes come up again and again because we, as a society, have yet to get this right.

We have so many systems in place and yet women are still killed by their partners and children are still physically and sexually abused by those who are supposed to care for them. Until we find a way to stop that happening, I believe that writers will have to keep telling these stories. Like Molly, I don't want these children to simply be statistics, or a short article in the newspaper that people shake their heads at and forget about. I want to make their pain real, their experiences visceral and the truth of their damaged little lives something that people cannot forget.

I have loved writing about the bond of sisterhood and family, and I hope you've enjoyed Molly's, Lexie's, Alice's and even Margaret's stories – as sad as they may be. These characters live on in my head and heart and I hope it is the same for you.

I usually end my novels on a note of hope because that's what I want for the world and for those women and children who suffer.

If you have enjoyed this novel, it would be lovely if you could take the time to leave a review. I read them all, and on days when I question whether or not I have another book in me, they lift me up and help me get back to work.

I would also love to hear from you. You can find me on Facebook and Twitter, and I'm always happy to connect with readers.

Thanks again for reading.
Nicole x

NicoleTrope

@nicoletrope

ACKNOWLEDGEMENTS

I would like to, once again, thank Christina Demosthenous for her exceptional editing. I know I can count on her to push me to do my best work, and every book I publish with her is better because of her skills. I am beyond delighted to have been able to work with her again.

I would also like to thank Kim Nash and Noelle Holten, publicity and social media wizards, for helping my novels into the world. Thanks to the whole team at Bookouture, including Alexandra Holmes, Martina Arzu and Lauren Finger. Thanks to DeAndra Lupu for another sterling copy edit.

I would also like to thank, as always, my mother, Hilary, for being my first reader and for reading my books with a fresh eye each and every time.

Thanks also to David, Mikhayla, Isabella, Jacob and Jax (sock bandit and annoying writing companion).

And once again thank you to those who read, review and blog about my work. You make it all worth it.

Made in the USA
Monee, IL
08 December 2022

20191064R00187